I0598354

As much as he loved her, he feared she would never be his, and he could not continue breaking his own heart…

"What are you saying, Rick?"

"This may ruin my life, but I'm going to have to leave you and get on with my life."

"Oh, no, Rick, please don't say that. Please don't do this. I'll quit school."

"No, you won't. I won't let you. You've got a mind and skills the world needs. How selfish it would be for me to ask you to do that, or even allow you to do it. No, you will go on and fulfill your destiny. I will stay the same, but I cannot labor over you, I miss you too much. I have to free my mind of needing you every minute of every day. I'll lose it if I don't. When you reach your goals and if you decide you want me, my folks will know where I am. If you call me in four years, eight years, or longer, and tell me you've decided to be a bird, then I will be a bird too. I will still love you, but for my self-preservation, I have to try and forget you."

She was crying now, almost uncontrollably.

"What I'm saying, Lizzy Bee, my love, my one and only love, is that whatever you have to do or be, that is what I want you to do or be."

"Will you kiss me," she asked him.

"Has anyone ever told you no to that question?"

"I've never asked anyone but you that question."

He took her in his arms and kissed her passionately for only a brief moment.

"If this ever happens again, you'll have to ask me that question again."

Rick Bennett and Elizabeth Meadow fell in love in their senior year of high school and knew they could never live without each other. But they both had dreams. Elizabeth planned to find a cure for breast cancer, the terrible disease that took her mother when she was only ten. And Rick wanted to teach college students. Each has a passion for their dream as real as their passion for each other. When, after graduating from college, Elizabeth asks Rick to wait for her to finish her post graduate work and get settled in her career before they get married, Rick makes the hardest choice of his life. He breaks up with Elizabeth, telling her if she ever decides she is ready, he will be waiting, but he has to move on with his life. Both devastated, the two go their separate ways, only to discover, too late, that they were both wrong. Can fate intervene to reconnect them, or are they doomed to pay for this mistake forever?

KUDOS for *A Bowl Full of Grapes*

In *A Bowl Full of Grapes* by Jack Sprouse, Rick Bennett and Elizabeth Meadows are high school sweethearts. They plan to be married after college, but Elizabeth changes her career plans halfway through college and asks Rick to wait while she finishes her research for her new career field. Rick fears they are never going to get married, and he breaks up with her, telling her that if she is ever ready to settle down, he will be waiting. But until then he has to move on with his life. Devastated, they both go their separate ways. Are they doomed to be unhappy forever? A poignant and touching story of two people who were meant to be, despite their divergent dreams, this is one you won't want to miss. ~ *Taylor Jones, The Review Team of Taylor Jones & Regan Murphy*

A Bowl Full of Grapes by Jack Sprouse is the story a love that was destined by fate, although the two people involved are determined to accomplish their dreams. Elizabeth Meadows wants to be a research doctor and find ways to prevent heart attacks, like the one that took her mother when she was ten. Rick Bennett wants to teach economics or history in college. When the two fall in love in high school, they agree to wait to marry until after their undergraduate work in college. But when Elizabeth decides to suddenly change careers in midstream and asks Rick to postpone their wedding, he breaks up with her, saying he can't compete with her career. They are both devastated and both make bad choices based on their hurt feelings. Can fate intervene with these two stubborn people, or is it too late for them? *A Bowl Full of Grapes* is both a love story and a family saga, filled with suspense and surprising plot twists. With charming and well-developed characters, this is a moving and heartwarming story mainstream romance fans will love. ~ *Regan Murphy, The Review Team of Taylor Jones & Regan Murphy*

ACKNOWLEDGMENTS

Thanks to my granddaughter, Cheyenne Middleton, for the great cover art

Jack Grimmer; Seth Grimmer; and Isaac Grimmer, Fredericksburg, Texas residents, for use of their names and personas in the book.

A Bowl Full of Grapes

A Love Story

Jack Sprouse

A Black Opal Books Publication

GENRE: WOMEN'S FICTION/ROMANCE/FAMILY LIFE

This is a work of fiction. Names, places, characters and incidents are either the product of the author's imagination or are used fictitiously, and any resemblance to any actual persons, living or dead, businesses, organizations, events or locales is entirely coincidental. All trademarks, service marks, registered trademarks, and registered service marks are the property of their respective owners and are used herein for identification purposes only. The publisher does not have any control over or assume any responsibility for author or third-party websites or their contents.

This book is dedicated to my daughter, Jeanne.

Chapter 1

Crash

2002:

Ed Whelan was the Owner and CEO of Optimum National Telecom "ONT," a telecommunications company that had ridden the telecom bubble to great success in the late nineties and early two-thousands. He sat at the head of the table in his conference room early on a Wednesday morning.

He looked around the table at his six-top sales people who had been instrumental in helping him create the success the company had enjoyed for the past few years. He did not relish the message he was going to have to deliver.

"Gentlemen, and lady." He sneaked a knowing look, and a wink, at Maggie Fletcher who was sitting at the other end of the table. The wink was not lost on the men at the table. He continued, "As you all know Networks unlimited, one of the two biggest telecom firms in the world filed for Chapter Eleven bankruptcy in June of last year. And yesterday, if any of you are not aware, Global Dynamics went belly-up."

"Oh shit," several voices said in unison. There was mumbling all around the table.

"What does this mean, Ed?" Adrian Bennett asked.

"Basically, Adrian, it means that the proclamation made by some technology gurus, in February of 2001, that those two telecom giants would battle for worldwide supremacy over a trillion-dollar market and that there would be no losers was…how shall I put this?…overly optimistic. The bottom has fallen out, and the proverbial feces has made contact with the rotary oscillator."

"The shit has hit the fan? Joe Reedy said.

"That's right, Joe," Ed replied. "There will be lots of losers, mainly banks and stockholders."

"What does it mean for ONT?" Adrian asked.

"We're still sorting that out. It may be a few days before I know how this will affect us. But it's going to shake up the industry very dramatically. I assure you that I'll do everything within my power to keep us solvent and to keep everyone employed. This bust is being estimated to be ten times bigger than the dotcom crash. We may be seeing the largest bubble in history. It's created a hole that the industry is going to have to climb out of.

"I'm hearing that WorldCom is very close to bankruptcy, and if WorldCom goes under it will be the biggest failure in business history. Even Enron's demise was not that severe. So, I'll call another meeting for next week about this same time, and we'll examine where we are and explore our options. Keep your chins up, guys, we've been through hard times before, we'll get through this."

About an hour after everyone had left the office, Ed heard the front doorbell ring, and he got up from his desk and went to the door. Maggie Fletcher stepped in, and he took her in his arms and kissed her passionately. "God, you are beautiful," he told her. "Let's go to my office."

"How bad is it really, Ed?" she asked.

"Pretty damned bad," he said. "I'll be fortunate to keep this place afloat. I'll have to keep Adrian Bennett on for at least a month or two—he's my best salesman—but everyone else will have to go. I may have to lay you off for a while, but don't worry. I'll bring you back when I get things settled down. We have to be discreet."

"Discreet? You think anyone in this office doesn't know we're sleeping together?"

"I just don't want anyone stirring up trouble. When I make the cuts, I'll bring you back to help Adrian handle the customer load we have left and then tell him a believable story that you're going to do the accounting…or something like that. In the meantime, we have to figure out how to stay in business."

The following week, Ed asked Adrian to come into his office, prior to the scheduled conference, so he could apprise him of the ongoing situation. Adrian showed up early that morning and went to the boss' office as requested.

"Thanks for coming, Adrian," Ed said. "I wanted to go over with you what is going to happen at the meeting this morning."

"I'm assuming the news is not good, Ed."

"That's an accurate assumption, Adrian. I can keep 'you' on for about another two months, but I'm going to have to let everyone else go within the week. Now, you'll have a fairly generous severance package. It won't replace your salary of course, but we're talking somewhere around three-hundred K. You'll draw your regular salary for the next two months, and I'll give you a very good reference and do everything I can to help you get employed."

"Well, I was kind of expecting this, from what I've been reading and seeing on the news. I appreciate your keeping me on as long as you can. I'm thinking I'll have to downsize my house and living standards pretty much across the board. But if that's what it takes, so be it."

The meeting was not a pleasant affair for either the employees or the employer. Ed Whelan tried to put a positive spin on the situation, but it was a poor attempt. He told them their severance compensation packages would be available at the end of the week and that their jobs with ONT would then be over, it was as simple as that. Lives were impacted and sometimes traumatized just that easily. He wished them all well and assured them that he would give them all positive references when they applied for jobs elsewhere.

Afterward, he spoke with Adrian about his situation. "Have you talked to your family about this yet, Adrian," he asked him.

"I've been holding off, Ed. I'm going to do it tonight after dinner."

"The industry is going to be struggling for a while. We face years of painful reorganization in order to get the over-supply of capacity built during the boom years brought into line with demand and the massive debt that will have to be restructured."

"I'm not sure what all that means, Ed," Adrian replied.

"There will most likely be more bankruptcies and many among some pretty big companies. Bottom line is it may be tough getting a job for a while. What you said about downsizing might be your best option. You might even consider looking out of state for a job."

"Out of state? Wow, I don't know how that would go over with my family. I hope it doesn't come to that."

"I do too," Ed responded. "I just wanted to be as honest as I can with you."

"I appreciate that. I'd hate to leave California. My family is pretty entrenched here."

"Maybe it won't come to that, Adrian. Maybe things will turn in our favor. Start putting your resume out right away and if you have to take off for interviews, feel free to do so."

Thanks, Ed," Adrian said. "I'll be okay."

Ed was on the verge of panic, but he had managed not to show it to his employees or to his wife and family. At forty-five-years of age, he'd been at the top of his game and at the top of his business world. Ed had made a fortune through his telecom company. Starting in 1995, with a half-million-dollar loan from his wife's father, Julian Stroud, he'd rode the bubble to a lucrative life-style and had paid the loan back with interest. In the last two years, he'd started to bank money. And now he was in fear that he might lose it all.

Ed found himself in a cold and loveless marriage from which it would be almost an impossibility to extricate himself without stirring up a fire-storm of biblical proportions. His wife Fran came from a very powerful family in the Santa Barbara area, and Ed knew that, if he tried to divorce Fran, they would take him for everything he had worked so hard to achieve over that past seven years.

Ed was desperately in love with Maggie Fletcher, a woman ten-years his junior, without whom he was convinced he could not live. He was so enamored with the woman that he was willing to risk almost anything just to be with her, anything but his business. But now, with the business at risk, his mind began to calculate how it might work out to his advantage.

"It's going to result in some life-changing events for us," Adrian Bennett told his family. "I apologize for not foreseeing this, but the truth is nobody at my level in the industry could have foreseen it happening. I'm just going to be brutally honest with you and give you some worst-case scenarios. First, unless I can find a new job making as much money as I am making at ONT in a month, then we're going to have to sell the house." He paused to gauge their reaction.

His wife, Leeann appeared to be traumatized. "Oh God, Adrian," she said, "you know how I love our house."

"I know, Lee, I love the house too, but without the same steady income, we just won't be able to make the payments. We can sell the house and use the equity to buy another house outright."

"Mom, it's just a house," Rick, the Bennetts' seventeen-year-old son, said. "If Dad can't get another job right away, we just have to roll with the punches."

"I don't know what that means, Rick. I just don't want to sell my house."

"Would you rather have it repossessed and lose all the equity?

"That's okay, Rick," Adrian said. 'Thank you, son. Lee, we have a month for me to look for another job. Please just keep an open mind about this. Families must take drastic measures sometimes to survive."

"What if you don't find another job, Dad?" Rick asked him.

"Well, the house is valued at a million-five. I still owe the bank the bulk of that, about a million, on the note so after all the closing cost and such, we'll have five-hundred thousand or so. My severance from ONT will be about three-hundred thousand, so it's not like we'll be destitute. A decent house will run us about half of our bankroll, about four-hundred thousand. Or—"

"Or what?" Leeann asked.

"Ed Whelan suggested I seek a position with a company in another state. There are some areas that are not as negatively affected by this crash as California is. The cost of living is also cheaper in some other places."

"What other places are you talking about," his wife asked.

"Ed mentioned Texas, specifically, and maybe Florida. I'll have to put my resume out online and see if I arouse any interest. That's only if I don't find anything right away in state."

"Texas, Oh my God, Adrian, Texas? Please don't tell me we have to go to Texas.

"I'm not telling you we have to go anywhere, Lee, but I have to support this family, and I intend to do that, no matter what I have to do. If I have to go by myself, I'll do it, but I'd rather keep the family together. It's going to be hard enough to get through this mess, but if we don't stick together, it could ruin all our lives."

"Dad is right, Mom," Rick said. "We stay together, no matter what."

"But our lives are here," Leeann said. "I have so many things to do here and people counting on me."

"Shit happens, Mom, we roll with the punches. Whatever is best for Dad is best for the family. The Ladies Auxiliary, or whatever all those gossip-fests are called, will just have to find someone else to organize their cake-bake."

"That's just not fair, son," she replied to him.

"Life is not always fair, Mom, but it does go on."

Adrian Bennett watched his seventeen-year-old, son with a sense of love and pride he'd not felt for him in quite some time, as the boy walked out of the room. "Come on, Amanda," he said to his fourteen-year-old sister, "let's go for a ride."

The girl got up from the table and followed him out the door to his truck. "Where are we going, Rick?" she asked him.

"I want to talk to you about everything that's happened," he told her. He drove to Stearns Wharf and found a parking spot along West Cabrillo Boulevard. He opened the truck door for his sister and took her hand. "Let's sit on the retaining wall," he said. "Amanda, it's actually a good thing that we, you and I, are going through this crisis when we are young because this will be an excellent learning experience for both of us."

"I don't know what you mean, Rick."

"Did you see how Mom is handling the issue? Mom has been living a pampered life so long that she cannot bear to face reality. She has no idea how to shift gears and divest oneself of burdensome things that we can no longer afford. She's going to be an albatross around Dad's neck throughout this whole ordeal. I can see it coming."

"I might be able to see it too, Rick, if I knew what you were talking about."

"I'm sorry, Amanda, I forget that you're only fourteen. You look so grown up. I swear, I'm going to be beating up boys to keep them from bothering you before too much longer."

The girl giggled. "You better not."

"Okay, okay, I'll try to be a little clearer. You know the house we live in?"

"Yes."

"It's a nice house, it's a very nice house, but it is way too big a house for a family of four and for the income Dad has. He bought that house because of Mom. Your mother is a very pretentious woman."

"My mother? She's your mother, too."

"I know, and I said that for emphasis, not to assign any blame to you, or to me. Actually, if there is any blame to be applied here, it probably should go to Dad."

"To Dad, why?" she asked. "What did Daddy do? He lost his job."

"I know he did, but for years now we have been living above our means, or more accurately, above Dad's means. I know he couldn't foresee this economic downturn, but he had to know he was way over his head in debt. Now it's going to take some serious cutting back for us to survive. For you and me, it means we may have to move somewhere away from friends we have now and live a more frugal life-style. You do know what frugal means, don't you?"

"I know what frugal means," she said.

"I just don't want you to look at all this as a blow to your self-respect and 'who you are.' If we have to cut back on vacations, new clothes, going out to eat at expensive restaurants, and stuff like that, you've become accustomed to, don't let it make you feel like you're any less of a person. You are still Amanda Bennett, a smart, a very smart, girl who will go far and do well in life no matter how much money her daddy makes. Do you understand what I'm telling you?"

"I understand, Rick," she said, "thank you. We both need to help Daddy get through this."

"Yes, we do, and I'm so glad we see eye to eye on this." He bent over, put his nose to hers, and looked directly into her eyes to emphasize his 'eye to eye' remark. Amanda started giggling. "Now, let's get some lunch at Moby Dick," he suggested.

"Really," she said, "you're going to take me to lunch?"

"I am," he said and took her hand in his. They started walking toward the wharf.

"I'm pretending I'm on a real date," Amanda said.

"That'll come soon enough, Amanda. I hope Dad is ready for it because I'm not."

"Why not, Rick? I'm almost fifteen."

"You're just too pretty to be fourteen. You're growing up too quickly."

They were seated, and both ordered the Moby's Fish & Chips. As they were eating, Amanda kept looking around.

"What are you looking for?" Rick asked her.

"I was hoping some of my friends would see me here with a guy and think I was on a date."

"Don't you think that anyone who knows you would know that I'm your brother?"

"No, not everyone I know at school even knows I have a brother, especially such a good-looking brother."

"Well, thanks for that bit of encouragement," he told her.

When they were back at home, he walked her to the door, took her head in his hands, and kissed her on the top of her head. "Every great date should end with a kiss, don't you agree?"

She giggled loudly. "Yes, and it was a great date, thank you, Rick."

"It was my pleasure, sprite," he said. "Mom will probably grill you on what we talked about. Try to tell her just as little as you can get away with."

Adrian received a call from Ed Whelan, who was in a near frenzy. "Adrian," he began, "Julian Stroud, my wife's father, is threatening to have his lawyer slap an injunction on the company to bar me from making any large payouts until he can have the accountant assess our ability to stay afloat for the long term. I need to meet with you and resolve your severance package issue. Can you meet me at Buddy's Diner this afternoon?"

"Of course, Ed, but how can he do that? You're not filing for bankruptcy, are you?"

"No, but I'll explain it to you when we meet. Can you be there at three this afternoon?"

"I'll be there at three, Ed. Something is going on with Ed," Adrian told his wife.

"Why, what did he say?"

"He wants to meet with me this afternoon, not at the office, at Buddy's Diner."

"That's really strange," Leeann said.

"Yes, it is," he replied. "In the meantime, I got a buzz from a company in Minnesota that wants me to come out there and talk to them about a job."

"Minnesota? I don't know but what that would be worse than Texas, Adrian."

"I know, Lee, I'm pre-disposed to not even want to go for the interview, but I think I owe it to us to pursue every possibility. I don't know. Let me see what Ed has to say this afternoon, and then I'll decide what to do about the Minnesota thing."

When Adrian met Ed at three at the diner, Adrian ordered coffee and Ed ordered a club sandwich. "I haven't eaten anything all day, my nerves are shot," he told Adrian.

"You sounded pretty distraught on the phone. What's going on?"

"You know my father-in-law, Julian Stroud, Fran's old man. He's all up in the air, thinking the business is going to fail. Fran owns half the stock, that was part of the deal when he loaned me the money for the start-up. Now he's having their attorney slap an injunction on me to keep me from making any large capital expenditures."

"Aw shit, I see where this is going," Adrian said, "my bonus."

"All the bonuses," Ed told him, "but not to worry. It's not business with us, Adrian, it never has been. You've been with me since the beginning, and you've done as much to build ONT as I have, so you'll get your bonus, I promise you that."

"But?

"But the three-hundred grand is in an offshore bank account in Belize. I set up an account for you at the same bank I use. I had the paperwork Fed-Exed to me for you to sign. Once it's all signed, we'll send it back to the bank, and they'll email you receipts and updates, so you'll be able to keep tabs on the money."

Adrian looked over the documents that Ed laid out in front of him on the table. Everything seemed to be legitimate. "So, what if I need the money, Ed?"

"I want you to take a trip with me to Belize, Adrian. I'll buy the plane tickets, and we'll only be there maybe two days. I think you should consider buying some rental property there and, using a property management to handle the leasing and upkeep on the place. It will give you a steady income and a place to go on vacation once you land in a job and get back on your feet."

"That all sounds great, Ed, but I've got a realtor putting my house on the market, and I'm looking for a job. And I still have to show up for work, although I don't think you really need me at the office. I think you are just keeping me on to help me out."

"That's another thing, Adrian. I'm going to have to cut your employment off at the end of the month. The injunction won't let me keep anyone on but office staff after that."

"By office staff, I assume you mean Maggie?"

"I hope there are no hard feelings about that, Adrian."

"No, Ed, that's your business. I don't fault you for anything in your personal life. You've always been fair with me. I am interested in the Belize thing, though. It's something that might really help me out in the future."

"Good, then I'll make the arrangements and let you know when we leave."

"I'm going to decline the Minnesota thing," Adrian told his wife." "I'm going to Belize with Ed this week sometime."

"Belize?" she said, astounded. "Why in the world are you going to Belize?"

She was surprisingly open to the idea when he told her about the possibility of owning property in Belize that would produce a second income for them.

Ed picked Adrian up early on Monday of the following week. They drove to LAX and caught a Delta flight to Belize City International Airport. They picked up a rental car and drove to the Radisson Fort George Hotel and Marina.

"I made reservations for two days. If we need a third day, it won't be a problem. We'll be taking a water taxi to Ambergris Caye where I have two houses. There's one available for sale just down the street from me that I want to show you. You don't have to make a decision right away, but I'm going to encourage you to do so."

"What's a caye?" Adrian asked.

"A caye is a small, low-elevation, sandy island on the surface of a coral reef. It's like a key, as in the Florida Keys."

Adrian nodded.

"When we get to San Pedro, that's the major town on the caye," Ed told him, "we'll rent one of the golf carts they have to get around in. This is one of mine," Ed said as he passed an exquisite condominium with an all-glass front and a wharf that jutted out into the inlet between the caye and mainland.

"That's beautiful, Ed," Adrian said. "How much did that cost?"

"That one is a little out of your budget, Adrian. You'll have to start small, but in time you can build up an enterprise here if you invest your time and money just right. This house was a half million five years ago. My other one is farther away from here. We're coming up on the one I was telling you about. It's right over there." He pointed at a beautiful one-story house surrounded by trees and shrubbery.

"It's a good-looking place. It's off the water, I see."

"It's about a two-minute walk to the beach. That's no big deal. They still rent out very easily. You'll have a steady income year-round, and you can call the management company and reserve it for you and your family any time you want to. Most clients rent for a week or two at a time."

"How much is this house?"

"I think this one is a hundred and seventy grand. With closing costs and all the initial set up with the management company, you're looking at two-hundred K. It will earn you about forty-five thousand a year pre-tax, and yes, you will have to pay taxes on the money, but that's after the management fees. You should clear maybe thirty grand in the end."

"How do I reconcile the three-hundred thousand dollars on my taxes? Will you send me a 1099 or what?" Adrian said.

"No, I can't do that. I can't have anybody know I had that money, and by anybody, I mean my wife and her father."

"So how do I explain where I got the money?"

"You saved the money, Adrian."

"What?"

"You saved the money. You didn't put it in the bank. You saved it and rat-holed it in a safe in your house. Listen, you've worked for me for ten years. What would you have had to do to save that much money in those ten years?"

"I would have had to divorce my wife the day I went to work for you," Adrian said, and Ed burst out laughing.

"Okay, but seriously, you could have saved thirty grand a

year, conceivably? Some of your bonuses were twenty thousand or so, and a couple of years you made thirty-five, if I recall."

Adrian nodded. "In the proverbial perfect world, perhaps, but—"

"Relax, Adrian," Ed said. "You made me a lot of money the ten years you worked for me. Now my asshole father-in-law and his shrew daughter are preventing me from doing right by you. This is the only way I can do the right thing. This is not business, it's personal, not as an employee, as a friend. Take the money, buy the house, and don't worry about it. Okay?"

"Okay, Ed, thank you. Let's get the paperwork done."

Back at home, Leeann opened the door for Adrian, and her expression demanded an explanation. He just smiled at her until he set his bags down in the living room.

"We own a house in Belize, Lee. I have pictures and a brochure, oh, and some papers for you to sign. I put ownership in both our names."

"We're not going to live there, are we?" she asked.

"No, but I bet you would like it. It's a beautiful place. It's income property, about a two-minute walk from the beach, right on the Caribbean. If it's half as profitable, as Ed Whelan says it will be, then it will be a good deal for us. I'll explain it all in time, but right now I'm really tired. I need to get some rest. Tomorrow I have to start looking for a job for real."

Adrian received an email from a company in Dallas, referencing his resume on the internet. The email had an attached "fillable" application form they were asking him to complete and return, along with references, college degrees, and other work-related information. He'd never received such an inquiry before but thought it would simplify the process, so he filled out the form and gathered all the other requested information, along with a picture of himself, and sent it back to them.

Two days later he got a call on his cell phone. "Hello, this is Adrian Bennett."

"Mister Bennett," a male voice said, "this is Brian Hancock with DTS in Dallas. How are you doing?"

"Oh, Mister Hancock, I'm doing just fine. I appreciate your calling, I wasn't expecting to hear from you so quickly, but I'm glad you called."

"Well, we like what we see on your résumé, Mister Bennett, and we'd like to ask you to come to Dallas and sit down and talk to us if you're interested."

"Yes…Mister Hancock, is it?…I am interested. When would you like for me to be there?"

"Well, first off, let's get past this 'Mister' business. Call me Brian and, if it's okay with you, I'll call you Adrian."

"Yes, of course, it's okay, that was getting a bit awkward. I'm pretty much available any day of the week."

"I'll have my office arrange for your flight and for a hotel room here. How far is Santa Barbara from LAX? Do you need a flight from there to LA?"

"No, I can drive to LAX faster than I can get to the airport and go through all that mess."

"Okay, then we'll get you a round trip from LAX into DFW, and I'll pick you up. I'll Fed-Ex the stuff to your house as soon as we have all the info in hand."

"That sounds great, Brian, I appreciate it and look forward to meeting you."

Adrian immediately thought of his son Rick and his having to leave Santa Barbara. It had the potential to affect his life possibly more than anyone else in the family. He went up the stairs to the boy's room and knocked on the door."

"Come on in," Rick said, and when he saw his dad, he motioned to him to enter. "What's up, Dad?"

"I need to discuss something with you, son. You were very convincing in your argument to your mother about keeping the family together, when we were discussing the possibility of my having to take a job out of state."

"Yes, I was, and I meant it," he said.

"Well, I got a call from a company in Dallas, and they seem very interested in me, based on my resume. I know that doesn't mean I'm on the payroll yet, but they want me to come in and talk to them. If they make me a decent offer, I'm inclined to think that I have to consider taking it. Texans have a reputation for being rude, crude, and socially unacceptable, as the saying goes. But Texas always seems to be booming. Texas is like magic. We have to give it a chance, I think."

"Absolutely, Dad, but now you're worried what it will do to my football career?"

"Well, yes, I am, Rick," Adrian replied. "You're an integral part of your team, and they're counting on you. Will you still be willing to move with us or should I try to make arrangements for you to stay here and finish your last year in high school at your school?"

"I can play football anywhere, Dad. Football is a means to an end for me. I want a full scholarship, and that's all. I'll earn it, but I don't plan to make a career out of football, I don't want to play in the NFL, so if you get a job in another state, I'm on board. My bigger disappointment is having to leave Grandpa. Ever since Grandma died, he's been all alone and having me working with him in the summer seems to be a really big thing for him."

"I know, Rick, but we'll just have to come and visit as often as we can. He's my father, and I'm concerned about him too, but he's tough and independent. We need you with us during this difficult time."

"Don't worry, Dad, I'll go with the family. Not going was never an option."

"Thank you, son, I would have hated to have you be separated from us, if even for just one school year."

Brian Hancock was not what Adrian had expected. He supposed he was thinking the man would be wearing a white Stetson like J R Ewing of the *Dallas* TV show fame, but Hancock was well-dressed in a fitted suit and matching shoes and tie. He was a presentable man, if not one who might be considered handsome. He was about six feet tall, as best Adrian could tell, at least two inches taller than Adrian, but plumper. He appeared to be a few years older than Adrian although his hair was still fully brown while Adrian's had started graying around the temples. They shook hands at the baggage claim station.

"Great to see you, Adrian," Brian said, "thanks for coming."

"Thank 'you' Brian, I'm happy to be here. Let me get my bag, and we'll be good to go."

They took LBJ—I-635—Freeway into Dallas and exited at Preston Road. The DTS facility was located in an office complex on the north side of the freeway. Brian pulled into the parking lot, and he and Adrian got out of the car and went into the company office.

"Adrian, this is Emma Jones, our receptionist."

The attractive young woman stood up and extended her hand toward Adrian. "Welcome to DTS, Mister Bennett," she said, as he shook her hand.

"Thank you, Miss Jones," Adrian replied, "I'm happy to be here."

"That office right there," Brian said, pointing, "belongs to Cindy Morrow, our office manager. I expect she is already in the conference room with the boss."

The office facility was nice but not opulent. There appeared to be no wasted money on frivolities. All expenditures appeared to Adrian to be for expediency and functionality. That was a good thing, in his estimation.

Kenny Morrison was a short man, at least a couple of inches shorter than Adrian, but he carried himself like a much larger man, with confidence and what Adrian would describe as *stage presence*. He was overweight and plumpish and was losing his hair.

He didn't appear to be a drinker but probably indulged himself in too much rich food. He was fifty years old, Brian would tell Adrian at a later date, and was a *marketing genius*, one of the best in the business, according to Brian.

Kenny met Adrian almost like he was an old friend. "Damned glad to meet you, Adrian," he said, as he pumped Adrian's hand. "Let me say first that your resume really caught my eye. It looked to me like you were doing a hell of a job out there at ONT, damned shame about their trouble."

"Yes, sir, it was. I guess the bust caught a lot of folks by surprise."

"I talked to Ed Whelan about you. He says you were pretty much the prime mover in his success in over the last ten years."

"Ed is a good guy," Adrian said, "but he tends to downplay his own role in the success of the company. It was a team effort. I did my part, and he did his. We had a good run. Ed was a fair man to all his employees."

"Yeah, he told me you would probably say something like that."

Adrian laughed out loud. "You'd have to meet Ed, he's quite a character."

"Well, suffice it to say, he spoke very highly of you, and we may have a place for you here if you will just give me a run-down on what you did for Ed."

"Of course, Mister Morrison—"

"Call me Kenny."

"Oh, sure, Kenny, well, in addition to canvassing and creating new accounts for telecom systems, I assisted our engineer in designing and expanding server room facilities and assisting in the design and installing of back-up generator and UPS services to ensure that a company will not suffer from loss of utility electrical power. I handled clients all up and down the Pacific coast, to Oregon and Washington."

"So, traveling for a night or two out of town is no problem for you?"

"No, not at all," Adrian said.

"Have you had any experience with solar power systems?" Brian asked him.

"We were starting to explore the possible uses it might provide for our industry, and currently, I just don't think it's cost effective. Most of the available systems are direct current and therefore require inverters. Also, the panels just don't produce enough wattage to be all that helpful. It takes too many of them to make enough power to make it worth the effort. Now, this is just my opinion. I'm sure there are some experts who might say otherwise."

"Well, kiss my ass," Kenny said. "Okay, Brian, you win, you, sneaky bastard. How did you know Adrian was going to say the same thing you've been telling me for the past year?"

"I didn't know, Boss, I swear. We didn't talk about that before we got here."

Kenny looked at Adrian and Adrian was shaking his head. "Okay," Kenny said, "then I'll defer to the experts."

"I owe you a lunch, Adrian," Brian said, and they all laughed.

"Okay, Adrian," Kenny said, "we have a need here for you, if we can come to terms. As I said, I talked to Ed Whelan, and he told me you were making a hundred and fifty K with annual bonuses. I'll be honest, we are just not budgeted for that level at this time."

Adrian smiled. "Ed's a good guy, Kenny. I love the man, I really do. He's a friend as much as he was a boss, but I wasn't making that much money."

Kenny's eyebrows went up, and he started laughing.

"My base salary was a hundred-thousand and close to a hundred-twenty with bonuses," Adrian continued. "I've done some research, however, and with the difference in the costs of living between here and California, my need will not be as much."

"Eighty-thousand is what I had in mind, Adrian, and that's in addition to full benefits, a company car, expense account, and bonuses. The bonuses may not be as large as you were used to. We're still growing, but who knows? We may get there."

"I have a realtor putting my house on the market. Once it sells, I'll be able to buy a house here with my equity, so I'm okay with your pay scale."

"So, you're telling me you'll take the job?" Kenny said.

"If you're offering me the job, then yes, sir, I'll be happy to take it."

"Hell, yes, I'm offering you the job. Welcome aboard." Kenny reached across the table and shook Adrian's hand. "Is ten-thousand dollars enough to cover your moving expense?

"Yes, of course, it is. Thank you," Adrian said.

Brian shook his hand and welcomed him to the company as did Cindy Morrow.

"You'll need to sit down with Cindy and fill out all the paperwork. When that is done, we'll go to lunch. Cindy made a reservation for you at the Hyatt Regency at the airport, so you won't be rushed to get to your flight in the morning."

They went to The Capital Grille, an upscale restaurant near downtown Dallas. Kenny immediately started trying to order for Cindy. Cindy was a very attractive woman. At five feet, four inches, and weighing only a hundred and ten pounds, she was well built and drew admiring looks from men everywhere she went.

"Come on, Cindy, get the French Onion soup," he kept insisting.

Adrian watched their interaction with amusement.

"She loves the stuff, Adrian, but it makes her fart like a plow horse."

Cindy covered her eyes with her hands.

Brian started laughing. "Poor Cindy, we treat her like one of the guys, Adrian, so she won't let her good looks go to her head."

The waiter came to take their order, and Cindy told him she was still looking at the menu, so Kenny ordered first.

"I'll have the eight-ounce Filet twice."

"Twice, sir?" the waiter asked, bewildered.

"Yes," Kenny said, "two of them."

Brian and Adrian chuckled. Both of them ordered the fourteen-ounce Strip Sirloin.

"I'll have the Maine Lobster salad as my main course," Cindy said.

"Will that be all, miss?"

"Please bring me a bowl of the French Onion soup."

All three of the men at the table started laughing. The waiter looked confused but left to turn in their order.

"Every time I have to pass gas this afternoon, Kenny Morrison, I'm going to come into your office."

"Oh, that's right, I have jobsite meeting I have to go to this afternoon," Kenny said.

"You can fart in my office anytime you want to, Cindy," Brian said.

Adrian chuckled and shook his head in amusement. "I think I'm starting to love Texas already," he said.

Chapter 2

Moving

T hey made me an offer I couldn't refuse," Adrian told Leeann on the phone after he'd gotten back to his room at the DFW Hyatt Regency.

"Oh, Adrian, please don't tell me we're moving to Texas," she said, whining into his ear.

"Come on, Lee, be reasonable. I have to make us a living. It's time you came into the real world. This is a good company here, and they'll pay me pretty close to what I was making with Ed. The cost of living will be substantially less, so we'll get along much better."

"We have to stay until the kids are out of school," she said.

"I have a plan. I'll go over it with you when I get back home tomorrow. I start to work in two weeks, so we have to move quickly. We have to get the house sold and make arrangements for a mover. The company is giving me ten grand for moving expenses."

"How much are they going to pay you?"

"Eighty-thousand a year plus benefits and bonuses," he told her.

"Oh, well, that's not so bad."

"It's pretty damned good at this point in our lives, and I'm thankful to have it," Adrian said. "I'll be in tomorrow and fill you in on what has to happen next."

It was three in the afternoon when he pulled into the driveway at home. Leeann had dinner ready by five and, immediately after dinner, she cleared the table, and they all sat down in their usual spots.

"Okay, family, here's the news," Adrian said. "It's good news and bad news, depending on one's perspective. I was offered the job in Dallas. It is a very good offer. I felt like, for the sake of the family, I could not turn it down. The job market here is just too erratic and uncertain. I know we all have lives here, but sometimes life throws people a curve. Life has thrown us a curve. But the almighty has fielded the curve for us and given us a way forward. I have to do this. It's my responsibility to support this family. I need for you all to come with me."

"Of course, we'll go with you, Dad," Rick said. "There was never any doubt about that."

"I'll go with you, Daddy," Amanda said.

"Thank you, darling, it wouldn't be the same without you. So, what about the mother?"

"Well, you're not taking my children and leaving me here by myself," Leeann said and sighed deeply.

"Good, then it's settled. Here is what I want to do. I'm going to rent a small moving truck and load up all my stuff and Rick's stuff and take our two vehicles to Dallas. The lady at the office has a realtor setting up some houses for me to look at when I get back. If I can't find anything right away, Rick and I can stay at a Regency Inn or a place like that. I'll put the stuff we don't need in storage until we find a house. I'll find us a house, Lee. You'll just have to trust our judgement, your son's and mine. I promise you we'll get you a nice house."

"But what about Rick's school?"

"He can start to school in Dallas. He'll have a couple of months to get familiar with the school, make a few friends, and go talk to the coaches about trying out for the quarterback position this coming school year. Football season is over now anyway. Is that okay with you, son?"

Rick nodded. "That's great, Dad, it sounds like fun."

"Then you'll have to deal with the people coming to see the house and the realtor, Lee. Once we get a buyer, I will fly back and sign the papers with you and make arrangements for the mover."

"I feel like my life is coming to an end, Adrian," Leeann said.

"It's not, Lee, you're just turning a page."

Adrian put his car on a car carrier and pulled it behind the rental truck while Rick followed in his truck. It was a grueling three-day trip across the southwest from Santa Barbara to Dallas. They rented a suite at the Regency and unloaded all their personal clothing, and gear, then found a storage facility and unloaded the rest of their things and returned the rental truck. Adrian checked in with the office and Cindy gave him the name and number of several realtors who had potential houses for him to look at.

"Okay, I guess school can wait a couple of days. I'd really like for you to look at some of these houses with me if you don't mind. I don't want your mother thinking I picked out a house all by myself."

"I think that's best, Dad. She can't get upset at both of us if we make her live in a hovel." Rick said.

They had three appointments the next day. The first two were very nice houses and well within their budget, but they were in far north Dallas, a little farther from the office than Adrian wanted to be. The third prospect was a colonial style house, on Azalea Lane just south of the office, maybe a mile or so. It was a five bedroom which offered an extra room for a home office and a guest room.

"What do you think, son?" Adrian said.

"I think it's perfect, Dad, and I think Mom will love it too."

"So, you say it's four-fifty," Adrian asked the realtor.

"Yes, sir," the man said. "Four-hundred-fifty-thousand.

"Go ahead and work up the paper on it. I'm in the process of selling my house in California. I can put down ten percent and finance it through my bank until my house sells, and then I'll pay it off. I'd like to have a home inspection done, but we can go ahead with the preliminary work."

"Can we meet at my office tomorrow, so I can get all your information, employment, bank, et cetera."

"Of course," Adrian said. "I'm pretty much free all day tomorrow. I'd like to get some pictures of the place and any brochures or online pictures you might have that I can send to my wife. She's still at home trying to sell our house."

"Sure, no problem, give me your e-mail address, and I'll send you links to everything I have on this property."

"Thank you. I'll call you in the morning to set up a time to come in to start the paperwork process."

Rick walked into William B. Travis High School and found his way to the administration office.

"Can I help you, young man?" a lady at the front desk asked him.

"Yes, ma'am," he said. "My name is Rick Bennett, and I'm a transfer from Bel Air High School in Santa Barbara, California. My family is in the process of moving to Dallas."

"Oh, okay," she said. "Do you have your transcripts?"

"I do," he said and handed his folder to her.

She opened it up and started to read through it. Then she shoved the form toward him along with a pen. "Can you fill out this form for me, please?"

"Our address is six-five-two-two Azalea Lane, but we haven't moved into the house yet. My dad is still in the process of buying it. I'm putting down his cell phone number and mine."

"That's fine," she told him. "Oh, I see you are an A-honorroll student. That is impressive and refreshing. And you were on the football team at your school?"

"Yes, I was."

"Well, we don't have a lot of football players on the A honor roll. No offense, Mister Bennett, but you are quite rare around these parts."

"No offense taken, ma'am."

"I'm Mrs. Donnelly, Ellen Donnelly. Do you plan to try out for the team here at Travis?"

"Yes, I do, Mrs. Donnelly," Rick said, "And I also intend to maintain my honor roll status."

"What position do you play, if I may ask?"

"I play quarterback, ma'am," he replied.

"That is just marvelous," the woman said. "You'll want to talk to Coach McNeal about the football team. I'll write down his name and other information for you, and, if you can have a seat, I'll get your schedule for you just as quickly as I can."

"Thank you," he said, and he took a seat in the waiting area.

He had waited about ten minutes when a man, wearing khaki slacks and a polo shirt, walked through the door. On his head was a baseball cap with the school logo on it. The man was wearing tennis shoes. Rick knew immediately that the man was the football coach.

He walked up to Rick, although there were several other students sitting in the waiting area. "You're Bennett, the quarterback, young man?"

"Yes, sir," Rick said, as he stood up.

"I'm Wade McNeal. I'm the coach of the football team. Ellen Donnelly tells me that you're transferring here from California. You want to try out for my team, is that right?"

"Yes, sir, I was starting quarterback at my school back home."

"Well, mighty fine. Let me tell her that I'm going to take you with me for about an hour while she puts your schedule together. Is that okay with you?"

"Sure," Rick said.

He left the office with McNeal. They walked out to the field house where the sports facilities were, and he directed Rick to his office. "Have a seat, Rick."

Rick sat down in the chair across from the coach's desk.

"What brings you to Dallas, Rick?" McNeal asked.

Rick gave him a brief explanation of their story and how he came to be in the office of Travis High School, registering as a new student.

"Mighty fine," the coach said. "So tell me about your experience with your team at…"

"Bel Air High School, I went to Bel Air High School in Santa Barbara. I was starting quarterback my sophomore and junior years. We played for the state title this past season but lost to De La Salle. We stayed with them until the fourth quarter, but they just out played us."

"De La Salle? Well, that's nothing to be ashamed of. That's one of the best teams in the country."

"I know. It was actually an honor to just be in the game against them. I really wanted to win that game, but I couldn't make it happen."

"Well, don't dwell on it. Next year is a new season. Listen, Rick, I've got two guys competing for the position, so you'll just have to jump into the mix. I frankly don't think you'll have any trouble beating these guys out. One is a junior, and the other one isn't that strong. Just bring you're A game. I'll tell Mrs. Donnelly to put you in my sixth period. The team practices every day until the end of the school year. Early training will start in August to get ready for the coming season. Are you starting today?"

"No, sir, tomorrow. I'm helping my dad get settled. We're still in the process of moving here."

"Okay, then I'll see you tomorrow afternoon. Glad to have you with us. I'll let you get back to Mrs. Donnelly."

Rick got his schedule from Ellen Donnelly and just as Coach McNeal had said, his sixth period was athletics, or more accurately, football. He had English Lit and Grammar for Home Room, first class in the morning, a teacher named Joan Culley.

That afternoon, Coach McNeal introduced Rick to the offensive coach, Randy Quigley, who was also the quarterback coach. They shook hands. "Okay, Rick, I'll get you some gear and then I want you to warm up. I want to check your speed against our fastest guys. From what Coach Wade told me, I know you're a good quarterback, but I need to know if you can run fast enough to get your ass out of trouble if you have to." He took Rick to the locker room and fitted him out with a helmet and pads, a jersey, and shorts and shoes. "If you make the team, we'll fit you for a uniform. What number did you have at your last school? If it's not taken, we'll let you wear it here."

"Number sixteen," Rick replied.

"Joe Montana fan, huh?" Quigley said.

"Yes, sir," Rick said.

"Yeah, me, too, okay let's go."

After Rick, had made a couple of laps around the field and completed some stretching exercises, Quigley motioned for him to come over. Then he called two other players over to the 100 meter track where he had three sets of starting blocks in place. One of the other players was a tall but stoutly built black kid named Jason Green, who was the team's kickoff and punt returner, and the fastest player on the team. The second player was Bobby Gladwyn, one of the wide receivers. "Gentlemen, he said, this is Rick Bennett. Rick is going to be trying out for the quarterback position for next year. He is a transfer from Bel Air High School in Santa Barbara, California."

Both boys shook hands with Rick and wished him good luck in the tryouts. Quigley told them to line up and get ready to start the run. He went through the call, fired his starting pistol, and the three boys shot of the starting blocks in a mad dash to the finish line.

Norman Pettigrew, the defensive coach, was waiting at the other end with his time clock. Two other players standing there watching as well, just for good measure. The three runners crossed the line so close together that Pettigrew could not say for certain which one had won the race.

"Are you shittin' me, Norman?" Quigley asked him. "Are you telling me that a quarterback kept up with the two fastest players on our team?"

"Green might have been a half-step ahead, but it wasn't any more than that, if it was that much. I clocked them at ten-thirty-two."

Wade McNeal just smiled at Quigley when he told him about the race. "Tomorrow, I want to see how this boy can throw a football. You hear me?" Quigley was nodding his head knowingly. "Put Gladwyn running some long routes and let's find out just what we've got here," McNeal said.

"I've got a feeling about this kid, Wade. I've got a feeling that a miracle might have just walked through our door."

"Let's see how he throws a football first, before we start dancing in the halls, Randy, but I'm kinda feeling that way, too."

The next afternoon, the entire team gathered around to watch the "new guy" show his stuff. Rick spoke with the center, a large rugged boy named Rufus Longley. Longley was red-faced and looked as if he was continually out of breath, but when the play began, he was surprisingly quick. Rick and Longley worked out the cadence they would use for the passing try-outs.

Rick set up under center as Bobby Gladwyn got ready to head down field on a "post" pattern, called by Randy Quigley. Longley snapped the ball, and Rick backpedaled quickly about ten yards and then advanced five yards back toward the line of scrimmage. Gladwyn was fifty yards away when he made his cut toward the goal post, and the ball hit him square in his numbers. He pulled it in and ran on into the end zone. Then he ran back to the huddle.

"Great pass, Rick," he said. "Let's try a slant in and out toward the corner, okay, Coach?"

"Go right ahead, guys," Quigley said.

Rick yelled at the coach. "Coach, can we get some defensive players on the field, add some feel of competition?"

"Good idea, Bennett. Hey, Norman, put your cornerbacks out there and see if they can stop Gladwyn."

Pettigrew waved and sent two of his defensive backs out onto the field.

They set up again, and Gladwyn headed toward the center of the field as Rick took the ball and moved backwards again. The two cornerbacks moved to cover Gladwyn, and he suddenly pivoted toward the corner marker of the end zone with one of them on his heels and the other trying to get an angle on him to beat him to the point at which he thought the ball would land.

Rick faked a throw toward the goal post, and the other cornerback hesitated, just long enough to break his stride, and Rick then threw the ball into Gladwyn's hands at the corner.

"Okay," Quigley said. "I've seen enough. Let's get the running backs in here and practice some hand-offs and options."

Bobby Gladwyn caught up with Rick on the way to the parking lot. "What are you going to be doing this summer?" he asked him.

"Don't know for sure," Rick replied. "Everything's pretty much up in the air at our place. We're just getting settled in. My dad and I came on ahead, and my mom is still at home selling our house. Once that happens, we'll go back and bring her and my little sister back here with us."

"So, you'll be here permanently?"

"Looks like. My dad got a good job, and he just bought a house here, so yeah, we're here for good."

"Must be kind of a culture shock moving from California to Texas."

"It was harder on my mother than any of the rest of us. My dad lost his job because of the telecom bubble, so he's just happy to have another one. I'm pretty much okay anywhere. I'm the adventurous type. I'd never been to Texas before. It's really not that different. I haven't seen any shootouts on Main Street since I got here."

"Nah, you gotta go over to Fort Worth for that," Gladwyn said, and Rick laughed.

"I'll try to steer clear of that, in that case," he said.

"I'm just happy to have a good quarterback," Bobby said.

"If I make the team, I'll be happy too."

"Oh, you made the team already. Don't worry about that. McNeal and Quigley are as happy as a puppy with two peckers. You threw two passes, and they started working on play calling and executions. Trust me, Rick, you're the quarterback."

"So, what do you do all summer, Bobby?"

"I've been working the last two summers for a construction company—actually, a remodeling company. It's decent pay, and I save a lot of money, in case I decide to go to college. Some of the guys from the team get together now and then, on the weekend, and play flag football or do cookouts. It would be a good thing for you to get in on, you know, get to know everybody before the season starts. McNeal starts training in August anyway."

"I wouldn't mind getting together with you guys. I'll give you my email addy and my cell phone number."

Adrian signed the papers on the Azalea Lane house and Fed-Exed copies to Leeann for her signature. He and Rick moved their stuff in on the weekend. The following week they had the cable TV, and internet service hooked up, so the house began to feel like home, except it lacked several rooms of furniture and other miscellaneous items, and a mother and a daughter/sister.

Adrian started to work full time, and Brian asked him to take on a client in Shreveport, Louisiana. The client was a man of Cajun descent named Louis Bertrand. Bertrand owned a business that installed telephone systems for startup companies and expanded and upgraded existing systems for growing businesses. Louis spoke with a noticeable Cajun accent, but Adrian immediately perceived that he was not an uneducated man.

"See here, Adrian, we've been growin' so fast that I had to build a whole new building, three times the size of the one I'm in now. I had to expand my territory down to Lake Charles and Lafayette. I've hired ten new people jus' this past week."

"Well, let's go look at the new building," Adrian said. "I'll need to see the plans, and if you can get me a set that would be helpful."

Louis nodded his head.

"Has the new server room been engineered?" Adrian asked.

"No," Louis said, "but the plans list the equipment and the modems and shows all the remote UPS desk stations."

"Okay, I can take all that back to my engineer and technicians in Dallas."

"I want you guys to do the design and installation for me. They've been doing my work for going on ten years now. You're new, aren't you?"

"Yes, sir, I just recently came on board. I relocated from California."

"Well, you seem to know what you're talking about, so I look forward to working with you. You like Cajun food?"

"I don't know," Adrian said. "I've never had any."

"Oh, well, we'll have to fix that."

Brian Hancock was the first person, Adrian ran into when he got back to the office. "Hey, Adrian," Brian said, "how'd it go with ol' Bertrand?"

"It went very well, Brian, I've got a set of plans, and I'll need, to get with Gary."

"Let me get Kenny and Gary, and we'll meet you in the conference room."

Adrian spread out the construction drawings on the conference room table and showed them the new server room facility. "It lists all the servers and UPS equipment and locations of the racks. Their electrician will provide the power receptacles at the racks. We will install the racks, equipment, and battery packs."

"Louis mentioned something about wanting a backup generator for his server room because he's been having a lot of utility power outages lately," Brian said. "Did he say anything to you about that?"

"Yes, he did," Adrian replied, "and I called an electrical contractor in the area that installs generators. I told Louis we could handle it as a turnkey contract. That was the only company in the area I could find that does that kind of work, so it might be kind of expensive."

"Yeah, it could be," Kenny said. "You might want to mention that to Louis and tell him that, in order to cut out our markup, he might want to handle that himself. He'll probably want us to do it anyway, but it'll be a nice gesture."

"Okay," Adrian said, "that is a good idea. Thanks, boss."

"Did he take you to that Cajun food restaurant?" Kenny asked him.

"He did, but I paid for it, he tried to, but I insisted."

"Good, I'm glad you did. That Louis is quite a character. At first glance, you'd think he's a rube, but he's got an MBA from LSU. He's no dummy."

"He told me a joke," Adrian said, "I probably shouldn't tell it, but…"

"Oh, come on," Brian said, "Cindy isn't here.

"Okay, well, there was this Cajun boy who had a—

"Is this the 'dick' joke," Kenny blurted out?"

Adrian threw his pen on the table and sighed. "Well, crap, I was looking forward to telling this all the way back home."

"Go ahead and tell it, Adrian, Gary hasn't heard it," Kenny insisted.

Gary nodded his head.

"Okay, as I was saying, and you have to imagine it with a Cajun accent. This Cajun boy was blessed or cursed, depending on one's perspective, with a twenty-five-inch pecker. So, he goes to a witch doctor to see what can be done about it. The doctor tells the boy he cannot help him, but he should go to a certain place in the swamp, look for this magic frog, and ask the frog to marry him. The frog will tell him 'No,' emphatically, but he will lose five inches off his pecker every time the frog says 'No.'

"The boy does as the witch doctor tells him. He goes to the place in the swamp, and he finds the frog. 'Will you marry me, Miss Frog?' the boy asks the frog. The frog says 'No,' and suddenly the boy loses five inches off his pecker. 'Hmm,' he thinks, 'it really works, but a twenty-inch pecker is still too big, so he asks the frog again, 'Will you marry me?' Again, the frog says 'No.' And poof, another five inches comes off his oversized member. Now it's fifteen inches long, and he thinks, one more time will give him a ten-inch member, and he would be a very well-endowed man, so he goes up to the frog one more time and says. 'Will you marry me, Miss Frog?' The frog looks up at him and says: 'How many times do I have to tell you this? No, No, No.'"

Everyone around the table burst into uncontrolled laughter, including Adrian.

Adrian received a call from Leeann telling him that they had a buyer for the house. The realtor had set up a meeting for the title transfer, payment, and payoff and all the associated business involved in the selling of one's home.

Leeann was both happy and sad. School would be out in a week, and Amanda would not have to leave early. She would lose the house she loved so dearly, but she would soon have her family back together again, and that was what mattered to her the most. Adrian would fly back when the mover had everything loaded and ready to move out. The three Bennetts would drive back in Leeann's car. When the business was all completed, they set out on their journey.

"How far is it to Dallas, Daddy?" Amanda asked.

"It's about fifteen-hundred miles, honey," Adrian told her, "so please don't say 'are we there yet' as soon as we leave California."

Amanda giggled. "I won't, Daddy, but that's a long way. Are we going to drive straight through or stop for the night somewhere?"

"I expect we'll spend one night in a motel. It's about a twenty-one-hour drive, so I don't think your mother, and I want to drive that far without at least one good night's sleep and a hot shower."

They stopped for dinner in Tucson and spent the night in Las Cruces, New Mexico, slept fairly late, until Nine o'clock, had breakfast, then headed for El Paso. When they got to El Paso, Amanda let out a cheer.

"Finally, we're in Texas. I can't wait to see our new house."

"You'll have to wait just a while longer, I'm afraid, honey. It's still over six-hundred miles to Dallas."

"Oh, my gosh, she said, "we're barely half way." She looked dejected.

"We're a little farther than half way," Leeann said, "but we're not there yet."

Amanda nodded. Leeann drove for four hours, while Adrian rested until they got to Big Spring, where they stopped for lunch.

"I wonder where the spring is," Amanda mused.

"No idea," Adrian said, "I wondered that too when Rick and I came through here."

"Well, if it's big enough to name the town after, it ought to be big enough to see."

"I agree," Adrian replied, "and I'm sure there is a spring somewhere around here of sufficient size to warrant naming a town after it, but we just don't have time to research it right now. We have to go home."

It was ten o'clock that night when they got to the house on Azalea Lane. "Here it is, Lee, it's not as big as the house in Bel Air, but it's a pretty decent house. I think you'll be happy here."

"It's fine, Adrian, I like it, I want to see the inside."

The porch light came on, and Rick stepped out onto the front porch and walked to the car.

He opened the back door and let Amanda out and hugged her first and then hugged his mother, who had already gotten out of the car.

"Come on in, Mom," he told her, "you gotta see this house. Dad did a great job."

Amanda ran on ahead and went inside.

"Where is my room, Daddy?" she shouted.

"Upstairs and down the hall, Manda. Rick picked the master upstairs because I gave him first choice. He was here first. Your mother and I are in the big room on the right end downstairs. You have your choice of the other three rooms upstairs. The hall bathroom will be yours."

"Oh, Adrian, it's really nice. In fact, it's beautiful. It's all the house we really need," Leeann said.

"I know, Lee, that's what I was trying to tell you, and this house will be paid for—no house payment. That will take such a load off my shoulders."

"When are the movers coming with the furniture?"

"I scheduled them for tomorrow. You'll have to play traffic cop because I have to get back to work."

"Where will Amanda sleep tonight?"

"Amanda will sleep in my bed," Rick said, "and I'll sleep on the floor. You and dad will sleep together. Just try not to disturb the rest of the family."

"Why, son, what *do* you mean?" Leeann said mischievously.

Adrian was up early and out the door to the office. Rick took his mother and sister to breakfast, and they hurried back to the house in time to be there for the movers.

By the time, Adrian came home from the office, the furniture was all in place and Leeann, Amanda, and Rick had busied themselves the entire day getting things put away. "You guys look worn out," he said. "I guess you're too tired to go out for dinner."

"Not on your life," Leeann said. "I'll make dinner tomorrow night but tonight let's go to a restaurant."

"How about Cheddars? It's not far from her, just up on Greenville Avenue and the food is good. Rick and I have been eating there quite a bit since we got here before you and Amanda."

"Cheddars sounds fine," Leeann said.

After training started, Rick's schedule was as full as it would be when school actually started. The coaches worked them on the field in the morning and then in the class room in the afternoon. They scrimmaged, ran plays and wind-sprints and pass routes. In the classroom, they studied plays and watched as many videos of their scheduled opponents that the staff could get their hands on. It was grueling work, and hot, a lot hotter than Rick had been accustomed to but he adapted.

The Friday before the start of classes, Coach Quigley asked Rick to meet him in his office after practice. Rick showed up as he'd been asked to do and knocked on the coach's door.

"Come on in," Quigley yelled through the door.

As he stepped into the office, the entire coaching staff was there waiting for him. Quigley tossed him a black jersey with a white number 16 on it.

"I want to win State," Quigley said.

"I do too," Rick replied. "I'll give you everything I've got."

"Then let's do it. You're my quarterback."

The coaching staff cheered and shook his hand and patted him on the back and thanked him for all his hard work. Rick remained humble and thanked them for the opportunity.

"The offense is going to Possum Kingdom for the weekend before school starts," Bobby Gladwyn told him. We're celebrating our new quarterback. Longley's old man has a cabin on the lake, and he lets us use it every so often."

"What's a Possum Kingdom?" Rick asked.

It's a big lake and resort area west of Fort Worth, really neat place. How many people can you carry in your truck?"

"I can carry six, my center console turns up into the upright position, unless I have to carry the front line, then I can only get about four."

"Okay, so we need two vehicles. Rufus has a van that can carry the big guys."

The *cabin* was more than a cabin. It was a two-story house. Rufus Longley's dad, Richard, was waiting for them, when they arrived, with the barbeque pit fired up and ready. Richard Longley was a big man, at six feet four inches he was three inches taller than his son and outweighed him by fifty pounds. He was a congenial man and seemed to genuinely enjoy being involved with his son's football team.

"Bring those briskets from the fridge for me, Rufus, Richard yelled at his son, and get some of the guys to help you with all the other stuff."

"Okay, Pop," Rufus said. Several of the guys went into the house to help bring out all the drinks and condiments and other necessities."

I brought twenty-two beers," Richard told them, "that's enough for two each for you little shits. You can't have any more because you're not old enough and I don't want to get in trouble with the law. Promise me you won't go find some ass-hole to buy you more beer."

"We promise, Mister Longley," Jason Green said. "I'll make sure they don't get any more."

"Thanks, Jason," Richard said, "I'm leaving you in charge when I leave here."

Once Richard had finished the briskets, and all the food and essentials were on the tables, he left to go back to town. "Be sure to lock the doors when you leave," he said. "The housekeeper will be here on Monday so just pick up all your personal shit when you leave."

Rufus Longley, Jason Green, and Billy Martindale were the captains of the football team—Martindale, being on the defensive squad, was not there. Rufus and Jason called a meeting together for the ostensive purpose of welcoming Rick to the team.

Jason Green spoke first. "We've struggled the last two seasons guys, and I think we all know that it was because we were weak at the quarterback position. I think we all believe now that we have us a quarterback who can take us all the way. This dude not only can run as fast as me, but he can run as fast as Bobby Gladwyn, and in case anybody here didn't know—that is fast. As they say in the movies, California's loss is our gain. Rick Bennett is our quarterback, and I just want everybody to let him know that we are glad to have him with us."

"I second that," Rufus said, "this guy is the real thing. Let's give a big cheer for our new quarterback, Rick Bennett."

A loud roar went up and clapping and shouting and calls for Rick to make a speech.

Rick raised his hands and called for quiet and, when everyone had calmed down, he stood up on a chair. "Aw, hell, guys," he said, "I don't think I'll be able to do this now."

The whole room broke out in laughter and yelling as they threw their beer cans and half-eaten sandwiches at him and anything else they could get their hands on. Then the five front linemen grabbed him off the chair, carried him down to the water's edge, and tossed him into the lake.

"It's official now, pal," Bobby Gladwyn told him, as he waded out of the water. "You're one of us."

Chapter 3

The Meadows

James Harley Meadows always went by his middle name because his father owned Harley Davidson motorcycles when Harley was born. Harley was a successful small construction contractor in the Dallas area for almost twenty years. He had taken over the business from his father, who had passed away at an inordinately early age when Harley was only twenty-one years of age. It was a task any normal person would have thought impossible, but Harley had been working for his dad since he was fifteen and knew the business almost as well as the older Meadows man did.

Not only had Harley continued the successful management of the company but he had expanded it into other areas south and west of the city. Harley had no interest in motorcycles, but he kept his father's machines in honor of the man. They had remained in a storage shop at the Meadow's place of business ever since the elder Meadows man had passed on.

Harley married Ann Marie Lewis in 1984. Ann Marie was a blonde-haired, blue-eyed beauty and had been the love of Harley's life since they met in middle school. They had a daughter in 1985, whom they named Elizabeth Ann, after Ann Marie's mother. Elizabeth was the perfect image of her mother and a blessing to Harley Meadows.

The following year, another daughter came, and they named her Rose Marie. Rose had brown hair and hazel eyes and looked like her father, Harley. Rose was a pretty girl but, was not as pretty as her sister, Elizabeth, but was nonetheless an equal blessing to her father.

Elizabeth was a gifted girl, being inherently bright and a quick study. As the sisters grew older, Learning came easy to Elizabeth. Schoolwork and good grades were effortless while her sister Rose had to work hard and study late into the night just to maintain grades acceptable to her parents. The two girls were like night and day, the younger Rose being demure and pliable and an all too willing "people pleaser."

Elizabeth was pushy and often arrogant, continually showing off her knowledge, and, at times, being hurtful to people who were not as intelligent as she was. As a result, she had few real friends and strived to exist in the company of adults more so than with kids her own age. She advanced to the honor roll early in her school years and maintained that status all through high school. Rose traveled in a constant circle of friends, females and males, and was genuinely one of the most popular girls in every school she attended.

During the summer months, both girls helped their father around the shop and office a couple of days a week. Rose helped the warehouse men put together material orders and mostly "got in the way," but they tolerated the pleasant young girl because she was such a sweetheart and because they had such great respect for their boss, Harley.

"What is this, Jimmy?" Rose asked as she struggled to pick up a long object.

"That's a two-by-four Rose," Jimmy Morales told her. "That may be too heavy for you. Let me help you with that."

"I can do it," she told him.

"Okay, but be careful. Put it on that stack over there by the big door," he said, pointing. He watched the girl drag the eight-foot piece of wood over to the big stack of lumber and push it up onto the top of the pile."

"What do you want me to do now, Jimmy," she asked him.

"It's about time for your break now."

"But I'm not tired," she said.

"No, but I am," he said very low. "Why don't you go see if you can help your sister?"

"Okay," Rose said and skipped off to the office.

Elizabeth worked in the office and the lady who ran the office, Amber Pearson, discovered that the girl was actually helpful to her. Elizabeth learned how to file work orders and other company-related paper and folders and access information on the computers. Once when Amber had gone to the restroom, she heard the telephone ring and, before the answering machine could pick up, she heard Elizabeth's voice on the phone.

"Hello, thank you for calling Meadows Construction. This is Elizabeth. How can I help you?"

The girl had repeated the exact greeting that Amber used when she answered the phone, and Elizabeth was eight years old at the time.

In 1995, Ann Marie Harley, wife and mother, died suddenly of a heart attack. There were no warning signs or symptoms or any evidence that she had been in ill health at all. It just happened. Harley Meadows was devastated. For Harley, it was almost as if he had died himself. He struggled to keep the business going. Many days he could not force himself to go to the office.

The girls were ten and nine when their mother died, and the loss hit them just as hard as it had their father, but they seemed to survive the immediate blow much better than he had.

Harley started coming home early from work during the work week, something very much unlike his normal routine, and would sit around the house in a morbid stupor. He didn't take to drinking heavily, although he did enjoy a couple of glasses of wine with his dinner every night. His strict devotion to his Catholic faith kept him free of drunkenness, but it offered him little comfort against the loss of his beloved wife. He almost lost focus of the fact that his two little girls were now his life's responsibility, and it would take a shock to bring him back into focus.

It happened one Monday morning in August when Harley could not get out of bed. He had spent a tormented night in despair and sorrow, questioning the almighty about his tortured station in life. The only woman he'd ever loved had died at far too young an age, and Harley could bring no closure to it. All the power of heaven seemed unable to help him make sense of it all. He had a job to do and a large briefcase full of the weekly projects that needed to be addressed that very morning. The phone was ringing, and he could not make himself answer it.

As he lay in bed, he heard the garage door going up and the engine in his wife's car cranking. He stumbled into his home office and found the briefcase missing. Confused, but still too distraught to think clearly, he sat down at his desk to try and clear his head. His daughter Rose walked into the room.

"Rose, what are you doing here?" he asked her.

"I just went back to bed after Elizabeth left," she said.

"Where is Elizabeth?"

"She took your briefcase to the office."

"What, she did what?" he asked her, dumfounded at what she had said.

"Elizabeth took your briefcase to the office."

"How did she get there, honey?"

"She took Momma's car, Daddy. She said they needed the work orders for the week."

"Oh, my God, I've got to get to the office. Get your clothes on, Rose, we've got to go."

When Harley got to the office, Elizabeth was sitting across from Amber's desk, talking to her and going over the work orders for the week. Amber was not even aware that the girl had driven her mother's car from her house to the office. Harley's demeanor told her that something was not normal.

"Elizabeth, baby, are you okay?" he said, as he took her in his arms and hugged her.

Amber looked confused. "Are you okay, Harley?"

"I'm fine, Amber. I've been going through some bad times lately."

"That's to be expected, boss. Nobody can blame you for that."

"I know, but I've got to get it together. It ends today. From here on out, I'll be here every day without fail."

"Well, you got us the workloads for the week. That was the critical thing. If you need to go back home now, I can handle everything here."

"You don't understand, Amber," Harley said. "I didn't get here this morning. Elizabeth brought the workload information in. I was at home, incapacitated."

"But how did—"

"She drove her mother's car."

"Oh, holy shit. Oh, I'm so sorry for saying that."

"It's okay," Harley said. "That was my first thought too." He pondered for a moment. "I'll get Jimmy to drive it home and ride back with me. I'll be back to work in just a bit."

Later that night, Harley sat the girl down at the kitchen table and looked at her lovingly. "Elizabeth, honey," he said, "I know you were trying to help, but, baby, you can't drive a car, you're too young."

"But it's an automatic shift, Daddy, it's easy. You put it in D to go forward and in R to go back. I watched Momma drive everywhere we went. I knew you were feeling bad over Momma, and I knew the stuff had to go to the office. It's not very far away."

My God, he was thinking. *She looks so much like her mother, it almost breaks my heart every time I look at her. And she is so smart, it's scary.* "Okay, baby, I appreciate what you did, but please don't ever do that again. Promise me you won't ever do it again."

"I promise, Daddy, I won't ever do it again, until I'm old enough to drive."

"Thank you, Elizabeth," he said." I'm not going to miss work anymore, I promise 'you' that."

At seventeen, Elizabeth was in her junior year at William B Travis High School and was an A honor roll student with a 4.0 GPA, with aspirations of becoming a scientist. Elizabeth was a walking, talking anomaly. She had determined that she would commit her life's work to finding ways to prevent people from having heart attacks. To this goal, she dedicated much time, effort, and passion.

She exuded intelligence, had perfect command of the language, was comfortable conversing with adults, of all professional persuasions and callings, and yet she was strikingly beautiful. Her blonde hair—that fell halfway between her ears and her shoulders—and brilliant blue eyes set upon a perfect face captured attention everywhere she went. And people had often commented that she would "be more likely to *cause* heart attacks than to prevent them," It was this sort of interaction between males and females that brought disdain from the young woman.

She disliked the *jocks* and the macho types, who strutted and preened and tried to impress her with inane *guy* talk. But she admired the strong, silent type, men like her father, who had fallen in love with her mother at an early age and would never love another as long as he lived. Elizabeth knew this about Harley Meadows and, for her, that was the only kind of love worth having.

Chapter 4

Elizabeth

It was early August, just before the football training began. Rick received a call from Bobby Gladwyn.

"Hey, Bobby, what's up?"

"I need a favor, Rick, I'm at work. Actually, I'm about to get off, and I've got a flat on my car. The spare is flat too. I was wondering if you could come and take me to get both tires fixed and then bring me back, so I can put the one back on my car and get out of here."

"Sure, Bobby, just tell me where it is."

Bobby gave him the address, and Rick wrote it down. The sign on the building said *Meadows Construction and Remodeling*. Rick pulled into a parking space and walked into the nearest door he saw. The sign on the door notified visitors that the room was the Office. Sitting at a desk in the Office was blonde haired-girl with blue eyes Rick could not help staring at.

"Can I help you?" she asked him.

"I'm looking for Bobby Gladwyn," Rick replied.

"He should be out in the shop," she said.

Rick looked around to see if there was a door leading from that room to the shop.

The girl stood up. "I'll show you where he is." She led him out the same door he came in, and he followed her down the side of the building to another door. She opened it and held it open for him, and he went into the building.

"What's your name," she asked.

"Rick Bennett," he said. "What's yours?"

"I'm Elizabeth Meadows."

"So, you own this place?"

She smiled sardonically. "My dad owns it. I work for him. Are you a friend of Bobby's?"

"I am. We're also teammates."

"Oh, you don't look like a jock."

"Really, so what does the stereotypical jock look like?"

"Well, the *stereotypical* jock—" She put up two fingers of both hands beside her head to indicate quotation marks. "—typically can't spell stereotypical."

"That might be true," he replied, "but the stereotypical *pedant*—" He mimicked her hand gestures and her voice, "—sometimes makes exaggerated assumptions, often baseless and inconsiderate."

Her demeanor changed. She was angry, but more at herself than at him. "Come on. I'll show you where Bobby is," she said. She turned sharply and took him to where his friend was, without speaking to him again.

"I see you met Miss Perfect," Bobby said as he began taking the flat tire off his car.

"Uh, yeah, as a matter of fact, I did."

"She's the boss's daughter."

"She told me that," Rick said.

"Really, I'm surprised she even spoke to you, I guess you're not bad looking. That had to have something to do with it. She usually assumes anyone who is friends with the hired help, is a peon."

"She's easy to look at," Rick said.

"Oh, no question about that," Bobby agreed. "A couple of the guys on the team asked her out, at different times, and she just laughed at them. Didn't say a word, just laughed and walked away from them. Her old man is a great guy, though. It's hard to believe she is his daughter. Harley Meadows is as good as gold. He would have taken me to get my tires fixed today, but he's out on a job and won't be back until later."

"Don't worry about that, Bobby," Rick said. "I don't mind doing this one bit. It's no trouble."

"This is a really nice truck, Rick, it's almost new. When did you get it?" Bobby asked him.

"I started working for my grandpa every summer when I was fourteen. He paid me, and I saved most of the money. He bought a new truck every year, and I got my license when I was sixteen, so he gave me this truck—called it a bonus."

"That's a really good grandpa."

"He's a good man. I'll miss him the most about leaving California."

"Oh, I meant to say, Harley has another daughter named Rose, and Rose is the exact opposite of Elizabeth, just not as pretty and not as smart. Rose is a year younger and very outgoing."

"Why is the other girl so uptight?"

"Their mother died when they were both young. I don't know if that's what caused it because, if it did, it didn't make Rose like that. Elizabeth is smart, very smart, and when I say smart, I mean four-point-oh GPA and honor roll her whole school life. She's so smart, she's stupid, I guess, but damn is she good looking. Such a waste that is."

The first day of the new school year, Rick picked up his schedule and discovered that he had the same home room teacher as Elizabeth for English Grammar. He entered the class and asked the teacher, Mrs. Culley, if she had assigned seating.

"You can sit anywhere you like," she said. "You're Rick Bennett, right?"

"Yes, ma'am," Rick said, and he looked around for a seat. He took a seat on the center row, one seat back from the front desk.

Mrs. Culley went on about her business without paying much attention to the students coming into the room. She was a studious woman who appeared to Rick to be about his mother's age, maybe a few years younger. She was not unattractive but was not a head-turner.

She was married, so Rick assumed that she had been able to attract at least one man in her life. He wondered if she had kids, but she never mentioned having any during the school year. He didn't want to pry into her personal business, so he never asked.

Almost every seat in the class was taken except the one in front of him when, to his shock and surprise, in the door rushes the girl from the construction company. She had an armload of books and notebooks. She made a quick obligatory apology to Mrs. Culley for being late.

"Take the seat in front right there, Elizabeth," Mrs. Culley said, pointing to the desk in front of Rick.

The girl sat down without even noticing that Rick was sitting right behind her. He was enjoying the moment. He decided to stare at the back of her neck to see if he could make her nervous, subconsciously. He began fantasizing about lifting her hair and kissing her neck and lost track of what the teacher was saying, so he diverted his eyes. There just didn't seem to be anything imperfect about her physical appearance. Mrs. Culley was telling them that the seats they were in would be their permanent seats for the year. They were to sit in the same seats for every class, so she could more easily get to know their names.

About twenty-minutes into the class, the teacher got a message on her pager. "I have to go to the office for a few minutes, I won't be long. You guys can just talk among yourselves but don't get rowdy."

Some of the students chuckled at that.

After she left, a boy in the seat next to Elizabeth began holding his nose up in the air in an obvious attempt to get her attention. She ignored him but that only made him try just that much harder. "Hey, stuck up," he said to her, "do you cover your nose when you go out in the rain, to keep from drowning?"

The girl gave no indication that she had even heard him.

"Hey, bitch!" he continued, more loudly, and she reacted physically but said nothing.

For Rick, the boy had then crossed a line that should not be crossed. He raised his voice to the rude boy. "Knock it off, asshole," he told him.

The boy turned to look at Rick. "Who are you?"

"It doesn't matter who I am," Rick said. "Don't talk to her like that."

"Do you know her?" the boy replied.

"No," Rick responded.

"Then why do you care?"

"She's a girl. Don't talk to girls like that."

"What's gonna happen if I don't stop?" the boy said rudely.

Rick started to stand up. "Let's go out in the hall, and we'll find out."

The boy's face showed fear, and his demeanor changed dramatically as Rick's six-foot-two-inch frame started toward him with deliberate seriousness.

"No, that's okay," the boy said. "I was just teasing her. I meant no harm."

Rick sat back down, and the girl continued to stare straight ahead. Several girls in the class applauded briefly. They had a new hero. When class was over, Rick stood up and walked past Elizabeth as if nothing had happened.

When the bell rang, Mrs. Culley motioned to Elizabeth. "Can I see you for a minute before you go to your next class," she said.

The girl went over to the teacher's desk as all the other kids left the room.

Later that day, after school, Rick and Bobby Gladwyn were talking outside the field house.

"You won't believe who is in my home room class, sitting right in front of me," Rick said.

"Elizabeth Meadows?" Bobby said.

"How did you know that?"

"Who else would you even mention? She's the only girl we both know in common."

"I guess that makes sense."

"So what are you going to do?"

"I'm going to take her out."

"No shit?" Bobby said, surprised. "Did you ask her?"

"Not yet, not sure how I'm going to do it, but I know I am."

"Is this like a challenge or something?"

"No," Rick said. "I just started looking at the back of her neck and—well…"

"Damn, Buddy, I hope you don't fall for this girl. She's a ball-buster," Bobby said.

"I started imagining what it would be like to kiss her neck. I'm going to have to look at that neck the whole school year."

"Oh, crap, I think it may be too late. What are you thinking, Rick?"

"I'm thinking I have to take her out. Just don't tell anyone about this, please. I have to plan this out."

"I won't tell anyone, don't worry about that. But be careful, that's my advice."

Rick watched Elizabeth for the next few days, waiting for a chance to talk to her without interruption. He couldn't approach her after class because they both would be rushing to their next class.

But purely by chance, one afternoon after school, he saw her siting on a bench in the student center. She looked up at him just as he walked up to where she sat.

"Can you spare a minute?" he asked her.

"Sure," she said.

He assumed she was more amenable to him because of the incident with the rude boy in the classroom on their first day at school. He sat down beside her. "I perceived from our first meeting, at your father's place of business, that you are not overly fond of athletes or, as you referred to me, 'jocks.'"

"I may have been presumptuous," she said.

"Perhaps, but regardless, I have a challenge for you. It has come to my attention that there is at least one player on our team, with whom I am familiar, who like you, has a four-point-oh GPA and is also an honor roll student."

"How do you know that I have a four-point-oh GPA and that I am an honor roll student?"

"I have my sources," he said. "Anyway, my challenge is this, if I can show you this fella's transcript, would you be willing to have dinner with him one night?"

"What does this guy look like," she asked.

"Quite handsome, as a matter of fact, movie star looks, actually," he said.

She smiled. "Well, I suppose I'd have to say yes to such a

challenge like that, if you can actually produce this particular individual."

"Well, perhaps I'm presumptuous, but I brought his transcript with me just on the outside chance that you might be receptive to my challenge." He opened his notebook to get his transcript out.

"Don't waste your time, smart guy," she said, "I'm way ahead of you. Mrs. Culley filled me in on you the first day of school."

"Are you serious?" he said, looking like the air had just been let out of him.

She started laughing. "Yes, I'm serious, and thank you for what you said to that rude boy who was ragging on me. Oh, and yes, I'd like to have dinner with you. Where do you want to take me?"

"Where would you like to go?"

"It's up to you, you asked me," she said.

"How does Macaroni Grill sound?"

"Yes, I love Macaroni Grill."

"This Saturday night, about seven okay. I have a game on Friday,"

"Yes, that's fine. I'll write down my address and phone number. You're going to love this. My address is 1109 W Ricks Circle."

"Ricks Circle?" he repeated. "That has to be prophetic."

"Maybe," she said. "Stranger things have happened. I'll see you tomorrow at school."

"I have a date, Daddy," Elizabeth told Harley.

"Really, you finally found someone who can walk on water?"

"Oh, Daddy, that's not fair."

"I'm sorry, honey, it's just that you expect so much from people. Who is this boy?"

"He's the quarterback of the football team."

Harley Meadows just looked at his daughter and didn't know what to say. "Come on now, Lizzy, who is this boy you're going out with?"

"I'm serious, Daddy, he's the quarterback of the football

team. He's in my homeroom class, and he has a four-point-oh GPA and has been on the honor roll since he was in middle school. I've seen his transcript."

"How did you see his transcript?"

"Mrs. Culley got a copy of it and showed it to me."

"And why would she do that?" Harley asked her.

"Mrs. Culley thought it was really interesting that a football player could maintain such a GPA level for that long a time in school. The guy is smart. His family has just moved to Dallas from California."

"Well, the whole family must be smart if they left California and came to Texas."

"Yeah, that's kind of what I was thinking, Daddy. He's friends with the guy who works for you, Bobby something."

Bobby Gladwyn?"

"Yeah, Rick is friends with him."

"Then he must be okay because Bobby is a great kid. So, this Rick kid, what does he look like?"

"He's good looking, really good looking."

"Why am I not surprised? Smart and good looking, you're a perfect couple."

"It's just a date, Daddy, he didn't propose marriage."

The Saturday morning newspaper headline read *WB Travis beats Abilene Cooper 42-0.*

The follow-up story revealed that Rick Bennett had thrown for four touchdowns and Jason Green had run for two in the lop-sided victory against a very good team.

Rick found the house on Ricks Circle. *Wow*, he thought, *these folks must be loaded.* The house was plush.

He went to the door and rang the bell. Harley Meadows came to the door.

"That was one hell of a game last night, Rick," he said.

"Well, thank you, Mister Meadows. We had some good luck, and the team played well on both sides of the ball."

"Forty-two-zip is not luck, son. I was at the game. You're one hell of a quarterback."

Elizabeth came to the door. She was wearing a white dress that came down to just above her knees. It was just a plain dress, nothing expensive or elaborate, but it fit her perfectly, and she was beautiful in it, Rick noted.

She was trying to turn Rick around to walk to his truck. Harley followed them all the way to the truck, and, after Rick opened the door for her and helped her into the seat, Harley went around to the driver's window and was still talking football to Rick.

"Daddy," she said, "he's taking *me* to dinner, not you."

"Oh, I'm sorry, I just love football. You kids have a good time."

"So, your father doesn't share your opinion of jocks, I take it," Rick said as he drove away from her house."

"I'm sorry about that," she said.

"Water under the bridge. Now, I think the nearest Macaroni Grill is on Northwest Highway."

"It is," she said. "Tell me about where you came from."

"Well, we lived in Santa Barbara in a section of town called Bel Air. I went to Bel Air High School, coincidentally. My dad was a slave to the telecom bubble, over extended, living in a house he couldn't afford. It all blew up, and he had to sell the house and take a job here. Thank God for Texas is all the Bennett family has to say. He got a job making enough money to afford a reasonable lifestyle. Even my mother seems to be happy here, and she was the one who was most devastated over losing her house."

"Where do you live now?"

"Actually, not far from you. We bought a house on Azalea Lane, you access it off Hillcrest."

"That's not far at all."

"I'll drive you past the house on the way back from dinner."

"So, you like pickups. You'll be right at home in Texas."

"I like this particular one, the Ford F-150 with the extended cab. The console comes up, see—he pulled up the center console to the upright position. "Someone can sit in the middle, you know, like a girl for instance if she were so inclined."

"Okay, I can take a hint," she said, and she slid over next to him in the seat.

The hostess led them to their table and gave them their menus. "I assume you like Italian food," he said, "since you said you like the Macaroni Grill."

"I do, my dad brings my sister and me here occasionally. He fancies himself a great chef, so he cooks a lot at home, but he takes us out a lot too."

There was a downpour going on outside. They could hear the thunder and see the lightning flashes through the windows on the restaurant.

"You have to have the cheesecake. It's still raining, and we can't leave right now anyway."

She agreed and, in a little while, it sounded as if the rain had stopped. He paid the check, and they left the building. The parking lot was flooded, and water was almost up to the curb at the edge of the lot.

"Let's see," Rick said, "I can either go get the truck and bring it over here right next to the curb and get you in, or I can carry you to the truck."

She started laughing while he pretended to be contemplating which course of action to take. At that moment, someone in another truck came roaring through the parking lot right next to the curb where they were standing. The wheels of the vehicle pushed up a wall of water that was soaking everyone standing along the curb. As it approached Rick and Elizabeth, Rick stepped in front of her and put his arms around her. He drew her into him and covered her with his body as the water sprayed all over his back and legs.

"Oh, my gosh," she said, as she stepped back away from him, "You're soaked, Rick. I can't believe you did that."

"It's such a beautiful dress, I couldn't let it get wet."

"I don't know what to say," she said, looking at him with a mixture of awe and disbelief.

"Don't say anything, just wait here. I'll go get the truck."

He drove his truck over to the curb where she was standing, got out, picked her up in his arms, and set her in the driver's side so she would be next to him, then he got in beside her and started the engine.

"Don't leave yet," she said.

He turned and looked at her. "Okay," he said, but let me get away from all this activity here." He drove around to a secluded location in the parking lot and shut off the engine, then turned and looked at her again.

"Thank you, Rick. No guy has ever been so nice to me before, and so chivalrous. I'm just a bit overwhelmed."

"Maybe you never gave anyone a chance to be nice to you before."

"I don't know, you may be right, but I really enjoyed this evening. I mean that."

"Will you go out with me again?" he asked.

"Will you kiss me?" she said.

"Has any guy ever told you no to that question?"

"I've never asked a guy that question before."

He looked deeply into those unbelievably beautiful blue eyes for a moment and then put his arm around her and pulled her gently to him. He put his left hand behind her neck and placed his lips gently on hers. Their lips moved together like choreographed dancers moving in perfect unison. After a minute, he pulled away."

"Why not?" he asked.

"Why not what?"

"Why have you never asked a guy that question before?"

"Because the only guys I've ever gone out with never asked or waited to be asked, they just tried to take what they wanted, like it was a forgone conclusion that it was okay."

"I'll never touch you without your permission, Elizabeth, I promise you that."

They spent another mad few minutes locked in lip service to each other until, breathless, they wrapped themselves around each other in a lover's embrace.

He murmured over her shoulder, "We'd better stop this, or you're going to have me on life-support."

She laughed and let go of him. "Well, we can't have that, can we?"

He drove by his house to show her where he lived and then drove her home.

"So, what about next Saturday?" he said.

"What are you doing Saturday morning?" she asked him.

"What have you got in mind?"

"My dad goes to a small church thing that feeds homeless people. He does it once a month, and my sister and I go with him. If you're not busy, I'd like for you to come along. And then Saturday night, why don't you come to my house for dinner? Would you like that?"

"Yes, to all the above," he said. "What time do I need to be here Saturday morning?"

"Around nine o'clock, okay?"

He walked her to the door, and they stood there a moment looking at each other.

"You know, Rick," she said, "there is such a thing as non-verbal permission."

"Oh, right," he said, and he took her in his arms and kissed her goodnight. "Okay, Lizzy Bee, I will see you Saturday Morning."

"What did you just call me?"

"It was kind of a take-off on Elizabeth, I suppose. I didn't plan it, it just kind of came out. "You're not mad, are you?"

"No, I think it's kind of cute."

"It's kind of appropriate," he said. "You're like a busy bee, the way you rushed into class the first day of school all loaded down with books, so Lizzy Bee just seemed to fit."

The following Friday was an away game against Midland Lee, and Travis won by a slim margin of 14-7. The team had a good game but likewise did the Midland team.

"A win is a win," the coaches said, philosophically.

Rick was up early on Saturday morning and headed to Elizabeth's house at around nine. He didn't want to be late. It turned out he was early by about fifteen minutes. Rose came to the door. "You must be Rick," she said, "come on, Dad and Elizabeth are in the back getting ready."

Harley had a trailer attached to his pickup truck. He'd been barbequing brisket since the night before. He spotted Rick and waved. "Hey, Rick, good win last night, sorry I couldn't make it, but I had to get ready for today."

"That's okay," Rick said, "what do you need me to do?"

"Just help the girls load up the stuff onto the trailer."

Elizabeth was coming out the back door of the house with an armload of boxes.

"Let me get that," Rick said and took it from her.

"I'm glad you came, thank you," she said.

"I wouldn't miss it."

"We leave about nine-thirty and get there around ten to set up then serve lunch, starting at eleven until about two."

"Okay."

"Man, of few words, huh?"

"Mine is not to reason why, mine is just to do what I'm told."

"Tennyson, right?"

"Tennyson."

The target facility was small Catholic Church in south Dallas. They had a large room that was used for various events. One priest and a couple of parishioners were starting to set up tables and chairs when Harley and his crew arrived.

"I'll help them set up, Mister Meadows, unless you want me to unload the truck," Rick said.

"No, go ahead, Rick, the girls and I can unload the truck."

Rick began helping the three men set up the hall with tables and chairs. In a half hour, the job was complete. Harley then went over with him the procedure for serving the folks who came in for the food. Rick helped Harley prepare the brisket while the girls opened cans of vegetables, heated them, and put them in metal serving dishes. The priest would greet the visitors at the door, and his parishioners would circulate through the room, as the meals were being served, attending to any needs anyone might have.

In the end, there were about a hundred people who came through the door for the free meal. The priest, Father Benson, had busied himself mostly with attracting new members to his church. He would have to wait until the next day to see just how successful his efforts had been.

After the crowd had left, and everything was cleaned up and put away, Rick and the others broke down the tables and the chairs and stowed them away in their proper location.

Harley, Father Benson, and the rest of them sat around the one remaining table, drinking coffee and tea, more or less debriefing and discussing the work of the day.

"You're a life saver Harley," Father Benson said, "you and your two lovely girls. You help more than you can possibly know. And this young man—" He pointed at Rick. "—he's an absolute dynamo."

"Rick is Elizabeth's boyfriend," Rose said, and Elizabeth glanced quickly at Rick, who smiled at her."

"Ah, I see, and are you Catholic, Rick?"

"No, sir," Rick said, "my family is Lutheran."

"Good, good, and where do you worship Jesus—meaning where do you go to church?"

"Wherever I happen to be when the spirit moves me," Rick said, and Father Benson chuckled.

Back at the Meadows' home, Rick helped them unload the truck and clean up.

"I'm going home to clean up, and I'll be back at seven, is that what you said?"

"You can come earlier if you want to," Elizabeth said.

"Why don't I come at six, so we can talk a while?"

"Then I'll look for you at six."

"So, you must really like this guy, Rick," Harley said, "inviting him to dinner after only one date."

"I do like him, Daddy," Elizabeth said. "He's different, he's just not like any other boys I've ever known."

"Well, I hope you don't mind if I talk football with him some of the time."

"I guess not, as long as you don't want to go on dates with us."

"No, no, I'll stay home and cook."

Rick showed up dutifully at six, and Elizabeth took him into the back yard where Harley had built a Koi pond and a small Oriental garden. An elevated area directed a stream that flowed into the pond over a mound of rocks and over a waterfall. It created a babbling brook effect that was soothing and comforting. They sat down in two chairs facing each other, and he looked at her for a few minutes.

"This is really nice," he said.

"I come out here on occasion, when I'm feeling down, and sit and listen to the waterfall. It helps sometime."

"I want to know about you, Elizabeth. I want to know how you feel about things and what you plan to do with your life."

"That's going to take a while," she said.

"I think it's worth the investment."

"Did you have a girlfriend back in California?"

"No, I dated girls, quite a few, but that all seems irrelevant now. I have feelings for you I've never had for anyone else."

"After one date, how did that happen?"

"I don't know, it just happened," he told her.

"Well, don't you think it's something you should figure out before you go off to college on a football scholarship and then become a big-time NFL star? Suppose I don't want to be part of all that."

"I'm not going to play in the NFL."

"You're not?"

"No, I'm not, what gave you that idea?"

"It just seems like the typically logical progression for a football player."

"I'm not your typically logical football player."

"No, I guess you're not, then what do you plan to do?"

"I do plan to use football to go to college, but I want to teach either economics or history, or both at the college level."

Her eyebrows went up. "Really?" she said.

"Yes, really, but now you've got me talking about me again. I want to know about you."

"I plan to go to medical school, genetics, bio-medical science, I want to do research for preventive methods and treatments for heart attacks," she said.

"I'm not surprised. You certainly have the brains for it."

"My mom died from a heart attack when I was ten, and somehow that made me want to do something to help keep people from having heart attacks, if I can in some way."

"That is truly awesome, Elizabeth. Not many people have that much courage and ambition, and the stamina to actually do it. I hope you see it through."

"I intend to see it through. There is a lot more that we need to know about each other, but we can't cover all that before dinner. I like you, too, Rick, and I suppose that happened just as suddenly. I don't really know how it happened either, just that it did. So, we may need to spend more time together."

"That was going to be my suggestion," he said. "I'm keeping Saturday nights open for the time being, unless you advise me otherwise."

"I don't have anything pressing at the moment, so, Saturdays are reserved."

Rick discovered that Harley Meadows was indeed a man of many talents. He prepared what he called an Alsatian stew or more accurately a casserole made with cuts of lamb, pork, and beef, simmered with potatoes and onions.

Harley explained, with magnificent stage presentation that the dish was originally a peasant dish that was traditionally cooked in a community setting. He called it Bacheofe but said an alternate spelling was Bachenoff which was much easier to pronounce.

Harley opened a bottle of Cabernet Sauvignon, a French red wine, and poured a glass for each of them. "One glass each, mind you," he said, "I do not intend to go to jail for contributing to the delinquency of minors."

"Oh, come on, Daddy," Rose said. "We won't tell. You won't tell, will you, Rick?"

"Tell what?" he said.

"See, Daddy, we can have two glasses each."

"No, daughter," he said, "there's a greater principle at play here. If I give you kids two glasses of wine, I would never forgive myself, for that would not leave enough for me."

The three kids started laughing, and Rick stood up. "Then I propose a toast." He lifted his glass, and they all clinked theirs to his. "To Mister Harley Meadows and his two beautiful daughters."

"I'll drink to that," Harley said.

"You'll drink to your laundry, Daddy," Elizabeth said.

Later, Elizabeth walked Rick out to his truck. They kissed, and she opened the door for him.

"Will you take me somewhere tomorrow?" she asked him. "We still have a lot to talk about."

"I would love to do that, just tell me what time."

"I'll call you in the morning."

His mom and dad were sitting in the living room when he got back home. "Hello, son," Adrian said. "How was your date?"

"It was cool, Dad. Elizabeth's dad fixed dinner, and it was some kind of French dish, really good, he's a really interesting guy."

"You're kinda sweet on this girl, aren't you, honey?" his mother said.

"Kinda," he replied.

"The look in your eyes says more than kinda," Leeann prodded.

"I like her very much, Mom."

"When are you going to bring her to meet us?" Adrian asked him.

"I think it's a little early for that just yet, but I will."

The next morning, Elizabeth called. "I want to go over to White Rock Lake," she said.

"I don't know where that is."

"I'll show you."

She directed him to a place, and he turned the truck into it and parked. She leaned back against the passenger side door and drew her knees up into the seat and wrapped her arms around them.

He turned to face her. "I haven't dated much since I got old enough to date. I guess that's why most kids at school think I'm a snob. That kid in class, the one you called down when you came to my rescue, he asked me out once, and I told him no. He got mad about it and took every opportunity to rag on me about it."

"He didn't have the right to talk to you like that," Rick said.

"I know, but what I'm saying is that it was partially my fault, maybe, because I was rude to him. With you, this is the first time I've ever gone out more than once with a guy. I really like you, but I think this is probably a temporary thing with you."

"Why?" he asked. "I don't want it to be."

"I have some strange ways about me."

"Yes, you do, and I'm sure I do too, but you have some very special qualities too. Seeing what you do with you dad and your sister at that church, and your drive to help people, those are not just superficial things. Those are not strange ways."

"When my mother was sick, I made a promise to her, and to my dad, that I would remain celibate until I got married. I don't sleep around. Every guy I have dated before you, and there haven't been that many, but that was all they wanted. Once they learned that I would not have sex with them, they lost interest in me."

"Oh," he said, "well, in that case, I might as well take you home. Put your seat belt on."

The look of disbelief on her face made him start laughing.

"Elizabeth, if you're trying to get rid of me, you're going to have to tell me, because it's going to take more than that to make me go."

"I thought you were serious for a moment there," she said.

"Look, I'm not going to tell you I love you because I'm not a hundred percent sure yet, and I don't want to spook you, but I can't stop thinking about you. I think about you just about every minute of the day. I have to force you out of my mind so I can get up for the games. I want to go with you and your dad every Saturday on that church thing just so I can be around you. I want to walk you to class at school, holding your hand. I dream about you at night, and you don't want to know what goes on there. That's how I feel. I hope you can live with that."

"I'm kind of where you are, Rick," she said. "I'd like to do the hand holding thing. I've never had that with a guy but, with you, I think it would be very special. We have about seven months before we have to make decisions on college. Then we'll have to find out if this thing will survive a cell phone and email relationship."

"I know, I've already started worrying about that," he said.

"Perhaps you should kiss me," she said, "that might stop your worry for a while."

"It's worth a try, Lizzy Bee," he said, and he took her hand as she moved across the seat beside him.

Chapter 5

Winning

By the end of September, the William B Travis High School football team was at 4 and 0, having beaten Abilene Cooper, Midland Lee, Plano, and Abilene High, in Rick Bennett's first four starts with the team. By Halloween, they were 9 and 0 with one game left on November seventh and threatening to go undefeated for the first time ever in the history of the school.

Adrian spent the last week of October in Louisiana, wrapping up the work on Louis Bertrand's new server room facility. The new backup generator was installed and tested and all local inspections made. The city of Shreveport issued an occupancy permit, and Bertrand started moving his staff into the space as Adrian was preparing to leave for home.

Rick was receiving preliminary letters from a few schools around the country, and several phone calls, to which he responded that he had not even begun to think about what he would do after his final year in school.

"Yes," he told them, "I do intend to accept a scholarship to play ball in college, but right now, my goal is to help my team win the state championship of Texas."

Both Bennett men were having a good year. Kenny and Brian were extremely pleased with Adrian's work on the Bertrand contract, and they wanted to expand his territory to the rest of Louisiana and the panhandle of Florida. Adrian was pleased with the confidence the company had placed in him, but it did mean being away from home for longer periods of time.

On the seventh of November, Travis beat Arlington 21-10 for an undefeated season and faced some even tougher competition in the coming playoffs. Rick received a call from Harley Meadows, asking him to come by the office for a talk. Rick immediately drove to the Construction office and went to Harley's office.

"Thanks for coming, Rick," Harley said.

"No problem, Mister Meadows, what's up?"

"You've got a tough row to hoe ahead of you, now with the playoffs coming up. I want you to skip helping us out at the church this, next time and rest up if you think that will help you in the game."

"I really look forward to doing that with you on Saturdays," Rick said, "and it's not hard work. I tell you what. If we have a practice that Saturday, I'll skip, but if we don't, I'd like to keep doing it."

"Well, okay, do what you think is best, Rick. Have you gotten any offers from colleges yet?"

"I'm starting to, but I'm deflecting them. I don't want to get distracted from the playoffs."

"Can I ask you a non-football question, Rick?"

"Of course, Mister Meadows," he said.

"First, stop calling me Mister Meadows, call me Harley. Everyone who works for me calls me Harley."

"Okay, I'll call you Harley, Harley."

"I'd like to ask you what you intend to do with my daughter when you both go off to college and points beyond."

Rick thought seriously for a moment about what Harley had said. "I love her, Harley. She's the only girl I've ever loved. I want everything that goes with that, as long as she agrees and consents, and even if she doesn't, that's still what I want."

"You know she wants to be a geneticist, and that takes a long time in school. And she's a headstrong girl who will, I have no doubt, become a headstrong woman. It's going to take a patient and self-controlled man to live with her."

"I wouldn't be here talking to you now if I didn't know that. I'll do what it takes, and I'll wait as long as it takes."

"Well, I hope it works out for both of you. I've been praying for years that the right man would come along for her."

"Neither of us is a compulsive person. We're both are very deliberate. She's made it clear that she intends to remain celibate until she's married. I have to respect that, although I believe I could have made a good case for not keeping that tenet. But I chose not to try. Even if she does not decide to marry me at some point in time, I hope the man she does marry has the good sense to respect her decision, as well."

"Have you asked her? Does she know you love her?"

"I haven't told her, but she knows," Rick said.

"Yes, I expect she does. Well, I won't tell her anything about our conversation. It's best that you work it out with her on you own timeline without any outside interference."

"Thank you, Harley, I really appreciate it."

It was after the last game of September when Bobby Gladwyn, who had become Rick's best friend in addition to being his favorite passing target, spotted him walking down the hall, holding hands with Elizabeth. Bobby immediately contracted a case of lockjaw and could not speak. He stood there like a statue and watched them walk on by. Neither of them noticed him.

Later at practice, he approached Rick. "Please tell me we are going to win State," he said.

"Okay, we're going to win State," Rick replied.

"Now I know it will happen," Bobby said gleefully."

"What do you mean?"

"Everything you say you're going to do, you do."

Rick shrugged and looked confused.

"I saw you in the hall with Elizabeth Meadows. You said you were going to take her out and apparently, you did more than take her out."

"We've been dating for a while now," Rick told him.

"That's unbelievable," Bobby said. "You're my new hero—check that, you were already my hero. Now you're my super-hero. I am in awe. Do I still have to keep it quiet?"

"I'd rather not spread it all over the school. She's kind of funny about that sort of thing. She doesn't like a lot of public attention, even though she seems to enjoy the looks we get when we walk in the hall holding hands."

"Well, I'm happy for you, Buddy, there are going to be a lot of jealous dudes around school when this gets out."

"I just don't want her to think I'm flaunting her."

"What if she starts flaunting you?" Bobby said.

"Well, that's okay, I don't mind the attention." Rick decided it was time for his folks to meet his girl. "I'd like to bring Elizabeth over for dinner this Saturday, Mom, if that would be okay."

"That would be wonderful, Rick, if your father is back from Louisiana. I would like for him to be here to meet her."

"When is he due back?"

"He should be back in by Friday afternoon. What should I fix, what does she like?"

"She likes Italian, French, just about anything I guess. She's a Texan. They pretty much eat anything, don't they?"

"I think my son is fast becoming a Texan too, and I think that pretty blonde-haired girl may have something to do with it."

"It's not such a bad place, Mom. There are some good people here."

"You're not falling for this girl, are you?"

"Would that be so bad if I did?"

"No, I guess not, she sounds like she might be a perfect match for you."

Adrian didn't get home until Saturday afternoon, but he was there in time for dinner with his son's love interest. One look at Elizabeth made Adrian understand why Rick was initially attracted to her but listening to her talk captivated the whole family just as it had their son and brother. She was a delightful girl whose knowledge of so many things belied her stereotypical blonde beauty physical persona. The dinner turned out to be a very pleasant affair. Elizabeth asked Adrian questions about his job, and she gave him the impression that she was sincerely interested in his answers, not just making small talk.

"I am currently working with a startup radio and TV station

in Alexandria, Louisiana. For instance, we'll install a satellite system, which includes a tower. These systems are integral to contemporary telecommunications as communications today often involve bouncing signals off receptors located miles above the earth, but I'm sure you're familiar with that concept."

"Well, insofar as using a cell phone corresponds to that," she said.

"It's similar, and we install cell site towers too, without which your cell phones would be useless. But anyway, we provide the supplementary equipment and wiring, hardware and software, and do the installation, testing, and training. We do a turnkey contract."

"That's a lot more involved and complicated than I imagined," Elizabeth said.

"But not as complicated as the human heart," Adrian replied. "I understand you plan to become a geneticist."

"I do, at least that is my dream."

"Well, I hope you stick with it, it's a noble calling."

"She will," Rick interjected, "Nothing gets in her way."

"Well, almost nothing," she said, smiling at Rick.

"Are you Rick's girlfriend?" Amanda asked her.

"I don't know," she said, "Am I your girlfriend, Rick."

"Yes, Elizabeth, you are my girlfriend."

"Then it's official, yes, Amanda, I'm your brother's girlfriend."

"That's good," Amanda said, "because I like you."

"Well, I like you too, Amanda."

"We're playing for the state championship next week," Rick said, as he drove her home.

"Are you confident that you'll win?"

"I have to win."

"Why" losing isn't the end of the world."

"It will be for Bobby Gladwyn."

"For Bobby Gladwyn, why?"

"Well, when I discovered that you were sitting right in front of me in home room, on the first day of school, I told him I was going to take you out—on a date, I mean. He thought I was wasting my time, but then when he saw us together in the hall, he begged me to guarantee him we would win state. I did it."

"So, he thinks because you got me to go out with you that you can do anything you set your mind to?"

"Pretty much."

"That's going to be pretty Earth-shattering for him if you don't deliver."

"There's a lot riding on the game. It won't really affect my scholarship offers, but it will be a big letdown for the team and for the school. I really want to win it."

"Then do it," she said matter-of-factly.

The new radio and TV station in Alexandria was owned and operated by a company called Interstate Communications, and its CEO was a man named Andrew Guidry. Despite the pretentious name, Interstate Communications was an ambitiously small company, albeit with a large budget. Andy Guidry was a hands-on CEO, and he was on site most of the time while the new facility was being constructed and the equipment was being installed. Adrian had remained on site as well for four days of the week, typically driving back to Dallas on Thursday evening to be in the office on Friday to fill in the bosses on his progress.

"We're gearing up for the 'oh-four election coming up next year," Guidry told Adrian. "We're contemplating putting a facility in New Orleans if your company can handle it."

"Will it be similar to the one we're doing here, Andy?" Adrian asked him.

"Pretty much the same, but it will start up very soon, before this one is wrapped up. Will you need some help with that?"

"Possibly, but I'll see how my office wants to handle it. I don't want to break off this project at this stage in the game to start another one. We may put another project manager on the New Orleans facility."

"DTS is the only company I've found that can do a complete turnkey project without having to sub-out parts of the work load."

"We're pretty well staffed and have several installation

crews. It does get hectic sometimes shuffling them around all over Texas and Louisiana keeping up with the workload, but so far, we've been able to deliver. At the current time, like most telcos, the only service we don't provide is what's called the *last mile* connections, like your domestic phone line, you know, Verizon, et cetera. We provide *points of presence* where companies can interconnect to them. Other than that, we can do pretty much anything you need."

"We're going to proceed with it, so I would like to get the ball rolling," Guidry said.

"If I can get a set of plans from you, I'll send them to my office, and our engineer can get a head start on it before I get back."

"That sounds like a plan," Guidry said. "Thanks, Adrian."

Brian Hancock suggested he handle the New Orleans project since Adrian was tied up in Alexandria and Kenny wanted to avoid subjecting Adrian to burnout.

Kenny called Adrian. "Adrian, you've been on the road ever since you started with us, and I want you to take a week off, as soon as you're finished up there in Alexandria."

"I'm okay, Kenny," Adrian said. "I could do the New Orleans job if you need me to."

"No, I want Brian to take that one and give you some time at home. You've done a hell of a job, and I appreciate it, but I'm not going to wear you out."

"Okay," Adrian said. "My wife will appreciate it."

"I thought you might want to go home for a few days."

"Home is in Dallas, Kenny, that's where my family is."

"I'm glad you feel that way, Adrian," Kenny said. "We're mighty happy to have you with us. Take a week off and go somewhere."

"I'll do that, boss, thanks." Adrian called his wife. "Would you like to go to Belize for a few days, Lee?"

"You know I would, when?" she said.

"When I'm through with this project, maybe a week or ten days."

"Just the two of us?"

"Yes, the kids are still in school. Rick can take Amanda to school. We'll be back before Thanksgiving."

"I'll start packing," Leeann said.

Adrian was in Louisiana when Travis High played South-lake Carroll for the 5-A Division 2 State Championship of Texas. He hated himself for not going home to go to the game, but the job was at a critical stage, and he felt obligated to be there. At the motel, later, he searched for information on the game and finally found the score: William B Travis 20, Carroll 14. The copy read that, as time was running out and with the score tied 14-14, Travis drove to the ten-yard line. Travis quarterback Rick Bennett threw a short pass to Jason Green in the right flat. Green was wrapped up at the five-yard line and flipped the ball back to his quarterback, Bennett, who had followed the play, and Bennett ran it into the end zone for the go-ahead score as the clock ran out. Travis was 14-0 for the season and High School Football Champions of the State of Texas.

"I guess Bobby was right," Elizabeth said, on the phone. "You *are* magic."

"I need to see you, beautiful," he told her.

"Little ol' me?" She said, in an exaggerated southern voice. "I thought you'd want to be celebrating with your fellow jocks."

"No, I need to see you."

"Well, I'm in the parking lot with my dad and Rose. I'll wait for you."

"I might be a while, I have to shower. Why don't I pick you up at home later, okay?"

"Yes, I'll be waiting for you at home."

They gave Rick the game ball, and he gave it to Jason Green. "Jason had the presence of mind to toss the ball off instead of trying to fight it into the end zone and running out the clock. He deserves this more than I do," Rick said.

"I don't know about that having that presence of mind stuff," Jason said. "I just know they had me locked up tight. I looked around, and there was Rick right behind me. I said, 'here, you take this muthafucker, I don't want it.'"

The whole locker room erupted in laughter.

Some reporters were there wanting to talk to Rick. "I have to go pick up my girl, guys," He told them. "She's waiting for me." And he hustled out of the building.

Harley was the first one to come to the door at the Meadows' house. He was ecstatic when he saw Rick. "That was one of the greatest plays in the history of high school football, Son," Harley said.

"It was a lucky play, Harley. I didn't plan it like that."

"Well, it worked out, regardless, and we won the game. I couldn't be prouder, and I know the whole school is too. I bet McNeal and Quigley wish you could play one more year."

"Yeah, well, this was my last hurrah, as they say."

Elizabeth came to the door, "Let's get out of here," she said.

"Where do you want to go?"

"Where we can be alone."

"White Rock Lake?"

He was leaning back against the door of his truck, and she was leaning against him. He had his arms around her and was nuzzling her hair and kissing her neck. "You'll probably slap me when I tell you this, but I'm going to tell you anyway."

"Okay," she said.

"First day of school, you were sitting right in front of me. I started staring at your neck and imagining what it would feel like to do what I'm doing right now."

"Are you serious?"

"I am serious, Elizabeth. You are so beautiful, you take my breath away sometimes."

"I'm glad you see me that way. I doubt you would have wanted anything to do with me just for my mind."

"I might have enjoyed talking to you, but I can't guarantee that I wouldn't have fantasized about kissing your neck. But you being beautiful has not hampered our relationship, as far as I can tell."

"Well, you're not exactly hard to look at, yourself, Rick Bennett."

"Thank you, ma'am, you could do better, but I hope you don't."

Rick drove his parents to DFW Airport to catch their flight to Belize. It was about a three-hour flight to the airport in Belize City. From there they caught a shuttle to the water taxi to take them to San Pedro on Ambergris Caye, where their house was located.

Leeann had become quite amorous on the ride out in the taxi. She was so obvious that she had drawn the attention of some of the other passengers. She was hugging and kissing on Adrian like a teenager.

"I'm afraid you're going to have to wait until we get to the house, my love," he said.

"But you've been gone so much lately, and I've been sleeping alone. I've been having impure thoughts, Adrian. I need to be punished." She giggled like a young girl.

His wife was still very attractive, at forty years old. She still had her slender figure that Adrian remembered when they met in college. Her shoulder-length brown hair she kept brushed so that it always looked shiny and clean and she always smelled good. Her blue eyes were still inviting.

"I'll be gentle, I'll use tough love," he told her, speaking low so no one else could hear.

"But I've been very bad, Adrian, I really need to be punished."

He chuckled. She was beginning her role playing. Lee loved to morph into her "naughty lady" routine on occasion when they had been away from each other for extended periods of time. The house in Santa Barbara was a little more conducive to such playful games because it was much bigger than their current house, and Lee was always aware that the kids might hear them.

They arrived in San Pedro, and Adrian rented a golf cart for them to get around in while they were on the island,

"We should stop and pick up some groceries before we go to the house," Adrian said.

"How far is it to the house?" she asked him.

"It's not far."

"Can't we go to the house first? I'd like to see it."

He nodded his head and drove on toward the place.

"Oh, my goodness," she said, "it's beautiful, Adrian, I love it."

"Take a look at the bedroom, I'll get the bags," he told her.

Adrian retrieved their bags and took them into the bedroom to Leeann.

"It's really nice. Hurry," she said.

"I've got to park the golf cart and take a leak, I'll be right back." He drove the cart under the shed on the side of the house then went to the bathroom.

When he walked into the bedroom, Leeann was standing by the bed in a pair of red cowboy boots, and nothing else.

"Really, Lee," he said, "red cowboy boots?" You don't even like Texas."

"You'd better get over here right now, cowboy. This ride is going to last a lot longer than eight seconds."

"Listen, lady, I'm going to give you two hours to knock off this foolishness."

"And if I don't knock it off in two hours, what are you going to do then?" she said.

"I'm going to give you two more hours."

She squealed with angelic delight and jumped onto the bed, boots and all.

Adrian walked over to the bed and took off his clothes.

"Take off the boots, lady," he told her.

"No way," she said, "the boots go with the package."

The next half hour reminded him once again why he had fallen in love with Leeann Owens, and why their marriage had withstood the storms and pitfalls that often come between a couple.

Afterward, they lay next to each other. He cradled her in his right arm, and she lay her head on his chest. "It's late," he said, suddenly, "I've got to get you back to that bar where I picked you up."

"You didn't pick me up in a bar, Mister. You brought me here from *Dallas, Texas.*" She attempted to mimic the Texas accent, and he started laughing.

"Okay, lady, I'll get you back to Texas, but after that, I can't be responsible for anything that happens."

"Don't mess with me, Mister Bennett, I'll cut your balls off.

"That would hurt," he said.

"I didn't mean it. It would hurt me as much as it would you."

"Oh, I doubt that," he said.

Later they went out to dinner and had drinks on the beach looking out over the Caribbean.

They made love again that night with more control, and without the antics, but with no less passion, and twice every day for the remaining days they were there. On the ride, back to the mainland in the water taxi, Leeann was a bit more subdued. "I'd like to do this again sometimes," Leeann said.

"Well, I lived through it, I thought for a while there I might not, but I did, so yeah, let's plan on doing it again."

Rick and Amanda were waiting for them at the airport when they got back into DFW.

"Did you guys have fun?" Amanda asked them.

"We did," Leeann said.

"Can we go with you next time?"

"I don't know, Manda, we'll see," Adrian told her.

At the end of March, Rick was rapidly approaching the point at which he was going to have to make a life changing decision about his education. He'd received offers from many schools around the country wanting him to come play football for them. All of them had made it clear that he could pretty much name his own price. His price, however, was that he wanted to go to school on an academic scholarship. He didn't really want to play football in college. The truth was, though, that he may not have any other choice.

"I need your help," he told Elizabeth on the phone.

"Okay, what do you need me to do?"

"I need to compile a list of my priorities before the next school year begins. I was thinking we could go to the lake. I'll bring a pad, and you can help me arrange my thoughts on paper."

"Pick me up."

When they got to the lake, Rick turned to her. "I have four priorities, as best I can tell. Are you ready to write?"

"Yes, go ahead."

"Number four, I have to list all the offers I have from the various schools, evaluate the benefits, the pros and cons, et cetera. I just want to write these down right now, we'll go over the details later.

"Okay," she said.

"Number three, I need to find out how to query a school about getting an academic scholarship. Number: two, I need to find out which school is the best one for the field I want to go into. I don't care where I play football, but I want to eventually write economic and/or historical non-fiction manuals for college classes."

"Wow, that is awesome, Rick," Elizabeth said. "So, what's number one?"

"Number 1, top priority, somehow, I need to find the courage within me to ask Elizabeth Meadows to marry me."

"Well, I think we should probably work on that one first, don't you?"

"I think that would be a good idea, yes."

"Good, I'm glad you agree. Then I have to ask you one question, Rick Bennett. Do you love me?"

"Yes, Elizabeth, I love you. I am 'in' love with you, I am crazy about you. I am insane over you. I—"

"Okay, you made your point, and I think it's only fair that I tell you that I love you too. But that only gets us past the most important hurdle. When do think we should get married?"

"I think that's pretty much up to you. I'm thinking maybe our second year in college. We'll both be twenty years old then, and we can wait longer if we get to that point and decide it's too early."

"You're more level headed than I thought you would be. I appreciate your thoughtfulness," she said.

"My concern is that, if you go off to some school half the country away from me, I'll lose my mind if I have to go months without seeing you."

"I don't want that either, Rick, maybe we can figure something out. We both have to go to a four-year program. Then I want to go to Johns Hopkins for medical school, you'll be graduated by then. We'll be married and together and we can live there in Baltimore until I finish."

"If you'll just pick a school that needs a quarterback, we'll be on our way," he said.

"Are you sure you're okay with not sleeping together until we get married?"

"I told you I love you, and I meant it, whatever it takes to make you happy and to make you my wife, that's what I'll do."

"I love you for that," she said. "So what do you want to do now?"

"Let's go tell your dad and then go tell my parents."

Chapter 6

New Beginnings

Early in June of 2003, Adrian got a phone call. It was a California area code from a number he did not recognize.

The caller identified himself as Julian Stroud. Adrian knew the name as that of Ed Whelan's father-in-law, but he gave no indication to the man that he did.

"How can I help you, Mister Stroud?"

"Call me Julian, Adrian. I don't know that we have ever met, but I understand that you worked for my son-in-law, Ed Whelan, for quite some time before the recent trouble."

"Yes, I did," Adrian said. "What's going on?"

"I'm trying to locate Ed. It seems he has disappeared, along with a half million dollars of company money, as best I can figure. Have you heard from him lately?"

"No, I haven't seen or talked to Ed since I left his employment over a year ago. I wish I could help you, but I just don't have a clue where he is."

"Did you know he was having an affair with one of his female employees, a woman named Maggie Fletcher?"

"There were rumors going around the office, but I never saw any concrete evidence of anything. I pretty much minded my own business and did my job."

"Well, if you hear from him, I'd appreciate it if you'd let me know. He's cost me a lot of money."

"It's been over a year, Julian, I doubt that he'll contact me after this much time but, if he does, I will advise him to contact you."

"I would certainly appreciate that, Adrian, thank you," Julian said.

Adrian chuckled. So Ed had run off with Maggie. Adrian marveled at the power a skirt—or a pantsuit, as the case might be—had over a man. He never figured Ed Whelan for the type who would so easily throw away the business he'd spent so many years building. But, in the end, Adrian guessed that waking up in the morning on Ambergris Caye next to Maggie Fletcher topped everything Santa Barbara had to offer. And, of course, the half million dollars Ed had allegedly absconded with would help assuage any homesickness he might incur for California.

Elizabeth applied to and was accepted by Johns Hopkins University for her Pre-Med major. This was not the news Rick wanted to hear.

"I was hoping you'd be closer to me," he said. "Now I have to decide what to do. JHU doesn't have a football team."

She laughed out loud. "No, doctors don't play football," she said. "What do you want to do?"

"I want to go to school without playing football."

"Can you do that, I mean, financially?"

"I think so, my folks started putting money in a fund for me, and for my sister, when we were kids, and I've worked every summer and after school during the year. I save most of my money, except what I spend on you. I have quite a bit of spending money saved up. I hope to spend most of it on you before you leave me."

She laughed and punched him on the shoulder. "I'll never leave you," she said

"I hope not."

"Can't you get an academic scholarship?"

"I can get some help from a school because of my grades, but I don't know how much."

"But a football scholarship will pay for everything, won't it?"

"Yes, but then football will take up all my time."

"I'm sorry, Rick," she said. "I didn't mean to complicate things for you. It's just that Johns Hopkins is the best medical school in the country, and I can do my pre-med there and then my medical too. I really want to do it."

"I want you to, it's not about me. We're still on track. I've just gotten spoiled seeing you every day. I'll miss you so much."

"But we'll have email and cell phones, and we'll see each other at Christmas and Thanksgiving."

"You're not helping me very much. I need to put my hands on you, come here."

"I will miss this," she said as he kissed her passionately. "Listen, Rick, if you want to go to bed with other girls before we're married, I'll understand."

He pushed her away from him. "What the hell are you talking about, Elizabeth? I don't want other girls, I want you. I understand your position on marriage, and I'm okay with it. You're a Catholic and, as Billy Joel said, 'Catholic girls start a little later than other girls.'"

She started laughing. "That's not exactly what he said, Rick. But I guess I sort of mislead you. I haven't remained a virgin because I'm a Catholic. It's just my personal choice. I promised my mother. I don't even know for sure what I am, religiously speaking I mean. I just want to save myself for the man I marry."

"And I want that man to be me, baby. It doesn't matter why you decided to drive me insane, I'm okay with it."

"Oh, don't be so melodramatic."

"Well, I don't intend to go to bed with any girl, any woman, until you and I are married. So, don't even let that cross your mind."

"Okay, sorry, now will you start kissing me again?"

"Oh, okay," he said, feigning hesitance, "if I have to."

Rick spent the better part of June and July explaining why he would not be accepting scholarships to the many football programs that had offered them to him. He'd decided to attend SMU for his BS in Economics. SMU was close to home, so he'd save money on lodging. He would get some help from the school because of his excellent GPA, but he would not play football. His friend Bobby Gladwin would be playing wide receiver for the Mustangs, and Rick looked forward to hanging out with him on occasion.

"I sure wish you would be there throwing me the ball, ol' buddy," Bobby told him, one evening when they had gotten together.

"You don't need me, Bobby," Rick said. "You're a star. I'll come to the home games and watch you play."

"It's just strange that the best quarterback in the state decided not to play college football. That's a bigger story than it would have been if you'd chosen to play for the Longhorns."

"I've just got other plans, Bobby."

"I probably would too, if I had your brains. I envy people like you who are so damned smart. And being a star quarterback too, how often does that happen? You're a…what's the word for that?"

"Anomaly."

"That's it," Bobby said. "You're an anomaly. People like you just don't come along very often. And your girl too. How often do you see a girl who looks like Elizabeth and is as smart as she is?"

"Not very often," Rick acknowledged.

"And the two of you are going to get married one day, that just blows my mind."

"Yeah, mine too."

"Well, I'm dating her sister," Bobby said, "but it's not like she's a consolation prize. Rose is the coolest girl I've ever known."

"That's great, Bobby, I didn't know. Elizabeth never mentioned it to me."

"Harley knows, and he's happy about it. I'm still working for him in the summer, probably will every summer, unless I get picked up by an NFL team. Then I won't need the money."

"So, are you planning on marrying Rose?"

"I don't know," Bobby replied. "I'd marry her just to have Harley for a father-in-law, but I don't know if it will come to that or not."

"Well, we'll have to get together more often. You can come by my house anytime you have the time."

"I'd like that, and I'll be at the Meadows' for Christmas. I'm sure you will too. Rose said Elizabeth is coming home for the holidays."

"Yeah, I got an email from her the other day about that," Rick said. "She wants me to pick her up at the airport when she gets in."

When the day finally came, Rick could hardly wait to see Elizabeth. He picked her up at the airport.

"White Rock Lake," she said as soon as they were in his truck and away from the terminal."

"I missed you," he told her.

"Yeah, me, too, how's SMU?"

"Kinda boring actually. Bobby Gladwyn is on the football team. I run into him on occasion. He says he's dating your sister Rose."

"That won't last long. She won't put out."

"You don't think it's possible that he could fall in love with her and they might get married?"

"I suppose it's possible, but Bobby Gladwyn is not you."

"And what do you mean by that?"

"Well, he's not nearly as good-looking, and he's not as patient and as understanding as you are."

"Don't be so hasty in your heaping of ego-boosting bullshit on me."

"It's not bullshit."

"Okay, whatever, but before I met you, if somebody had told me that I would go with a girl for two or three years without going to bed with her, I would have thought they were insane. What I'm saying is that a man in love will deviate from the norm, sometimes very seriously from the norm."

"I'm in love too, Rick, I'm in love with you, and I want it to be perfect."

They parked at the lake. She leaned back into his arms, and he kissed her long and tenderly. He kissed her cheeks and nuzzled her hair with his face. "I'm gonna have to bring an oxygen bottle with me on these escapades in the future."

She laughed. "Take it easy, my love, I'm not a doctor yet."

"Then I may have to have an ambulance follow us on future dates."

"Do you want to make love to me, Rick?"

"What?" he said, looking at her incredulously.

"I'm asking you, do you want for us to make love?"

"Yes, Elizabeth, you know I do."

"Then we'll do it while I'm home for the holidays."

Rick perked up a bit, suddenly growing excited by her conversation and wondering where it was going. "But I thought you wanted to wait until we're married."

"I do, but I want to do whatever makes you happy."

"That's not fair. You're telling me to make you do something against your principles."

"No, I'm telling you if you want me, I want to make love with you."

"Is this a test?"

"Just tell me the truth, do you want me?"

"Yes, Elizabeth, I want you. I want you so much that sometimes I think I'm going insane."

"Then take me to my house. Daddy and Rose are out of town, visiting some old friends. They aren't expecting me until tomorrow."

He just shook his head in disbelief and started the truck. It occurred to him that she had planned this all along, but he wasn't going to say anything to her that might change the direction in which she had set them.

She led him to her room upstairs and locked the door behind them then turned off the light. The night light from her bathroom was just bright enough for him to see her take off her clothes and come into his arms, completely nude.

He picked her up and carried her to her bed and lay her down. He could have been dreaming again, but for the lovely creature lying there in the flesh next to him. He grew dizzy from kissing her lips as he pulled her next to him and they made love.

Finally, consumed with each other's passion, they remained in a lover's embrace. She lay in his arms while he stared at her in an almost dream-like wonder.

"Nothing has ever happened to me like what just happened here, baby," he said.

"Me neither, you were wonderful, Rick."

"No, it's you, it's all you. You're everything I could ever want or need."

"I'm so glad my first time was with you. You truly are wonderful, you were gentle and tender, my perfect lover."

"I never thought I could ever love someone like I love you.

"I'm glad I talked you into this," she said.

"I didn't put up much of a fight."

She smiled at him. "I want you to stay the night with me."

He just nodded and began kissing her again.

They awoke about nine the next morning and showered together, then she straightened up her room. He kissed her again several times.

"I'll see you tonight for dinner," he told her.

She followed him all the way to the front door, kissing him and squeezing him around his waist.

"Where have you been?" his mother asked him when he walked into the house.

"Elizabeth and I fell asleep in the truck at the lake."

"Okay," she said, "if that's your story, let's go with that one."

Harley baked a turkey for Christmas dinner and, along with mashed potatoes, candied yams and an assortment of other vegetables and giblet gravy, the table was full when he called everyone in from the living room.

"I must say," he began, "that I am blessed to have my wayward daughter, Elizabeth, who is home from visiting foreign lands, and my daughter, Rose, along with my future son-in-law, Rick, and the only football player left in the family—" He looked at Rick and winked. "—perhaps my potential son-in-law, Bobby, here for our Christmas dinner celebration of the birth of our Lord, Jesus Christ.

"That was a run-on sentence, Daddy," Elizabeth told him. "Remember we have an English major at the table."

"I thought it was a very well-constructed sentence, Elizabeth," Rick said. "And, not that it matters, but my major is economics. English is my minor."

"Well, excuse me, sir," Elizabeth said.

"It's okay, I promise not to turn into a Grammar Nazi."

"Do you guys know that, when Rick and Elizabeth get married, who she will be?" Bobby spoke up.

"Of course, Bobby," Harley said, but before he could answer, Rick butted in.

"The Bennets' second daughter from *Pride and Prejudice*."

"And you'll be my Mister Darcy," Elizabeth added.

"Aw crap," Bobby said, with mild frustration, "I should have known better than to try and show off my intellect in a family of egg-heads."

This brought a roaring laugh from everyone at the table.

"You must have seen the movie recently, Bobby," Harley said.

"It was an old movie I watched last night."

When it was time for Elizabeth to leave, Rick took her back to the airport. "Do you still love me?" she asked him, as she was getting her bags together.

"Are you kidding me? I've seen you naked now. I love you more than ever."

"Oh, you cad," she said. "I take back all the nice things I said about you."

"Really?" he said.

"No, of course not. I love you more than ever too. I'll call you when I get to my dorm."

One thing that Johns Hopkins offered freshman was a program called *covered grades*. This meant that, for the first semester, each freshman would take his or her enrolled courses and earn a grade, but nobody would see those grades but the freshman. Everyone else would see only a Pass or Fail. This was the school's way of letting the student ease into the college experience and give them some academic freedom to get out and be social and meet people, to keep them from feeling so isolated.

Elizabeth had determined that she would maintain her 4.0 GPA throughout her college career. She soon learned just what a task that would be. High school was like two plus two compared to what she was up against in the world of higher learning. In the Johns Hopkins environment, Elizabeth Meadows was nobody special. She would have to earn any respect. She was a blonde-haired girl from Texas, and nobody expected her to be anything but that.

Her looks would cause her some minor annoyance for most of her college career. It would not be until she entered post-graduate medical school and became a real factor in her field that she would be taken seriously for her skills more than for her physical appearance.

'*Men are always going to see a beautiful woman first and the doctor second. That's just the way men are,*' she remembered Rick telling her on several occasions.

She was reminded again one afternoon when she was having lunch in one of the many campus eating facilities. A man approached her table and asked her if he could join her.

"Why?" she asked him, "there are a lot of empty tables."

He was a well-dressed upper classman who appeared to Elizabeth to smell of money.

"My name is Gerald Morrissett, and I wanted to ask you if you would do me the honor of having dinner with me one evening."

"Thank you, Gerald, but I am engaged, so I do not date."

"What is your name, if I may ask, and from where have you come to Johns Hopkins?"

"I'm Elizabeth Meadows, and I'm from Dallas."

"Dallas," he said. "then you are a long way from home. Is this alleged fiancé back home in Dallas?"

"You're asking a lot of questions. I already indulged you by telling you my name. What is it you want?"

"I wanted to take you out. We have some very exclusive restaurants here in Baltimore that you might enjoy."

"Oh, gee, an exclusive restaurant, that might be a nice change. All we can get in Dallas is beans and chili."

"Yes, well, your sarcasm is noted. But with your boyfriend back in Dallas, what would be the harm in going out to dinner with me?"

"First, he's not my boyfriend, nor is he my alleged fiancé. We are engaged to be married. Now I would appreciate it if you would leave and let me finish my lunch."

"Ah, now you seem upset, did you just get tossed off the cheerleading squad?"

"No, did you just get accepted by them?"

"I'll have you know I don't appreciate being insulted by an undergraduate trollop."

"And I don't appreciate having my lunch interrupted by a supercilious asshole who won't take no for an answer."

With that, the man stormed away from her table.

I can't wait to tell Rick about this, she thought.

In Dallas, Rick was having little trouble with his studies. He'd purposely taken a heavy schedule so he would have to keep busy to take his mind off of Elizabeth. He quickly discovered that it didn't work. Occasionally, he found himself regretting that he'd decided not to play football. He didn't miss the attention and the constant pressure to win. But he could have gone to the University of Maryland and played football and been a stone's throw, figuratively speaking, from Elizabeth.

At least he spent his nights at home and ate his mother's cooking. That was some consolation but not much. He still took Amanda out on occasion, but it was beginning to get awkward because she had matured to the point that it was no longer obvious that she was his little sister. He would call her "sis" in public, mainly to relieve his own perception that he was dating an underage but early blossoming girl. When he thought about it, the truth was that, most likely, no one even noticed.

The contrast, from his life as a high school football star, and a serious college student, was dramatic. He finished his first full year of college in his self-imposed obscurity.

Chapter 7

Changes

2004 ~ 2005:

Elizabeth came home for the summer to help her father in the business. Her first year at JHU had been both successful and disappointing for her. The first semester her GPA dropped to 3.7, still considered "excellent" by the school, but next to being traumatic for the obsessive perfectionist. Second semester she brought it back up to 4.0. It was a simple difference between an A-plus and an A-minus, but her prolonged proverbial hand-wringing, to Rick over the telephone, made him worry about her sense of perspective.

"Calm down, baby," he told her on more than one occasion. You're going to make yourself sick."

"But I want to be the best, Rick. I have to be the best."

"You are the best, Elizabeth, you will graduate with honors. I know you will."

"I'm thinking maybe I should stay here for the summer and take extra classes and accelerate my course."

"No!" he shouted, and she laughed.

"That's what Daddy said. He wants me to come home too."

"You can't do that to me, Elizabeth. I'm losing my mind here without you."

"It was just a thought, Rick. I'd like to get through this just as fast as I can. I'm not here to party or to find a husband, like some of the others I had to live with in the freshman dorms. The work is much harder than high school."

"I haven't found that to be the case," Rick said.

"You're smarter than I am," she replied.

"No, I'm not. I'm studying economics and English. You're going to be a scientist. Of course, you have a greater challenge than I do."

"I couldn't have done it this year anyway because Daddy really wanted me to help him in the office until he can hire someone. Rose has been filling in since Mrs. Pearson left, but Rose doesn't know the office like I do."

The Bennetts were going back to Belize, and they were taking Amanda with them. Rick chose not to go along. More exciting to him was the possibility of having the house, and Elizabeth, to himself for a few days.

Adrian was hoping to find Ed Whelan when he got to Belize. He went to the bank when he got into Belize City and took out some money. The income from the rental property had averaged about eighteen hundred a month. It did not total the thirty thousand a year Ed Whelan had prophesied, but it was close enough not to quibble about.

He showed Leeann the bank statement and told her how much the house had made them since he bought it."

"I'm starting to get horny, darling," she said.

"We brought our daughter with us, Lee," he reminded her.

"You sure know how to spoil a mood."

The bank manager told Adrian that Ed Whelan had indeed settled permanently in Belize with his wife and was living in one of his "three" houses on Ambergris Caye. He remembered Adrian from the time Ed brought him to the bank to open up his account.

"I'm under strict orders not to tell anyone that Mister Whelan is in Belize, but I know that you and he are good friends. He will be happy to see you, I'm sure."

Adrian found the house by the direction the bank man had given him and, when he knocked, on the door, Ed opened it and yelled his name loudly when he saw them.

"Adrian! I was hoping you'd show up down here one day. How in the world are you?"

"We're doing well, Ed. Lee and I came here about a year ago, just the two of us, and spent four days. I thought about you, but I didn't think that you might be living here."

"We came down right about that time, Adrian. Hey, you have to come over for dinner tonight. Turns out that Maggie is a world-class cook. In addition to being great in the sack. Why don't you come back over around seven or so? Amanda can swim in the pool or the ocean if she wants to. Damn, she's growing up, isn't she?"

"It's been a while, Ed," Adrian said. "We'd love to do that. We'll see you at seven."

When he got home, they took their things into the house and walked down to the beach. There was an open drink stand, and Adrian and Leeann had a couple of pina coladas, and Amanda had a coke.

When they got back to Ed's house, Maggie was setting the table. "Dinner will be in about a half hour," she told them.

"Let's go out on the patio and talk a while, Adrian," Ed said.

"Get a glass of iced tea first, Adrian," Maggie said and poured it for him.

"I guess you're probably wondering why I'm here with Maggie Fletcher," Ed said to him after they had sat down on the back patio,

"No, actually, I already knew you were here."

Ed looked confused.

"I got a call from your father-in-law, some time back, asking me if I knew where you were. I told him I had no clue, because I hadn't seen you since I left ONT, so it wasn't a lie. Well, it was sort of a lie. I really hadn't seen you, but I had a pretty good idea where you were. Anyway, I didn't tell him anything."

"I appreciate that, Adrian. He's still looking, as far as I know."

"So, you just threw all caution to the wind and ran off with Maggie? And, by the way, I'd forgotten how good looking she is. I guess if a man is going to give everything up for a woman, it might as well be for a woman who looks like Maggie."

"I think she really loves me, Adrian. She says she does. Of course, she could be just playing me, but she cooks and keeps the place cleaned up. She acts like a wife, and we have a lot of fun together. She stays horny all the time. I have a hard time keeping up with her."

"It must be something in the air, Ed. The last time we were here, I thought Lee was trying to give me a heart attack. I was afraid I was going to need a paramedic before we left."

Ed chuckled and nodded his head.

"So, what happened with you and the business, you just got tired?"

"Yeah, it wasn't long after you left and went to Texas, that I just got tired of all the bullshit. They were nit-picking me to death. You know they blocked me from paying bonuses to all the other employees, and that pissed me off. I couldn't bring them all down here to Belize and square up with them like I did with you. I felt like a real asshole for having to shortchange those guys like that."

"Julian told me you took a half-million dollars out of the company before you disappeared. He was really upset."

"That lying sonofabitch. He was trying to scam his own daughter and the few shareholders we had. He probably has that money in a Swiss bank account, that crooked bastard."

"So, you didn't abscond with a half million bucks? Those were his words, not mine."

"No, hell no, don't believe anything that thief says. He's a snake in the grass, no way I'd take half a million dollars from my wife. She's an angry shrew, but she's still my wife. It was more like three-hundred and fifty thousand."

Adrian started laughing and couldn't stop for a few minutes. "You're an evil genius, Ed Whelan, but you're a good friend."

"Well, I had a new wife to support. I had to think of her."

"You married Maggie?"

"Here in Belize, I did."

"You do realize, don't you, that's against the law? And taking that money, damn, Ed, you could get in big trouble. I'm not trying to throw a wet blanket on your fire, but you could end up in jail, and I'd hate like hell to see that happen."

"Meh," Ed said, "I'm hoping Maggie screws me to death before that happens."

Rick and Elizabeth were lying in Rick's bed in his room, in The Bennett home, after making love. She was in her panties and one of his T-shirts. He had put on a pair of sweat pants. They were lying on their sides, facing each other.

"I won't ever get tired of looking at your face," he said.

"Not even when I'm eighty years old?"

"I'll be eighty, too."

"No, you won't. We're the same age."

"I'll be eighty, as well, I mean."

"Do you really want to live that long?" she said

"If you do, I do."

"Right now, I just want to live long enough for you to make love to me again."

"No problem, baby. I love you, Elizabeth Meadows, I'll always love you."

Summer ended, and she was gone again. Rick began his sophomore year, thinking about writing a book. He had originally intended to write a historical piece on some little-known subject of American history, but he'd done no research, and he had no time to travel and search. Anything he might find on the internet was already in print and, therefore, not original. He decided, instead, to begin research on the book he planned to write for his final thesis. He would focus on economics because he would have access to many experts on the subject.

He entertained the notion of writing on Reaganomics, a decidedly controversial subject with as many pros as cons on both sides of the political aisle. His own father, a self-described Reagan Conservative, had been somewhat critical of President Reagan's economic programs, so Rick might be able to get him to sit for an interview. He made the decision and then tabled it for the time being.

Elizabeth moved into an efficiency apartment at Bradford Apartments, Number Nine East 33rd Street in Baltimore. The Bradford was an off-campus facility and thusly did not require the purchase of a meal ticket. Sophomore students switched from freshman year banquet-style food hall to *dining dollars* that could be used at several cafes on campus.

Sophomores typically were required to declare their major by the end of their sophomore year, but Elizabeth did that as soon as classes started. Her GPA being a solid 4.0, she would be able to start taking some upper level classes. This would fit in perfectly with her accelerated plan to complete her full courses early. She loved the seclusion and privacy of the efficiency apartment. Having a roommate was such a distraction from her studies. But she eventually found that she missed having a friend to talk to. Rick's emails came with less frequency, so she assumed that he was as busy as she was. His last note to her was a week ago.

Lizzy Bee, still missing you, and I thought about your suggestion that I use my full name for my pen name when, and if, no, make that when I do write my first book. My middle name is Owens (my mother's maiden name). I can't believe I never told you that. So hopefully you will see my name Richard Owens Bennett on a best sellers list one day.

Until I see you again, I love you, Rick

She looked forward to getting his emails, although she was often remiss about responding. She decided that she would take summer classes at the end of her sophomore year with an eye toward leap-frogging past her *bridge year* after her senior year.

Chance provided her with the friend she needed in the person of a girl named Eva Graham. Elizabeth was having lunch at one of the on-campus cafes, and the place was packed. A plain-looking girl was searching for an empty table, but there were none.

Elizabeth spotted her and waved. "You can join me," she said.

"Oh, thank you so much, I'm Eva. What's your name?"

"Elizabeth Meadows, you look familiar, don't you reside at Bradford?"

"I do," she said, "I think I've seen you. Do you have roommates?"

"No, I rented an efficiency, because last year I had trouble studying with two other people in the room."

"I know what you mean. I have the same problem now," Eva said. "They want to party, and I have enough trouble making my grades without all the distractions. What are you at JHU for?"

"Genetics, bio-medical science," Elizabeth said.

"That's a mouthful," Eva replied, "what exactly does that mean?"

"I want to be a scientist. Basically, I want to study ways to prevent heart attacks."

"Oh, that's a noble pursuit. Most people I've known, who go into fields like yours, are motivated by some personal event or loss. Did you..."

"My mother—died of a heart attack when I was ten years old."

"I see. I'm sorry, but that one tragedy may result in you being instrumental in the saving of millions of lives."

"You never know," Elizabeth said. "I hope so.

"God works in wondrous ways," Eva replied.

"That's what I've always heard. What is your major, Eva?"

"Environmental Engineering," Eva said.

"That sounds noble too," Elizabeth said. "What will you do with it?"

"My parents have a farm near Gettysburg, not too far from here. They raise grass-fed beef and are in the process of employing a system called permaculture. That's agricultural design principles centered on simulating or directly utilizing the patterns and features observed in natural ecosystems. I plan to help them by developing more and better ways to prepare the soil for food production."

"Now that's a mouthful too," Elizabeth said. "I'd be curious to hear more about it, but I've got to get to a class. If you're having trouble studying in your dorm room, you're more than welcome to come to my room and study. It's small, but I have a desk where I keep my laptop and a table. There's plenty of room."

"I'd like that, Elizabeth, I could use a quiet place to study, and a friend would be nice, too."

"Yeah, me too. I'll write down my room number and my cell phone number so you can call me to make sure I'm there. I'm always there."

Eva began a regular study routine in Elizabeth's apartment. Elizabeth learned that the Graham family were sort of *pioneers* in a new world of food production that was gaining greater popularity worldwide with each passing day.

Eva was a very pleasant person, Elizabeth discovered, and quite intelligent. She had a passion for her calling, as did Elizabeth, and had apparently been brought up by her parents to be a religious person. A friendship quickly developed, and Eva happened to be on a bench outside the Bradford one afternoon when Elizabeth came home from class.

"Hi Eva," she said. "You want to come up?"

Elizabeth checked her voice mail and noticed that she had a message from Rick. She put it on speaker so Eva could hear his voice.

"Hey, Lizzy Bee, I need you to call me. If you don't call me tonight, I'm going to slash my wrists."

Eva laughed, "Lizzy Bee?" she said. "That must be your guy."

"That's him, that's Rick, he's my guy."

"He sounds like a great guy," Eva said. "Is Lizzy Bee his pet name for you?"

"Yeah, he always said I was like a busy bee, because I never slow down, but he changed it to Lizzy instead of busy."

"When are you getting married?"

"Well, we had originally planned to get married after our sophomore year, but I'm not sure I can handle a marriage and the work load I have here."

"Do you think Rick will be okay with that?"

"I don't know. I hope so."

"What's he doing now?"

"He's at SMU in Dallas, he's in economics, wants to teach college kids. Get this, he was a star quarterback in high school. He had offers from all over the country for scholarships to play football, Alabama, LSU, USC, and a lot of others, but he gave it up to go on his own. He chose SMU so he could live at home."

"Okay, now for the important question."

"Yes, he is good looking," Elizabeth said and retrieved a picture of Rick from her phone.

"Oh, my gosh, he certainly is," Eva said. "You're both very lucky."

"Thank you, Eva. I'm going to call him if you don't mind."

Elizabeth dialed Rick's number, and he picked up.

"Okay, I'm putting the knife down," he said.

She started laughing, and Eva looked at her, smiled, then went back to her work.

"He says he's putting the knife down."

Eva smiled again.

"Who are you talking to? Rick asked her.

"That's my friend, Eva," Elizabeth said, "she lives in the building. Eva is from Pennsylvania."

"When are you coming home, baby? I miss you."

"I'll be home for Christmas, and I'll spend every minute with you."

"Well, that's not too far off, I guess I can make it until then," he told her.

"Have you started your book yet?"

"I've started the first page."

"How much have you written?"

"Chapter One," he said.

"You've written the first chapter?"

"No, I wrote the heading, Chapter One, I need your inspiration."

Elizabeth started laughing. "You're just teasing me."

"I am, baby, I'm sorry. I just haven't gotten into it yet. I'm keeping my grades up, though, so I should get a reward when you get back home."

"Hold that thought. I've got just the thing in mind."

"Oh, really, and what is that?"

"I can't tell you, remember, I have a friend in the room."

After she had finished the phone call, Elizabeth made some coffee, and she and Eva took a break.

"You should come home with me one weekend," Eva suggested.

"I might do that, maybe a break in the routine would be good."

"I'd like for you to meet my folks. They're sort of in the same field you are, just with a different approach."

"Oh, how so?" Elizabeth asked.

"Well, you will be looking for ways to save lives through medical research, and they are trying to do it through the development of better and safer food."

"I'm interested in whatever works."

"Yeah, I figured you would be," Eva replied.

The Graham farm was a hundred-acre spread off of Highway 97 about halfway between Gettysburg and Littlestown. The two girls arrived about eleven o'clock on a Saturday morning.

"This is really pretty country," Elizabeth said, as they pulled into the driveway of the two-story country home where Eva had grown up.

"I loved it here when I was a kid. It was hard work, living on a farm, but it was good experience. Let's find my folks, I told them about you."

They walked toward the barn and, just as they got to the double door, a lanky young man came walking out. He was about five feet, ten inches, and weighed maybe 165 pounds or so. He was wearing Levis, cowboy boots, and no shirt. His tanned chest rippled with finely-tuned, sinewy muscles and locks of brown curly hair protruded from beneath a baseball cap, on which was a symbol of the Philadelphia Eagles.

When he spotted Elizabeth, he smiled broadly. "Ah, my package has arrived," he said.

"What are you talking about, Josh?" Eva asked him.

"I told you, the next time you come home, to bring the prettiest girl in your school for me to keep for my very own."

"Knock off the bullshit, Josh."

"I'm not bullshittin', sis, this has to be the prettiest girl in your school. She's the prettiest girl I've ever seen in my life."

"Just mind your manners. This is Elizabeth Meadows, Josh. She's majoring in something you can't even pronounce. Elizabeth, this is my half-witted brother, Josh Graham."

Elizabeth smiled, and Josh reached to shake her hand. She took his hand and returned the cordiality. "I'm happy to meet you, Josh. Any brother of Eva's is a friend of mine."

"Wait a minute, are you telling me she didn't bring you here for me?"

"I'm afraid not," Elizabeth said, "but I appreciate the offer."

"Next time you come home, sis, bring one who looks just like this one."

"Where are the folks, Josh?" Eva said.

"They're in the barn," he said, pointing over his shoulder with his thumb.

"I apologize for my brother," Eva said. "He thinks he's God's gift to women."

"He is kind of cute, Eva, but he seems harmless," Elizabeth said.

"Here are my parents," Eva said, as a man and a woman walked out of the barn. "Mom, Dad, this is my friend, Elizabeth Meadows."

"Well, hello, Elizabeth, I'm Jocelyn Graham, Eva's mother and this is William, her dad." Both parents shook hands with her. "Come on into the house, we'll get you settled in."

"She met Josh already," Eva said.

"Oh my," Jocelyn said, "I hope he didn't hit on you."

"He was very complimentary."

"Oh, I bet he was," William said, winking at Elizabeth. "The boy is incorrigible."

"He seemed nice enough. I took it all in fun."

William Graham was an imposing man, strongly built. About forty years of age, as best Elizabeth could figure, maybe six feet tall and two-hundred pounds. He looked to be an older version of his son. His wife was slightly taller than her daughter, had the same color hair, but wore it shorter. Jocelyn Graham most likely had been an attractive woman, in her younger days. But years of farm life in the sun had weathered her skin and made her look older than she was. Both of Eva's parents were passionate about their farm, and they had invested much in sending their daughter to Johns Hopkins in the hope of applying her learned skills to the family's benefit, once Eva had graduated.

"These steaks are from grass-fed beef cows, Elizabeth," William explained. "And all the vegetables are grown here on the farm in ground prepared without chemicals or pesticides of any kind."

Elizabeth was curious about their farming techniques and expressed that to the Grahams.

"We'll show you tomorrow how we do it. Of course, it will be a crash course. It would take much longer to learn the entire process from top to bottom."

"I look forward to that. I love learning new things."

"I'd like to learn the best place to go dancing in Baltimore," Josh interjected. "How about I come down sometime and pick you up, and you can show me around?"

"Shut up, Josh," Eva said, "Elizabeth is engaged to be married. She's not interested in going out with a seventeen-year-old kid."

"Oh, well, excuse me," he said, "but he's in Texas, ain't he?"

"Oh, come on, Josh," Elizabeth said, "don't tell me that a good-looking guy like you can't find a bus-load of girls here in Pennsylvania."

"Well, of course, I can," Josh said, smiling. "I probably could put together two bus-loads, given an hour or so, but they don't look like you."

"Leave the girl alone, son," William said. "She came here to learn about Graham Farm's cow shit, not Joshua Graham's bullshit. Right, Elizabeth?"

"Right, Mister Graham," Elizabeth replied. "If I needed any bullshit, I'd go back to Texas."

And everyone at the table burst into laughter, especially Josh.

"Oh, now I *know* I love you," he said.

The next morning, Jocelyn and William took Elizabeth for a walk around the farm.

"As you can see," William told her. "Josh is not just our court jester, he actually does work when he's not in school," he said as the boy drove by on their tractor. "We began five years ago to convert the property from traditional farming to a grass-fed beef ranch, so to speak. And permaculture type preparation of the soil for the planting of crops. Vegetables and fruits. To produce enough grass on a smaller acreage farm, we use a paddock rotation system."

Elizabeth opened a spiral notebook and began writing. "Paddock rotation?" she said.

"Yes," William said, "here's how it works, briefly. We set aside a certain number of acres and divide them into individual 'paddocks' of an acre or two, each, or larger depending on the number of cattle we want to produce in a particular year. The number of paddocks depends on how fast the grass will grow back as we move the cattle along in the rotation.

"We move the cows into the first paddock and leave them a full day. They eat the grass that has already grown up there. The do their business, you know, poop all day long and trample it down. Then we move them to the next paddock, and they repeat the process. About four days later, the poop in the first paddock starts to get really ripe, the maggots start crawling, I'm not trying to make you sick, that's just what happens."

"No, I'm okay," Elizabeth said, "I'm writing this all down."

"Then," William continued, "we send the chickens into the paddock, and they do what chickens do. They eat the maggots and poop all over the place and fertilize the soil even more. The grass starts to grow up again. Then we rotate the chickens right along behind the cows in the rotation. The system is designed to ensure that there is always grass for the cattle to eat.

We produce beef that is completely free of grain feed. It healthier for people and for the cattle, too."

"What kind of grass is this?" she asked, as she kneeled down and brushed her hand over it.

"We use orchard grass mainly, which is common to Pennsylvania, and in the cooler months, we either use a blend of some rye grasses, or we bale some of our own grass. We always keep a few of the paddocks just for the production of baled grass for winter."

"This is really interesting, Mister Graham. It's given me something to think about. I'm studying neuroscience at JHU because I want to help find ways to prevent heart attacks."

"Well, you see, Elizabeth," Jocelyn said, "producing healthy food is the most basic thing we can do to achieve that goal."

"I do see," she replied, "and I'd like to learn more about this."

"You're welcome back anytime, we'd be happy to help you any way we can."

"What I'm thinking is, that I might want to write my senior thesis on your system of farming, as an addendum to the quest to find ways to prevent heart attacks and cancer and any other disease that threatens humanity."

"You could come home with Eva in the summer and work on the farm with us, if you want to. You'd have enough material then to write a book and your thesis."

"I'd like to do that, Elizabeth said, but I can't this summer. I've already registered for extra classes that I need to take. I'm thinking of next summer between my junior and senior year."

"That's a great idea," Jocelyn said. "We'll pay you the standard wage we pay our regular summer help."

"No, I don't want you to pay me. It will be research for me, but I'll work hard. I've worked for my dad all my life growing up."

"Then I insist on paying you and providing you with room and board too. We'll work out the terms when the time comes."

"Fair enough," Elizabeth said. "I'll stay in touch with you through Eva. We've decided to get a two-person room together next year."

Sophomore year ended, and Eva left for home. Elizabeth decided to go home for a week to see her family and Rick. He picked her up at the airport and took her to her house. No one was home, so she took his hand and led her to her room. They filled each other's romantic needs and then showered together.

"Let's go to the garden," she said. "I need to fill you in on what's happening with me and find out how your book is coming."

"It's been so long, baby," he told her, "I really missed you. Are we going to get married?" The look on her face gave him her answer.

"I can't right now, Rick, I just can't. Can we wait?"

"I guess we'll have to. If you can't, I can't get married alone."

"Something new has come up that is going to affect how I approach my career in the medical field."

"You didn't meet another man, did you?"

"What? No, no of course not. Why would you even ask that?"

"I'm sorry. I didn't mean it. What is this new thing?"

She told him about her visit to the Graham Farm and about the work they did there and that she was going to work on the farm the following summer.

"It's such critical work. I just have to be involved in it."

"I know you do, Elizabeth but I want to be involved in you."

"I want it to happen, Rick, but there is just so much I have to do. Will you wait for me?"

"Do you remember the movie we saw when you came home for the Christmas holidays?"

"*The Notebook*?"

"Yeah, the scene where they're at the beach, and the girl is flapping her arms and telling him she's a bird."

"I remember."

"She tells him to say she's a bird, and he says she's a bird. Then she tells him to say *he's* a bird, and he says, if you're a bird, I'm a bird. Did you grasp the significance of that scene?"

"It was just lover's play, I guess. Why, what did I miss?

"Maybe it was just me, but I took it to mean that the guy was so in love with her, that anything she wanted to do or be, he was okay with it. I mean if she wanted to be a bird then, as silly as that might sound, he would be a bird too."

"So, you're saying if I want to be a bird, you will be a bird too?"

"Basically, yes, that's what I'm saying. I love you, Elizabeth, and I'll always love you. This is never going to end for me, but I'm not certain it's ever going to start for you."

"What are you saying, Rick?"

"This may ruin my life, but I'm going to have to leave you and get on with my life."

"Oh, no, Rick, please don't say that. Please don't do this. I'll quit school."

"No, you won't. I won't let you. You've got a mind and skills the world needs. How selfish it would be for me to ask you to do that, or even allow you to do it. No, you will go on and fulfill your destiny. I will stay the same, but I cannot labor over you, I miss you too much. I have to free my mind of needing you every minute of every day. I'll lose it if I don't. When you reach your goals and if you decide you want me, my folks will know where I am. If you call me in four years, eight years, or longer, and tell me you've decided to be a bird, then I will be a bird too. I will still love you, but for my self-preservation, I have to try and forget you."

She was crying now, almost uncontrollably.

"What I'm saying, Lizzy Bee, my love, my one and only love, is that whatever you have to do or be, that is what I want you to do or be."

"Will you kiss me?" she asked him.

"Has anyone ever told you no to that question?"

"I've never asked anyone but you that question."

He took her in his arms and kissed her passionately for only a brief moment. "If this ever happens again, you'll have to ask me that question again."

Chapter 8

Grapes

2006 ~ 2007:

Nearing the end of his junior year, Rick was almost finished with his book, although he'd not yet decided on a title yet.

Given that his dad had been a Reagan Conservative, something of an oddity in California—at least in Santa Barbara, it was—he had discussed with him his plan to write the book on the subject of Reaganomics.

Adrian, surprisingly, did not render the ideological subjective defense of President Reagan's economic plan that Rick had expected he would. His dad gave him what he believed were the positives and the negatives of Reagan's signature program.

"You see, Rick," Adrian said, "President Reagan promised to reduce the growth of government spending, income and capital gains taxes and government regulations. He also said that he could reduce inflation by controlling the money supply."

"Did he actually do it?" Rick asked him.

"Well, yes and no. Reaganomics was based on what they called *supply side* economics. This meant cutting taxes, pretty much across the board, which would give companies more cash to expand, hire workers, and create a greater supply of goods and services. It would also give wage earners more buying power and more incentive to work."

"But I keep hearing from the *political opposition* that Reagan's policies didn't really work all that well."

"It didn't reduce government spending, it just shifted it from domestic programs to defense. That suited the Republicans just fine, but it pissed off the Democrats."

"But he did cut taxes, didn't he?" Rick said.

"Yes, he did, quite a bit, actually. If I recall correctly— remember I'm doing this from memory—but I think he lowered the top income tax rate down to about twenty-eight percent from a high of around seventy."

"That had to help a lot of people," Rick said.

"The overall sentiment was that it helped the rich folks more than it helped the poor. At least that's the way Reagan's detractors portrayed it."

"I want to present the subject fairly. I don't want to sugarcoat anything."

"I hope you don't, but you'll have to do lots of research. Get information from all opinions and sort it out as best you can. Let it come out as truthful as you can possibly be."

There were days when he didn't think about Elizabeth, but they were few and far between, as the old saying went. His self-imposed exile from her, he questioned every day. He'd changed his cell phone number and his email address, not out of anger at her but to protect himself. Her voice on the phone would have destroyed any illusion he might have had about ever going on without her. An occasional email from her would only have had him checking his mail a hundred times a day, hoping for another one.

He called his friend Bobby and asked him to meet him for a couple of beers and burgers later that night. Rick was already at a table when Bobby walked in.

"What's up, pal?" Bobby said as he sat down.

"I sort of broke up with Elizabeth," he said.

"Aw bullshit, I know better than that." But Rick's demeanor made him think otherwise. "You're serious."

"Let's just say I called a time out. She wanted to wait until she finishes her medical schooling before we got married. She is just so driven that she doesn't have time for a serious relationship. I wanted to give her the time, without bogging her down with encumbrances."

"What did she say, or do?" Bobby asked.

"She was hurt, offered to quit school."

"Wow, then she really loves you."

"I couldn't let her do that, Bobby."

"I know you couldn't or wouldn't. But what now?"

"I told her that I would be waiting for her if she ever gets the time for me. I've changed my cell phone and email because I know if I hear from her, my plan will go to hell very quickly. I'm going to give you my new information so you can get in touch with me. Please don't tell her how to contact me. I told her to contact my parents when she decides if she wants to marry me and live our lives together."

"I won't tell her, I promise. I hope you are doing the right thing. If any two people were ever meant for each other, it's you and Elizabeth."

"I know, and if it's meant to be, it will happen."

A year had passed since the break-up, and Rick had immersed himself in the book. He hoped to finish it sometime before the end of the first semester of his senior year. He found a Dallas literary agent, a man named Morris Templeton of the Templeton Agency, to push the book to a New York publisher. He knew he would need another time-consuming project to occupy his mind, after the book either sailed or failed, because he would surely fall back into the same depressed state he'd experienced the first few months after he and Elizabeth had parted.

He hoped book sales would demand his time being involved in promoting and making personal appearances. He had to chuckle when he thought about the things going through his mind. He was already preparing himself for fame or notoriety.

At this same time, Elizabeth was making plans to spend the summer at the Graham Farm to learn about permaculture and how to prepare the soil for the production of chemical free vegetables and fruits and the staples of life. She bought three pairs of overalls and several sweatshirts, and a good pair of work boots.

"My folks have prepared the guest room upstairs for you. You'll be just down the hall from me, and you'll have your own bathroom."

"I hope they don't go to too much trouble," Elizabeth said. "I really appreciate the opportunity to do this. I think it will be a valuable lesson for me."

"It will help you in your career, Elizabeth," Eva said. "I firmly believe that my parents are thrilled to have you coming for the summer. Oh, and by the way, Josh is sleeping in the barn."

"Oh, no, I hope I'm not taking his room."

"No, he has an efficiency in the loft above the barn. He likes it there, anyway. He's been living out there for the last couple of years. He sneaks girls in sometimes. I've threatened to tell Mom, but I'm not going to."

At the farm, the work started early, right after breakfast. Elizabeth came down in her overalls and a blue sweat shirt, wearing a Dallas Cowboys baseball cap.

"Have you ever ridden a horse, Elizabeth?" Josh asked her.

"Nope, sorry," she said.

"You're from Texas, and you never rode a horse?"

"I live in Dallas, Josh," she said. "We do have cars, though. I can drive a car."

"You gotta lose that cap," he said.

"You can forget that."

"Okay, stay there, I'll be right back."

She watched him walk to the barn. He'd grown a couple of inches since she had first come to the farm and was as tall as his dad. A minute later, he came riding out of the barn on his horse. He really looked handsome, and he sat on the horse like a real cowboy, Elizabeth couldn't help but notice. He rode right up to Elizabeth and held out his left arm for her to grab on to.

"Come on," he said, "let's go bring in the herd."

She extended her arm up to him.

He scooted up in the saddle, reached for her arm, and lifted her up on the horse in the saddle behind him. "Hang on," he said and spurred the horse into a gallop.

She wrapped her arms around him, to keep from falling off, as they rode at what seemed to Elizabeth to be breakneck speed. She figured that Josh was showing off for her benefit, but she was enjoying the ride and the attention, so she just went with it.

"We have to drive them toward the paddocks," he said.

"Shouldn't I have stayed back at the barn to help the others?"

"No, I needed the help here."

"What exactly am I doing to help you, Josh?" she asked.

"Hugging me, Elizabeth, that's what I needed you to help me with."

"Oh, you are such a bullshitter, Josh Graham," she said and slapped him on his shoulder. "Take me back so I can start earning my keep."

"Okay, but hang on a little tighter." He spurred his horse, and the animal took off like a rocket.

"Where you been, Elizabeth?" Eva asked her when she and Josh had returned to the barn.

"Your smooth-talking brother told me he needed help driving the herd in."

"Josh," Eva yelled at him, "what is wrong with you?"

Josh raised both arms, shrugged, and looked at her quizzically. "What?" he said. "She never rode a horse. She's from Texas, and she never rode a horse. I was just showing her around the farm."

"You could have taken the jeep," Eva replied.

"But riding on Boonie is so much more—"

"You mean she wouldn't have to put her arms around you in the jeep."

"Something like that," Josh said.

"It's okay, Eva," Elizabeth said. "I enjoyed it, I really did."

They started walking the cows into the next paddock.

"Cows are pliable and agreeable creatures. They will follow a person who walks ahead of them," William Graham told her.

Once the cows were in the paddock, William or Josh would close the wire and shut them in. The cows would be taken out in the late afternoon and put back in the pasture, and the process would be repeated the next morning.

"So you don't fence them in?" Elizabeth asked William.

"Standard wooden or barbed-wire fences are much too expensive. We use an electric fence system. Once a cow rubs against it, they learn to stay clear. It's a cheap way to control them. It works with the chickens, too."

"When do we put the chickens in?"

"The chickens go in about four days after the cows come out. It takes about that long for the maggots to start growing. The chickens are just like the cows. They'll follow me into the paddock. And they stay there as long as necessary. The wire is low enough to zap them if they walk into it, so they don't try to get out."

"It's fascinating," Elizabeth said, "the whole process is fascinating to me."

"You're going to learn a lot this summer, but before we go any further, I need for you to come into the office with me and Jocelyn to discuss your wages."

"I didn't expect to be paid for this, Mister Graham."

"Nonsense, Elizabeth, you're not here to play at farming. You're going to be working, and I don't believe in a person working and not getting paid."

"What we are going to propose to you," Jocelyn said, "is that we pay you what we pay any new hand we hire. That will be ten dollars an hour, plus your room and board while you're here. It's not a lot of pay, but it's farm work, and it's honestly about all the job pays."

"That is more than generous, Mrs. Graham, and I am more than happy with that arrangement."

"Good, then it's a done deal," William said, "but one more thing, for heaven's sake call us by our names. This Mister and Mrs. business is just too burdensome."

Elizabeth laughed. "Okay," she said, "it's a deal, thank you both."

The work was hard, but Elizabeth had grown up working for her dad and, although she had done office work, she had developed a good work ethic. That work experience had helped her in school all through her public-school days and now in her college career. The Grahams discovered that the beautiful young woman from Texas was not afraid to get dirty. She came in from the field every evening covered with sweat and dirt and, more often than not, cow flop. She would jump in with Josh and all the hired men whenever there was work to be done.

One afternoon after work, Josh and Eva were sitting on the bench by the barn watching Elizabeth approach from the field.

"Got to love the Lord for making things like that," Josh said.

"You really have got a *thing* for her, don't you?"

"I could if she was available, sis, but she has no interest in me or anyone else. She's a woman in love, and I have nothing to offer but bullshit. It's too late for me. Nobody is going to get in between her and that lucky bastard in Texas. But damn, is she good looking, and so real."

"I know," Eva said, "most women who look like Elizabeth are all into themselves."

"And she acts like she doesn't even know she's beautiful," Josh said.

"I don't know how she could not know, Josh, you tell her every day."

"I didn't tell her yesterday," he replied."

"Okay, so every other day."

They were laughing when Elizabeth came up to where they were.

"What's so funny?" she asked.

"I can't tell you," Eva said. "It might embarrass Josh."

"Nothing embarrasses me."

"Was he talking about me?"

"Would that surprise you?" Eva said.

"I would give him a big hug right now," Elizabeth said, "but I've got pig shit all over me."

"That's okay, come on," Josh said, and they all started laughing.

The cow and chicken rotation work seemed like child's play to bringing in the harvest. The Grahams leased equipment that contained platforms on which pickers would lay as the machine passed over the rows of various types of crops. As they passed over the crops, the employees lying on the platforms would pick the crop and place it in bags or containers. It was hot and uncomfortable.

After the gathering, they had to crate and label the product for shipment to the various markets.

"We sell some of the beef directly to restaurants in Littlestown and Hanover, but most of it goes to processing plants in the area," Jocelyn explained to Elizabeth.

"What about all the vegetables and fruits?"

"Mostly, we sell through farmers' markets. A lot of our customers buy directly from us right here on the farm. Eva usually runs a stand when she's here in the summer, Josh does it sometimes. He's actually not as dumb as he acts."

"I sort of figured that out from watching and listening to him on the job this summer," Elizabeth said.

The day before they were to leave, Eva, Elizabeth, and the two older Grahams were gathered by the barn, talking about Elizabeth's experience over the past few months.

"You've really been a blessing to us all this summer," Jocelyn told her. "I hope you'll come back often with Eva."

"I look forward to that, Jocelyn. I certainly will," Elizabeth responded.

Josh came riding out of the barn on Boonie and rode up to Elizabeth. "You want to take another ride with me around the farm before you leave?" he said to her.

She looked at him demurely. "I don't know, Josh, I probably better not."

"Oh, come on," he said, "why not?"

"I'm afraid I might enjoy it as much as I did the first time," she said.

He looked at her for a moment as if he were trying to decipher the meaning of what she said. Finally, he smiled broadly, spurred his horse, and rode off toward the pasture.

"You almost knocked him out of the saddle with that one, young lady," William said.

"Oh, yeah, Lizzy," Eva said, "you lit a fire in my little brother that won't go out for a while."

The next morning at breakfast, Elizabeth thanked the Grahams for their hospitality and for allowing her to come and work and research their business.

"I have reams of information on my laptop that I plan to compile and organize into a book for my post-graduate work. I want to ask you if it's okay if I mention you guys and the farm in the book."

"Of course," William said. "That might be good for business."

Rick got word from his agent that the book had been accepted by a well-known New York firm. That was the good news. The bad news was that it would take over three years to edit and process the manuscript before it would go into print.

He had not expected that. He would be graduated before the book was in the bookstores. So, he would graduate and work on getting his masters. At least this solved his problem of finding that time-consuming project he thought he would need to keep his mind off Elizabeth.

Early in May of 2007, Rick got a call from his agent, Morris Templeton. "The publisher has taken a second look at the book and wants to do some preliminary promotional work on it. We need to talk to them about it. Can you come into my office for a conference call?"

"Well, sure, just tell me when."

"I'll set up a time with them and let you know."

The meeting was set for a few days later, in the afternoon. Rick had to skip two classes, but he figured he could make them up. In the agent's office, Morris took him to the conference room where monitors were set up. "This will be a video conference, Rick," he said, "we'll be able to see them, and they'll be able to see us."

"Okay," Rick said. "I'm not overdressed, am I?"

Morris laughed. "No, Rick, shorts and tennis shoes are fine."

Introductions were made. The New York element introduced themselves: "Hello, Mister Templeton and Mister Bennett, I am Harold Briggs, CEO of Briggs and Fredericks Publishing, my assistances are Gloria Richards and Manny Flores. I'd prefer you call us by our first names."

"Thank you, Harold," Morris said, "I am Morris Templeton and, by all means, call me Morris. I am here with Richard Owens Bennett, our author, who goes by Rick, in person, so feel free to be informal with us as well."

"Okay, Morris and Rick," Harold said, "first, we really like the book. I guess that goes without saying, or we wouldn't be publishing it. But Gloria did some research on our author and found out some interesting things that we'd like to use in promoting the book if Rick has no objection."

Morris looked at Rick quizzically and raised his eyebrows.

"Yes, Harold, go on."

"She discovered that Rick was a star quarterback in high school and turned down not a small number of scholarship offers from major schools around the country, to play football, because he wants to teach school at the college level."

"That's a true fact, Harold. Rick led his team to an undefeated season in 2002 and won the championship of the State of Texas."

"That's what we'd like to use, Morris and Rick. We'd like to play up, for instance, the 'quarterback to economist' meme. Manny here read the manuscript and pointed out something to me that convinces me that the book will be a best seller."

"What is that?" Morris asked.

"The very first line of the book," Harold said, "probably the best hook I've seen in a very long time. 'The Trickle-Down theory didn't work because that's all it did, trickle down.' That's brilliance, Rick. Now if you have no objection to our using your football past to promote your book, we'll proceed with the project. And we will be getting it out a lot sooner than usual. Probably within a year."

"I have no objection whatsoever, thank you, Harold," Rick said."

"Then I'll have my accountant Fed-Ex a check to Morris, for an advance against sales for fifty-thousand dollars."

"No shit?" Rick exclaimed.

"No shit, Rick," Harold said. "Thank you.

He had forty-five grand after the agent took his ten percent. *I'll have to pay taxes on it, of course*, he was thinking. He thought, at first, he might put half of it in the bank and just piss away the rest, but his brain took over and talked him out of that course of action. He took his family out to dinner.

"They liked the line you gave me about the trickle-down theory, Dad. I didn't tell them it wasn't my idea. They were so busy patting me on the back, I just couldn't say anything."

"No problem, son," Adrian said. "Behind every genius is a dad who inspired him a little."

"I've got an idea for an investment, Dad."

"Really, what are you thinking?"

"Remember when you used to take me and Amanda to the wineries in California when we were kids?"

"I remember," Adrian said.

"I loved visiting those wineries."

"I know you did, you used to say you were going to start a winery one day. You were twelve-years-old."

"I passed a vineyard the other day when I was driving up north of Dallas."

"You're thinking about buying a vineyard?"

"I'm thinking that might be better than starting one. If I can buy one that is already established, it will save me a lot of time getting into production."

"You won't remember the Van Dykes, but they had a vineyard up near Santa Ynez. That's where we used to take you and Amanda when you were kids."

"I remember the place and people but nothing specific."

"Your mom and I got to be pretty good friends with them over the years. I'm going to give them a call and see if they have any advice for you about starting a winery here in Texas."

"Okay, Dad, I appreciate that, I really do. That would be helpful."

Rick graduated with honors in May. He had to decide if he would take classes during the summer and apply that toward his master's degree. Typically, it takes one and a half to two years after acquiring the bachelor's degree to get your masters. To teach at a four-year college or university, one must have a masters' degree. Rick felt like he could get the sufficient credits in a year and a half. He decided to attend the summer session.

It all seemed like wasted time to him now. His passion for teaching had slowly diminished right along with his relationship with the woman he loved. He felt himself yearning to make a turn in a different direction. Nevertheless, he determined that he would continue the pursuit of his master's, if for no other reason than to edify his own ego.

He couldn't stop himself from wondering about Elizabeth. She would undoubtedly be starting her graduate studies, going all the way for her MD/PhD. He fought the temptation to go see Harley Meadows, and he won the fight.

"God how I miss her," he said to himself, out loud, on many occasions.

He went to sleep at night, thinking about her, and woke up in the morning, thinking about her. He had turned into a somber, almost unapproachable man who women found attractive and often made it clear to him.

In the local sports bar, where he occasionally went for dinner, and to watch a baseball or football game, depending on the season, a woman approached his table one evening. She was well-built and pretty and looked as if she worked out regularly and took good care of herself.

"Are you all alone?" she asked him.

"I'm all alone," he replied.

"My name is Mona. I've seen you here a few times now. Do you mind if I join you?"

"I guess not, Mona," he said, "have a seat."

"What's your name?" Mona asked as she sat down next to him.

"Rick, Rick Bennett," he replied.

"Rick Bennett? I've heard that name somewhere. Are you from around here?"

"I've been in Dallas since 2002. I go to SMU."

"You played football for Travis, didn't you? I remember you."

"Nah, you must have me mixed up with somebody else, Mona."

"No, I didn't," she said, chuckling. "You won the state championship and then gave up a lot of scholarships to play football. Come on, you're teasing me, right."

"Right, I'm teasing you. I'm that guy. I just graduated, and I'm studying for my master's, so I can teach in college."

"You're a good-looking guy, but I never see you with anyone, do you have a girlfriend?"

"I'm engaged to be married, Mona."

"Oh, wow, then why do I never see you with her?"

"She's going to school at Johns Hopkins in Baltimore, Maryland. We're going to get married when we get all settled down."

"Oh, I see," she said. "Well, in the meantime, would you like to come home with me for the night, Rick?"

Rick pursed his lips. "I really can't, Mona. You're very attractive, but I'm about as taken as any man could ever be. I appreciate the offer, though."

"Okay," she said. "It's just that you have the most beautiful blue eyes I've ever seen on a man."

"You're not making this any easier for me, Mona, but I have to say again that I'm in love with my woman, and I'm not going to cheat on her. I made a promise."

"She's a lucky girl, and I envy her, I just thought I'd try. Good luck to you."

"You take care of yourself, Mona."

She got up from the table and left the bar.

When Rick walked into the house, Amanda was watching television.

"Where are the folks?" he asked her.

"They went out to eat."

"And they didn't take you?"

"I wanted to watch Dancing with the Stars."

"You really like that show, don't you?"

"Yeah, I really do," she said.

He went upstairs to his room and turned on his laptop. A few minutes later, Amanda was yelling at him. He walked out to the stairs.

"What is it?" he yelled back at her.

"Come down here."

"Why, what's up?"

"Elizabeth is on Dancing with the Stars."

"Don't be silly, Amanda, she can't be."

"It looks like her, come see."

He walked down the stairs to humor her and looked at the TV. "That's not Elizabeth, Amanda, that girl is a professional dancer."

"Well, she looks like Elizabeth," Amanda insisted. "What's her name?"

"I don't know," he said.

A little later, she showed up in his room. "It wasn't Elizabeth," she told him.

"I tried to tell you, who was she?"

The announcer said she was Juliann Huff, or something like that, I'm not sure."

"I think I've heard of her, but it's spelled differently from how it sounds," Rick said. "She does look like Elizabeth, though, but not as pretty, whoever she is. I have to agree with you on that."

At JHU, Elizabeth graduated very near the top of her class and, like Rick, had decided to take the fast track to her master's. She had registered for summer classes and, since Eva had graduated and gone home to work with her family on their farm, Elizabeth had leased an efficiency apartment at the Bradford, for the summer months.

She went to bed every night, thinking about Rick, and awoke every morning, imagining he was lying there in the bed beside her. She had become despondent when she first discovered he'd changed his cell phone number and email address. She went through several weeks of almost debilitating depression, crying herself to sleep every night.

But through it all, she had managed to maintain her high GPA and honor roll status. Her drive to succeed was all that kept her sane. Her cell phone rang, and she looked at it, it was her father.

"Hi, Daddy," she said.

"Hello, baby, I have some news."

"Okay, what's up?"

"Your sister is getting married."

"Are you kidding me, Rose is getting married? So, Bobby finally popped the question?"

"He did, and Rose is happy, and so am I. Bobby is a great kid. He graduated from SMU and has been drafted by the New Orleans Saints. They're getting married in June. I hope you can come home for the wedding. Rose wants you to be her maid-of-honor, or whatever it is they call that sort of thing."

"I wouldn't miss it, Daddy," she said. "I'll call Rose and let her know I'll be there."

Elizabeth was giddy. She was certain that Rick would be at the wedding. He and Bobby Gladwyn were best friends. Bobby would surely want Rick to be his best man. She made up her mind that she would reconcile with him at the wedding. She would ask him to marry her now, and they could work out the living arrangements for the best of both their needs and plans. They could make it work, she knew they could.

But Bobby sat down with Harley and told him that Rick had made the decision to remain separated from Elizabeth until she had completed her schooling and was completely free to be with him if she still wanted to. She would have to make that decision of her own free will with no influence from him. Rick loved Elizabeth and always would. He was not seeing anyone else and had told Bobby that he would wait for Elizabeth until she was ready to be his wife, no matter how long it took. He had asked Bobby not to tell Elizabeth how to contact him before that time.

Harley agreed that Rick had made the right decision. Harley loved his daughter, but he respected Rick's decision and would not try to intervene or interfere in their affairs.

Elizabeth was devastated. Not knowing his whereabouts was worse than the fact that he had avoided her on purpose.

Rick had begun to question his decision not to go to the wedding when Bobby called him. He didn't know at the time that Elizabeth had planned to give up her goals and ask him to marry her. Had she called his parents, like he'd asked her to do, they could have reconciled and been happy again. He could only deduce from all this that she had given up on him and just didn't want to see him ever again.

Perhaps she had met someone. He hoped not. At least, according to Bobby, if there was another man in her life, she didn't bring him to the wedding.

He knew he would never love another woman again, as long as he lived. He might meet a woman one day he could live with—a man had needs, after all—but he'd probably ruin her life. To the casual observer, Rick Bennett looked like a man on a steadily increasing upward path. He would soon have his master's degree, he had a book that would soon hit the bookstores nationwide, and he was a handsome young man with endless possibilities. His was a brilliant résumé, but it wasn't bright enough to hide his broken heart.

Chapter 9

Summer in the Dirt

2008:

"Hey, Rick," Adrian yelled up the stairs to his son's bedroom, one evening.

Rick walked out to the top of the stairway. "Yeah, Dad, what's up?"

"I got a call back from James Van Dyke, out in Santa Ynez. Come on down when you get a minute."

Rick went down the stairs, and he and Adrian sat down at the dining room table. "James has some old friends who left Santa Ynez about thirty years ago, moved to Fredericksburg, Texas, and started a vineyard. George and Millicent Humphries, she goes by Milly, are an elderly couple who are ready to retire. He's in his late sixties or early seventies, James couldn't say for sure which, but they want to find a buyer for their vineyard. They haven't advertised it, just by word of mouth. After I called him last week, he looked around for me and came up with this opportunity. You may want to check it out."

"Where is it, exactly?" Rick asked.

"It's on Highway Two-Ninety, just outside Fredericksburg."

"I'll pull it up on the Google map and take a look. This might work out for me, if I can make a deal with these folks."

He placed a call to George Humphries, at the number his dad had given him, and made an appointment to meet with them the following week.

It was a fairly pleasant drive down. He crossed the Colorado River at Marble Falls and turned onto Highway 290 at Johnson City, drove toward Fredericksburg, found the Humphries place, and turned into the driveway. It didn't appear to be a very large facility. There was a house—a nice-looking one—a couple of out buildings, and a large barn. But he didn't see any buildings or equipment for pressing the grapes and producing the wine.

Mrs. Humphries met him at the door. "You're Rick, I assume," she said.

"I am," he told her. "And you are Mrs. Humphries?"

"I'm Millicent Humphries, but everyone calls me Millie. My husband is in the office. Would you like some coffee, Rick?"

"Yes, ma'am, if you're making some for Mister Humphries."

She led him to the office where the older man was seated at a wood desk that looked as if it were as old as the man himself.

"How are you, sir?" Rick said and shook the man's hand."

"I'm getting too old for this shit, young man," he said.

Rick laughed. "Sometimes I feel that way to, Mister Humphries."

"So why do you want to buy my vineyard?"

"When my sister and I were young, my parents took us every summer to the Van Dykes vineyard and winery in Santa Ynez. They were good friends with my folks, and we would stay with them for a weekend. I was fascinated with the place. I guess it was sort of a boyhood dream to own a winery. I never thought we would leave California back then, but circumstances brought us to Texas. I drove by a vineyard one day, near Dallas, and realized that I never lost that desire. My dad said he would call the Van Dykes and ask their advice, and they gave us your name and number."

"Well, I'm glad they did, and I'm glad you came to see me. Milly and I don't have any children to take the place. I have one nephew who is even more worthless than his old man, who is Milly's brother, so I wouldn't give him the sweat off my balls."

"Now, George, watch your mouth," Milly yelled at him from the kitchen. "You don't know that young man well enough yet to talk like that."

Rick started chuckling.

"I'm sorry, Milly," George yelled back. "She's a little too mild mannered sometimes, but I put up with her."

"I understand," Rick said and chuckled at the old man's *gentle* gruffness.

Milly brought them coffee, cream, and sugar, and Rick pulled up a chair and sat down across from George.

"First off, Rick," George said, "call me George. I've got twenty acres of planting area here. I plant ten acres with red and ten with green for red and white wine. I can't keep cows, so I buy cow manure to spread on the soil around the vines every year. Also, I keep free-range chickens that I let loose in the fields after the manure starts to ripen.

"Is that like that permaculture thing I've been hearing a little about?"

"Yes, it's as pure as leaving ground fallow, but we don't do that with grape vines," George said. "We trim them back once each year and then harvest the next growth. If I'd had the acreage and the money, I would have gotten my own herd of cows, but I just don't have the time left and the energy to do it." He sighed. "The barn is for storage of the wine and the other buildings you saw coming in, are where we store the equipment. We have a tractor and tools and miscellaneous stuff like that. I'll get you an inventory list."

"What about actually mashing the grapes and bottling the wine, where do you do that?" Rick asked.

"We send the product to a winery about ten miles east of here on Highway Two-Ninety. I have a crew come in and harvest it, weigh it, and deliver it to the facility. They turn it into the product and put it in barrels and then bottle it as soon as it's aged sufficiently. We have our own label. You can create your own brand if you choose to buy the place."

"I am certainly interested, George, but there is just so much I don't know."

"I can teach you, but it will take some time. You will need help. I have a few helpers that I'm sure will stay on with you. It's a lot of work that I can no longer do."

"What kind of time frame are you thinking to make your move out of here?" Rick asked.

"I'd like to be sold out in six months," George said.

"The time is sufficient for me. Here's my situation, George. I'm in graduate school, I want to get my master's degree, but I'm not married to that course of action. I really want to do this. I've written a book that is being published by a firm in New York. I am hopeful it will create a steady income for me. I don't know yet how big an income but, again, hopefully."

"No kidding?" George said. "What's the book about?"

"It's a treatise on the Reagan economy."

"Well, I'll be damned," he said, "then you're sure as hell smart enough to run a vineyard."

"Let's hope so," Rick said, "but I guess I should ask you what you want for the place."

"Half a million bucks for the whole package, land, house, equipment, and buildings. That's a lot less than what I could get if I was willing to wait a year or two."

"Yes, sir, it's not a bad price. I think I'd like to pursue it. I'll have to go to my bank so if you can get me an assessment and an inventory, like you were talking about."

"Why don't I finance it for you?"

"You can do that?" Rick said.

"I don't have to have the entire amount all at one time. You can get up and running and use the earnings from the vineyard to make your payments."

"I'll have to learn the business first, and I'll have to make payroll. How much down payment do you need to make the deal, George?"

"I don't have to have a down payment," George said. "Once we sign the papers, we can set up a payment plan based on a percentage of your yearly production. I want to get paid for the place, but I don't want to cripple you with debt before you even get started."

"I'll need to learn the business before I can do anything," Rick said.

"I have a...foreman, I guess you'd call him...who can show you the ropes, so to speak. We have a crop in the ground now that will be ready for production in a couple of months. You can apply half of that to your first annual payment. How much money do you have available?"

"I've got forty-thousand dollars."

"Well, hell, Rick, that'll be more than enough to easily make payroll through a harvest," George said.

"Then why don't you get the paperwork done and give me a call? I'll come back down, and we'll do the deal."

"Done," George said, "I'll have Carlos here to walk the property with you and show you how to make it work."

"Okay, George," Rick said, "what's left?"

"Shake hands on it, and we have a deal."

They shook hands, and Rick told Milly goodbye and that he would see her again soon.

He called his dad and told him about the deal he made. "You don't think I was too presumptuous, do you, Dad?

"James Van Dyke spoke very highly of George Humphries, but I'll give him a call and tell him about the deal you made and see what he says."

"Okay, I'll be driving back home tonight, and we'll talk more about it."

Rick stopped at a small café and bar for dinner on the way back to Dallas. The place was what he had come to expect as typical to Texas. The menu had chicken fried steak, cheese-burgers, club sandwiches, and chef salad. He ordered the chicken fried steak, and it was pretty good, he decided. He turned on the radio in his truck but could not get any Dallas stations. The only local stations were country and western. He wasn't fond of C&W, but there was nothing else, so he left it on.

After a few songs, the voice announced that the next song was by the Statler Brothers, a group Rick had never heard of.

The name of the song was *Elizabeth*. "Are you kidding me," he said out loud, but he listened just to see what it was.

It was a heart-wrenching song about a man who was away from the woman he loved and how he longed to be with her. The man wasn't certain he would be able to go on without her. Rick listened to the sad, beautiful song and marveled at how similar his circumstances were.

By now he was tearing up and feeling like his life was over. He turned the radio off, pulled off to the side of the road, and just sat there staring out into the beam of his headlights. He covered his face with his hands, leaned over into the steering wheel, and wept uncontrollably for about two minutes. He was only vaguely aware of the red and blue flashing lights of the Texas DPS cruiser that had pulled up behind him.

When the trooper knocked on his window, Rick sat up, lowered the window, and turned on the overhead light in the cab.

"Are you okay, sir?" the trooper asked him.

"Yes, sir, I'm fine," Rick said. "I just have a headache. I stopped for a minute to rest."

"Can I see your license, insurance, and registration?"

Rick got his license out of his wallet, retrieved the other info from the glove box, and handed them to the officer.

"Have you been drinking, Mister Bennett?"

"No, sir," Rick said. "I stopped at a café back down the road, but I just had dinner and a coke, no alcohol.'"

"Would you be willing to take a breathalyzer test?"

"Sure," Rick said.

"Okay, that won't be necessary. Here's your paperwork back, drive carefully."

"Thank you," Rick said.

"Oh, one other thing, are you the Rick Bennett who played for William B Travis High School?"

"Yes, sir, back in 2002."

"You should have played for UT."

"Yeah, I probably should have."

Elizabeth completed the manuscript that she began the summer she worked for the Grahams on their farm. She entitled the book *My Summer in the Dirt* with a subtitle: *and other foreign matter.*

She applied for a copyright and emailed a copy to Eva for her parents to read and make suggestions and offer any corrections for mistakes they might find. She received a response from Eva very quickly:

Elizabeth, so good to hear from you, and so proud of you for completing the book. Mom and Dad want me to ask you to come and spend a weekend with us. They have some suggestions on where you can get the book published. Let me know.
Eva.

The Grahams were waiting for her when she arrived. William and Jocelyn hugged her and beckoned her into the house.

"I hope you brought your work clothes, girl," William said and then laughed.

"I absolutely love the book, honey," Jocelyn said. "It is so well written. If you ever decide against being a scientist, you can always be a writer."

"Well, that's kind of why I wanted to come and talk to you. I'm thinking of maybe bouncing off in a different direction."

"Really," Jocelyn said, looking confused. "But that was your life's goal."

"I know. All my life, after my mother died, that was all I wanted to do. But ever since I came here and discovered what you guys do, I've had what might be called an epiphany, of sorts."

"What do you mean, Elizabeth," Eva asked her.

"I think I've come to believe that what you guys do is more important than anything that modern medicine can or does do. I think what you do is basic to preventing health problems. I just believe this is the way I should be using my talent to help people."

"You're not going to drop out of school, are you?" Eva said.

"I'm going to get my master's degree," she said, "but I'm not going any further than that. I'm going to lecture and write."

"I think that's wonderful, Elizabeth," Jocelyn said. "You're willing to give up a lot of money and fame for something you think is right. Not many people have the courage and the moral strength to do that."

"Listen, Elizabeth," William said, "there are publishers who specialize in subjects like your book. Jocelyn and I will write a reference for you, and your mention of our farm in your book will draw attention to the industry."

"One other thing you should consider, though," Jocelyn added," is this. You should use a pen name to write under. This subject could bring you some negative publicity that might hurt you in anything you might decide to do in the medical field in the future."

"What name should I use?"

"Maybe Beth Meadows or…what's your middle name?"

"Ann."

"Ann Meadows, or Beth Ann Meadows has a nice ring,"

"All right then," Elizabeth said, "I'll be Beth Ann Meadows, thank you."

They heard a vehicle driving up outside. "There he is, Elizabeth," Eva said.

"Has to be Josh."

"Yep, but don't worry, Josh won't be bothering you."

"Josh got him a girlfriend, did he?" Elizabeth said.

"Better that that, Josh got married."

"Are you serious?" Elizabeth asked, astonished.

"She's a good girl," Jocelyn said. "You'll like her.

Josh walked in the door. "Whose car is that in the—oh shit," he said, when he saw Elizabeth.

Everyone in the room started laughing. Elizabeth stood up and hugged Josh.

"Hi, Josh, how are you? Been a long time. It's good to see you."

The girl standing behind him had long black hair, dark eyes, red lips, and was built like a movie star. He took her hand. "Come here, Crystal," he said, "I want you to meet an old friend of the family. This is Elizabeth Meadows. She was roommates with Eva at Johns Hopkins."

"This is the one you had the hots for? Yeah, I see why now. Hello, Elizabeth, I've heard a lot about you. I'm glad to finally meet you. Maybe now Josh will shut up about you."

"Aw hell, Crystal, why you gotta embarrass me like that? Elizabeth is like a sister to me."

"A sister, huh? I never hear you talk about Eva like you talk about her."

"Well, look, Crystal and I gotta go into town, we'll be back later."

After Josh and Crystal drove off, the four of them burst into laughter.

"That was just a bit surreal," Elizabeth said.

Rick's book launched in June of 2008 and was met with a mixture of both disdain and admiration. Reagan worshippers assailed the book as a betrayal of the great man's legacy, while those who hated him painted it as a whitewash of his administration. Sales amounted to just under a hundred thousand dollars over the first two years, enough to make back the advance the first year. In 2009, he would earn another fifty thousand. It wouldn't necessarily be a case of too little too late, but it was a far cry from what he had expected and needed.

He would make the deal with George Humphries, though. Humphries turned out to be an honest man and kept his promise to Rick. Carlos Ramirez taught Rick the basics of the vineyard—everything that required actually walking around the property and doing "hands-on" work. George taught him the business side.

"We set the rows eight feet apart, Mister Rick—" Carlos pronounced his name Reek. "—and the vines are planted six feet apart in each row. That adds up to nine hundred and seven vines para acre. Mister George, he'll tell you about the wine we get para acre." Carlos occasionally inserted Spanish words into his dialogue.

"Our fields typically yield four tons of grapes per acre," George explained to Rick. "One ton of grapes will result in a little more than two barrels of wine. Each barrel contains sixty gallons, twenty-five cases, or three-hundred bottles. So basically, we reap right at seven hundred twenty bottles from each harvested acre. Twenty acres multiplied by seven hundred twenty bottles will give us fourteen thousand, four hundred bottles of product. The red can be bottled for sale after a year because we introduce sugar into it during the cooking process, but the white takes at least three years. We store the red in wooden barrels in our barn and the white in steel tanks at the winery. They do the bottling and labeling for us as part of the cost of their processing."

Rick earned his master's, but it was of precious little value to him now. His passion for teaching was gone, and his passion for life was hanging by a very thin thread. His major goal now was one of necessity, more than passion. He had to make a living.

He wanted to make a success of the vineyard, and he threw himself into that with all his available enthusiasm. The Humphries moved out of the house, and Rick moved in. He bought a bed, that was about all he could afford at first. But as his profits from the book began to trickle in, he slowly began to make the place look like a home that people actually lived in.

He changed the name of the business to Lizzy Bee Vineyard. No one understood the name, but no one argued against it. He had a sign erected over the entry, informing people that they had arrived at the Lizzy Bee Vineyard. The Humphries had sold a lot of wine from a stand they had at the edge of the property near the highway. He had to apply for a liquor license to engage in that endeavor, but it was worth the trouble, Rick decided. He enjoyed working at the stand and talking to the people who stopped to check out the product. One particularly busy day, a lady stopped at the stand. The girl he had running the stand was occupied with another customer, so Rick walked up to the new customer.

"Anything I can help you with, ma'am?" he asked her.

"I've seen your stuff in stores in the San Marcos area," the lady told him. "I bought a bottle on a whim and found it quite delightful. When I passed here and saw the sign, I just had to turn around and stop and see where it comes from."

"I'm glad you did," Rick said. "I'm the owner, Rick Bennett. Would you like to take a tour of the place?"

"I'd love to," she said.

She was older than he was, mid-thirties, he guessed, sort of plain looking but not unattractive. He showed her the rows of vines and the big barn with the barrels of wine that they kept in storage for aging.

"I see you have chickens on some of the unplanted ground," she said. "Do you raise chickens?"

"No, I treat the fields with a soil preparation technique called permaculture. It creates a soil that is chemical free and results in a tastier and healthier product."

"Coincidentally, I know some people who are likewise interested in this technique. They might like to do a story on your vineyard, if you wouldn't mind."

"Heck no, I wouldn't mind," he said. "I can use any publicity I can get."

"I have a book, back at my apartment in Austin. I'll bring it to you next week when I pass through here again."

"I look forward to that. Here, take a few bottles of my red and white, complimentary, for your friends to try."

"Well, thank you, Rick. My name is Val, short for Valerie, Chambers. I live in Austin, and I teach at a community college."

"Really, what do you teach?" Rick asked her.

"I'm involved in environmental studies," she said.

"Good for you, Val, that's apparently a growing industry. I look forward to seeing you again."

Rick came to realize that he would have to hire someone to manage the office, make the payroll, and pay the bills. He didn't want to hire a service to do it, that was too impersonal. He suddenly got what he thought was a brilliant idea. He called his sister, Amanda.

"Hey, Rick, what's going on?" Amanda asked.

"Hello, sis, what are you doing?

"I'm watching TV," she said

"No, I mean what are you doing with your life?"

"I just finished my second year at community college."

"What are you going to do now?" he said.

"I don't know, why?"

"I want you to come down here and help me run the vine-yard."

Oh, my gosh, Rick, are you serious?" Amanda shrieked.

"Yes, I'm serious. I need you to manage the office and keep the books and stuff."

"Yes, I'd love to do that. Where would I stay?"

"You'll live in the house with me, silly."

"Can you come and get me?"

"Pack your things and call me when you're ready. I'll come and get you. We'll need to bring your bedroom furniture too. Let Mom and Dad know and make sure they're okay with this."

"Okay," she said, "I'll be ready tomorrow."

"Let's make it the day after tomorrow, okay?" he said

"Okay, Rick, I'll be ready, thank you so much."

Rick was looking forward to having Amanda around. She had always been such a pleasant girl, and she and Rick had always been close. Amanda had a way of bringing light and joy into a room, and he needed the positivity he knew she would bring back into his life.

The Humphries house—now the Bennett house—was a single story with four bedrooms, one of which had been made into the office. Rick had taken the master bedroom, so Amanda would have her choice of either of the remaining two. She picked the one closest to the hall bathroom.

Val Chambers returned the following week. When Amanda answered the door, Val was a bit surprised.

"Oh," she said." I was looking for Rick."

"He's in the office, I'll get him. I'm Amanda, Rick's sister." There was no mistaking Val's relief at hearing that Amanda was Rick's sister.

"Come on in, Val," Rick said. "I was just finishing up some paperwork in the office. Would you like some coffee?"

"Sure, that would be nice," she said.

He led her to the living room, and they sat down.

"I'll put on a pot," Amanda said and skipped off to the kitchen.

"My sister just came down from Dallas to manage the office for me. I was getting overwhelmed."

"She's very outgoing and pleasant. She'll make a nice addition to your business."

"That's what I was thinking. So, you're going in to Fredericksburg?"

"Yes," she said. "I love coming to Fredericksburg, it's such a unique place."

"I haven't had much opportunity yet to get acquainted with the town since I moved in here."

Amanda brought the coffee, and they doctored their cups with the desired amounts of cream and sugar.

"I'll be in the office if you need me, Rick," Amanda said, and she left.

"Here's the book I was telling you about. I don't know much about the lady who wrote it, but she writes and lectures all over on the soil preparation industry to which you alluded."

He picked up the book and looked at it.

"My Summer in the Dirt? That's an interesting title."

"I know, apparently, she worked on a farm in Pennsylvania one whole summer, learning from the family that owned the farm everything she wrote about in the book. This book has become the de-facto primer for the entire industry."

"I hate to take your only copy. Can I buy this somewhere?"

"I can get another copy in Austin, don't worry about it."

"What's her name?" He looked at the cover again and looked stupefied.

"Is something wrong Rick? Val asked him.

"I don't think so," he said. "Her name is Beth Ann Meadows. That is eerily similar to my ex-fiancée's name, Elizabeth Meadows, but it has to be a coincidence."

"Really, why?"

"Elizabeth was a genetics-bio-medical science major at Johns Hopkins. She was obsessively dedicated to becoming a scientist-slash-researcher to find ways to prevent heart attacks.

Her mother died from a heart attack when she was ten. Nothing, and I mean nothing, would have diverted her from her career path."

"Not even you, I assume."

"Not even me."

"I'd like to take you to dinner tonight if you're not too busy," Val said.

"I think that would be nice, Val," he said. "I can meet you somewhere, you know the town probably better than I do."

"I like the Altdorf on Main Street. Can you meet me there around seven?"

"I'll Google the address and be there at seven, thanks, Val." After she left, he went back to the office. "She wants to talk about how to get better and healthier crop production out of the soil, by using permaculture management techniques," he told Amanda.

"She wants to talk about how to get you out of your pants and into her bed," Amanda replied.

"Oh? And when did you get so worldly and in tune with other people's hidden agendas?"

"Are you kidding me? The woman was practically licking her lips when you walked her to her car."

"It's just dinner, sis, I'm not going to bed with her."

"Then you're going to hurt her *feelings*," she said, emphasizing the last word, as she smiled at him playfully.

The Altdorf was a very popular German restaurant, established in Fredericksburg in the seventies. It featured some of the finest German food in the state as well as popular American and Tex-Mex favorites.

The waiters knew Val and ushered her and Rick to a table in the courtyard outside, right away.

"I brought a bottle of wine from a local Fredericksburg Vineyard. I hope it's okay to bring it in."

"Of course, Miss Chambers," the waiter said, as he handed them their menus. "I'll bring a couple of glasses."

"Do you own stock in this place?" Rick asked her."

"I should by now," she replied, "I come here often enough.

"So, what do you suggest?"

"I'd suggest a glass of this local rose wine. I know the owner of the vineyard, and he is meticulously obsessive about his grapes."

"That's very flattering, and I am overwhelmed. I think I will have a glass. Yes, it's an excellent wine."

"Let me guess," she said. "Lizzy Bee has something to do with that ex-fiancée to whom you alluded back at your house."

"You're very perceptive, Val. Yes, the name is a nickname I used to call her."

"I get the impression that it's not over for you."

"You may be too perceptive for my own good. I won't be much fun if you insist on taking me back in time."

"Then, by all means, let's go forward. I like the wiener schnitzel, that's a pork cutlet with lemon. Do you see anything you like?"

"I like the looks of this jaeger schnitzel with, the brown gravy. I think I'll have that."

After they finished eating, she raised the wine bottle and saw that it was empty. "I have another one in my room. Will you come back with me? There's something I want to talk to you about."

He'd consumed just enough wine to believe that Val really wanted to talk to him about some important subject matter. And the truth was that he was really enjoying the conversation with her and didn't want it to end. It had been so long since he'd had an actual conversation with a woman that he'd almost forgotten what it felt like.

In her room, she opened the second bottle of wine, and they each had another glass.

"I want to tell you my story, Rick."

"Only if you want to, Val, it's not necessary."

"I want to. You see, I'm married. My husband is much older than I am, by twenty years, and he's rich. I didn't marry him because he was rich, I married him because I loved him. But now he's crippled and in a wheel chair. He encourages me to teach, because I love to do it, not because I need the money."

"I'm sorry, Val," Rick said." I'm not judging you for anything."

"The reason I'm telling you this is that I'm thirty-five years old, still relatively young, and I still have needs, and I think you know what those needs are. I can tell you're hurting and I'm not going to pry into the reasons for that. I'm hurting, too. We can make each other's hurt go away, even if it's only for a little while. No strings attached, no expectations, I won't complicate your life. I just need you to make love to me tonight."

He looked at her for a moment, contemplating the right and wrong of what he was considering doing. Perhaps it was the wine, or her vulnerability, but just her asking him to make love to her, so desperately it seemed, somehow made her beautiful to him. She had been sort of plain looking when he first met her. But now she was a good-looking woman, very desirable, and he could try to convince himself that he should not give in to temptation, but he wanted her. Perhaps it could have been any woman. He wouldn't try and sort that out. Val wasn't Elizabeth, no woman would ever be Elizabeth, but Val was here, and Elizabeth was not.

He stood up and took her hand, and she stood up. He kissed her, gently at first and then more forcefully. The need of so many lost years started raging through his body like a firestorm. She began shaking and grasping at him desperately.

They managed to remove their clothing and get into the bed. Val was not lax in voicing her appreciation for the effort he was putting forth to make her happy. When they caught their breath, after they had rescued each other from sexual deprivation, they lie there, a while before she spoke.

"How long has it been for you, Rick," she said.

"I don't know, I can't remember."

"Well, I'm awfully happy you decided to end your sabbatical with me."

"Yeah, me too. You're incredible, Val."

"Will you do it for me again?"

"Yeah, if you can wait about a half hour."

"I'll wait all night, if that's what it takes," she said.

"Did she let you keep your pecker?" Amanda asked him, as he came in the door, at two in the morning.

"Where in the world did you learn to talk like that?" Rick said, shocked at her language.

"From Mom," she said.

Chapter 10

Convergence

2009:

Elizabeth started working in Richmond, Virginia, out of the office of an organization called The Society for the Promotion of Chemical-Free Food, commonly referred to by its abbreviation, SPCFF—pronounced Spicuf. They took messages for her, contacted her when she had a request for a lecture, and provided her an office free of charge. Elizabeth had brought much positive attention, and donations, to the organization.

She turned down a salary because she was making quite a substantial amount of money from her lectures and from royalties from her first book: *My Summer in the Dirt*.

A package arrived for Elizabeth, and one of the staffers put it in her office for her. When she came in, she read the label and saw that it was postmarked Austin, Texas. There were two bottles of wine in the package. There was a note in the box that said:

I am a fellow chem-free food advocate, and I found that this wine is from a vineyard that employees the same practices you advocate in your book. I thought you might enjoy this.
Signed, Valerie, from Austin, TX

Elizabeth looked at the labels on the bottles. *Lizzy Bee Vineyard. How can this be*? she was thinking. The label said Fredericksburg, Texas. She was dumbfounded. "This has to be the most impossible coincidence, or an extremely cruel joke, she said to herself. There is no way this can be from Rick. He could not possibly know that I'm at this address."

The manager of the office, a man named Corley McKnight, walked into her office. "Is everything all right, Beth?" he asked.

"I'm not sure," she said.

"I don't understand. You're not sick, are you?"

"No, it's not that. I got two bottles of wine, from someone I don't know, and the label on the bottles is a pet-name that my ex-fiancé used to call me. It makes no sense to me."

"This is the guy you parted ways with a couple of years ago?"

"Yes, he broke it off with me."

"Oh, here we go with that bullshit again. Beth, men do not break up with women who look like you. They may kill themselves over them, but they don't break up with them."

"It was complicated, Corley. We were going to get married in our second year in college, but my schedule and agenda just wouldn't permit it. I asked him to wait until I finished medical school, but he said no. He told me that if I ever found the time for him, to look him up and we'd start over."

"Then why didn't you look him up?"

"I tried, but he had left, and I don't know where he is. I'm convinced that he doesn't want to see me anymore."

"Are you still in love with this guy, Beth?"

"Yes, I am, I think I will always love him," She said.

"Then tell me his name, and I'll find him for you."

"I don't want to do that' I'm leaving it in God's hands now."

"God?" he said, incredulously. "I thought you said you were an agnostic."

"I was for most of my adult life, but my summer on the Grahams' farm changed my way of thinking, in more ways than one. They were down-to-earth people, and they were Godly people. Something changed in me while I was with them. I dropped out of medical school and rededicated my life to what I'm doing now."

"Well, that's all very nice, but if I were that guy, and I was in Tiera Del Fuego, and I got an email telling me that Beth Meadows was in love with me, I would *walk* to the Rio Grande and then *walk* to Virginia or to wherever you were."

"That's really sweet, Corley, but if Rick and I are meant to be together, I believe it will happen. It will happen if God is willing and, in his time, when our hearts are ready."

"Is there any chance that these two wine bottles came from your guy's winery?"

"I don't know," Elizabeth said. "He's from California originally, and his parents used to take him and his sister to a winery every year just for a weekend. Rick often talked about owning a vineyard and winery one day. But his greater passion was teaching."

Corley took a closer look at the label on the wine bottles. "It says this place is in Fredericksburg, Texas, Beth, that's close to Austin."

"I doubt that it's him, it has to be a coincidence."

"Okay, I guess you know what's best for you. So, what's our next campaign, Beth? Are you working on another book, or should I start scheduling the lecture circuit?"

"I'm just starting to form the book in my mind. I'll write an outline while I'm on the next tour, but I'm not going to rush into it. I've got time. Can you go ahead and set me up for the next campaign?"

"Indeed, I can," Corley said. "I have to make some confirmations with the promoters, and I'll have that to you in the morning."

"Good, thank you, Corley."

At the vineyard, the second year proved to be more successful than the first. Rick paid half the profits to George Humphries for the yearly installment and kept the other half for operating and living expenses. He bought a new truck and let Amanda drive it to Dallas when she wanted to go home and see Mom and Dad.

"You will come back, won't you, sis? Don't me leave high and dry here."

"Are you kidding me, Rick? I love it here. I'm just going for the weekend."

"Good, because I can't run this place without you."

Amanda beamed when he told her that.

He walked out to the road where the local girl he'd hired was selling wine to tourists who stopped. He took her some iced tea and water. He remembered that was how he'd first met Val Chambers. He was surprised, and yet kind of relieved that he'd not heard from her again.

"Hi, Lacey," he said, "any business?"

"I sold four bottes to two people in a car this morning, Rick, but nothing since then. I feel like I'm wasting your money. They stop and talk but don't buy much."

"Don't worry about it. You give them brochures and answer any questions they have. It's publicity. Let's give away a bottle every so often."

"Give it away?" she said, looking confused

"Yeah, not to everyone who stops, and don't give any to kids, of course. But it won't hurt to give away a bottle or two every morning. It's good *word of mouth* advertising."

"Okay, I'll try that, but I'll use good sense. I won't give away the store."

Rick chuckled. "That's good, Lacey, by the way, are you going to college after you graduate this year?"

"Yes, I'm going to Texas State in San Marcos."

"Now that's interesting, I was planning to apply for a teaching job there before I bought the vineyard."

"Are you serious, Rick?" I wouldn't have figured you for a teacher."

"Well, that was my plan, but it didn't work out that way."

"I bet you would have been a great professor, Rick."

"You think so, Lacey?"

"Yeah, I do, because you're so smart."

"Well, thank you, miss," he said, "that's quite a compliment."

When Amanda came back on Sunday, he told her he was taking her out to eat.

"Where are we going, Rick?"

"We're going to The Altdorf."

"What is that?" she asked him.

"The Altdorf is a German restaurant. It's a very good German restaurant."

"Is that where that woman took you that night you didn't come home?"

"Yes, it was, and I came home. I just came home late."

"I don't want to hear any details."

"Well, that's good because I wasn't going to share any details with you."

As they were eating, Rick looked across the courtyard and noticed an elderly man sitting in a wheelchair. It drew his attention because the courtyard was covered with a smooth rock surface, so it must have been some trouble rolling the chair to the table. Then he noticed the woman at the table with the man. It was Val Chambers. "Oh shit," he uttered under his breath, low enough that his sister did not notice. He tried to avoid looking at Val, hoping she wouldn't notice him, but it didn't work.

Their eyes met, and the look on Val's face was one of fear and pleading. Rick was almost angry at her. *What the hell does she think I'm going to do?*" he was thinking, *come over to her table and tell the old man...hey, I screwed your wife the other night.*

He averted his eyes, to let her know that he was not going to make any sign at all that he even knew her. He was careful not to let Amanda see him looking in that direction. When they had finished eating, he paid the check, walked Amanda out, and shielded her from the side Val was sitting on. Amanda never knew she was there.

A few days later Rick received a call from Val.

"Hello, Rick, I'm sorry about the other night in the restaurant in Fredericksburg," she said.

"You're sorry about going to a restaurant with your husband?"

"That's really not what I meant. But thank you for avoiding me."

"What did you think I was going to do, Val, come over and introduce myself?"

"I don't know, I just sort of panicked when I saw you," she said.

"There was no reason to. Listen, Val, we had a one-time thing. It was good, really good. But it was also really wrong. You're a married woman and what happened between us cannot happen again. Under different circumstances, maybe, but as it is now, we can't see each other again."

"I know that, Rick. You're right, thank you, for the night at my room and for the other night at the restaurant."

"No reason to thank me, Val. You gave me something I needed very badly, but it was a one-time thing and has to stay that."

"I just want you to know, Rick, that the way you feel about the woman you love, is the same way I feel about my husband. He got sick and can no longer give me what I need in bed. That does not mean I no longer love him, I still do. What I needed from you was intimacy that I cannot get from the man I love, and I think that it was the same with you."

"Yes, it was, Val, it wasn't just physical, although it filled a very great need I'd had for a long time. I appreciate your honesty. I respect your marriage and your feelings for your husband."

Relieved, he hung up and breathed easy. He had not wanted the thing with Val to go any further, and now he knew it would not.

In the SPCFF Office, Richmond, Virginia, Corley went over the schedule. "Listen up, Beth, I've got your schedule set. You're going to be on lectures for the entire month of June. Nine events. I'm going send Peggy with you and Jerry in the RV, Jerry will drive. I'm not making motel reservations. You can do that when, or if, you need to stop for the night. Please get two rooms, if you don't mind. You and Peggy in one and Jerry in the other. I've got five farm visits set up for you. Stay with them overnight if they ask you. People love that, and it is great publicity."

"You mean I can't sleep with Jerry?" Peggy yelled from just outside the door.

"Am I talking too loud, Beth?"

"No, Corley, you're doing fine," Elizabeth said, chuckling, "two rooms."

"Okay, here is the schedule: Charlotte, North Carolina, Thursday, June fourth; Atlanta, Georgia, Monday, June eighth; Birmingham, Alabama, Thursday June eleventh; Tuscaloosa, Alabama, Monday June fifteenth; Shreveport, Louisiana, Friday June nineteenth; Beaumont, Texas, Tuesday June twenty-third; Houston, Texas, Wednesday June twenty-fourth; San Antonio, Texas, Thursday June twenty-fifth; Austin, Texas, Monday June twenty-ninth."

"Finishing up in Austin? Elizabeth said. "I may go home for a few days and let Peggy and Jerry bring the RV back to the office. I can fly back later."

"If that's what you want to do, then do it, Beth, you're the star."

Jerry Meisner, the driver and all around go to guy at SPCFF, was, pretty much Corley McKnight's right-hand man. Jerry was a muscular, powerfully-built man about five feet, ten inches tall. He weighed maybe 165 and didn't have an ounce of fat on him.

Jerry claimed to be Randy Meisner's brother, even though he was over thirty years younger than the renowned bassist of the band The Eagles, and despite the fact that Jerry was a black man.

It was a running joke that everyone went along with. Jerry knew the lyrics to every Eagles' song ever made.

He was also skilled in martial arts and wasn't afraid of the devil himself.

For that reason, Corley asked Jerry to go along on every lecture circuit that Elizabeth and her assistants went on. He knew they would be safe with Jerry Meisner.

Peggy Boyd had accompanied Elizabeth on several circuits in the past. She was fiercely loyal to her. Peggy was not an attractive woman, but she was dedicated to her job and so likable that she made every trip more fun.

"Okay team," Jerry said as they pulled out of the parking lot. "It's two hundred ninety-three miles to Charlotte so try to relax. We're eastbound and down."

"Eastbound?" Elizabeth said. "Shouldn't we be going west, or southwest?"

"Don't you remember, Beth?" Peggy said, "Jerry likes to use movie lines and song lyrics in general conversation just to see if anybody catches on."

"I remember now," Elizabeth replied. 'I never catch on because I never watch movies."

"See how much you missed by being a nerd?" Jerry said to her."

"Who are you calling a nerd, Randy Meisner?" Elizabeth yelled and threw a pillow at him.

"I'm *Jerry* Meisner, peaches, Randy is my brother, and yeah, you definitely have a few nerd-like qualities about you."

"Well, that hurts my feelings, Jerry," she said.

"Then I take it back, peaches."

"Okay, thank you."

The first lecture went well. Elizabeth had delivered the *My Summer in the Dirt* lecture so many times now that she was flawless. Jerry typically sat in a seat on the front row on the outside chance that some guy made the ill-advised decision to approach Elizabeth at the podium. It only happened once in the several years she had been doing the job. That time two guys in the audience stopped the man. But Corley was sufficiently concerned about it that he began sending Jerry along with her after that.

"Isn't our first farm stop, in Georgia?" Jerry said.

"Yes, the Nash farm is on first on our list, John and Emma. Take the exit at Four-Forty-One and go south, left down Homer Road."

Peggy started poking fun at the Southern-sounding name. "Hey, Homer, is this here your road?"

"My father's name was Homer," Jerry said. "You making fun of my father?"

"You told me your father's name was Harold."

"Harold was his middle name, Peggy."

"Oh, you're so full of shit, Jerry. I never know when you're telling the truth."

Jerry started laughing so hard he almost ran off the road.

"Anyway." Elizabeth took the conversation back. "Go eight-point-four miles down Homer Road and The Nash farm is on the left."

Elizabeth and Peggy changed into work clothes before they got to the farm and, as Jerry drove the RV onto the property, a man waved at him from the barn and motioned for him to come on over.

"Can I help you with something, young man?" John Nash asked Jerry.

"Are you Mister John Nash?" Jerry asked him.

"I'm what's left of him, son," Nash replied.

Jerry laughed. "We're from the Chemical-Free Food Society in Virginia, sir, and we received a letter with some questions, regarding the permaculture agriculture management techniques, that we promote."

"Yes, sir, I did write you folks a letter, but I wasn't expecting a personal visit. This is quite a surprise."

"We're on a speaking tour, and you're just off our route so we thought we'd stop and show you the answers to your questions rather than write a letter back. The lady who wrote the book is here and another lady too. They are going to answer all your questions and show you some things."

Elizabeth and Peggy got out of the RV wearing their overalls and work boots, ready to go to work. Both shook hands with Nash, and he yelled for his wife, Emma, to come out of the house.

"You can park your rig next to my barn here," Nash told Jerry. "I've got a hook-up on the side next to the electrical panel. There's a bathroom with a shower inside the barn if you need it."

"That's mighty nice of you, Mister Nash," Jerry said. "Right now, I'm going to get some shut-eye, I've been driving a while. The blonde-haired lady there is the brains of the operation, by the way."

Elizabeth and Peggy walked with John and Emma down to their paddocks. Elizabeth surmised quickly that the paddocks were too large for the number of cows they had.

"You either need more cows, if you leave them just one day, or you need to make the paddocks smaller. That's why your grass is not coming back quickly enough. You could add more paddocks, but your acreage is limited.

"I can't really afford more cows right now," Nash said.

"Let me do some figuring," Elizabeth said. She went to the RV, came back with a rolling measuring tape, and rolled off the lengths and widths of each paddock. Then she pulled a small calculator out of her pocket and punched around on it for a few minutes, writing down information as she continued. "If you cut them in half, they will then be too small. I would suggest rearranging the sizes to three-quarters what they are now."

"I'd have to move the fence posts and re-run the electric wiring. That's going to take a lot of work, but if you think that will fix the problem, that's what I'll have to do."

"Do you have any help, John?" she asked him.

"No, miss, it's just me and the wife."

"Well, look, we don't have to be in Atlanta until the eighth. That gives us three days to get it done. If we can connect at your barn, and you said there's a bathroom in the barn, we can stay there. We can leave on the eighth and get to Atlanta in time for the show that evening."

"You mean you guys would do that for us. I'll be happy to feed you while you're here but that's a lot of work and—"

"I'm not as soft as I look, John," Elizabeth said.

Elizabeth and Peggy pitched in immediately, taking down the electric fencing wire. They let Jerry sleep a few hours and then gave him the news. Elizabeth laid out the spots for the fence posts, and Jerry started with the post-hole digger. John Nash was no slouch for a man his age. He made Jerry let him take over after a while. Emma kept them supplied with iced tea and sandwiches.

They worked until dark on Friday and Saturday. Emma made a meal of roast beef and mashed potatoes and other vegetables on Friday and catfish, hush puppies, and creamed corn on Saturday. She made them breakfast every morning—ham and eggs and biscuits, hot coffee, and all the milk they wanted. Emma went to church on Sunday, but John stayed and worked with Elizabeth and the others. They finished the job around six o'clock on Sunday evening. They ate dinner, and Elizabeth went over some final details with John about the rotation system of his paddocks.

After Monday morning breakfast, and heartfelt thanks, and they told John and Emma Nash goodbye and headed for Atlanta. After the Atlanta event, they had two days to kill before Birmingham and Tuscaloosa, so they rented motel rooms. They stayed one day with a farm family in Louisiana on their way to Shreveport. Only information was needed for that family, and Elizabeth was the provider of same. Peggy and Jerry were relieved that job required no digging.

Back on the road, Elizabeth and Peggy were trying to snooze, and Jerry started singing an Eagles song, "Take it to the Limit."

"Why do you always sing that song, Jerry?" Peggy asked him.

"My brother sang that song, Peg. It's my favorite Eagles song."

"You have a good voice, Jerry," Elizabeth chimed in. "You should have gotten your brother to get you a tryout with the band."

"Now you're just blowing smoke, peaches. I can carry a tune," he said. "That's a long way from being in a band like the Eagles."

"Rick's favorite Eagles song is 'Tequila Sunrise,'" she said.

"Really? And why is that?"

"He says it reminds him of me."

"Oh, yeah, I can understand that, from what you've told me about him."

"What, what is it," Elizabeth prodded him. "What is it about that song?"

"There's a line in it about she wasn't just another woman. That had to be the reason he related the song to you, because you are *not* just another woman."

The Bowers farm near Beaumont, still inside Louisiana, was in need of a similar reconfiguration as the Nash farm, but those folks had five sons and two daughters who had grown up working on their farm, so Elizabeth directed the operation, and the kids on the farm did the work. They stayed with Ted and Nina Bowers, and their seven offspring for two days.

"We're going to have to stop eating with these folks, peaches," Jerry said, "or I'm going to be as fat as a house."

"I was thinking the same thing," Elizabeth said, and Peggy agreed.

Before too long they were in Texas, and Elizabeth was getting homesick. She wanted to see her dad. She knew that Rose was probably in New Orleans with Bobby, but it would be good to be back at home and to sleep in *her* bed, the bed she and Rick had made love in the first time.

She did the event in San Antonio on the twenty-fifth of June. They would spend the weekend on the Riverwalk in San Antonio and head for Austin on Monday, and then for Dallas.

At the Lizzy Bee Vineyard, in Fredericksburg, Texas, Amanda brought the mail in and lay it on Rick's desk.

"You have a letter with a postmark from Fredericksburg, Rick," she yelled at him from the kitchen.

"Okay, sis, thanks."

He picked up the letter from his desk and looked at it. It was a plain white envelope with no return address. It had a Fredericksburg postmark, like Amanda said.

There was something stiff inside it. He opened it and took out what appeared to be a ticket to some event. *This is very strange*, he was thinking.

He read the information on the ticket.

This ticket will admit one guest to:
My Summer in the Dirt
A lecture by: Beth Ann Meadows
Time: 8:00 p.m.

Where: Austin Convention Center
When: June 29, 2009
500 E Cesar Chavez Street,
Austin, TX.

He sat down in his desk chair and stared at the ticket. Then he reached for the book that Val had given him. He leafed through the book for any clue to who had written it and how this ticket had come to him. The inside cover of the book had an extensive Bio on Beth Ann Meadows. It listed her accomplishments in the permaculture industry, her long resume of lecture appearances, and all the visits her teams had made to family farms. But it gave no clue to who she really was, where she came from, where she went to school, and no picture. "What does this mean," he muttered to himself. It left him just as frustrated and as alone as he'd ever been.

The woman in the book had worked on a farm all summer, shoveling cow flop and chicken squat, and getting dirty and hot and sweaty. She had discovered God and a new lease on life, dedicated her life to helping people learn how to grow chemical-free food and eat healthier.

That just might be Elizabeth, his Elizabeth, although it was no longer proper for him to call her *his* Elizabeth, but Elizabeth Meadows was no stranger to hard work. She had worked selflessly at the church in Dallas, helping feed homeless people.

He could not rule out that this Beth Ann Meadows and his Elizabeth were one and the same person. It was either that, or it had to be a cruel coincidence. But who sent him this ticket from Fredericksburg? He didn't know anyone in Fredericksburg, except for Val. Could Val have sent him the ticket? That was possible, he supposed, but why?

"There is only one way to find out," he said, talking out loud to himself now. "I have to go to that lecture."

Chapter 11

The Road Home

The Austin Convention Center was a huge complex. Rick parked his truck and found his way inside the building. Signs directed attendees of the lecture to a ballroom where the event would take place. The place was almost full when he arrived, but he found a seat on the aisle about six rows back from the front.

Jerry and Peggy were directing the set-up of the screen for Elizabeth's Power Point presentation, and employees of the convention center were putting the finishing touches on the lighting equipment.

Rick had not seen Beth Ann Meadows yet, so he still wasn't sure who she was. But suddenly, with no introduction, a blonde-haired woman, in a blue skirt and white blouse walked briskly to the podium. There was a murmur in the crowd. Men and women alike almost gasped when they saw her. Applause went up and continued until she asked for quiet. Her blonde hair shone brightly in the stage lighting, and her face was full of confidence and self-awareness. She seemed, to many, to be too attractive for such a venue, more suited perhaps for the opening of a Hollywood premiere in which she was the star.

When she turned and faced the audience, Rick saw her and almost lost control of himself. *It is Elizabeth*, he was thinking, and immediately, he went back, in his mind, seven years in time to their home room class. He was sitting behind her, staring at her neck, fantasizing about kissing her. He remembered their first kiss, when she asked him to kiss her.

In the space of a few moments, he relived their lives together, up until the time they parted. "My God," he thought, "she's so beautiful." He couldn't wait to hear her speak again.

Facility personnel were taking names of guests who wanted to ask questions, while Elizabeth continued her lecture. Rick gave his name as, Richard, to the one on his side of the aisle and sat back down,

"Cattle were never meant to be fed grain," she was saying.

Something about twisting their stomachs out of whack. She went into an elaborate explanation of all the dangers, results, and debilitating effects of feeding grain to cattle and how unhealthy it was for consumption of the meat by humans. He couldn't concentrate on what she was saying. He just wanted to hear her voice.

"Damn, she's a looker, ain't she?" the man sitting next to him said. "I'd pay good money just to watch her recite the alphabet."

Rick just smiled and brushed him off. There was much applause, but Rick wasn't sure if it was for Elizabeth's presentation or for her appearance.

She did a Power Point show that lasted about a half hour, during which time Rick just stared at her. She did not see him sitting in the audience, as far as he knew.

She then spoke another half hour and then opened the floor up for questions. There were quite a few serious questions from folks who seemed genuinely interested in the process Elizabeth was promoting. She fielded the questions with perfect acumen and professionalism. The crowd was almost mesmerized, it seemed.

The lady who had taken Rick's name came to him, asked him to stand up, and informed him that Miss Meadows would get to him directly.

Elizabeth was taking notes as she was asked questions. When Rick's turn came up, she turned and looked at him. "Holy shit!" she exclaimed loudly, and the audience reacted in surprise. Her face changed expressions, and she was visibly moved. She stepped back from the podium for a moment and then moved back to it and steadied herself by placing her left hand on it. She raised her right hand and covered the right side of her face for just a moment. She could feel her heartbeat increase dramatically. Then, forcing herself to regain her composure, she took several deep breaths and addressed him. "Yes," she said, pointing at Rick, "the gentleman on the right-side aisle over there."

"Yes, thank you, Miss Meadows, my name is Rick Bennett, I own the Lizzy Bee Vineyard near Fredericksburg, Texas, and uh—uh—" Rick started stammering and couldn't speak.

"Yes, sir, Mister Bennett," she said. "Do you have a question?"

Rick just stood there trying to find words to say to her. Then he just started smiling at her.

"Something is going on here," Jerry said to Peggy.

"What?"

"I don't know, something about her reaction to this guy, it's just a feeling I've got."

Elizabeth smiled at Rick for a brief moment, brushed her hair back, and then said, "Will you kiss me, Mister Bennett?"

The audience was stupefied. Every head turned to look at him and then back at Elizabeth. It was a strange turn of events.

"Has anyone ever told you no to that question?" he said.

"I've never asked anyone that question, except you—so, what's it going to be, Rick?"

"Yes, Elizabeth, I will kiss you, and I'll never kiss anyone else for the rest of my life if you'll marry me."

And with that, she kicked off her high heels, left the podium, ran barefoot down the steps, jumped into his arms, and embraced him.

He lifted her up and swung her around as their lips met, and they kissed long and passionately while the audience started cheering and clapping. Cameras were flashing, and reporters were rushing to get closer to them with their video recorders.

Jerry ran over to where they were, more out of habit than concern. Rick set Elizabeth back down on the floor, but they were still locked in each other's arms.

"It's okay, Jerry," Elizabeth said. "This one is my guy."

"Holy cow, Beth," Jerry said, "give me a heads up next time, won't you?"

"There won't be a next time, Jerry," she said.

Later outside the Convention Center, they were at the RV.

"So, this is the Rick you've been talking about for the last two years?" Jerry asked her.

"This is the one," she said as she was retrieving her things from the RV. "Tell Corley, I'll get in touch with him when I come back down to Earth."

"I'll do that, Beth," Jerry said. "It was nice meeting you, Rick. I have to tell you, I was not expecting what happened here tonight. She usually just graciously declines those offers."

"You mean that has happened before?"

"It's happened before. That's why I'm here, in case some guy won't take no for an answer."

"Well, I'm glad she told me yes, in that case," Rick said, and Jerry laughed.

"I almost fainted when I saw you standing there," Elizabeth said, on the drive back to Rick's place.

"I could tell it caught you by surprise," he said.

"So where do you teach? You do teach, don't you?"

"No, never had the heart for it after I lost you."

"You didn't lose me, Rick, you dismissed me."

"And I paid the price for it too, baby."

"Then we both did. I so wanted to see you at my sister's wedding. I was going to tell you that I would give up everything if you would marry me and get on with our lives together. I called your parents at the home number, but no one answered. I tried their cell phones, and no one answered them either. I was dumfounded and devastated. I thought you had quit me for good."

"That was a comedy of errors. My folks were in Belize with Amanda, so they just missed your call, I guess. It was just a freaky turn of events. I'd asked Bobby not to give you my number unless you were ready to marry me. Bobby is a fiercely loyal friend. I wish Bobby had called me and told me you wanted to see me. I would have come to that wedding in a heartbeat. I came away from that thinking that you never wanted to see me again."

"So much time lost and so much misunderstanding. How did you know about my lecture in Austin?"

"I got a ticket in the mail. It came in an unmarked envelope. I had no clue what it was all about, but the name was so close to yours. I guess I was just hoping, by some miracle, that it would be you. What's with the name change?"

"There's a story behind that, I'll explain it later. I have an idea who sent the ticket. I'll check that out too, later."

"Did you finish medical school?"

"Nope, I gave it up to pursue what I'm doing now."

"Unbelievable, I just assumed you would be working in a research lab somewhere, by now. I've been so caught up in my own problems, I'm sorry. I should have at least kept up with your career. What made you decide to not finish medical school?"

"I found something I believe is more important."

"I have your book. A lady who stopped by the vineyard gave me the copy. But I didn't know for sure that it was you until tonight."

"Really? That's strange. Somebody I don't know, from somewhere in Texas, Austin, I think it was, sent two bottles of your wine to my office in Virginia. The name on the label really threw me for a loop."

"That's kind of weird too, the lady who gave me your book wouldn't take any money for it, so I gave her several bottles of the wine—some red and a white."

"That's what they were, I really freaked out over the name. I couldn't imagine you owning a vineyard, but I couldn't imagine anyone else naming their vineyard the Lizzy Bee, either."

"I think it might have been the same person who sent the wine and the ticket."

"Nothing will surprise me after all this."

"What a roller coaster we've been on, Elizabeth. I can't believe I found you like I did."

"After all this time, Rick, it's almost like a miracle."

"It *is* a miracle baby."

"I want to get married before we go to Dallas," she said.

"Are you sure, you don't want a big wedding?"

"Do you want a big wedding?"

"No, I just want you."

"Then let's get married tomorrow."

"Tomorrow?"

"You asked me to marry you, Rick, did you mean it?"

"More than I've ever meant anything in my life, Lizzy."

"They have a justice of the peace in Fredericksburg, don't they?"

"I expect they do, but we'll have to get a license first. It might take two days."

"Then marry me Wednesday. I have only one condition."

"Ah, a condition, I should have known. What is your condition, Miss Meadows?"

"We must both agree to live together on your vineyard in total obscurity from the world. And you must swear your undying love for me."

He pulled the truck to the side of the road and turned off the engine. He turned toward her and took her hands in his. He looked deeply into her eyes and told her: "I agree to your condition without hesitation and with unbridled joy and I do hereby swear to you that I will love you as long as there is breath left in my body. Thank you, Elizabeth Bennett, I love you."

"Thank *you*, Mister Darcy," she said, "I love you too."

Chapter 12

The Vineyard

2009:

Rick and Elizabeth were married at the justice of the peace in Fredericksburg, Texas on July first. It was a Wednesday, just as she had requested, two days after she had leapt into Rick's arms at her last lecture, in the Austin Convention Center.

"I've got breakfast ready, baby," Rick said, "if you can get out of bed."

"Again?" she asked.

"Yep, I intend to pamper you for at least a year or so."

"I'll be there in just a few," she said, threw back the covers, sat up in the bed, and put both feet on the floor."

She walked out to the kitchen table after putting on a T-shirt over her panties. He'd set the table and had the silverware lined up perfectly on a folded napkin. There was scrambled eggs and bacon and a coffee cup already sitting next to her plate. "Biscuits are in the oven," he told her, "They'll be right out."

"I'm not used to this," she said.

"Well, I'm not used to having the love of my life sleeping beside me all night long."

"So, your plan is to fatten me up?"

"No, this is just for our honeymoon. I spent four years of my life without you, and I'm just happy to have you back with me."

"I'm happy to be back too, darling. I don't ever want to be away from you again."

"We need to go to Dallas, Lizzy, and tell the folks about us. Amanda should be back today. Once she gets back, I'll feel comfortable about leaving the place in her hands, and we'll go."

"Okay, my daddy is going to be so happy to have you in the family."

"And my folks are going to be just as happy to know I found you. They've been almost panic-stricken the last few years over me."

When Rick's sister Amanda returned from Dallas the next day and pulled into the driveway, Rick and Elizabeth were standing in the front yard. Amanda shrieked and ran to her, and Elizabeth ran to her. They embraced, and Amanda was overcome with emotion.

"O—oh, my God, E—Elizabeth, you're here," she stammered. "What happened, how did he find you?"

"Rick showed up at my lecture in Austin on his white horse and swept me away and brought me back here to his castle."

"And you're staying? Please tell me you're staying."

"We were married yesterday, sis," Rick said.

"Married, you finally got married? Oh, my gosh, that's wonderful, I'm so happy for you. Have you told your dad or our parents?"

"We're going to do that tomorrow, Manda," Rick said. "If you don't mind running things while I'm gone."

"No, of course not, I don't mind a bit," Amanda said.

"Now don't call them. We want it to be a secret."

"I won't tell them," Amanda said.

When Harley Meadows opened the door of his house and saw his daughter and Rick Bennett standing there, he burst into tears and grabbed them both. After he gained control of himself, they went into the living room and sat down.

"You just don't know what a blessing it is to see you two together again," Harley said. "How did this happen?"

"Rick showed up at my lecture in Austin, Daddy, stood up for the question and answer session. I almost peed on myself when I saw him. Long story short, he asked me to marry him, I said yes, and we did." She held up her ring finger to show him the ring.

"It's a temporary ring," Rick said, "we were in a hurry. I'm going to get a better one here in Dallas."

"I insisted on getting married right away. I wanted to get him before he had a chance to change his mind."

"Yeah, like that would happen," Rick said.

"I would have loved to have had a wedding for you guys here, but I'm just so happy it finally happened. Did you call your sister?" Harley said.

"I called Rose and told her not to tell you. I wanted it to be a surprise."

"So, what are you going to do now?"

"We're going to tell my folks," Rick said.

"Oh, I know that, but I mean in the future, what are you going to do?"

"We're going to make wine, Daddy. Rick has a Vineyard near Fredericksburg. We're going to live there and make wine and love."

"Well, I've been praying for you two for all this time, and I won't stop. I'm so happy for you. I am blessed so much, with both my girls married to fine young men. But this big ol' house is mighty lonely now without my two chattering magpies running around in it."

The Bennetts were equally ecstatic to see their son and to learn that he had found and married his lost love. Elizabeth repeated the story of how she and Rick had gotten back together, and everybody hugged. Rick's mother started crying.

"So, what are you doing now, Elizabeth?" Adrian asked her. 'Did you get your PhD?"

"No, I dropped out."

"Seriously?" he said. "What happened to that girl who was going to conquer the world?"

"Well, the first thing that happened was that your son broke my heart."

"Oh, come on, baby," Rick said.

"Well, you did, but anyway, I met this friend at school, whose family in Pennsylvania owned a farm. They raised grass-fed beef and practiced chemical-free soil preparation for the growing of fruits and vegetables. I spent one summer on their farm, working and learning all about it. I wrote a book about it and started doing lectures on the subject. I became quite popular in that particular niche industry. It was at my last lecture in Austin where your son showed up and made me an offer I couldn't refuse, to quote *The Godfather*."

"Oh, my," Leeann said, "how in the world did that happen?"

"It was the conclusion of several strange occurrences, Mom," Rick said.

"Someone sent Rick a ticket to the lecture," Elizabeth said. "We don't know who yet, I thought it was my office manager in Virginia, Corley McKnight, but he said no, so it's still a mystery."

"Well, we're happy for you," Leeann said, "but I would appreciate it if you would send my daughter back to me on a permanent basis. Now that you have Elizabeth back can't you get along without your sister?"

"Amanda loves it in Fredericksburg, Mom. I don't think she wants to come back to Dallas. She's been a big help to me, and I know you don't want to hear this. But your little girl has met a guy."

"Oh, hell, don't tell me that, Rick. Who is this boy? Have you met him?"

"I've met him, Mom, and he's not a boy, he's a man. Dave is about twenty-five, has a well-drilling business, or something like that. I don't know him well, but he seems okay. Amanda is twenty-one-years old now. You may have forgotten that helpful bit of information."

"You keep an eye on her, Rick, don't let her get mixed up with the wrong kind."

"I will, Mom, and I won't, don't worry."

"How long can you and Elizabeth stay with us?" Adrian asked him.

"We're staying the night, Dad. We have to get back and get ready for harvest. We start harvest in mid-July."

"I wish you could stay a few days, but I understand, business is business."

Carlos Ramirez brought in his grape-harvesting crew, and they were busying themselves with the work at hand as Rick showed Elizabeth the process.

"They gather and weigh the product and deliver it to the winery for crushing and fermentation, and then they bring it back to us to store for aging. We ship directly from town to our largest distributors but some of the smaller stores in the area, I deliver myself."

"That's a nice touch," Elizabeth said. "What about new business? How are we expanding sales?"

"I've been doing that myself, but I've got an idea now that you're here."

"Oh, what's your idea?"

"I was thinking that you might start making sales calls to some stores in the Austin area and points farther north. I don't want to move too fast and out sell what we can produce."

"I'd like to do it, Rick, but I'd want you to come with me for the first few calls just so I don't mess up."

"Lizzy, once they look at your face, they'll be grabbing the order form out of your hands."

"Oh, so all I am to you is a pretty face?"

"No, no, honey, of course not," he replied and smiled. "Your body is—"

"What?" she interrupted him. "You sexist pig! Okay, mister, I'll flaunt myself to your customers for the benefit of your capitalist enterprise. Should I wear short shorts or maybe my bikini?"

"You have a bikini?"

"Yes, Rick, I have a bikini."

"Go put it on," he said as he started walking toward her, "I want to see it."

She squealed and started running toward the house, and he gave chase. She ran through the front door and into the bedroom with Rick right behind her. He grabbed her, picked her up, and, tossing her onto the bed, started kissing her.

"I'll go with you on the first few sales calls," he said.

"What are you going to do to me right now?" she asked.

He whispered something in her ear, and she squealed loudly.

Amanda yelled from the office: "Can you two at least close the door?"

"Put on your bikini," Rick said, "I'm going to close the door."

Snyder's Good Time Liquor Stores was a chain store facility in Austin. Rick had tried to get his foot in the door—or more accurately, his wine on the shelves—for the past year. To date, he had made no impression on the managers of the individual outlets. He made an appointment with Doug Snyder, the general manager of the organization, and he and Elizabeth went to his office with two cases of Lizzy Bee's finest.

"Mister Snyder," Rick said, shaking the man's hand after they were shown to his office, "I'm Rick Bennett, and this is my wife, Elizabeth. I've been trying for some time to get a placement in your stores for my product but, although your managers have tasted my wine and all have made positive comments, they cannot seem to find room on their shelves for me."

"Well, Rick, and please call me Doug, our space is limited, but if the wine is a good product, I don't see why we couldn't accommodate you. Did you bring some with you?"

"I have two cases in the truck, Doug," Elizabeth said, as she reached out and shook his hand. "But I don't think you'll need that much to check it out."

"Uh…no, if you could bring a bottle in, I'll have my secretary bring in a couple of glasses, and I'll try it out." He almost could not stop staring at Elizabeth.

Finally, she turned away from him. "I'll be right back," she said, went out to the truck, retrieved two bottles of wine, and brought them back to the man's office.

"Try a glass of this, Evelyn," Doug said to his secretary, an elderly woman in her sixties.

"Don't be silly, boss, I'm still working."

"This is part of your job description, Evelyn. I'm ordering you to try this wine and let me know what you think." He poured himself a glass as well and took a sip. "It has a very good taste, Elizabeth," he said.

Evelyn was reaching for the bottle to pour herself another glass. Rick picked it up and did it for her.

Doug was staring at Elizabeth. "Are you the Lizzy in the Lizzy Bee?" he asked.

"I am," she answered.

"That's pretty clever, that had to be Rick's idea, I'm assuming."

"It was his idea. It was a nickname he used to call me when we were in high school."

"And where was that? I mean, where did you two go to high school?"

"We went to William B Travis in Dallas," Elizabeth said.

"Of course, Rick Bennett, I thought the name was familiar. You quarterbacked Travis to the state championship back in..."

"2002," Elizabeth said.

"That's right, I remember now. You must have been a cheerleader, right?"

The question struck fear in Rick over what Elizabeth might say or do. He knew it must have cut her to the bone.

"I was Rick's cheerleader long before he was a football star."

"Elizabeth has a master's degree in bio-molecular engineering from Johns Hopkins University," Rick said.

Doug looked dumbfounded. "And she looks like that?" he said, pointing at Elizabeth. "I'm sorry about the cheerleader comment, Elizabeth. My wife says I'm a Neanderthal. I don't have a clue what it is Rick just said you have a degree in. But I know you must be smarter than me, so I'm sorry, again." He made the form of a pistol with his right hand and pretended to shoot himself in the head.

"It's okay, Doug," Elizabeth said, "I don't offend easily. You're smart enough to manage a large multi-faceted enterprise, and that is something of which you can be very proud. I'm guessing you're smart enough to stock Lizzy Bee Vineyard Wines on your shelves too. What do you think, Doug?"

"I was so afraid you were going to go off on him when he made the cheerleader remark," Rick said, on the drive back home.

"I would have jumped up and done a 'beat 'em bust 'em, that's our custom, G*oooo*, Travis!' if it would have made a sale."

"He seemed to like our wine."

"You think? He drank a whole bottle all by himself, and the little old lady was practically in a stupor," she said.

"I know. I was afraid, for a minute there, that Doug was going to put his hands on you."

"I would have drawn the line there."

"I would have drawn it first," Rick said.

Rick Took Elizabeth on her first official tour of the property because he wanted to get her input on how he might improve production and the quality of the soil in which they were planting their vines. "We have twenty acres of active planting area. George Humphry, the man I bought the vineyard from, planted ten acres red and ten acres green every year. I kept that same formula. George was buying manure for the preparation of the soil, but I've made a deal with a couple of dairy farms to dump their manure on our planting acreage. I can't take it all because we just don't have enough land."

"We don't have room for our own cows," Elizabeth said.

"I know. I wish we did, but the land around us is locked in, and nobody wants to sell, so, we just have to make do."

"Yes, and we have to anticipate the increase in advance by a year or so, or we'll have a demand we cannot meet. If we over produce, we can store the wine in the barn and cut back on production the next season. The last two years we have produced more than fourteen-thousand bottles of wine each year. But we'll have to either buy or lease additional land if we want to increase production. I think we should consider that,

once the property is paid off. I plan to increase our sales substantially."

"I think so too, Lizzy," Rick said. "I have confidence in
you. We'll want to plant more red on the additional acreage
because we introduce sugar into the red that makes it good for
consumption in a year. The white takes at least three years before we can bottle it. Once the harvesting crew is all done,
Carlos Ramirez, our foreman, leases his men to other vineyards, and to farmers in the area for seasonal work. Mister
Ramirez is quite a successful capitalist on his own. I was very
fortunate to get him from George Humphries when I bought
this place. Carlos knows more about running a vineyard than
anyone I've met since I've been here. We set the rows eight
feet apart, and the vines are planted six feet apart in each row.
That adds up to nine-hundred and seven vines per acre."

"And how much wine will that produce, approximately,
Rick?" she asked him.

"Our fields typically yield four tons of grapes per acre. One
ton of grapes will result in a little more than two barrels of
wine. Each barrel contains sixty gallons, twenty-five cases, or
three-hundred bottles. So basically, we reap right at seven
hundred twenty bottles from each harvested acre. Twenty
acres multiplied by seven hundred twenty bottles will give us
fourteen thousand, four hundred bottles of product. If we increase that by ten percent next year...well, do the math—
fourteen hundred and forty additional bottles of wine. We
store the red in wooden barrels in our barn and the white in
steel tanks at the winery. They do the bottling and labeling for
us."

"I'd like to see the winery where they turn it into the juice."

"Okay, baby, I'll call them and tell them we want to come
and visit, once they start bottling our product."

The Brighton-Ford Winery was located ten miles east of
the Lizzy Bee on Highway 290. It was a large facility and was
always bustling with activity. Megyn Ford, granddaughter of
Charles Nathan "Charlie" Ford, one of the original founders of
the winery, was the current managing CEO. Megyn had agreed
to give Rick and Elizabeth a tour of the facility.

"My grandfather, Charlie Ford and his best friend, Joseph Brighton, started the winery in 1949, not long after they came back from the war. Neither of them knew much about growing grapes but Joe Brighton's family had owned a winery, and he'd been raised in the business, so they bought this plot of land and built the winery from the ground up. We processed George Humphries's wine for thirty years, long before I started managing the place. I was sorry to see him leave the business, but it looks like his vineyard is in good hands."

"It was a learning process for me," Rick said, "but I'm getting the hang of it. This is my wife, Elizabeth. She's going to be helping me run the business. She wanted to see how things work here."

"Hello, Elizabeth," Megyn said, and they shook hands. "I assume you are the Lizzy, in the Lizzy Bee?"

"Guilty," Elizabeth said.

"That's a nice touch," Megyn replied.

"It was Rick's idea."

"I figured as much. So, let's get started." She led them into the main building. "There are five basic steps in the wine making process. You have just completed the first step, the harvest."

Elizabeth had her notebook out and was taking notes as Megyn talked.

"Grapes are the only fruits that have all the necessary elements to consistently make natural and stable wine."

"What are these elements?" Elizabeth asked her.

"Right, there are acids, esters, and tannins. These are all-natural elements."

"I'll research these when I get back to the office."

"Right," Megyn said. "Now harvesting can be done by mechanical means and is in some larger vineyards. But many winemakers prefer to do it manually because mechanical harvesting is often damaging to the grapes. Once the grapes are taken to the winery, they are sorted into bunches so the rotten or under ripe grapes can be removed. Mechanical presses have replaced the foot-stomping method that was employed in the old days. The mechanical presses 'stomp' the grapes into what is called 'must.' The must contains the skins and seeds. For the white wine, the grapes are quickly crushed and pressed in order to separate the juice from the skins, seeds, and solids to keep color and tannins from leaching into the wine. In the red wine, though, the skins are left in contact with the juice to acquire flavor, color, and additional tannins."

"I'm writing," Elizabeth said. "I'm amazed that you can remember all this without notes."

"I've been doing it for twenty years," Megyn said. "After all the crushing and pressing is done, we start the fermentation process. We add a commercially cultured yeast to ensure consistency and predict the result. Fermentation continues until all the sugar is converted into alcohol and dry wine is produced. For a sweet wine, we stop the process before all of the sugar is converted."

"How long does the fermentation process take?" Elizabeth asked.

"Fermentation can take anywhere from ten days to a month or longer. Once the fermentation is complete, we begin what is called clarification. Clarification is the process of removing all the solids, such as dead yeast cells, tannins, and proteins. Then we transfer the wine into either oak barrels or stainless-steel tanks. George Humphries always stored his red wine in barrels in his barn and his white in our tanks. It adds a little cost in transporting the barrels back and forth, but it saves on the cost of storage space. Rick decided to do it the same way when he bought the vineyard."

"Do you age the wine in the barrels or do you bottle it first and age it in the bottles?"

"It can be done either way," Megyn said. "We believe it is best aged in the barrels and tanks. Aging the wine in oak barrels produces a smoother, rounder wine. The steel tanks are used primarily for white wines.

"Thank you, Megyn," Elizabeth said." I've been enlightened. I now have a much better understanding of what we're doing."

"You are quite welcome," Megyn replied. "Call me anytime if you have any questions."

"So, what do you think, baby?" Rick asked her on the way back to the house.

"How much do you owe on the property?" Elizabeth asked.

"Oh, roughly about three-hundred-thousand or so, why?"

"Until we get the Vineyard paid off, it's going to be hard to generate a lot of income, with the operating expenses and taxes and all."

"I know. I determined that I would pay it off in five years. George didn't demand that, and he's not charging me any interest, but I thought it would show good faith to pay it off as quickly as possible."

"I've looked at the books, and I don't see how you've made enough to live on the past two years," Elizabeth said as they got out of the car and went into the house.

"I've been averaging about twenty-five grand a year from royalties on my book. I use that for my personal expenses. I bought the new truck and some new furniture for the house—stuff like that."

"Oh, I didn't realize that. Rick, that's wonderful. But we need to acquire more land so we can produce more grapes. If we don't, we won't be able to meet the demand for the new customers I intend to develop."

"Well, I suppose we can take a look down the highway for some more acreage, maybe put a trailer house on the property, and hire someone to live there and tend to it. But that will take financing. We don't have enough money to do it 'in house.'"

"Actually, we do, darling."

"What do you mean?" he said, looking at her questioningly.

"I have the money," she said.

"I'm not going to use your money."

"Oh, but you think I should use yours?"

"You're my wife, Elizabeth. I'm supposed to take care of you."

"You do take care of me, Rick, in more ways than you can know. I thought our marriage would be different from the traditional thing that people get trapped in. I'm not a helpless little woman who needs a big strong man to support her and give her an allowance. I don't need protecting from the cruel world. I thought our marriage would be a partnership, an equal partnership.

"Our marriage is all that, honey," he said. "I'm just starting to feel like everything I've tried has been a failure. I thought I would make a million bucks off the book, find you, and really impress you. Then I really wanted to make a go of the vineyard, and it's really hard making ends meet. If I didn't have the little bit of money from the book, I would have had to ask George Humphries to let me make reduced payments on the property, and that would have made me feel really bad. Finding you is the only thing that saved me from losing hope."

"Then let me help you. I want to be a part of this. I want to be a part of you and everything you do. Just let me make the yearly payments until we're free and clear, and then we'll look into buying some more land. That's three years, and then we can start expanding the business."

He looked at her for a few moments while appearing to be in deep thought. "Okay," he said, finally, "but when I get the title on the property, I'm going to have it put in both our names. I want it to be legally yours, too."

"I'm okay with that," she said.

"I'm going down the road to the Walmart. You want to come along?"

"No, thank you, I'm a little tired. I think I'll stay here and rest a while."

"Do you need anything?"

"Can you pick me up a pregnancy test?"

"What?" Rick said, his jaw dropping as he stared at her, speechless.

"Well, don't just stand there looking at me, say something," she said.

"You're pregnant?"

"I'm pretty sure I am," she said, "that's why I want you to pick up a pregnancy test for me."

"Okay," he said.

He was almost in a stupor all the way to the store. When he got back, he handed her the pregnancy test.

"I'll be waiting right out here," he said.

She went into the bathroom and administered the test as he stood outside the door. She came out and walked around to the other side of the room without looking at him. He watched her every step and when she looked up at him, he stared at her. "Okay, stop teasing me," he said, "what did it say?

"Oh," she said, "what do you want to name him?"

Rick yelled as loud as he could, went to her, put his arms around her, and picked her up. He started kissing her. "We have to find you a doctor right away," he said.

"I know, but we have time for that. Right now, I want you to make love to me."

"Is it okay? It won't hurt you?" he said.

"It will only hurt me if you won't do it."

"I'd never do anything to hurt you, baby," he said. "Go put on your bikini."

"I can't wait that long, Rick."

Chapter 13

Offspring

2010:

Elizabeth was two months away from giving birth and, against Rick's pleading, was still waddling around the grounds of the vineyard. She liked to help out at the roadside stand where people stopped to taste samples of the wine and, as often as not, to purchase a bottle or two.

"When are you due?" had become the popular question of late.

"February twenty-fifth, give or take," Elizabeth would respond.

One afternoon, a late model Toyota, Tacoma, double-cab pick-up truck came driving up onto the property. Elizabeth was nearest the entry, so she approached the vehicle. A handsome man with a neatly trimmed beard, wearing a baseball cap backward on his head, stopped where she was standing.

"Can I help you?" she asked him.

"I'm looking for Amanda," he said. "Is this the right place?"

"It is," Elizabeth said. "You want to come in or would you like for me to get her for you?"

"I have to be at a job in about an hour so, if you don't mind, can you tell her I came by? I don't want to make you walk all the way up to the house in your condition."

"I can call her," Elizabeth said. "What's your name?"

"Dave Braddock," the man said.

"Oh, yes, Dave, Rick and Amanda have both mentioned you. I'll call her."

Elizabeth called Amanda and, a moment later, she was rushing out the door and was sprinting out to Dave's truck. When she was almost there, Dave got out of his truck and walked toward her. Elizabeth noted that he was a well-built man who looked like he took good care of himself. He stood about six feet. His Levis fit his body tightly, and his arms looked very muscular and bulged out around the T-shirt he was wearing.

"Hi, Dave," Amanda said as she jumped up on him and put her arms around his neck.

He held her to him by wrapping his arms around her legs and butt.

They kissed so passionately that Elizabeth almost felt like she should turn her head. She had almost forgotten that Rick's baby sister was twenty-one-years-old now and no longer a little girl. It was just strange to see her interacting in such manner with an obviously older man.

"Are you still coming to pick me up tonight?" Amanda asked him.

"I am, baby-doll, but I have a job to go to right now. I just wanted to come by and see you for a minute."

"I'm glad you did. I want you to meet my sister-in-law. This is Elizabeth Bennett, my brother's wife. Elizabeth is going to have a baby."

"Really," Dave said, "I'm glad you told me. I thought maybe she was just putting on weight."

Amanda and Elizabeth both started laughing.

"I'm glad to meet you, Dave," Elizabeth said. "Rick went into town, but he'll be back later. Maybe you can see him tonight."

"I hope so," he said. He kissed Amanda again and then got into his truck and left.

"Wow, this must be more serious than I thought, Manda," Elizabeth said. "I thought it was just a 'hanging out' kind of thing with you and Dave."

"He wants to marry me," Amanda said. "But he had to get his divorce finalized first. He just got the papers back last week, so he's free now."

"Does Rick know all this?"

"I'm going to tell him."

"When did you plan on telling him, Manda? Don't you think this is kind of rushing into this thing?"

"No, I've known Dave for almost a year now."

"Well, just talk it over with Rick."

When Amanda brought it up later, Rick was not pleased. "This is bullshit, Amanda," he said to her, his voice elevated. "You've been going with a married man who's been cheating on his wife with you?"

"It's not like that, Rick. He was separated, and they're now divorced."

"And he wants to jump right into another marriage before the ink is dry on the divorce papers?"

"The ink *is* dry on the papers."

Elizabeth chuckled to herself when Amanda said that, but she remained silent.

"That's an expression, honey. It means it's too soon after the divorce. Dave seems like a nice guy, but I have to question his judgement."

"I love him, Rick, and I told him I'd marry him. I want to. I want to have what you and Elizabeth have."

"How can you know you love him, sis, you're too young to know that."

"Too young? How old were you when you knew you were in love with Elizabeth?"

"That's different," Rick said.

"No, it's not."

"We were more mature than you are."

"You're not my father, Rick."

"I'm responsible for you, Manda, because Dad is not here. Maybe you should at least call Dad, or Mom, and talk to them before you do something rash."

"I'll call Mom, but I still get to make this decision. Dave is coming to pick me up tonight. We're going to Silver Creek on

Main Street. It's Dave's favorite place. Maybe you guys could come along with us and get to know Dave."

"We'll see about that, I'm not sure Lizzy and the boy are up for that. But I want to talk to Dave when he comes tonight."

Later than night, when Dave came to pick up Amanda, Rick confronted him.

"I know you're just getting one side of the story, Rick, and this is going to sound self-serving, but the woman is a psycho," Dave said. "We married way too young, right out of high school, and it was volatile right out of the gate. She was insanely jealous. She imagined I was cheating on her, and I never did. She used to follow me around. She'd show up at my jobs and go off on me in front of customers. It caused me a lot of trouble."

"How did you meet my sister?"

"We met at the Walmart," Dave said. "She was shopping and couldn't reach something on a top shelf."

"I asked him to reach something for me, and he picked me up instead, so I could reach it."

"I was flirting," Dave said. "I had filed for separation at the time, so it wasn't like I was cheating on my wife. I liked Amanda the first time I saw her."

"Well, she's my baby sister. Our parents are in Dallas, so I'm pretty much responsible for her. I know she's old enough to make her own decisions. I just don't want to see her get hurt."

"I won't hurt her, Rick," Dave said, "I promise you that."

"That is my only concern, Dave."

"Like Amanda said, we're going to Silver Creek. It's a popular place right on Main Street in town. It's a restaurant with really good food and a beer garden right out front. They have live entertainment on the weekends. We'd love to have you come along."

"If Elizabeth feels like it, I'm okay with it."

Elizabeth was nodding her head. "It's a little cool, so I'll bring a coat," she said.

"My friend Billy is one of the managers tonight," Dave

said. "I'll call him and tell him we're coming with a pregnant lady, and he'll save us a table."

Silver Creek, at 310 Main Street in Fredericksburg, was always jumping on Saturday night. Local talent showed up with their guitars and fiddles or whatever their musical instrument of choice. They sang everything from blues, to country, to folk and, even rock and roll on occasion. As Dave and Amanda and Rick and Elizabeth were being seated, a fella was playing an acoustical guitar and singing "La Bamba," the Ritchie Valens' song from 1958. A few, who knew the words were singing along.

"What's he saying, Dave?" Amanda asked him.

"How would I know? I don't speak Spanish."

"But you're from Texas. You should know how to speak Spanish, shouldn't you?"

"Well, you and Ritchie Valens are from California. Why don't you speak Spanish, baby-doll?"

"I took Spanish a year in school, but all I remember is gracias."

"That's quite an extensive vocabulary, sis," Rick said."

They ordered food and, just as Dave had told them, it was really delicious.

"We'll have to come back her often, Lizzy," Rick said.

"Right now, I think I need to get home and get in my bed," she replied. "My stomach is hurting."

"Okay, baby. We're going to bug on out, guys. Let's do this another time, maybe after the baby comes."

He went to get his truck which he'd parked about two blocks down the street, so Dave and Amanda walked Elizabeth to the truck. Dave picked her up gently and set her in the seat.

"Thanks, Dave, we'll see you later," Rick said

In Late February, Elizabeth gave birth to a boy, whom they named Harley Adrian, after both their fathers. They decided that they would call him Harley. Both families were there to see the baby.

The boy was a spitting image of his father, with black hair and blue eyes, but the doctor estimated that he would not be as tall as Rick was.

"So now we need a girl, Lizzy," he told Elizabeth. "I want one who looks just like you."

"Can you let me get back in shape before you knock me up again, please?"

"Well, of course, baby. I'm looking forward to seeing you back in shape again."

Bobby and Rose were home for the off season and living with Harley Meadows in Dallas. They came to the Bennett home with Harley to see the newest addition to the Bennett family.

"So, you won the Super Bowl, Bobby," Rick said, "congratulations. You're at the top of your game."

"Yeah, I think it might be time for me to quit," Bobby said.

"Seriously? I figured you'd be in for the long haul now."

"Rose is homesick and wants to come home. Harley is not in very good health, and he needs somebody to help him run the business."

"You can't need money, Bobby. Are you going to be happy not playing football?"

"It's okay. But you're right, I don't, in fact, I've got more money than I ever thought I would have and money is really all I needed football for. I'm ready to quit and have some kids like you and Elizabeth. We don't squander our money. Rose is very frugal, and I've invested quite a bit in some real estate. I don't need money, but Harley needs help, and Rose wants to be with him, in case something happens. He's all alone now with both his daughters married and gone."

"Well, that's mighty decent of you. You're never were a media hound, so I'm sure you'll be happy. I'm really glad it worked out for you and Rose."

"Yeah, me, too, Rick, I really love her. She's a good wife. How is everything going with you here?"

"It was a struggle the first couple of years. My book makes just enough money to help me with my personal living expenses, and not much else. Turns out that Elizabeth did a lot better in her career than I did. She insisted on paying off the loan for me. I had three yearly payments to make. She's already made one and is going to make the other two when they come due. She basically saved my ass, in more ways than one."

"That didn't hurt your masculine ego, did it?"

"Nope."

Bobby laughed. "Nope, just nope?"

"I'd have preferred to pay it off myself, but we're partners. When we got back together and got married, it really did save my life. She made the case that, if I loved her, then I would let her be a part of everything I am and want to be and do. Besides, I really needed the money."

In March of 2011, a daughter was born. They named the girl Ann Marie, after Elizabeth's mother. Rick was ecstatic, he had his girl, and indications were that she would indeed look like her mother.

Elizabeth had her hands full with a one-year-old and a newborn, so she was confined to the house for quite some time. Amanda continued to work for them in the office, and she helped with the babies. Elizabeth, being the naturalist that she was, had chosen to breast-fed both her children. It was healthy for them but somewhat restrictive for her. Breast-feeding two babies pretty much kept her home bound all the time.

"Hey, when do I get a turn?" Rick asked her.

"Whenever you can explain to your son and daughter why they're being put to bed hungry," she responded.

"Oh, I'm not going there. I'll wait."

Elizabeth was as obsessive about her body as she had always been about her mind. She began an intensive workout program that, in a few weeks, had her body back down to her pre-pregnancy weight and shape. She took it easy, not working too hard, but she did enjoy helping at the roadside stand. She also would take people on tours of the vineyard if they showed an interest in it.

Lacey Hunter, the girl who had been working for Rick during her summers off from Texas State in San Marcos, and Elizabeth became good friends. Lacey was fascinated with Harley Bennett, the one-year-old and, subsequently, with Ann Marie.

"I want to have kids someday," she told Elizabeth, "when I get married, I mean."

"That's a good idea, to wait until you're married," Elizabeth said, and Lacey laughed.

"I think it's so cool that Rick was going to be a teacher. He would have been a good one, I think."

"Yes, I believe he would have too, but he got sidetracked, and I can't complain too much. We're together now, and that's all that matters to me."

"I'm glad you did. I could tell there was something missing in his life. He wouldn't talk about it, but when you showed up, I realized what it was that was missing."

"It was the same thing that was missing in both our lives, Lacey. Once you find your young man, and you know he's the one you want to spend the rest of your life with, don't let anything get in the way of that. It will only cause you heartache. I was lucky, I got a second chance, and I won't ever risk losing it again."

A car approached the stand and stopped. An attractive woman, who looked to Elizabeth to be in her mid to late thirties, got out of the car and walked up to the stand. Lacey had gone to the house to use the rest room, so Elizabeth greeted the lady.

"Can I help you?" she said.

"I need to pick up a couple of bottles of your wine," the woman said. She was looking around as if looking for someone.

"Do you want red or white?" Elizabeth asked her.

"One of each, I think."

Elizabeth put the two bottles in a bag, took the woman's money, and handed her the bag.

The woman continued looking toward the house. "Is Rick around?" she asked.

"Rick went into town to pick up some supplies. I'm Elizabeth Bennett, his wife. Is there something I can help you with?"

"Are you the Lizzy in the Lizzy Bee?" she asked.

"I am," Elizabeth replied, "it's a nickname Rick used to call me when we were younger."

"Are you the former Beth Ann Meadows?"

"Yes, I am, how did you know that?

"I've read your book, it's fantastic."

"My gosh, I'm overwhelmed, thank you so much."

"So, you *were* the one, I'm so glad he found you."

"Well, thank you again. Do you want to come in and wait for Rick?"

"No, I, have to get back home, but thank you."

"Okay, well, thanks for stopping, drive safely, and have a good day, and enjoy the wine."

The woman went back to her car and drove away.

"The strangest thing happened today," Elizabeth told Rick after he was back in the office.

"This lady stopped at the roadside stand and bought a couple of bottles of wine. Then she asked if you were around. I told her my name and said I was your wife and she asked me if I was the former Beth Ann Meadows."

Rick became noticeably uncomfortable as Elizabeth continued.

"Then she said she'd read my book and liked it. I thanked her, of course, and then she said, 'So you were the one. I'm so glad Rick found you.' Do you find that as strange as I do?"

"That was probably a lady named Val, who stopped by once, been a couple of years now, and I offered to show her around the place. When I told her what I was trying to do with the chemical-free soil thing, she told me about your book. Then on another trip, she dropped off a copy of the book, and we talked about it. I mentioned that the name was very similar to my fiancée's name, Elizabeth. I told how we had been apart for several years, and that I hoped to find you one day."

"Does she live in Austin?"

"I think that's where she said she lives," Rick replied.

"The name on the card, that came with the two bottles of wine from your vineyard, was Valerie, from Austin, Texas."

"Really?"

"Yes, do you think she might have sent you the ticket to my lecture?"

"I've suspected as much," he said, "but I didn't know for sure. It was just such a strange thing that happened."

"It seems we may have a benefactor," she said.

"It could be," he responded.

"Should we try and find her and let her know how grateful we are for her help?"

"I don't think that's a good idea. Most good Samaritans would rather remain anonymous than have a lot of attention brought to them, don't you think?"

"I just think it would be a nice gesture."

"We don't know where she lives or how to get in touch with her. I'd just let it drop and be happy she did what she did."

Elizabeth was reading his body language as their conversation continued. She perceived that there was more about the woman he was not telling her. He was unwilling to talk about this mysterious woman, and Elizabeth was pretty sure she knew why. But she was not going to ask the question that her husband, sitting there in front of her, was afraid she would ask him. She would do as he'd suggested and let it drop. She would put the woman, and whatever might have happened between them, out of her mind. "You're right, darling, she did us a great favor, and I'm happy she did."

Dave Braddock came to Rick one afternoon and told him that he was in love with Amanda and wanted to marry her. "I'll drive to Dallas and ask your dad if you think it's a good idea, but you said you were responsible for her so I'm asking you for permission to ask her to marry me."

"That's quaintly old fashion, Dave, and I'm sure you know that it's strictly Amanda's decision, but I do appreciate you making the effort. If Amanda says yes, then I have no objection. I'll call my dad about it. They may come down before the wedding to meet you, so I wouldn't drive all the way to Dallas to do that. My folks are not old fashion. They'll certainly come down for the wedding and give you their blessing."

"I know it's just a ritual that not many guys do anymore, but I just thought it would be respectful to you and Amanda."

"And to yourself, too, Dave. You're a good man, and I know Amanda is crazy about you. I still think of her as a child, but she's twenty-two, and that is still hard for me to comprehend."

"She's not a girl anymore," Dave said.

"I know, she's a woman. Do you think she can keep working at the Vineyard?" Rick said.

"That's her choice," Dave said. "She loves working with you and Elizabeth, and I wouldn't change that."

"Well, okay then, just let me know if your folks come down, and I'll be here."

Amanda wanted to have the wedding at the vineyard, and Rick and Elizabeth welcomed the idea. Adrian and Leeann came in from Dallas and met their future son-in-law for the first time. It was a quiet affair. Dave's family was there, such as it was. His father had died in a car wreck when Dave was very young. Dave's mother had raised him and his younger brother on her own and had never remarried. Dave and his brother Jeffrey had been given the water-well-drilling company by their uncle Eddie, their mother's brother, who was in poor health. They had worked together to make it a successful business.

Rick hired a three-person combo, for the wedding—a guitarist, a drummer, and a female singer—that performed regularly at Silver Creek. Adrian dutifully gave his daughter away to a man he barely knew, but who came referenced by his son, and he trusted his son's judgement.

A local restaurant catered the affair with ample servings of Texas barbeque. After everyone was as full as they could possibly get, Adrian and Leeann took Dave and Amanda aside and told them they had a wedding gift for them.

"We are going to send you two to Belize for a week for your honeymoon."

"I don't know where that is," Dave said.

"No problem, Dave," Adrian said, "the plane knows the way. Amanda has been to our place before, and a friend of mine is going to meet you at the airport, when you arrive and help you get to the place. When you can make arrangements to get off, just let me know, and I'll set everything up. You'll drive to Dallas, and I'll take you to the airport and pick you up when you get back.

"Wow, I don't know what to say, Adrian. I've never been out of the country before. Thank you"

"It's a beautiful place, Dave," Amanda said. "You'll love it."

"You're welcome, Dave," Adrian said. "I just want to welcome you to the family."

"Don't worry about Amanda. I'll take good care of her, Adrian, I promise."

"That's all I need you to say, Dave."

Ed Whelan was waiting at the airport for Dave and Amanda when they arrived. He barely recognized Amanda. After introductions, he shook hands with Dave and hugged Amanda. "My god, Amanda, it's been eight years since I've seen you, how old are you, now?"

"I'm twenty-two, mister Whelan," she said. "Daddy said to tell you hello."

"Well, I want you and your young man to come and have dinner with me and my wife after you get settled in and tell me all about your life in Texas. I want to know how your mom and dad are doing, and your brother too.

He showed them the Bennett house and told them how to get to his house. "Why don't you guys come over around seven, if you can work us into your schedule?"

They assured him they would be there for dinner that night at seven.

"This is a really nice place, baby," Dave said. "It was really great of your dad to let us come here. I appreciate it. I hope you'll let him know that."

"I'll tell him, Dave. He likes you a lot, he's impressed that you have your own business, and you're only twenty-five."

"Well, I'm in love with his daughter, you can tell him that too," he said.

"Oh, he already knows that," she told him.

"So, you want to go for a swim in the ocean?"

"No," she said, "I want you to take me to bed."

"Oh, well, that's my favorite thing." He grabbed her and carried her into the bedroom and laid her down on the bed. They undressed, and he got in beside her.

"I love you, Amanda," he said as they began kissing and groping at each other. "You're beautiful, and you're amazing in bed."

"Now we can go swimming," she said after their passion was assuaged.

They swam for about an hour and then had a couple of drinks at a beachfront bar.

Back at the house, they showered, and she dried off quickly and went back to the bed. She was watching him as he came out of the bathroom, toweling off.

"How do you keep from tripping over that thing, baby?" she asked him, giggling.

"What?" He looked at her and realized what she was talking about. "Oh, I usually tuck it up in my belt."

"You look like a Greek god, Dave. You're the prettiest naked man I've ever seen."

"How many naked men have you seen, Amanda?" he asked her, puzzled.

"I've seen pictures," she said, "and I've seen my brother in his boxer shorts, but he doesn't come close to you."

"Well, I'm so glad you approve, sweetie. I kinda like the way you look naked too. But I also like the way you look with your clothes on. You're beautiful just the way you are."

"Don't put your clothes on, come over here," she said.

He smiled at her. "You're trying to kill me on our honeymoon, aren't you?"

"No, I'm trying to make you glad you married me."

He got back into the bed beside her, and she lay her head on his chest. She began caressing his body from his chest down to his stomach and lower. "I want to do something for you," she said.

A bit puzzled, he asked her, "Okay, baby, what?

She started kissing his chest, very slowly and passionately, working her way down his body. She kissed and ran her tongue along his stomach. He tensed up, not believing what his young bride seemed intent on doing. Her hand found his manhood and her lips continued moving along his body. Dave leaned back and closed his eyes for a moment and then opened them again to watch her.

Later, they lay in a lover's embrace in each other's arms.

"Amanda, I have to ask you this. Where did you learn how to do that?"

"It's not where you think, Dave," she said.

"I sure hope not, baby."

"You're the only man I've ever been with, I promise you that. In my little circle of friends at college, there was this friend of mine, an upperclassman named Jacey. Jacey had some video's...sort of training films I guess you could call them. And Jacey, by the way, knew how to do it already, and she learned by on the job training, if you know what I mean."

"I know what you mean, Amanda."

"That's how I learned how to do it, from the videos. Jacey said that men like it and that, when we get married, our husbands would appreciate it if we do it for them. So, what do you think?"

"Jacey was right, baby."

She squealed and hugged him tightly. "So, you won't mind if I do it again sometimes?"

"No, Amanda, I won't mind," he said.

"Are you glad you married me, Dave?"

"Yes, Amanda, I am so glad I married you."

"I'm glad I married you too, Dave."

Chapter 14

World Upside Down

2012:

Late one night, Rick was staring at Elizabeth in a very familiar way. Amanda was now living with Dave, and the children were sleeping. They were alone.

"What?" Elizabeth said, smiling at him.

"I need some loving," he said.

"If you catch me, you can have me," she said, as she jumped up from the couch and started running toward the bedroom.

He was on his feet immediately and caught her at the door, picked her up, and slung her over his shoulder. He carried her to the bed and laid her gently down. She took off her T-shirt. They stared into each other's eyes as she took off her shorts and unzipped his pants. He struggled to remove her bra but was having trouble with the snap.

"Aw hell," he said, "take this thing off."

She chuckled, reached behind her back, unsnapped her bra, and tossed it across the room. She started to take off her panties, but he stopped her."

"No, no, that's my favorite thing," he said as he pulled them down off her legs. He only broke contact with her eyes to turn back the covers on the bed.

He finished removing his clothing and got in the bed beside her. Her lips were soft and sweet and her body against his was warm and like something out of a dream.

When he entered her, she drew up, as if in pain, and her

face reacted the same way. He continued for a moment but then stopped.

"Am I hurting you, baby?"

"A little," she said, "but it's okay, don't stop."

He continued, slowly, but she cried out in pain. He stopped again and lay down beside her with his arm around her.

"Is something wrong, Lizzy?"

"I don't know Rick," she said. "This has never happened before."

"Did you pull a muscle or something? You know I keep telling you you're working too hard in that garden."

"I don't think so. If I did, I don't remember doing it. I just felt a shooting pain going up inside me."

"You should go to the doctor. Make an appointment as soon as they can get you in."

"I'm sorry, Rick," she said.

"For what?

"For letting you down."

"Don't be silly, baby, you've never let me down, and you never will."

He pushed the cover back off him and looked down at his legs.

"Holy hell, Elizabeth, I'm covered in blood. Are you okay? Check yourself."

"Oh, my god, Rick, I'm bleeding."

She tossed back the sheet, and he could see that it was covered with blood. Her hands were covered in blood, too.

He rushed to the bathroom and got a towel and washrag, ran water on it, and brought them to her. She tried to clean herself up as much as she could.

"Quick, get some sweat pants on. I've got to get you to the hospital. I'll get some more towels and wet washrags. I'll start the truck while you're getting dressed. Don't try to walk. I'll carry you to the truck."

When she was dressed, he placed some towels in the passenger seat of the truck, carried her out, set her into it, and made her as comfortable as possible. Then he retrieved the two babies and put them in their car seats in the back. On the way to the hospital, he called his sister Amanda and asked her to meet them and take the two kids back to the house with her.

Hill Country Memorial Hospital was on South Adams Street, which was Highway 16, heading out of Fredericksburg. Once they had checked in, the emergency room staff assigned Elizabeth to a room, took her vital sign measurements, set her up for IV fluids, and called her Gynecologist, Doctor Fred Merrill.

"I'm going to order a sonogram to determine where the bleeding is coming from," he told them. "Once we know the source of the bleeding, I can see what the next step will be in finding out what happened to you."

"Will you call my daddy, Rick?" Elizabeth said. "He'll come and help you with the kids."

"I will, baby," he replied, "just as soon as we know something."

Doctor Merrill took Rick with him into the lab to look at the images from the sonogram. "It looks like she has a tumor on her ovaries that has ruptured and ripped open a blood vessel. The bleeding is coming from the ruptured blood vessel."

"What do we do now, Doc?"

"We'll have to go in and cauterize the vessel to stop it from bleeding, and we'll do a biopsy on the tumor to see if it's malignant or not. Hopefully, it's benign."

"I have to ask you this, Doctor Merrill, is it possible this could be my fault? We were in the process of…uh…"

"Having sex?" the doctor said.

"Yes," Rick replied.

"I seriously doubt it, Rick. You don't look like the kind of couple that would engage in rough sex to such an extent that it could cause this kind of damage, are you?"

"Uh, no, Doctor, we're not, but we were playing, and right before, she was running away from me, in fun I mean."

The doctor nodded his head and smiled.

"I caught her, picked her up, and put her up over my shoulder."

"The tumor could have ruptured at any time. She could have been bending over or squatting down, picking up one of the kids. It wasn't anything you did and, even if your putting her over your shoulder caused it, it would have happened anyway. So, don't put yourself on a guilt trip over it. Nothing will be gained by blaming yourself for this."

"Okay, thank you, Doctor," Rick said, nodding his head.

Rick went outside the building and called Harley Meadows. He told him about Elizabeth's condition, and Harley said he was on his way. Six hours later, he walked into Elizabeth's room at the hospital.

Rick took Harley's hand and held it. "Thank you for coming, Harley," he said. "She's asleep right now, but she'll be happy to see you." He filled him in on Elizabeth's condition and told him they were doing a biopsy on the tumor. "It will be a few hours before we know if it's malignant or not."

Harley walked over to the bed and put his hand on his daughter's head. He lowered his head and was silent for a few moments. Rick perceived that he was praying. When he stopped, Harley began crying and then weeping almost uncontrollably.

Rick went to him and put his arm around him. "She'll be okay, Harley," he said. "Whatever happens, we'll get through this, and she'll be okay."

"I can't lose her, Rick," Harley said. "My girls are my whole life, I can't lose my Lizzy."

"I can't lose her either, Harley. We're not going to lose her. She'll be okay. I know she will. We'll do whatever it takes to get her through this."

After the surgeon had cauterized the torn blood vessel, Doctor Merrill came to the room and told Rick the results of the biopsy had come back, and he wanted to discuss it with him and Elizabeth.

"Elizabeth's father is here with us now, Doctor, I'd like for him to join us, if you don't mind."

They gathered around her bed, and Doctor Merrill explained to Elizabeth that the tumor, unfortunately, had turned out to be malignant. "We need to begin treatment right away," he told her. "I can give you the names of several oncologists here in town, and you can discuss with whichever one you choose to treat you how to proceed."

Rick and Harley were immediately distraught. Harley Meadows had become very emotional after he had become a grandfather. And his two daughters, having been gone from home for the past few years, had become even more precious to him. Now, with this latest devastating news, he had broken down, and Elizabeth was trying to console him.

"I know you're worried, Daddy, you always worried about me and Rose. But I'll be okay, I promise you."

"But people die from chemotherapy sometimes, Lizzy. It ravages a person's body."

"I'm not going to do chemotherapy, Daddy."

"What do you mean, baby?" Rick said. "You'll have to do it to get rid of the cancer."

"I'll do alternative treatments," she said. "There are other ways to fight cancer than chemotherapy. Chemo kills everything in your body. I'm not going to do it."

"Let's just wait and see what the oncologist has to say, okay?" Rick replied.

Rick asked Harley to go to the house. "You look worn out," he told him. "Why don't you get some rest? My sister, Amanda, is there with the kids and she can show you the guest room."

Harley agreed. "I am pretty tired, but please let me know if anything happens."

"I'll keep you posted, Harley, don't worry."

Elizabeth advised Doctor Merrill to pick an oncologist he was most familiar with, and she agreed to see him. A man named Samuel Morton came to her room. "I'm Doctor Samuel Morton," he told her. "I've seen your workup and the pictures, and I think we need to move quickly to get you on the road to recovery. I want to remove the tumor first."

"I don't think we should remove the tumor," Elizabeth said.

"And why would we not remove the tumor, Mrs. Bennett?"

"Won't the cancer spread if we disturb the growth?"

"That's a possibility, but it's an acceptable risk we have to take. We'll start you on chemo and radiation right away before the cells have time to spread."

"What options do I have if I choose not to do the chemo and radiation?"

"You have no other options," he said, somewhat annoyed by her question.

"There are alternative treatments for cancer."

"In the land of fools and dreamers there are, but if you want to survive this, you must start traditional treatment immediately."

"I think we have to listen to the doctor, Elizabeth," Rick said. "He's the specialist. Please, at least hear what he has to say."

"Thank you, Rick," Doctor Morton said, "at least we have one clear head in the family."

"I am hearing what he's saying, Rick, and I don't want to put my body through the torture of chemotherapy. It kills everything in the body. I believe there's a better way. There are alternative methods to fight it."

"I know, baby, but I just don't want you to die. I don't care if you lose your hair and puke all over the house. I'll take care of you for as long as it takes. I won't leave your side for as long as you're sick. I just can't lose you, Elizabeth. I love you."

"You need to listen to your husband, Mrs. Bennett," Doctor Morton said, reiterating his contention that chemo and radiation was the best path to recovery.

But Elizabeth remained adamant.

Harley implored her as well. "Rick is right, honey, maybe it is best to do what the doctor says is best for you. We both just want what's best for you."

"I appreciate what you and Rick are trying to tell me, Daddy. But doctors are in the business to create patients, not cure them. They're in bed with Big Pharma, and that's all about money. There is big money in 'treating' cancer but no value in 'curing' it. I love you both for loving me and for being concerned for me, but I'm going to use alternative treatments. I know a little something about it, and I have more trust in that direction than I do in Big Pharma."

"Oh, hell, you sound like that whacko, Winona Pearson," Doctor Morton exclaimed in frustration. "She should have been run out of the medical profession years ago. Okay, there's nothing more than I can do. She's signing her death warrant, and I'm not going to sign off on it. You folks had better find another oncologist very quickly, and I suggest you get one who can talk some sense into this young lady."

Elizabeth asked Doctor Merrill to contact the oncologist named Winona Pearson, whom Doctor Morton had maligned in his rant, and ask her to visit Elizabeth to discuss her situation.

The next morning, Doctor Pearson came to Elizabeth's room, approached her bed, and shook her hand as she introduced herself. "I've seen your X-rays and the lab report, Elizabeth," she said, "and Doctor Merrill tells me that you are interested in alternative treatment instead of the traditional chemo and radiation route."

"Yes, Doctor, I am. I'm a naturalist, of sorts, and I don't trust chemotherapy. I want to beat this thing with diet and exercise, and I suppose what you might call it the power of positive thinking."

"Well, I admire your courage. Most people take what they perceive as the 'easy' way out and go with the traditional chemo and radiation. It's going to be a long hard road for you, Elizabeth. I won't bullshit you about that."

"Thank you, Doctor, I appreciate that. I'm ready for whatever it takes."

"You'll need a strict diet, and you'll have to start right away," Pearson said. "You'll also need a health coach."

"I'm not familiar with that term, Doctor," Elizabeth replied.

"A health coach is a professional trainer, cook, and baby sitter, so to speak, all rolled into one. He, or she, depending on whom you chose to hire, will oversee your workout and exercise routine, plan your diet for you, and encourage you. It will be expensive because the person will be involved with you twenty-four/seven. They will live with you and be with you at least for the first six months or so. Then their presence in your home and in your life might taper off a bit, maybe to five days a week. It will be disruptive, so we need to make sure your husband is on board with your desire to enter into this."

"Rick is scared. He wants me to go the traditional route with the chemo. My daddy does too. They're afraid I'll die if I don't."

"I understand, Elizabeth. We'll have to convince them that the truth is you'll most likely die if you do take the traditional route."

Rick was open to Doctor Pearson's explanation of the natural healing process, but his fear was not alleviated. Elizabeth was adamant and remained firm in her desire to seek a cure from a natural-foods-and-exercise regimen.

"Okay, baby." He eventually relented. "Whatever you and Doctor Pearson think is best for you. I'll help anyway I can. What do we do first?"

"First, you call me Winona and, second, I'm going to make some calls and find us a health coach—Elizabeth will explain what that is to you—then I'll start putting together some information on diets, juices, vegetables, nut fruits, stuff like that. We need to get Elizabeth home and start her doing some mild exercise right away. I'll see you the day after tomorrow with more information on how we proceed."

Then next day, they met with Winona in her office. "I've contacted a man," she told them. "His name is Jules Frenkin, and he's a health coach, certified and trained at a medical school in Austin. He is highly recommended. I've known a couple of patients with similar circumstances to yours who have hired him and were extremely pleased with his professionalism and skill."

"How much will he charge us?" Elizabeth asked.

"It doesn't matter how much he charges, Lizzy, if he helps you get through this," Rick countered.

"No, she's right to ask, Rick," Winona replied. "You'll need him for probably six months, and he usually charges around eight-hundred a week plus some living expenses."

Rick didn't flinch. "Will he stay in the house with us?"

"Jules has an RV that he often parks on the property of his patients. He'll have to have electrical and water hookups. That will be less invasive than having him staying in the house with you and less expensive than renting a room or an apartment in town."

"That's not a problem," Rick said. "I can have contractors provide for the hookups for his RV. How does he work, five days a week, or what?"

"He'll work six days a week for the first six months. I'm only suggesting you hire a health coach because, with cancer, the body is weakened. And it's very easy for a patient to give in to the temptation to rest. The healing process can be grueling, and a health coach won't let you give up. I know you are a strong young woman, Elizabeth, but you've been dealt a potential death blow. It's going to take a strong will to beat it. You can do it, but Jules will help you. I've seen him work. You won't regret taking this course of action."

Jules showed up the two days later, and Rick directed him to a parking space next to the electrical service on the house. He'd hired a plumber to tie in a line to the house water system and another to the septic tank. An electrician had installed a set of receptacles for the power hookup to the RV. "Looks like you're ready for me, Rick," Jules said, "thank you."

"I didn't want to wait until you got here to start the work, Jules. I'll call the plumber now and get him out here to make the final connection to your rig."

"That's fine, but let's go meet your lady."

Elizabeth was coming out the door of the house as Rick and Jules approached. "Ah, you're on your feet," Jules said. "I see you're a fighter."

"I'm Elizabeth Bennett," she said, extending her hand.

Jules took her hand and kissed it. "And I have already met your Mister Darcy, my dear Elizabeth. He's quite a handsome fellow, I must admit. I am happy to meet you both. I am so sorry for your misfortune, but do not worry, we will beat this thing together, the three of us."

"We are glad to meet you too, Jules," Elizabeth said. "Thank you so much for taking my case."

"Yes, Jules, Winona Pearson speaks very highly of you. Lizzy and I are very grateful for you agreeing to help us."

"It's what I do, folks, it's what makes me happy. I'll have to make a point to see Winona while I'm this close. She is a rebel in the medical field, a rebel and a crusader."

"The first oncologist I talked to at the hospital said she was a whacko. That's why I decided to call her instead of using him," Elizabeth said.

"Winona has been trying to get the state of Texas to approve the use of medical marijuana for a number of years now. But the anal-retentive Republicans are too afraid of Big Pharma and the Baptists to do it. Don't misunderstand me, Winona is no hippie. She's a professional, one of the best oncologists in the business. Winona just came to realize that chemotherapy kills way more people than it cures. Anyway, that's a discussion for a later time. Right now, let's go inside, and I'll go over with you our plan of action."

In the house, Elizabeth started to make some coffee, but Rick insisted she sit down. "I'll make the coffee, baby, you talk to Jules, and I'll be right there."

"The first thing I want you to start doing is spending about thirty minutes a day lying in the sun, sometime between ten and two. Wear your bathing suit or don't wear anything, if you like, but you need that much time in the sun every day when we have bright sunshine."

"I can put up a screening fence," Rick said from the kitchen. "She can wear her robe out and take it off when she's inside the fence."

"Perfect," Jules replied, "that way the sun hits your entire body. Remember, do fifteen minutes on your back and fifteen on your stomach."

"I'll start today," Elizabeth said.

"Good. Now, I have a list of Alkaline-based foods I'll need Rick to find a source for in the area. They must be organic. All our fruits and vegetables must be organic. Some of them you won't be able to get organic, so we'll just have to do the best we can. The root cause of cancer is oxygen deficiency, which creates an acidic condition in the human body. Cancer cells do not live on oxygen and cannot survive where there are high levels of oxygen. An alkaline diet creates high levels of oxygen in the body, and that is our goal with you, Elizabeth."

The list included lemon, asparagus, kale, watermelon, avocados, grapes, collard greens, cauliflower, artichoke, sweet potatoes, green tea, bananas, blueberries, kiwi, figs, eggplant, limes, and cucumbers.

"We want to work as many of these foods as we can get in the area, that have been produced organically, into your daily diet. In addition, fresh-pressed juices from raw foods provide the most effective way of providing high-quality nutrition. You need to drink the juice from vegetables, such as raw carrots or apples. I have a two-step juicer we can use for this purpose."

"We already buy and use some of these foods now, Jules," Rick said. "I'll have to fill you in on my wife's history when we get some free time. She'll be a willing student for you because she's been into the 'natural' health thing for several years."

"I look forward to hearing that, Rick. Do you guys cook with bone broth?"

"Um, no, I've seen it on sale at the stores, but we've never used it."

"I'll show you how to make your own. You can use it in just about everything you make—soups, stews, mashed potatoes, other vegetables. It's good for you. You'll need to find a place to buy grass-fed beef and buy your roasts, ribs, and steaks there. We'll use the bones to make the broth."

Jules was up early the following morning, working in the kitchen while Elizabeth was slow running on the treadmill. He brought her a glass of juice he'd just squeezed in his presser. "How are you feeling this morning?" he asked her.

"Not too bad," she answered. "I've been working on the treadmill for several years now. I don't get fatigued so much. It's the normal routine around the house that makes me tired."

"That's what my main function is, besides making sure you stick to your diet. Here drink this," he said, handing her the glass.

"What is it?"

"Apple juice, I just pressed it. I've got some orange and pineapple in the fridge. You need to drink at least ten or twelve glasses a day. I'll exercise with you on every routine, like synergy. It will help keep you from getting fatigued. I won't let you get fatigued."

Later that night, Rick and Jules were sitting outside his RV having a couple of glasses of wine and engaging in casual conversation. Jules inquired about Elizabeth's medical history.

"As far as I know, Jules, she's never been sick a day in her life, at least she hasn't since I've known her. I met her when we were both eighteen."

"What about her family history. Any relative ever have cancer?"

"I'd have to ask her or her father, I don't know. Her mother died of a heart attack when Elizabeth was ten-years-old. That hit her hard and set her on a course to become a researcher for preventive measures for heart attacks. Elizabeth has a BS in bio-molecular engineering from Johns Hopkins University."

"Are you kidding me?"

"No, I'm not, Jules. She carried a four-point-oh GPA from middle school all through high school and came out of JHL graduate school with a three-point-eight.

"Holy cow," Jules said. "Why did she not tell me this?"

"I guess she didn't think it was relevant."

"Why is she not working in her chosen field?"

"Well, she kind of is. You see, Elizabeth met a friend in college, whose family owned a farm in Pennsylvania. They raised grass-fed cattle with the paddock rotation method of feeding and grass growing. Elizabeth became so enamored with the concept of chemical-free soil creation to produce fruits and vegetables and cattle that she gave up her original pursuits and changed to that industry. She wrote a book, a very successful book as a matter of fact, and began touring on lecture circuits for a company in Virginia."

"That is utterly amazing, and I thought she was just a beautiful woman."

"Well, she is that too. That's what initially attracted me to her, but once I got past her intellectual snobbery, I found a delightful, wonderful person. But it was love at first sight for me. It took a couple of dates for her to come around to liking me."

Jules chuckled. "You do seem to be the perfect couple, but how did you end up here?"

"That's an even longer story, maybe for another time. Suffice it to say, my wife is a brilliant woman, but right now she only needs what you know and what your skills can do to help her—help us."

"I'm going to help her, Rick, trust me."

"I do trust you, Jules, thank you."

The exercise regimen started the next morning.

"First, I want you to do two miles on the treadmill to get warmed up. I'll monitor your technique, then we'll begin our squats," Jules told Elizabeth while Rick began preparing food for the day's meals.

"You'll practice with a real chair first to learn how to do this move. Sit all the way down on the chair then stand back up in a squatting position. We'll do it at the same time, ten repetitions and ten sets. Let's go."

They faced each other, and Jules did the repetitions as Elizabeth did them. He was faster than she was, so he slowed a bit to keep pace with her. They completed the ten sets, and both were winded, but Elizabeth was obviously more winded than Jules. He was in extremely good physical condition.

"You want to walk it off a bit while you catch your breath?" he asked her.

"No, I'm good," she said. "What's next?"

"That's my girl," he said. "Now we do the routine again but don't sit down in the chair, just touch your butt to the chair and stand up, keeping the same form. This is going to be a little harder."

When they finished these ten sets, he brought her some juice and told her to sit down for a few minutes.

After a ten-minute break, he had her up again and doing lunges. "Lunges work all the major muscles in your lower body, and improve your balance," Jules told her. "Take a big step forward, keeping your back straight. Bend your front knee to about ninety degrees. Keep your weight on your back toes and drop the back knee toward the floor but don't let it touch the floor."

He demonstrated the move as he explained it.

They completed the routine, and Jules made Elizabeth drink some more juice. Then he had them do the lunges again. Once Elizabeth had become proficient at the move he had her do the move again, but this time he told her to take the step forward and out to the side. Then, when she had mastered that, he had her hold a five-pound dumbbell in each hand.

Next, they did a series of push-ups, ten push-ups, stand up and shake it off, then down and do ten more for ten sets.

"Do you need to rest, Elizabeth?" he asked her.

Elizabeth, sweating profusely, answered, "No, I'm fine."

"Now you don't have to show off for me, lamb chop. The goal here is not to wear you out. Our goal is to set a good exercise routine that you can handle and yet works you hard enough to accomplish what we need to accomplish.

"I'm not showing off, Jules," she replied. "I can do this."

"Okay, then on your back. We're going to do crunches."

"I know how to do crunches."

"Show me."

She lay on her back with her head resting on the palms of her hands, pressed her lower back down, then, in one smooth move, raised her head, then her neck, shoulders, and upper back off the floor, tucked in her chin, and lowered her back down. She repeated the process a couple of times.

"Okay, perfect," he said. "Now let's do ten and ten." He got down on the floor and started counting them off. Once they were finished, he had her rest a moment while he took some dumbbells out of his bag. "Okay, this will be the last routine in your repertoire, Elizabeth," Jules said, "The Bent-Over Row. Stand up and place your feet shoulder-width apart, bend your knees, and bend forward at the hips. Engage your abs without hunching your back. Hold the weights beneath your shoulders, keeping hands shoulder-width apart. Bend your elbows and lift both hands toward the sides of your body. Pause then slowly lower your hands back to the starting position. We'll start with the five-pound weights and increase as you get comfortable with more weight."

They completed that routine, and he asked her how she felt.

"I'm pretty tired, Jules," she said, "but I can do this every day."

"Good, this will be our daily routine for maybe a month, then, if you think you're up to it, we might increase the number of sets. Keep in mind, this is just until we beat the cancer. After that, you should seriously consider sticking to the routine we've just begun, as a daily starter. Make it your lifestyle. You and Rick both would be smart to do that."

"That's a definite, Jules. I intend to do that and, if I can cajole my husband into doing it with me, it will make me even more driven."

"Rick seems to be in pretty good shape. He must either work out or work hard on the vineyard."

"He stays busy, that's for sure. My husband was a football player in high school. He's always been lean and mean—figuratively speaking I mean."

"So how did a four-point-oh scholar hook up with a jock football player?"

"Are you kidding me, look at him," she said.

"Oh, I have. He's quite handsome, I have to agree with you on that."

"But there is more to him than that, Jules. Rick was an A honor roll student all through school, too, and maintained a four-point-oh GPA right along with me. That's what brought us together. He gave up scholarships to play football at several top universities, to get a BS in economics because he wanted to teach in college."

"And yet you both ended up, instead, running a vineyard, forsaking your chosen fields to be together. How did that happen?"

"It turned out that was the only way we could be together, and that was more important than all the rest."

"Well, good for you both, lamb chop. It's good that he is with you now, in your time of tribulation."

"What's with the lamb chop thing."

"I don't know. It just seems appropriate. I often give my clients pet name. You're just such a beautiful woman, Elizabeth."

"Well, thank you, Jules. I haven't felt very beautiful lately."

"Oh, but you still are, trust me on that. And don't get offended by anything I say. I'm as gay as a maypole, Elizabeth."

"Just how gay is a maypole, Jules?" Elizabeth said, laughing.

"I don't know. It's a line from the movie, *Love Actually*."

A month later, Rick took Elizabeth to see Doctor Pearson.

"You seem to be in good spirits," Winona said. "How is Jules working out?"

"Jules is wonderful," Elizabeth told her. "He's working my ass off, but I feel really great."

"That's good news. I'm going to draw some blood, and we'll see how things look. In another month or so, we'll do a thermography and check out the tumor. But it's too soon for that now."

Jules told them he was anxious to see the results from the blood work and, after morning exercises the next day, he asked them to sit down so he could talk to them. "I want to suggest something to you. If you don't want to do it, then I won't try to persuade you, and I won't mention it again."

"Okay, Jules," Rick said. "What is it?"

"I know you guys are pretty straight-laced and mainstream, and I would never suggest doing something that would offend your sense of right and wrong, but—"

"You want me to smoke pot, Jules?" Elizabeth said.

"No, Elizabeth, I want to make cannabis oil. Medical marijuana is not legal in Texas, but I can get it, and cannabis oil has some amazing healing qualities. It's been proven many times."

Elizabeth nodded. "My friends in Pennsylvania used it, Mrs. Graham, my friend's mother, had breast cancer, and she made cannabis oil, put it under her tongue every day. She showed me how to make it in a crock pot, using coconut oil. We'll just need an ounce of pot."

"Well, I'll be damned. I was worried about how you would take this, and you took it very well. I'll get the pot, though. I don't want you or Rick getting involved in that. It is against the law, you know. There is no money to be made in healing cancer in the United States, only in treating it."

Winona called Elizabeth and asked her to come in to her office to discuss the results of her blood work. "Your white blood cell count has gone down slightly, and that's good news Elizabeth. It's a small improvement but improvement, none-theless, and that's encouraging. An elevated WBC count, white blood cells, like you had when you first came in to the hospital, is indicative of distress in the body. As we now know, yours was the malignant ovarian tumor. A decreased or decreasing WBC count may tell us that the distress is being relieved. It's a little early yet, but I'm hopeful. Keep up with what you're doing. We'll check you again in about a month."

Rick was relieved and more inclined to give up his reticence about Elizabeth's foregoing traditional approaches to cancer cures such as chemo and radiation.

Jules increased the number of sets in their exercise routines, and Elizabeth began to falter.

"I'm wearing out," she told Jules." I can't keep up."

"You have to keep up, Elizabeth. I want to get us to twenty sets within three months."

"It's too much. I can't do it."

"That's bullshit, lamb chop. I'm ten years older than you, and I can do it. I am not going to let you die. Do you want to die, Elizabeth? Do you want to leave your husband all alone to raise your children without you?"

"No, Jules, I don't want to die."

"Then get off your lovely ass and get busy."

"Fuck you, Jules," she yelled at him. "I'm going to work you till you drop." She got up and restarted her routines, clenching her teeth with a steely look of determination on her face.

"Then do it," he said, and they began working like two fanatics.

Elizabeth, Jules, and Amanda were sitting at the kitchen table, eating lunch when Rick came in the front door with some material he'd purchased to make repairs to the greenhouse.

"Hey, Amanda," he said to his sister. "I ran into Dave at the Home Depot in Kerrville. He was in a really good mood."

Amanda smiled, nodded her head, and said, "Well, he ought to be. I gave him a blow job before I left the house this morning."

"Aw hell, sis," Rick responded. "Why do you have to tell me stuff like that?"

Elizabeth and Jules laughed uproariously.

"I just thought that maybe Elizabeth might take a hint from my experience," Amanda said.

"Did it ever occur to you that some of us just don't 'share' bedroom secrets around the kitchen table, or anywhere else?" Elizabeth replied.

Amanda looked at her sheepishly. "Oh, my bad, I'm sorry, Elizabeth."

Rick and Jules were chuckling at Amanda's embarrassment.

Jules made a trip to Austin and returned with an ounce of marijuana, which he dangled in front of Elizabeth. "Let's start cooking, lamb chop," he said.

"Rick!" she yelled to him in the next room, "my connection is here."

Rick walked in, looking confused until he saw Jules with the bag of weed. "I bought a jar of coconut oil and mentioned to the cashier that I brush my teeth with it," Rick said.

He went back to the store the next day and got the cheesecloth.

She took the pot, put it in the blender, ground it up to as fine a powder as she could, then emptied it out into a bowl. She then used a small brush to get all the residue out of the blender. Laying out the cheesecloth on the counter, Elizabeth spread half the marijuana onto it. She then rolled it up like a burrito and tied it up with tightly with string.

She retrieved a small glass cooking pot from the cabinet, put in a cup of water, and set it on the burner. Then she added three tablespoons of coconut oil and brought it to a boil. She added the weed burrito, mashed it down into the mix, and brought the bowl to a simmer. Then she covered it and left it for two hours. After two hours, she turned the burrito over, mashed it down again, covered the bowl again, and let it simmer another two hours. After it was fully cooked, she put it in the freezer and, when it was frozen, she took it out and stuck a fork through the cannabis pancake that had formed above the water. The water drained out through the hole made by the fork. What was left was the final product.

"Just put a small amount under your tongue every day for four days, Elizabeth," Jules told her. "Then two times a day for four days. You have to get acclimated to it. If you move too quickly, you'll end up on your ass on the couch ordering sweet and sour pork from the local Chinese restaurant. When you're ready, you'll do it three times a day, and then we'll see some progress with the tumor shrinkage. It's a damned shame people have to break the law just to use a natural cure that grows freely for all people to use."

"It's a gift from God," Rick said, "but the government knows better."

"Exactly," Jules replied. "Fuck 'em is all I have to say."

"My sentiments exactly," Elizabeth added.

Jules started a jogging routine for him and Elizabeth, in the reasonably cool of the evenings. He laid out a mile-long point east on Highway 290 to which they would jog, turn around, and return. Traffic was generally light, but they kept on the side of the rode and ran facing traffic. They had continued for a month without incident but, inevitably, that one pickup truck eventually came along with its compliment of drunk rednecks.

Spotting an attractive blonde-haired girl in jogging shorts and a halter top was just too much for the two men to remain silent. The passenger called out with some especially crude and disgusting comments about Elizabeth.

Jules and Elizabeth kept running, but Jules flipped the men off and, being too drunk to let it go, the driver turned the truck around and sped back to where the two were jogging along, unaware. The truck screeched off the road onto the grass in front of them.

The driver scowled at Jules. "Did you flip us off?" he yelled.

"I did," Jules replied. "You insulted my friend."

"How would you like for me to whip your ass?" the man shouted at him, still sitting inside the truck.

"I wouldn't like that," Jules said.

"Well, then you get her to take off her top, and we'll let it go."

"No, it looks like you're just going to have to whip my ass."

A little shocked at Jules's response, the man paused a moment. "Okay, pal. Come on, Bernie, let's get this guy."

Bernie got out of the truck and came around the front of it as the driver exited the driver-side door. Both men approached Jules with clenched fists.

"Come on, Jules, let's go," Elizabeth said.

"Get behind me, lamb chop," he told her, and she did.

The driver approached Jules first. Jules knocked him down and out with two quick punches. Then Bernie came at him. When he was a couple of steps away, Jules took a step to his right, planted his left foot, spun his right leg around, and hit the man on the right side of his face with his foot. The man went down immediately and did not get up.

"I'd advise you not to get up, Bernie," Jules told him. "If you decide to get up, I assure you, I will knock you down again."

The man just lay there and never said a word. Jules went to the truck, removed the keys, and threw them as far as he could out into the high grass on the other side of the fence that bordered the adjacent property.

"Let's finish our run, lamb chop."

"Holy shit, Jules, you're just full of surprises, aren't you? What was that thing you did with your leg?"

"That, my dear, was a back-spin crescent kick, Tae Kwon do, a Korean martial arts form."

"Well, you're my hero in more ways than one, now," she said. "Thank you."

"I told you I was going to take care of you, didn't I?"

At her three-month checkup, Winona was extremely positive about Elizabeth's progress. "Your WBC count has come down substantially, and the thermography shows that the tumor is being degraded. I am pleased, I am more than pleased. I can envision a complete recovery. Just don't quit what you're doing. The strong alkaline-content food diet you're on is working. Did Jules get you set with that 'oil' thing?"

Elizabeth was confused at first, but then she understood what Winona was talking about. "Oh, yes, Winona, he did, and it's working wonderfully."

"Okay, keep it up, and I'll see you in a month."

Elizabeth was walking Harley and pushing Ann Marie, in her stroller, around the vineyard one afternoon when an RV turned into the driveway. It looked familiar and then she saw the smiling face of Jerry Meisner behind the wheel and Corley McKnight in the passenger seat. She squealed and waved for them to come on up next to the house. Peggy Boyd got out first, and she and Elizabeth hugged.

"Oh, my gosh, I can't believe you guys are here," Elizabeth said. "How did you know—"

"Rick has been keeping us up to speed on your condition and your progress, peaches," Jerry said."

"That sneaky thing. He didn't tell me you were coming. What a wonderful surprise."

"So, when are you coming back to work?" Corley asked her.

"I can't promise you that, Corley. As you can see, I've got my hands full." She turned her palm up and swung her arm around to "present" her two babies. "These two are pretty much a full-time job for me and Rick both. And Rick's sister, Amanda, takes care of them most of the time while I'm working on getting better."

Peggy picked up Ann Marie and started walking around with her, Harley followed along behind her.

"I understand, Elizabeth," Corley said, "I really do. It's just that some of the light went out of our place when you left. Don't get me wrong, I'm happy for you, but we miss you."

"I miss you guys, too, and I am going to write another book as soon as I've beaten this cancer thing."

"Is the new book going to be about your cancer treatment?" Corley asked.

"Part of it is, but mainly it's going to be about the chemical-free soil concept. Our space is limited here, so we're going to buy some more land not too far away, get some cows, and do the paddock rotation thing. We need more good dirt for our grapes. How long can you stay?"

"We planned to stay a couple of days if it won't be an imposition."

"Heck no, it won't be any trouble at all. Rick went into town, but he'll be back before too long."

When Rick walked in the door, Peggy was playing with the children on the living room floor. Jules and Jerry Meisner were talking at the far end of the kitchen table, and Elizabeth and Corley were sitting at the other end, talking about her planned new book.

Rick shook hands with Jerry and Corley and sat down at the table. "Glad you guys finally got here," he said. "I was expecting you last week."

"The only guy I trusted to leave minding the store is Jerry, and there was no way he was going to miss this trip, so I had to let Herman fill in. Herman won't do anything, but at least he won't do anything wrong."

"I'm glad you made it, I wanted it to be a surprise for Lizzy."

"It was," she said. "I was walking the kids, and they just drove in. I couldn't believe my eyes."

"I wish I could have been there at that last lecture when you took my star away from me," Corley said. "Jerry told me it was a mind-blower."

"Oh, it was," Jerry said. "I'm getting ready to kick this guy's ass, and peaches kicks her shoes off, runs over and jumps into his arms, throws her arms and legs around him, and lays a lip-lock on him that almost made me blush. I'm thinking, this guy must have some 'pull' or something. And peaches tells me to relax, or something like that, because this is her guy. It was one hell of a night."

Peggy joined in from the living room floor, "I finally got to sleep with Jerry, Beth."

"Are you serious, Peg?" Elizabeth asked her.

"Well, we slept in the same RV together, if I can count that."

Everyone in the room laughed uproariously.

"Jules, do you know that Jerry is Randy Meisner's brother, you know, from The Eagles?" Elizabeth asked him.

"Are you serious?" Jules said, looking at Jerry. "Your mother must have had you awfully late in life."

"She was almost eighty, Jules," Jerry said.

Jules just shook his head.

"We tolerate each other's fantasies in our business, Jules," Corley said. "It's a pretty easy-going workplace. We don't question another coworker's resume, as long as he or she performs well. And Jerry has never let us down."

Jules, smiled, knowingly. "I've always loved the Eagles," he said.

The Virginia crew stayed a couple of days, and that was about as much time as Corley could stay away from his office, being the workaholic that he was. They packed their things and loaded up the RV and, after hugging Elizabeth and the children and shaking hands with Rick, they bid their goodbyes and headed back down Highway 290 for the long drive home.

At the end of Jules's six-month contract, he believed Elizabeth was ready to continue her life-saving regimen on her own. "You know what you have to do, lamb chop. I must go home for a while and see my folks. Then I have another job to start. But I want you to know that you are the bravest and most inspiring person I've ever met. It has been an absolute pleasure knowing you and your beautiful family."

"It has been all that and more for me and Rick, Jules. And I don't want it to end here. I'm going to send you an invitation every Thanksgiving and Christmas to come and have dinner with us."

"I will endeavor to come to dinner at your house if possible, lamb chop, thank you," Jules said.

Elizabeth hugged him. "I love you, Jules," she said.

Baby Harley, seeing his mother hugging the man, threw up his arms, and Jules picked him up and hugged him.

"I love you too, Elizabeth, and you two squirts too. And don't think you're going to get out of hugging me too, Rick, come here."

"I wouldn't think of it, Jules," Rick said and hugged him. Towering over the shorter man by five inches, he gave him the obligatory male backslap.

"I put some of our wine in your RV," Elizabeth said. "Wait 'till you get home to drink it."

They stood and watched as Jules drove out of the vineyard and onto the highway.

Winona was ecstatic at Elizabeth's next appointment. "Your WBC count is stable, and the tumor has effectively been eradicated." You did it, you beat cancer. I am so proud of you. You are a case study. You should be in a medical manual."

"We did it, Winona. You and Jules and Rick and I did it. We all did it. If you want to use my case in your campaign to convince the state to approve the use of medical marijuana, you have my permission, and I'll put that in writing."

"That might be helpful, Elizabeth," Winona said, "thank you. Now, keep in mind, you must keep up the full regimen, diet, and exercise. You can cut back on the cannabis oil, I don't want you out trying to score dope from some weed-head on the street. If you get to that point, let me know, and I'll help you out."

Elizabeth's eyes widened. "Well, okay, Winona, I'll keep that in mind, thank you."

Back at home, Rick was staring at her pensively.

"What?" she asked him.

"Why is it, baby, that every nickname any other man gives you, is always something to eat?"

Chapter 15

Into the Light

Elizabeth put the children to bed and sang a song to them until they drifted off to sleep. Then she dressed for bed, got into bed on her side, and lie there, contemplating everything that had happened to her in the past year or so. She had faced death from a deadly disease and had survived. Her family was intact, her children asleep in their beds, and her husband puttering around in some other part of the house.

She started to count her blessings but decided there were so many that she could not possibly name them all. Instead, she closed her eyes and said a quiet prayer of thanks.

Rick walked into the room.

Hearing his footsteps, she opened her eyes and smiled at him. He walked over to her side of the bed and sat down. Taking her hand in his, he kissed it tenderly.

"I need to tell you how much I love you," he said.

"Okay, shoot."

"No, I mean I really need to make you understand how much I love you."

Sensing his seriousness, she said, "Then tell me, darling."

"Right after I made the deal with Mister Humphries, to buy the vineyard, we made a handshake deal. I left to go back to Dallas, to tell my dad that I was going to proceed, and to get my checkbook. I stopped to eat at a café on the way back, and suddenly I started missing you—badly."

"I wish I had been there with you," she said.

"Yeah, me too. I guess I was just thinking that this was something you should have been involved in with me. Anyway, I had the radio on and in that area, there was nothing but country music…well, you know I don't like country music."

She nodded.

"So, the voice on the radio announced that the next song was one by some group, I can't remember their name now, but the name of the song was—get this, 'Elizabeth.'"

"Really?"

"Yeah, really, it freaked me out. I started to turn it off, but my curiosity wouldn't let me, so I listened to it. And it was one of the prettiest songs I'd ever heard. It was about a guy who was in love with a woman, who apparently was not with him, far away, as a matter of fact, sound familiar? I googled the song later and learned some of the words, but I couldn't dwell on it because it drove me nuts thinking about you. He's talking to her and tells her how much he misses her and how he wishes he could be with her. I had to pull off the road, and I just buried my face in my hands and started bawling like a baby. At that moment, all I wanted to do was die. I was convinced I was never going to see you again. I was about to start the truck and get it up to eighty miles an hour and run off the road into a tree."

"Oh, my god, Rick, you've never told me this before, I'm so sorry," Elizabeth said. "What did you do?"

"I didn't do anything. A state trooper pulled up behind me and came up to the window. I gave him my license and paperwork. He asked me if I was okay. I told him I just had a headache and pulled over to rest a bit. He asked me if I had been drinking, and I told him no. Then he asked me if I would be willing to take a sobriety test, and I told him I would. He said that would not be necessary, and he handed me back my stuff. Then, as he was about to leave, he asked me if I was the Rick Bennett who played quarterback for Travis High School a few years back. I told him I was, and he told me I should have played for UT. I told him he was probably right. Then he let me go.

"So, you didn't kill yourself after all?"

"Nope, something about that guy remembering me gave me hope that I would find you one day. I know that sounds weird, but that's what happened."

"A country song and a Texas State Trooper. That's a country song right there," she said.

"Anyway, what I'm trying to say is this. That day that I walked into the office at your dad's construction company, looking for Bobby Gladwyn, but found you sitting behind the desk, and I saw those beautiful blue eyes, I knew that moment that I was going to love you for the rest of my life."

"I know I felt something, but I have to confess it was pretty superficial. You were so damned good looking. I had no idea you felt that way about me that quickly. You had no trouble putting me in my place right after that."

"Oh, right," he said, "I meant to apologize for that."

"No need, I had it coming."

"Yeah, you kinda did."

"I love you, Rick."

"I love you too, Elizabeth."

"Will you make love to me?"

He smiled at her mischievously.

"Oh, no, don't you dare say it."

"I have to," he said.

"Okay, if you must," she told him.

"Elizabeth Bennett, has anyone ever told you 'no' to that question?"

"You, silly man. You know I've never asked anyone but you, that question."

Chapter 16

Azalea Lane

2065:

The doorbell rang at a mid-sized Colonial-style home on Azalea Lane in Dallas. A graying man, in his middle fifties, got up from his chair and went to the door. A young man who appeared to be in his mid-thirties was standing there, briefcase in hand.

"You are Mister Bradley, I assume," the older man said.

"I am, sir, and, as I told you when I called, I am with People of Texas Magazine. I appreciate your affording me the time to visit with you."

"It is my pleasure, Mister Bradley."

"Please, sir, call me Ben," the man said.

"Ben Bradley, is it? I seem to recall that was the name of a well-known newspaper man back in the last century."

"You may be right, Mister Bennett. I've heard that before. I've always meant to research it but just have not gotten around to it."

"Well, I wouldn't have known the name except for my father, who kept up with such things and must have mentioned it to me once or twice. Come on into the living room, Ben, my sister Annie is waiting. She made some coffee for us, if you want some."

"Perhaps a little later, sir," he said, "I've been on the road for several hours, and I've had a lot of coffee.

The older man led him into the living room where the man's sister was sitting on the couch. Bradley noticed that she was an attractive woman with bright blue eyes, and only the beginning streaks of gray, invading her blonde hair. Her eyes seemed alive with interest and anticipation.

"This is my baby sister, Ann Marie Bennett Miller, she goes by Annie. She's only a year younger than I am but I still call her my baby sister."

Bradley walked over and took the woman's hand. "I am especially happy to meet you, ma'am," he said. You are very well talked about, in the hill country around Fredericksburg, as is your brother and your husband was, before his passing. My condolences to you."

"Thank you, Mister Bradley," she said, "and thank you for coming so far to talk to us."

"It is my honor, ma'am, and please call me Ben."

"I will do so, Ben, thank you."

"This is a beautiful home you have here, Mister Bennett."

"Our paternal grandfather, Adrian Bennett, bought this house back in 2002 when he brought his family to Dallas from California. Eventually, after he died and our grandmother, Leeann, later, she left it to our father and our Aunt Amanda. Rick and Elizabeth had no intentions of ever leaving Fredericksburg, and they didn't want to get rid of the house, so they leased it out for a number of years, and then when Annie and I were old enough to go to college, they gave it to us.

"Annie married Frank Miller and lived in Fredericksburg, and I decided to go to school at SMU where my dad had gone, so Annie agreed to let me live in the house. Now, I'm still here. I suppose, if it doesn't fall down, our kids will get it one day."

"Your mother's book made quite an impact on the folks around Fredericksburg, back when it first came out. Can you tell me what your parents were like?"

"I'll let Annie take this. She's the romantic in the family."

"My mother was beautiful," Annie began. "She was so beautiful that it was almost a curse to her. Elizabeth Meadows was an honor roll student and absolutely brilliant. That was the problem. No one took her seriously because they just could not believe that a blonde-haired beauty could be anything more than a cheerleader. According to our grandfather, Harley Meadows, our mother was an intellectual snob and was often arrogant and dismissive of people." She handed him a photo album. "Here are some pictures of our parents back in their younger days."

Bradley opened the album and began to peruse it. "Wow, I see what you mean. She was a beautiful woman. Your father was a handsome man too," he said.

"Oh, yes," Annie replied, "and he was also a brilliant man, with the same credentials as my mother, but he didn't flaunt his intelligence the way she did. Rick was more laid back and humble."

"How did they meet?

"They met in high school. My father always claimed that he fell in love with Elizabeth the first time he laid eyes on her.

"I don't have a problem believing that," Bradley said.

"Rick and Elizabeth were married July first, of 2009 at the justice of the peace in Fredericksburg, after being apart for four years."

"You say they were apart for four years? Now that sounds like there's a story behind that headline."

"There is, Ben, and it's a long one and a sad one. Perhaps you'd like some coffee now."

Chapter 17

The Bennetts

2016:

It was mid-morning at the Lizzy-Bee Vineyard, just outside Fredericksburg, Texas. A man was walking the rows of his vines, checking for any fungal activity, aphids, or rodent damage to the plants.

Two sets of bright blue eyes were peering out from behind a grape vine, one row adjacent to and a couple of plants down from where the man they were watching was carefully examining the vines. He would pause every so often and pick a grape, stick it in his mouth, and taste it. Occasionally, he would spit it out and move on. When he came to the end of a row and started down another one, the two sets of curious orbs followed him, keeping one row away from him and watching him from between the plants.

The blue eyes moved along with him, taking every precaution not to be seen. The inquisitive eyes belonged to two handsome faces which, in turn, were attached to the heads of two endearing moppets—a five-year-old boy and his four-year-old sister—who were watching their father in what they thought was total secrecy.

"HA, Ann Marie," a woman's voice called out from somewhere near the house.

The boy squatted down, and the girl did the same. He put his index finger over his lips, signaling his sister to remain quiet.

The woman called out again, "Rick, are the children with you?"

"They're over here with me, Lizzy," the man in the other row shouted to her.

The two kids stood up and walked through the vines into the row where their father was standing.

"Daddy, how did you know we were here?" the boy asked him.

"It's my job to know where you are," the man said. "It's my job to keep you two safe."

"But I was being quiet. Annie was making noise."

"I was not," the girl said, with a look of defiance on her face, "I was being quiet, Daddy."

"I know, darling, you were both very quiet, but I could see you through the plants. I just knew you were there. I have super powers when I need to keep up with you guys."

"You have super powers, Daddy?" the boy asked.

"Sort of," his father told him. "I'm taller than you are so I can see over things that you can't. I knew you were following me, and I didn't mind, but when your mother called you, I had to let her know where you were, so she wouldn't worry."

He sat down on the ground and pulled both children to him, placing one on either side, and put his arms around them. He looked down at their faces and marveled at how much they had grown. *It seems like only yesterday, such a cliché*, he was thinking, *they were babies. Now they have become carbon copies of me and their mother*. The boy had his father's black hair and facial characteristics, as well as his lanky frame. And his wife, Elizabeth's, childhood pictures were indistinguishable from the physical appearance of their daughter, a strikingly lovely little towhead with the same blue eyes, blonde hair, and captivating mannerisms.

They'd named the boy, Harley Adrian, after his and Elizabeth's fathers, and called him Harley for a while. But they eventually shortened it to, HA to avoid confusion, when Elizabeth's father, Harley, was around. The name stayed with him all his life. The girl was named Ann Marie, after Elizabeth's mother, who had died from a heart attack when Elizabeth was ten years old. They called her Annie because that was what Harley Meadows, had called Elizabeth's mother.

"Do you guys want to help me check out the grape vines?" Rick asked his children.

"Yes, Daddy," they both answered together.

"Okay, then follow me. We're looking for weeds at the bottom of the plants." He found one and showed them and then pulled it out of the ground. "Like that," he said, tossing it into the middle of the row. "You guys are closer to the ground so why don't you look for weeds, and I'll check the plants for pests."

"What's a pest, Daddy?" Harley asked.

"Bugs and stuff," Rick said.

"Ew, bugs," Annie replied, scrunching up her nose, "I don't like bugs, Daddy."

"Then you can just pull weeds with your brother, darling," Rick said.

In about fifteen minutes, the two kids had grown tired of their assigned task and were starting to wander off down the row.

"You want to go to the house and see if Mommy can make us something for lunch?"

Both children were in favor of that course of action. Rick picked them up, one in each arm, with the intention of carrying them back to the house.

"I want to walk, Daddy," HA said, so Rick put him down.

"What about you, baby doll, do you want to walk too?

"I want you to carry me, Daddy," Annie said.

HA was already inside the house when Rick and Annie arrived. Elizabeth was making them sandwiches, so the three of them took their places at the table.

After lunch, the kids played in the living room while Rick and Elizabeth went to the office to discuss the next crop. July was grape picking season, and they were gearing up. Picking the grapes now on the vines was only part of the process. Last years' red wine would be bottled and shipped and the white from three years' past would be bottled. The processing and storage of the current crop would begin the process all over again.

"I got a call from a man in Fredericksburg, who has some land on the south side of Two-Ninety that he'd be willing to sell or lease to us. Apparently, he saw my note in Home Depot."

"When are you going to see him?" Elizabeth asked.

"He's coming here tomorrow."

"Should we try to buy or lease, what do you think?"

"I don't know, what do you think?" he asked her.

"Dammit, Rick, I don't know either, that's why I asked you."

"But you're smarter than I am, Lizzy."

"Not in everything, I'm not. How much land does he have and how much does he want for it?"

"We won't know that until he gets here. Are you upset with me?"

"No, I'm sorry, Rick, I'm just tired. My daddy is coming to help me with the kids and, while I appreciate his help, but he sometimes gets in the way."

"Oh, come on, Elizabeth, Harley is no trouble. He helps us out a lot around her, I'm glad to have him."

"He wants to come for good."

"What do you mean?"

"For good. He wants to give his house to Rose and Bobby and move in with us."

"I don't have a problem with that," Rick said.

"Ever since I had cancer and beat it, he's obsessed with the fear that it's going to come back. He's afraid I'm going to die. He's afraid he's going to lose me."

"I went through the same thing for a couple of years, baby, I know how he feels. He's your father, that's to be expected. I didn't understand it completely until our kids got older. Now I know exactly why Harley worries about you. You're his firstborn daughter, he lost your mother, and now he's afraid he'll lose you. You had cancer, Elizabeth, of course we're going to worry about you."

"I know," she replied, "but I'm still sticking to the regimen that helped me beat it. It's a lifestyle for me now. I know what I have to do to stay alive, and I will stay alive, for you and for the kids."

"You have to, Lizzy. We all need you, and your dad needs you too. I think we should ask him to come here to live with us. Harley will be a lot of help around here. Besides, I've always enjoyed his company. I just like talking to him."

The next afternoon, a green van turned off the highway, pulled into the driveway, and approached the house. An elderly gentleman with graying hair and beard exited the vehicle. Rick walked toward him and extended his hand.

"Are you Mister Grimmer?" he asked, as they shook hands.

"I am," the man said, "call me Jack. I assume you're Rick."

"Rick Bennett, yes, sir, I appreciate you coming. So you have some land not far from here?"

"Just a few miles," the man said. "I have twenty acres off Thirteen Seventy-Six about three miles the other side of Luckenbach."

"I'd like to see it. Can we go take a look?"

"Of course, I can drive us there," Grimmer said.

"I want to take my wife along, and we have two kids, so why don't I follow you in my truck. I already have the car seats in the truck."

"That's fine," Grimmer said.

Rick brought Elizabeth and the kids out and introduced her to the man. "This is my wife, Elizabeth Bennett, and our kids, HA and Ann Marie. The HA is short for Harley Adrian. He was named after our fathers, and we call him by his initials, so we don't get him mixed up with his grandfather."

"I am happy to meet you all. I have two granddaughters just about your age, young lady," Grimmer said, pointing at Annie.

"What are their names?" Annie asked him.

"They are Ava Fe and Juniper Grace, and they are very pretty girls, just like you are."

Annie giggled.

Then Grimmer shook hands with Elizabeth. "This is appropriate," he said, "Elizabeth Bennett was, as I'm sure you know, the second and loveliest daughter of the Bennet family from *Pride and Prejudice*."

"And you've already met my Mister Darcy, Mister Grimmer," Elizabeth said.

"Indeed, I have," he said. "So, shall we go look at my ground?"

He turned back toward town, drove a short distance to Highway 1376, and turned left. Rick followed the man past the turn-off for the small community of Luckenbach. Three miles past Luckenbach, they turned left onto a driveway. The man got out of his vehicle, unlocked a metal gate, and swung it wide open. He then got back in and drove down a gravel road, a hundred yards or so, and stopped.

Rick followed, and they all exited the vehicles, Elizabeth carried Annie, and Rick put HA on his shoulders. Rick took a long look at the acreage.

After a walking tour of the property, they came back to the location where the vehicles were parked.

"There's a creek nearby," Grimmer said. "It doesn't border the property, but that doesn't matter much because it's what they call a *seasonal* water source. That means—"

"I know what that means," Rick said. "It means it only has water in it when it's raining everywhere else anyway."

Grimmer began chuckling. "You'll have to put in a well is what it means," he said.

"Why are you selling the land, Jack?" Rick asked him.

"This land has been in the family for many years. I used to plan on doing something with it but now my kids are grown, so the best I can do with it is either give it to them and start a big fight or sell it and split the money between them."

"I like this ground, Rick," Elizabeth said. "What are you asking for it, Mister Grimmer?"

"I need twelve thousand an acre, ma'am," Grimmer said.

Elizabeth didn't flinch. "That seems like a fair price," she said, and Rick nodded.

"Let us discuss this tonight, Jack, and I'll have an answer

for you tomorrow. I have your phone number. Thank you for your time."

"My pleasure, folks. If you have made the vineyard work with only twenty acres, then you should be able to double your production, theoretically, with twenty additional acres. You won't immediately realize a lot of extra profit until the new acreage is paid for. But it'd be a good investment in the long run."

He followed them back to the Lizzy Bee to thank them, say goodbye, and take a look around. "You have a nice-looking place, Rick. My son, Isaac, has a winery tours company. It might be a good idea to put your place on the tour list. It could create a lot of interest in your vineyard. I can have him come and talk to you about it if you're interested."

"Absolutely, Jack," Rick said. "I'd like that very much."

"It's two-hundred and forty thousand, Rick," Elizabeth said. "I have about a hundred grand in my account and a royalty check from my book due next month. We only have enough in the company account to ensure we can make payroll through the harvest in July. I don't think we should go into that money."

"What are you suggesting then?"

"Let's try to finance the whole amount, setting aside the money in my account, and use our property as collateral."

"But we'll need money to develop the new property, buy new vines, and pay labor to plant and install a structure of some kind for a caretaker," Rick said.

Elizabeth breathed a heavy sigh. "We may not be able to do this all at once, Rick," she said.

"Let's go to the bank, apply for a loan, and see what happens.

"Okay, she said, "and by the way, Daddy is coming in tomorrow."

"Good," Rick replied. "I'll call Mister Grimmer and tell him we're interested in buying the land and we're going to the bank to apply for a loan."

The next day, they went into town to the local bank.

"We actually have three accounts, Phil," Rick explained to

the manager of the bank, Phillip Creel. "My wife and I have separate accounts, and we have a business account for the vineyard."

"I see," Phil replied, "and you are applying for a loan of two-hundred-forty thousand using the property for collateral?"

"That's correct, that's to buy the land. We have enough operating capital on hand to get through the next harvest payroll and to pay the bills through the end of the year. We'll have to make some improvements on the land, a well, living quarters—probably a small trailer house—and the cost of labor and plants to start a new crop for next year."

"Mrs. Bennett has a substantial amount of money in her account. Are you going to use that for the purposes you mentioned?"

"Yes, that is our plan."

"After you called, I checked out the county assessment of the value of your property. It is owned jointly by you and Mrs. Bennett, and there are no liens or attachments. The property is appraised at eight hundred thousand dollars, so I don't see any problem getting the loan approved. Call me back tomorrow, and I'll let you know."

"Eight-hundred-thousand dollars," Rick said to Elizabeth after they were back in the truck. "Original price was five hundred thousand. I'd paid two when we got married, and you paid it off. Now we've got the three-hundred grand back that you spent paying off the mortgage. You want that in a check or hundred-dollar bills?"

"Elizabeth laughed. "Keep it, darling. I'll take it out in trade."

"I may not live long enough to pay that off, baby."

"You better," she said. "So, what now?"

"We'll wait for the loan approval and then get the deal worked out with Mister Grimmer, then…I don't know what to do then. We'll figure it out, Lizzy, we always do."

Harley Meadows arrived at the Bennett home, pulling a small travel trailer containing all his clothing and living necessities. His daughter settled him into the room that Rick's sister,

Amanda, had lived in until she married Dave Braddock three years ago.

"Your sister Rose and Bobby are going to start having babies, Lizzy. They tell me they'll go nuts in that big house in Dallas if they don't start filling it up with kids pretty quick."

"I'm glad Rose is happy, Daddy," Elizabeth said.

"She seems to be so, Lizzy," Harley said. "She was really tired of living in New Orleans when Bobby was playing for the Saints. I was afraid they'd have trouble over her wanting him to quit football and come back home to Dallas, but he said he was ready. When they won the Super Bowl, he said he'd never top that, so he quit while he was ahead."

"Rose always liked Bobby, even when he first came to work for you in the summers and on weekends. I think you always wanted a son, Daddy."

"Well, I had two beautiful girls, and now I have two sons-in-law, who are more like sons to me than anything else, so what more could an old man ask for?"

"You're not old, Daddy."

"I'm fifty-six, honey, that's getting pretty close to old."

"Well, I'm thirty-one, and I'm starting to feel old."

"Oh, I know. I can't get past thinking you're still ten years old. I remember when you drove your mother's car to the office when you were ten, when I was going through my bad times after your mother died. You scared the hell out of me."

"I know, Daddy, I'm sorry. It just seemed like something had to be done."

"And you did it," he said, looking at her like he used to look at her when she was a little girl. "You were so smart, Lizzy. I sometimes wish you had gone on and got your PhD—I know you're happy here with your family, and I wouldn't change any of that, but a doctorate from Johns Hopkins, my gosh. Do you know what that would mean?"

"It wouldn't have made me happy without Rick, Daddy," she said. "I have no regrets. I do miss the lecture tours sometimes, and I'm still planning to write another book."

"Why have you not done that?"

"The first one had such an impact on the permaculture industry, it was so successful, I guess I'm just afraid the next one won't be as successful. I don't have as much to say as I did then. I suppose I have what they call writer's block."

"Then write about something else, Lizzy."

"Like what, Daddy?

"Write about your life, your lives, yours and Rick's. Write about how you met, the incongruity of it all. Rick's family moving to Texas from California, you two meeting in high school and falling in love. Write about how you went away to a different school, got your master's but gave it all up to lecture and write about the production of chemical free food, your four-year breakup with Rick, and how he eventually found you again, and you got married. You ended up here in the winemaking business, you got cancer, and beat it with only natural remedies. Hell, Lizzy, you've got a family saga right there."

Elizabeth pursed her lips. "I don't know, Daddy, but I'll think about it."

A short time later, mid-morning one day, an SUV pulled into the driveway. Elizabeth was in the front yard with the children and walked over to greet the visitor. Behind the wheel was a handsome young man who appeared to be in his late twenties or early thirties.

"Can I help you?" she asked him.

"Yes, ma'am," he said. "My name is Isaac Grimmer. I own a company called Two-Ninety Wine Shuttle. My dad was here about some land he had for sale and told me you might be interested in adding your vineyard to my list of tour stops."

"Yes indeed," Elizabeth said., "I'm Elizabeth Bennett. I'll go get my husband. Just park anywhere and come on in. He's in the office."

As they were approaching the door of the house, Rick stepped out.

"Oh, here he is now. Rick," she yelled to him, motioning for him to come to them. "This is Isaac Grimmer. Mister Grimmer's son, who has the winery-touring company."

"We've been expecting you, Isaac," Rick said as they shook hands. "I'm happy to meet you. How would you like for us to present the place to your customers?"

"Well, why not just show me around the property and tell me all about it, how long you've been in business, and all about your process, and we'll work out a format for a presentation that you're both comfortable with."

"My wife will most likely do the presentations," Rick said. "She's sort of the de facto face of the vineyard—at least her face is on every bottle of wine we sell."

"Well, and this is just a suggestion, I think it would be nice if both of you do the presentations. Show the public an attractive young couple running a successful winery. You could divide the dialogue between you. Let Mrs. Bennett talk about the more feminine stuff, the grapes and the wine, et cetera, and you talk about the plants, harvesting the crops, and keeping the soil watered and treated. I'll have to leave the division of all that up to you because I don't really know much about the wine business."

"That makes sense to me, Isaac," Rick said, and Elizabeth nodded in agreement.

"I can write a program for us, Rick." She followed up with, "Is there any cost to us for this, Isaac?"

"No, the tourists pay me for the ride. If you want to offer them a glass of your wine, that adds a nice touch."

"How many people are usually on one of your tours?" she asked him.

"My bus seats twenty-five. We typically have fifteen or twenty. My van seats thirteen, and, usually, I have about ten. Occasionally, we'll fill up—you know, on holidays and during Octoberfest. The van tour, for some reason, almost always has only female tourists."

"If you'll let us know, ahead of time, the number of visitors, I'll have some refreshments and wine ready and available for them."

"Of course, they'll appreciate that. Your place is the closest to town, so I'll make it the first stop on every tour, but we'll always notify you before we show up."

"Thank you, Isaac," Elizabeth said. "We appreciate it and look forward to receiving your tours."

"Yes, Isaac," Rick added. "I'm glad your dad mentioned you to us. Thank you, for coming."

"It's my pleasure, folks. I'm happy to meet you both." They shook hands and Isaac got into his car and left.

Rick got a call from Phillip Creel at the bank, informing him that the loan had been approved. A title search had been done on the Grimmer property and revealed that is was free and clear of any liens and encumbrances. The Bennetts could pick up a cashier's check the next day, if they wanted to.

Rick thanked Creel and then called Grimmer to let him know. "If you can meet us at the Chase Bank on Main Street tomorrow, Jack, we'll finalize the deal."

Grimmer arrived at the bank, at the appointed time, with the deed and land survey document in hand. Phillip Creel had prepared the bill of sale. In his office, the proper paperwork was dutifully signed. Rick and Elizabeth endorsed the check for two-hundred-forty-thousand dollars and handed it over to Jack. They shook hands again and walked out of the bank together.

"Call me if I can be of any help to you," Grimmer said.

"I'll do that, Jack," Rick replied, "thank you." He turned to Elizabeth. "Okay, my beautiful bio-molecular engineer, from Johns Hopkins University, this is your field of expertise. What do we do now with our new twenty acres?"

"Well, my equally beautiful football star, impatient economics expert, you are probably not going to like what I'm going to suggest."

"I may not like it, but I will defer to your expertise, baby."

"We need to get it plowed under and tilled and plant grass. Let the grass grow as high as it will then bring some cows in to eat the grass and do their business, you know, crap all over the place, until the grass is eaten and covered with shit."

"And then bring in the chickens," he responded. "How many times do we need to do that?"

"Not that many, if we can find enough cows and chickens."

"You can calculate all that, can't you?"

"Yes, I can, but the problem will be housing the animals. We can't transport the animals every day."

"What do you suggest, Lizzy?"

"I think we'll have to divide the property into paddocks, maybe two paddocks per acre. That way we won't need as many cows and chickens. I think we should buy the cows and then sell them when we are finished with the process. We'll need a structure, not a full barn, but a place to keep them in foul weather. The chickens can free range. We'll lose a half acre, maybe a little more for a staging area and living quarters for a caretaker."

"You mentioned that, when you worked on the Graham farm, they used electric fencing between the paddocks to keep the animals in place."

"Yes, standard fencing is much too expensive and, besides, we'll have to take it down once we plant the vines."

We'll need a water well. I'll get Dave Braddock to drill a well for us."

Rick brought his foreman, Carlos Ramirez, to the property and offered to let him move his trailer house to the site and live there with his family rent-free. Carlos would have to pay for electrical utilities. Rick would provide his water, and they'd install a septic tank and a propane tank. Carlos would pay for the propane. Carlos would still provide, manage, and pay the crews during harvest season, for both sites, once the new property began producing grapes.

Isaac Grimmer arrived with his first busload. They were a chatty bunch, but most of them were genuinely interested in the vineyard and how things worked in a wine producing establishment. The majority of the visitors were women, and many of them seemed virtually hanging on every word that came out of Rick's mouth.

"I may have to stop coming to your place, Mrs. Bennett," Isaac told Elizabeth.

"Oh, for gosh sake, Isaac, call me Elizabeth, and why would you stop coming? They look like they're having fun."

"They are having fun, but your husband is even better looking than I am, and I like being the center of attention."

"Yeah, but Rick is not nearly as modest as you are," she said.

He looked at her for a moment and then burst out laughing. "I just don't practice *false* modesty," he replied.

After the tour, Elizabeth offered the visitors a glass of Lizzy Bee wine, at the roadside stand. She had purchased some French bread and cheese and sliced small portions for them to consume with their wine.

"We don't want to get them drunk before they get to the other wineries," Isaac had told her.

There were multiple questions for both Elizabeth and Rick, mostly about their private lives, how they met, how they came to own the vineyard at such a young age, and such and such.

"You should write a brochure about your vineyard, answering every question that you were asked today," Isaac said. "Otherwise, you're going to have to repeat yourself every time I bring a load of people out here. But you'll get some attention, I guarantee you."

"I'll work on that," Elizabeth said. "I think you're right, Isaac. They wore me out with all the questions."

Rick's sister, Amanda came out of the house with the kids. "Your dad is making lunch, Elizabeth. He asked me to come and get you guys."

"Tell him we'll be right in, Manda," Rick said.

"What are you making, Daddy?" Elizabeth asked Harley.

"Three-cheese ravioli," Harley answered.

"It sounds wonderful, but I can only eat a little. You know I'm on a strict regimen of diet and exercise."

"I know, Lizzy, but try a little. You know how I love to cook for my family."

"I know, Daddy. Rick and the kids will love it. The kids maybe not so much, but Rick and Amanda will for sure."

"I want to take the kids to town tomorrow, if you don't mind," Harley said.

"I'm okay with that. Just keep in mind that Saturday is really busy along Main Street and the traffic is really heavy. You have to watch them very closely."

"I've watched kids before, Lizzy."

"I know you have, Daddy, and I'm sure you worried about me and Rose just as much as I do about HA and Annie, but—"

"But these are *your* kids."

"Right," she said, laughing.

"And they're my grandkids, so don't worry, honey. I promise you, I won't let anything happen to your kids."

"Don't buy them any toys. They have enough stuff, and don't feed them too much ice cream or chocolate."

"But that's my job, Lizzy."

"The operative words were 'too much.' Please use good judgement."

"Good judgement, yes, I think I remember what that is."

Chapter 18

Into the Future

2065:

Mother began her book, Ben, at our grandfather Harley's persuasive suggestion that she document her and Rick's lives together. Rick was proud or her and gave her a lot of encouragement. But after the winter of 2016, and the very controversial election of that year, it was in early January of 2017 when Elizabeth received a phone call that lifted her spirits and started the juices flowing again in her veins and jump-started her competitive brain and heart."

"Tell me what happened, Annie," Bradley prodded her.

"Well, it was something that excited Elizabeth to no end, but something Rick feared the most. But first, let me backtrack just a bit."

"Take all the time you need, Annie," Bradley told her. "I'm on your schedule."

Annie nodded. "Rick and Elizabeth fell in love in high school, and they were crazy about each other. They planned to get married during their second year in college. Mother got a scholarship to attend Johns Hopkins University, in Baltimore. She wanted to do research on ways to prevent heart attacks. Now, she chose that as her field because her mother, Annie Meadows, after whom I was named, died when Elizabeth was ten years old. Mother majored in bio-molecular engineering and was absolutely driven to succeed.

"Daddy had many offers for scholarships to play football, but he wanted to teach in college, so he turned them down and went to SMU so he could live at home, this house we're in right now."

"Our father was a star quarterback in high school, Ben," HA Bennett interjected.

"Yes, he was and, when they entered their second year in college, he asked Elizabeth to marry him, but she asked him to wait until a little longer, so she could dedicate herself to her studies. Rick agreed although he was disappointed. During her junior year at Johns Hopkins, Elizabeth went home for a weekend with her college roommate. The roommate's family owned a farm in Pennsylvania, and the family raised grass-fed beef using a new method of chemical-free soil production, called permaculture. Elizabeth became interested in that industry, and the family invited her to come and spend the summer with them. She would be working on the farm, learning how they accomplished the task of growing enough grass to raise large numbers of cattle on smaller acreage, by efficient management of the land."

"Elizabeth didn't come back to Dallas that whole summer, and when she and Rick finally got together, she asked him to wait until after she had finished her post-graduate work before they got married."

"I'm thinking that didn't set too well with your father," Bradley said.

"No, it didn't, and that brings me to that time I mentioned that they were apart. Rick was hurt, but he didn't give her an ultimatum. He told her he was going to leave her, because waiting for her to marry him was driving him crazy. He told her that if she ever got ready to marry him, he would be waiting for her. Well, according to my mother, she was devastated by that and told Rick that she would give it all up and marry him right then. But he wouldn't let her. He said that what she had to offer the world was too valuable for him to interfere with.

"Now, keep in mind, Ben, it's been over forty years since Harley and I first started hearing my mother's stories of our parent's lives, but I still read her book again from time to time. After that, they both got their master's degrees in their chosen fields. Dad got his in economics because he wanted to teach, but after he and Elizabeth parted, he just lost his ambition for it. He finished a book he'd started in college, but it was never as successful as Mother's was. Rick made a deal with the owner of a vineyard to buy it, owner financed, and he struggled to make it work until 2009."

"What happened in 2009?" Ben asked.

"She'll get to that, Ben," Harley said, chuckling.

"Elizabeth had written a book about her experiences working on the farm in Pennsylvania and all she had learned about chemical free-soil preparation. The book was a smash hit and she made a lot of money from it. She began working for a company in Richmond Virginia, called SPCFF—they pronounced it Spiciff—which was an acronym for the Society for the Promotion of Chemical Free Food. She also started doing lectures, locally at first but later all over the country. It proved to be very lucrative.

"Mother was not afraid of work, and they had this van they travelled in. Often, they would stop at farms to visit with people, who had written, or called, the company with questions about the process. Sometimes they would help the farmers set up their property to do what they called the paddock rotation system of growing grass quickly and efficiently. My mother worked as hard as any of the men, despite her soft appearance."

"What was the name of her book, Annie?"

"She called it *My Summer in the Dirt*, and the sub-title was: *and other foreign matter*, which I assumed she meant cow shit."

Ben started laughing at the older woman's abrasive honesty.

"Now, Annie," HA said, "remember, we don't know Mister Bradley all that well."

"Don't worry about me, Harley," Ben told him, "I find your sister absolutely refreshing."

"So, that brings me to the best part, Ben," Annie said. "Elizabeth was on a lecture tour that ended in Austin, Texas, and some anonymous person had sent a ticket to the lecture to

Dad. They never found out who sent the ticket, but Elizabeth suspected it was a woman in Austin that Rick had slept with. She never told him about her suspicion, and Rick never confessed to it. But she told me that she believed he had.

"Rick went to that lecture and, to make a long story short, stood up during the question period and surprised Elizabeth. They had been apart for four years, and he asked her again to marry him. She kicked off her shoes and ran off the stage and jumped into his arms. They were married a few days later, and she left her life and came back into his. They lived happily ever after, had two babies—yours truly and my brother there in his easy chair. Their unbridled happiness lasted seven years until Elizabeth was asked by her publisher, and her former manager at the SPCFF company, to go on another lecture and book promotion tour. Rick was heartbroken, but he knew how much she wanted to do it, and he loved her so much that he always let her have her way.

"'Whatever makes you happy, Lizzy,' I heard him tell my mother a million times at least," Annie said.

Chapter 19

The Coming Storm

2016:

Market Place Square occupied the entire block encompassed by Crockett and Adams Streets and Main and Austin in Fredericksburg. Crockett and Adams formed the northwest/southeast border of the little park while Main and Austin were somewhat northeast and southwest. Fredericksburg was not laid out on a true north-south-east-west grid like many towns in West Texas. But leaving the downtown area, many neighborhoods did form an actual true directionally correct grid. It was almost as if, during construction of the town, somebody had a touch of wisdom, threw down his tools, and proclaimed loudly, "This is crazy, let's run the streets east and west, so people will know where the sun is supposed to come up and go down."

It might not have happened that way, but somewhere along the way, they changed the street layout in the town, and most folks were glad they did.

Harley Meadows discovered the Market Place Park one Saturday morning when he'd taken his grandkids, HA and Annie, downtown for the day.

In the center of the park area was an octagonal shaped building with, what Harley referred to as a cupola, although he wasn't sure that was the correct name. The building was white, and a sign outside identified it as Vereins Kirche Museum. Harley found a nearby bench and sat down while the two kids played nearby.

The warm afternoon sun shining through the leaves, of the surrounding trees, created shadows that danced all around the bench on which Harley sat, threatening to fall asleep. Additional voices jolted his eyes open, and he noticed two little girls playing in the same area where HA and Annie were playing a moment ago. HA was still there, but Annie was talking to an older man on another bench just across the area from him. Harley stood up and walked over to the bench to find out who his granddaughter was talking to. When Annie saw him, she motioned for him to come over.

"How are you, sir?" the man said. "I met your granddaughter at the vineyard when I went there to talk to the Bennetts about selling them some land I had."

"Oh, well that makes me feel better," Harley said, "I couldn't imagine who Annie was talking to."

"I can't blame you for being concerned, I would have been too. My name is Grimmer, Jack Grimmer, and I'm here doing the same thing you are, apparently. Have a seat, and we'll shoot the breeze."

"I'm Harley Meadows, and Elizabeth Bennett is my daughter. You've met her and my son-in-law, Rick?"

"Yes, I have. They bought twenty acres from me and, as far as I know, they are busying themselves with getting the ground ready to produce more grapes."

"They are," Harley said. "And I just moved in with them to help out with the kids and to get out of my other daughter's way in my house in Dallas. So, these two beautiful girls are your granddaughters?"

"They are. The one over there—" Jack pointed at one of the girls. "—that's Juniper Grace. And the other one is Ava Fe."

"Are they twins?" Harley asked him.

"No, they're cousins, Juniper is my son Seth's daughter, and Ava is my son Isaac's daughter. Isaac should be along any minute now to pick up Ava. You can meet him. He has a wine-touring business. He just made his first stop at the Lizzy Bee this past week."

"I look forward to meeting him," Harley said. "In the meantime, what can you tell me about this little building here? I've been studying it since I sat down here."

"This is the Vereins Kirche, which means People's Church in German. It is the oldest building in Fredericksburg. It was built not long after the arrival of the German settlers. The Vereins Kirche was the first public building in Fredericksburg and served as the town hall, school, fort, and as a church for all denominations."

"It looks to be in pretty good shape for such an old building," Harley commented, "I suppose they remodel it from time to time."

"It was built originally in 1847, torn down in 1897, and rebuilt in 1935, using the cornerstone from the original building. Each of the eight sides is eighteen feet wide and eighteen feet high, and the cupola is seven feet high," Grimmer told him. "And they do take very good care of the place. Fredericksburg is rich in German ancestry, and they take pride in their history and their architecture."

"I'm impressed, Jack," Harley said. "You know so much about the town."

"Well, I've lived here thirty years or so. You can't help but pick up loose bits of information if you keep your eyes and ears open."

"I grew up in Dallas, and I've heard of Fredericksburg, but I just never had any reason to come down this way until my daughter wound up here with her husband."

"I grew up in Arlington, Harley, went to Arlington High School, probably a little ahead of your time."

"Arlington, really? Well, it is a small world, like they say. My son-in-law Rick is from California, if you can believe that."

"I'll believe anything you tell me, Harley. They both seem like nice kids, a little out of their element it seems to me. Don't get me wrong, they are both very smart, they just seem kind of young to be taking on so much at this point in their lives."

"I've thought the same thing, but I wouldn't tell them that. They wouldn't listen to me if I did, anyway."

"I can certainly relate to that," Grimmer said. "Oh, here comes my boy, Isaac." He motioned for his son to come over to where they were. Ava saw him and ran to him, and he scooped her up and brought her to the bench where his dad and Harley were siting.

"Isaac, you remember the lady at the Lizzy Bee Vineyard, just out of town on Two-Ninety East?"

"Oh, my god, yes, how could I forget her?" Isaac began.

"Okay, before you put your foot any farther in your mouth, I'd like you to meet her father."

Isaac smiled sheepishly. "I was about to comment on how smart she is. I mean the way she conducted the tour with my first group was just brilliant."

"I had a feeling that was what he was going to say, Jack," Harley said, and both men started laughing.

Isaac took his daughter and left, while the two older men were still chuckling.

"I guess you get that a lot, don't you, Harley?"

"She used to almost get me in fights, Jack, but it wasn't her looks as much as her personality. I swear that girl was one obnoxious female when she was younger. I guess I'm lucky she found the only man in the world who was a perfect match for her."

"He's a very likable man," Grimmer said, "but he does give her some latitude. She's very knowledgeable about everything I had to discuss with them, and he let her go. He doesn't seem threatened by her intelligence at all."

"He's not," Harley said. "Rick is just as smart as my daughter is. He's just so crazy about her that whatever she wants, or wants to do, he's okay with it. I gotta tell you, Jack, when Lizzy went through her battle with cancer, Rick was as solid as a rock. After her health coach left, he helped her, did her exercises with her, prepared her food and fruit drinks for her. It helped me just knowing he was with her. I've got two really good sons-in-laws."

"You're a lucky man, Harley. A father's nightmare is to have his daughter married to a real shithead," Grimmer said. "Where is your other daughter?"

"Rose is in Dallas with her husband, Bobby Gladwyn. He's an ex-football player, played for the Saints. They don't have any kids yet, but I'm hoping soon they will. Rick and Bobby were teammates in high school."

"Really, Rick was a football player before he got into the winery business?"

"He was a star quarterback for William B Travis in 2002, took them to the state championship. Bobby was his primary receiver."

"I vaguely remember that, but I'm not a big football fanatic. He didn't get a scholarship to play football?"

"Rick had a lot of offers, but he turned them down to go to SMU. He wanted to teach economics in college. He has a BS degree, but he never got a teaching job. He bought the vineyard instead."

"I'd like to hear more, Harley, but I have to get this little one back home to her mother. Why don't we meet for lunch, maybe once a week somewhere and just talk?"

"I'd enjoy that, Jack. I'll give you my cell phone number, and I'll get yours so we can coordinate. You just tell me when and where and I'll be there."

"I don't have a cell phone, but I'll give you my home number. If I don't answer, just leave a message, and I'll call you back."

"You look like you're in pretty good spirits, Daddy," Elizabeth told him when he got back to the house. "How were the kids?"

"The kids were great," Harley said. "I took them to the little park on Main Street. And I met a friend."

"A woman?"

"No, silly, I ran into the man who sold you the land, Jack Grimmer. He was in the park with his two granddaughters, and we had a nice long talk. He's somewhat of a historian on Fredericksburg, apparently, being of German ancestry I assume by the name."

"Oh, Daddy, I think that's wonderful. I'm glad you found someone to talk to."

"We're going to meet for lunch or maybe breakfast once a week or so and just shoot the shit, oops, excuse me," he said, looking around to make sure the kids were not in earshot.

"I've thought a lot about your suggestion that I write a book about our family, Daddy," Elizabeth said. "I just can't convince myself that anyone would be interested in it."

"Would you write it as a work of fiction or like an autobi-ography?" Harley asked.

"I don't know, if I write it as fiction, then it would have to have a conclusion. I can't write a family saga because our saga has barely begun."

"Well, that's a good point, Lizzy, but you could write all that's happened up until now and fill in the rest as it happens. Wouldn't that work?"

"Maybe, but I really don't know if I'm that good a writer. The first book was successful, but it was about my field of expertise, and my passion, permaculture. The lectures helped sell the book. I just don't know. I need to discuss it with Rick, I suppose."

"Rick is your number one cheerleader, and then me. Be-tween the two of us, we'll keep you encouraged."

"I'll need it," she said and hugged him.

Whether it be called fate, coincidence, providence, or just blind luck, life occasionally throws a curve, unexpected, some-times unwanted and misunderstood, but always with the ability to change and redirect the present and the future and bring back the past.

Life threw Elizabeth a curve one morning, a couple of weeks before the turn of the new year in 2017. She was sitting at the dining room table, eating a bowl of cereal, when her cell phone rang.

"Hello, this is Elizabeth," she said.

A half hour later, Rick walked into the room.

Elizabeth put the phone down just as Rick sat down at the table. She stared at him until he spoke.

"Who was that?" he asked.

She hesitated for a moment.

"What, you don't want to tell me?"

"I'm processing it," she said.

"Who was on the phone, Lizzy?" he asked, growing uneasy.

"Corley McKnight."

"Aw, hell, Elizabeth. I thought that chapter of our lives was over. What did he want?"

"The publisher of my book is doing a third printing. They want to change the cover and put my picture on it this time."

"Oh, well that's no big deal. I don't blame them for putting your picture on the book. I never understood why they didn't have your face on it in the first place."

"I explained that to you. The chemical-free soil industry was a bit controversial back then, and they wanted to protect me from any possible harassment."

"I never bought into that theory," he said.

"Well, I guess they've decided that it's no longer a concern because they want me on the back cover."

"Then I'm okay with it," he said.

"There's more," she said.

"What?

"They want me to go on a lecture tour."

Her words fell on him like a cloud of doom, weighing him down, drawing the life out of him. He sat there as if in a stupor, staring at her, unable to speak.

"Please say something Rick," she implored him.

The cold winds of January were whistling around the edge of the house. Rick felt a shiver run up his spine. Although it was toasty warm in the house, he suddenly felt cold.

"You're shaking," she said.

"I'm cold," he replied. "It's cold in here."

"The heat is on, darling, it's not cold in the house. Are you getting sick?"

"No," he said, "I just had a sudden chill."

"Please talk to me, Rick," she said again.

"What is there to say, Elizabeth?

"What do you want me to do?"

"Does it matter what I want?"

"Of course, it matters what you want, Rick. You know it does," she said.

"I don't want you to go, baby."

She sat there for several minutes while he just gazed down at the table. Finally, she spoke. "Okay, darling, I won't go." Then she got up, went into their bedroom, and closed the door.

Amanda came out of the office to get a soft drink out of the fridge. Seeing her brother sitting at the table, looking down as if his world had just fallen apart, she walked over and put her hand on his shoulder. "Is everything alright, Rick?" she asked him.

"No," was all he said.

"Where is Elizabeth?"

"In the bedroom," he said, pointing in that direction.

She went to the door of their bedroom and knocked. Elizabeth opened the door.

"Can I come in, Elizabeth?"

The door opened, Amanda walked in, and the door closed behind her. She came out in a few minutes and went back to the office without saying anything to Rick.

They slept back to back that night with only the obligatory goodnight kiss and no further interaction between them. She lay awake for an hour or so after he had drifted off to sleep. She wanted him to make love to her but was afraid if she asked, he would say no, or worse would not say anything.

He was up early and out of the house before she awoke. She could hear her dad talking to Amanda and realized she had slept past eight. Amanda always started work at eight o'clock every morning. Elizabeth got up, went to the shower, put on sweat pants and a shirt, then went out to do her daily exercise routines.

"I have some checks that need to be signed, Elizabeth," Amanda said. She was polite but curt.

"Okay," she said, "I'll be there in just a minute."

Harley was getting ready to leave, and Elizabeth was curious about where he was going.

"You're not taking the kids are you, Daddy?"

"No, honey," he said, "I'm meeting Jack Grimmer for breakfast."

The Old German Bakery and Restaurant was located on Main Street in Fredericksburg, as it seemed was most everything else. Harley found Jack waiting outside, and they went into the restaurant. After a short wait, they were seated at a table near the window.

"What do you recommend, Jack?" Harley asked.

"I like the German pancakes," Grimmer said.

"The prices are reasonable," Harley said

"Yes, and the food is even better."

"I've been studying up on the history of Fredericksburg," Harley announced.

"Really?" Grimmer replied. "What have you learned?"

"The town was founded by a fella named John O. Meusbach who was originally a German baron with about six or eight names, but eventually he renounced his nobility and started going by that name. He made peace with the Comanche Indians and established a treaty between them and the settlers."

"You're right, Harley, good work. He founded a few other towns too, but I can't remember their names. They're not as big or as well-known as Fredericksburg."

"I also read that the Vereins Kirche, People's Church, was often referred to as the Kaffeemuhle," Harley said, butchering the pronunciation. "It looks like a coffee mill, they claimed."

"Kaffeemuhle," Jack repeated the word with a much better German tilt to it. "I had forgotten that, Harley, thanks for reminding me."

The place was always busy, and people were waiting for tables, so they paid their tab and left, vowing to meet the following week again for breakfast.

The tension in the Bennett house was noticeably oppressive. Harley Meadows had never seen his daughter and son-in-law at odds with each other. There was no arguing or yelling. Neither of them raised their voice to the other, but even the children sensed that something was wrong and soon grew uneasy and insecure. Harley sat down on the floor and played with them more than usual, but nothing could distract their attention from the obvious trouble brewing between their parents.

For the children of parents who were always hugging each other, teasing, kissing, and playing around the house, and now ignoring each other completely, it was very traumatic. The two kids were confused and in a state of emotional turmoil.

Three days after Elizabeth told him about the lecture tour, they had barely spoken to each other. Their nights consisted of a goodnight kiss and maintaining a space in the bed between them. Elizabeth was on the verge of falling into deep depression. Rick Bennett was the love of her life. She didn't want to hurt him. Had she misjudged how he would react to her embarking on another lecture tour? Apparently, she had.

She was sitting on the side of their bed, crying, when he walked into the room. She tried to wipe the tears from her eyes, before he noticed, but he walked over next to her and took her hand. Gently, he lifted her to a standing position and took her in his arms. He kissed her passionately and with such emotion that she was shocked and only realized after a moment what was happening. She returned his passion with her own and then just looked at him in confusion after he stopped.

"Is this something you have to do or is it something you want to do, Elizabeth?"

"I want to do it, Rick," she said. "I hope you can understand and forgive me, but I really want to do it."

"How long will you be gone?"

"They want me to do two lectures a month and some book signings and promotions in between. It's a one-year project."

"When will I see you again?"

"They'll fly me into San Antonio once a month, furnish me a rental car, and I'll stay home a week then fly back to Richmond."

"Okay, baby, if this is what you want to do, I'll be here when you come back."

"Will you make love to me, Rick?" she asked him after they had gotten into bed later that night.

"No," he said, "you need to be punished."

"Are you serious?" she said, pouting.

"No," he said, as he pulled her to him and buried his face in her neck. She squealed and kicked her legs like a teenager.

On January twenty-first, the day after Inauguration Day in Washington, Rick drove Elizabeth to San Antonio Airport and watched her board the plane for her flight to Richmond Virginia.

It would be their first time apart since they had been married. It brought back memories that Rick never wanted to recall again.

Chapter 20

The Deep Rolling Hills

The SPCFF office was a vortex of activity. People seem to be in a constant state of flux, doors were being opened and closed, people entering and exiting. Phones were ringing, and voices mixed together in an uninterruptable drone. The drone became just white noise, if one ignored it long enough, and did not attempt to make sense of it all.

Attention was on Corley McKnight's latest coup, Elizabeth Bennett. He had brought her out of her self-imposed retirement, brought her back to him in a last-ditch effort to save his business and his sanity. When the call came from Earth Publishing, asking Corley to organize a lecture and book signing tour for Elizabeth Bennett to promote the third printing of her book *My Summer in the Dirt,* Corley was ecstatic. He'd begged her to come back, her initial response being a resounding, No!

In the seven years since Elizabeth had left the company, Corley had gone broke. Beth Ann Meadows, as she was known when she worked for him and traveled the country speaking on the benefits of chemical free food, grass-fed beef, and soil preparation had virtually built his company for him. She made him rich and, when she left him suddenly, to run off and marry this love of her life, it ruined his life, and it ruined his business.

Now the publisher had agreed to advance him the money to start the project, contingent on his bringing Elizabeth into the fold. Corley had leveled with her and begged her to come and help him save his company. Elizabeth had kept that bit of information from her husband, thinking that he would not be sympathetic to Corley. The one time he met Corley, Rick took an instant dislike for him, although for Elizabeth's sake, he remained cordial until the man had left the vineyard.

"That man has the hots for you," he told her.

She disagreed with his assessment of Corley, but Rick was adamant about it.

"I've seen the way he looks at you when he thinks nobody is looking."

Now she was back in his office. "I'm getting a lot of attention, Corley," she said. "People keep asking me if I need anything, a coke or coffee, or anything else. It's starting to become annoying."

"I hired extra people just to keep you happy when you're in the office."

"Oh my, you're going to have to knock this off. I don't require such treatment," she said.

"But you're the star, Elizabeth," he said. "You were always the star. You made this company. We've got events booked solid for the whole year for you. We could conceivably book you for five years if you'd agree to do it."

"And ruin my marriage? There is no way I'm going to do that, Corley."

"You should have married me, Elizabeth," he said. "We would be millionaires by now."

"I hope you're joking, Corley," she said, looking at him sternly.

"I'm just joking," he said, laughing. "I was just thinking of the possibilities. Anyway, I have your schedule for the rest of January."

"What happened to Jerry?" she asked.

"When things got tough, I couldn't pay him what he was worth, so he moved on. I'm sure he'd come back if he knew you were here, but I don't know where he is. I no longer have the RV. I had to sell it. Peggy Boyd is still with me, and she'll go along to drive you to the events. We have a van. It's comfortable, and you guys will stay in hotels. You may stop at farms on the way, like you used to, but I don't want you working your asses off, rebuilding their fences, and restructuring their paddocks, like you did before. Just give them advice, nothing else."

"That's kind of a relief," Elizabeth said. "Oh, I didn't mind the work, neither did Jerry and Peggy, but those farmers fed us so much. I thought I was going to get as fat as a waterbed."

"Oh wow, that's funny," Corley said.

"That was one of Jerry Meisner's lines, I just borrowed it from him."

"You have a lecture on Friday in Alexandria. Three-thousand tickets have been sold, and there will probably be a thousand more by show time. These things have been highly promoted, and many of them have been booked for months."

"I've been staying in a hotel the last few days," Elizabeth said. "Where shall I plan on staying permanently when I'm in Richmond?"

"We have a couple of options," he replied. "I have a guest room at my house. It's a big house, and you'll have the full use of the whole house, if you want to—"

"I'm not staying with you, Corley. You should know better than to even ask that."

"I was just thinking of your comfort, Elizabeth."

"What's your alternative plan?"

"I can put you up at the Residence Inn."

"That will be fine," she said. "I'll check out for the time I leave and go home every month."

"I think if we rent it monthly, that won't be necessary. The cost will not be much different. You'll be able to leave anything you want to leave in your unit."

"That would certainly be easier," she said.

"Peggy will drive you to Alexandria in time for the event, and then you can come back after."

Elizabeth nodded. "I'll be updating my power-point program until Friday. I've added some stuff about the permaculture activity in the Texas Hill Country."

"Good," Corley said. "I look forward to seeing it."

That afternoon, Peggy Boyd walked into Elizabeth's office. They had not seen each other since she, Corley, and Jerry

Meisner visited the Vineyard in 2012. Both women hugged each other lovingly. When they let go of each other, Peggy was crying.

"I'm so glad to see you back here, Beth," she said. "It's like a dream come true."

"I'm happy to see you too, Peggy. It's been four years since you guys came to see me and seven years since I did a lecture. I'm hoping I can still perform."

"Oh, you'll be fine, you know you will. You'll knock 'em dead."

"Well, I hope not, that wouldn't look good on my résumé."

"Cute. I'm going to be your duty driver while you're here. Anyplace you need to go, day or night, just give me a call, and I'll come get you."

"I don't anticipate I'll be going anywhere at night. There are some restaurants pretty close, and I'll go to the grocery store during the day, so you can give me a ride, but I'll be working at night on my presentations and my books."

The event was taking place in an auditorium in downtown Alexandria. It was a hundred and four miles from Richmond to Alexandria, so they left Richmond around four, and Elizabeth and Peggy arrived in Alexandria around six o'clock for an eight o'clock starting time. Two people, a young man and a young woman, from Earth Publishing company were there already setting up a stand and stocking the shelves with Elizabeth's book. Some people were passing by, and a few were checking out the books, but no sales had been made at that time.

Elizabeth walked outside the building and called Rick. He sounded happy to hear from her. "Hey, baby, where are you?"

"I'm in Alexandria, Virginia, darling, about to do my first lecture. I just wanted to hear your voice and see how you and the kids are doing."

"We're all okay, Lizzy," he said. "Harley took the kids to the park. I'll have to tell them you called. Are you nervous?"

"A little, but I'll be okay. Don't worry about me."

"Is Jerry there to look out for you?"

"No, Jerry is no longer with the company. You remember

Peggy Boyd, the lady who came to the house with Jerry and Corley four years ago? She's my assistant and driver."

"Oh, well, I'd be more comfortable knowing Jerry Meisner was there, but I guess you'll be okay."

"I'll be back in Richmond tonight, and I'll call you and tell you how it went. But I have to go and start setting up my Power Point program. "I love you, Rick."

"I love you too, Lizzy, and I miss you."

Elizabeth was checking herself in the full-length mirror in her dressing room backstage. Peggy was putting the final comb to her hair. "How do I look, Peg?" she asked her.

"You're stunning, peaches," Peggy said. "If I were a man, I'd do you right here on the floor."

Elizabeth laughed. "Well, thank goodness you're not a man, or we'd be late for the show. And what's with the *peaches* thing, are your channeling Jerry?"

"Jerry called you that so much that, after he left, everyone just sort of adopted it. We started referring to you as peaches. New people who came in didn't even know your real name."

Elizabeth chuckled and shook her head. "Okay, here we go," she said, as she walked out through the side tunnel onto the stage and approached the podium.

The applause was deafening for several minutes. She stood there smiling and waving as four thousand attendees welcomed her in expectant anticipation of, they knew not what. Most had only word-of-mouth acclaim of Beth Ann Meadows, the name she had formerly toured under and the name on the original book.

Now the lady standing at the podium was identified as Elizabeth Meadows Bennett and the next two hours would prove, beyond all doubt, that she was still possessed the skill and the magic that had won her fame and success as a writer and speaker, and the beauty and personality that melted men's hearts.

It all came back to her, every word, every fact. She delivered the address as if she had never stopped lecturing. It was like her seven-year hiatus had never happened. On the ride, back to Richmond, Elizabeth was full of herself. "I had forgotten how much I loved this, Peg."

"You were good, Beth. It was amazing, absolutely amazing," Peggy said.

"I can't wait to get back to my room and call Rick. My gosh, it just seemed so natural to be doing it again. I wish he could have been here to see it."

"I can probably get some news video that you can send him."

"Oh, Peggy, that would be wonderful if you could do that, thank you."

The kids were asleep by the time Elizabeth got back to her room and called home. She told Rick all about her first lecture, and her excitement was not lost on him.

"I hope you don't get to having so much fun that you don't want to come home," he said.

She assured him that would not happen but the excitement in her voice, he perceived as being more for her new pursuit than for her anticipation of her next trip home.

"Okay, baby, I'll see you when you get home, come when you can."

Their next assignment was in Baltimore to a similar-sized crowd. Elizabeth's performance was no less brilliant than the Alexandria event, and the audience approval as enthusiastic, if not more so. Elizabeth spent an hour signing books after the main event. A couple hundred people waited in line to have their book signed and to offer comments to her. Most were complimentary of her performance, but not a small number of them—all men—told her how good she looked. One man asked her out.

"I'm married," she said, "but thank you."

He had the good sense not to pursue the matter. After it was over, Elizabeth put their things back in the van, and Peggy drove toward the Baltimore Washington Parkway.

"We can get a room, Beth, unless you want to get back home tonight."

"I can help you drive, Peg, if you feel up to making the trip back tonight."

"Are you hungry?" Peggy asked.

"Yes, as a matter of fact, I am. Let's find a place to grab a bite."

Peggy had missed her turn to the BW Parkway and was driving down Ritchie Highway, in Glen Burnie. She slowed down suddenly.

"There's a Denny's off to the right. It's not a four-star, but they're open twenty-four hours. You want to try that?"

"Denny's is fine," Elizabeth said, so Peggy pulled into the parking lot.

As they were walking toward the door of the restaurant, three men got out of a car that had been parked in a darkened area on the other side of the lot. They approached the two women, who quickened their steps, in an attempt to avoid them.

The three men, two whites and one black man, rushed to intercept them before they could get inside the restaurant. They were menacing, with torn Levis and dark hoodies, although the hoods were not pulled up over their heads. They were making no effort to conceal their faces.

"Hold up there a minute, foxy," the taller, dark-haired man yelled at Elizabeth. "You are way too fine to be out this late at night without a man. Imo look out for you tonight just to make sure nobody tries anything witchu. And all it's gonna cost you is a tap of that sweet ass. Whatcha say, Mama? Sound like a fair trade to you?"

"Get the fuck out of here, you scumbag," Peggy yelled at the man.

He just looked at her and sneered. "Now calm down, baby, I'm not gonna hurt your girlfriend, but I gotta have a slice of that, if you know what I mean. Don't worry, my man, Lamont, here will take care of you. Ain't nuthin he likes better than a fat white chick. You'll like Lamont, he got a big one, if you catch my drift."

"I catch your drift, all right, and you'd better catch mine. I'll say this one more time, you get your ugly head, your other moron, and Lamont and his big dick back in your car and get the fuck out of here, if you know what's good for you."

"Oh, she's a feisty one, ain't she Lamont. I bet you got a boner for her now."

"Yeah, I do," Lamont said. "Whatchu gonna do, bitch, if we *don't* get the fuck outa here?"

Peggy pulled up her sweatshirt, removed a .380 pistol from a waistband holster, and pointed it at the first man who had threatened Elizabeth. The men drew back when they saw the gun, but they didn't run.

She spoke to Lamont but kept the weapon pointed at the first man. "I'm going to shoot this asshole in the head, then I'm going to shoot you in the dick." Then she spoke to the third man who, heretofore, had remained silent. "You can leave, if you're smart, and I won't shoot you."

The man turned and started walking back toward the car from which the three of them had exited.

"Make up your feeble minds," she yelled at them again.

"You could get in trouble for carrying a gun in Maryland," the first man yelled at her. "You could go to jail for that."

"That won't bring you back from the dead," Peggy said, as she extended the gun toward him.

"All right, come on Lamont, I don't want to do it with a couple of lesbians, anyway."

"Do we look like lesbians?" Elizabeth asked Peggy after they had finished their meal.

"I might," Peggy replied, "but I'm not. I love men. I was crazy about Jerry Meisner, but he wouldn't touch me. But you, you're probably going to get me in a lot of fights before this tour is over."

"I had no idea you had a gun on you. I can't tell you how relieved I was when you whipped that thing out. Is it legal to carry a gun in Maryland?"

"I have a concealed handgun license in Maryland and Virginia. Corley paid for the training and expense for me to get it when he knew you were coming. He thought that, since Jerry would not be with us to protect you, I should be able to. Turns out it was a good decision."

"Why wouldn't Jerry make love to you?"

"He said he would have, but it turned out he was married, and apparently very happily married. I met his wife, right before he left the company. She was a good-looking woman. Still, it looks like he could have given me a mercy fuck just for old-time's sake. I mean, we had been pretty good friends all the time we worked together."

"Maybe we should spend the night somewhere, Peg. You have to be tired by now, I know I am, and it's a long drive to Richmond."

"There's a La Quinta just across the street. Why don't we stay there?"

"That sounds like a good idea," Elizabeth said.

Elizabeth was vaguely aware of activity in the hall outside her room. One glance at the other bed in the room told her that Peggy had already gotten up and was puttering around in the bathroom.

"Get up Beth," Peggy called to her. "They have a great breakfast buffet. I went and looked but didn't eat yet because I wanted to wait on you."

"I have to shower," Elizabeth said, "but I'll be quick." A half hour later, she had dressed and was finishing blow-drying her hair. "Let's go, Peg," she said.

The breakfast area was clearing out now, businessmen and travelling salesmen had gotten up early to partake of the complimentary fare and were quickly off to their meetings or sales calls or to whatever purpose their travels had brought them to Baltimore. The attractive blonde-haired woman, in sweat pants and a T-shirt, did not go unnoticed to the few remaining men in the place. Eyes followed her every step as she made her selections for breakfast. Peggy was already at the table eating when Elizabeth sat down.

Several men at another table laughed at something one of them had said as they all watched Elizabeth walk back to her table. She didn't bother guessing what evoked the laughter—some crude joke no doubt. She had gotten accustomed to such nonsense. Men away from home seemed to have a way of reverting back to their basic animal instincts. Not all men were like Rick Bennett, she kept telling herself every time some guy whistled at her or made some stupid remark.

She was afraid last night when the three thugs approached them, very afraid. *Thank God for Peggy and her handgun*, she thought. *What would we have done had Peggy, and Corley, not had the foresight to be prepared for just such an event. And thank goodness, the men were cowards and didn't have guns on them. Peggy and I could have been killed or raped then killed. We have to be more careful and more aware of where we go and at what time of the night we decide to stop for dinner.*

She took the next day off and just hung out around her apartment. She talked to Rick and the kids, but she didn't tell him about the incident. "We stayed at a La Quinta Inn last night and ate breakfast then drove back this morning."

"How did the lecture go?" Rick asked her.

"It went very well. I'm really good at this," she said and chuckled on the phone.

"I know you are baby, that's what scares me," Rick said.

"Why would that scare you, darling?"

"I'm afraid you might not want to give it up this time."

"You're the love of my life, Rick. I have nowhere else to go but back to you. I can make enough money this year to pay off the bank note for the land we bought. That's why I'm doing this."

"Oh, well, now you've got my attention. I just miss you, baby, this place is not a home without you. But if you can pay off the loan for the new ground, then you have my blessing."

"You are such a capitalist," she told him.

"Well, if I have to be away from you, there ought to be some money in it for me."

"Come and see me for the weekend. Dad and Amanda can take care of the kids, I need you, Rick."

"Do they have an airport in Richmond?"

"They do, can you believe it?" she said, laughing. "You'll have to rent a car. Peggy Boyd is my driver, but I don't want to put her out on the weekend."

"Okay, Lizzy, I'll be there sometime on Friday. I'll call you from the airport."

Elizabeth's cell phone was alerting her. It was Rick's ring tone, "California Dreaming." She answered quickly. "Hello, my darling, please tell me you're in Virginia."

"I am in Virginia, baby, now tell me how to get the part of Virginia that has you in it."

"Okay, you come into Richmond on Interstate Sixty-Four, all the way through town until you get to West Broad Street. Then at West Broad Street, turn left, that's kind of south, and you go a few blocks to Dickens Road and turn left again. Residence Inn is on the right, and you have my unit number."

When she heard the knock on her door, she checked the peep hole, to make sure it was Rick, and then opened the door. She was standing there in her panties and a tee-shirt that she had cut to fit just below her breasts.

"Now what if I had been here to fix the TV, lady," he said.

"You would have to fix me first, stud," she said and jumped into his arms.

They kissed like they had not been together for years. He lifted her into his arms and carried her into the bedroom. She had already turned back the covers in anticipation of his arrival. He laid her down on the bed, removed his clothing, and got in beside her. "I don't think I could have lived much longer without you," he whispered in her ear, as he took her in his arms.

Their ardor assuaged, she lay her head on his chest, and he caressed her arms and nuzzled her hair, breathing in her smell and beauty.

"When is your year up?" he asked her.

She began laughing. "I've only been here a month, honey, I've done two lectures and two book signings. My schedule prevented my coming home this month, but I had to see you. I promise I'll come home next month. I want to see the kids too."

"I hope you do. This could turn out to be one of those deals in which your schedule keeps you from coming home a lot."

"I don't think so, Rick. Corley was very clear about that, and I was too. He assured me that I could take a three-day weekend a month to go home."

"Three-day weekend, what happened to the one-week a month deal?"

"I'm afraid the schedule just won't allow it, Rick. We have to conform to when the facilities are available. There is a lot that goes into making it all happen. I'm sorry, I didn't know at the time. I hope you understand."

"Just promise me one thing, Elizabeth."

"Of course, what's that?"

"The first-time Corley tries to get you in bed, you'll quit right then."

"You've got Corley wrong, Rick. He's not going to do that. He's never done anything that made me think he had any feeling toward me like that."

"Just promise me that, baby."

"I promise, Rick, of course, I promise you that. Now, will you make love to me again?"

"Right now?" he said.

"I want to get my money's worth," she replied, smiling at him mischievously.

"I think you're trying to kill me, Lizzy."

"If I do, I promise to kiss you back to life, darling."

"Then it would be worth it. Come here," he said and pulled her to him.

They slept for several hours, after that, and then showered together. "I made reservations for dinner tonight. I'm taking you out," she said."

"So, where are we going?"

"We are going to Ruth's Chris Steak House, sir."

"I am impressed, ma'am. What time do we have to be there?"

"The reservation is for eight o'clock. I don't know how far away it is, but I have the address. I'll pull it up on the GPS on my phone." She tapped some numbers into the phone, quickly. "About twenty minutes it says, so let's leave about seven-thirty."

"So, you don't have a car here to get around in? I thought you told me they would furnish you a car."

"Corley is struggling to get back on his feet, so he has put Peggy Boyd at my disposal. She takes me to the grocery store and anywhere else I need to go. She picks me up in the morning to take me to the office and brings me back in the evening. I really don't need a car, Rick."

"That's not the point, baby. He's already starting to slough off on a very important promise he made. What if he tells you one month that he can't pay you?"

"No, my publisher is guaranteeing my commission agreement and the royalties on my book sales. There are folks from Earth Publishing at every event, managing the gate and the book sales. Corley is only involved because he put them in contact with me and the book in the first place, and he's a good event-planner."

"I'm telling you, Elizabeth, I don't trust that guy. He's going to either try to get in your pants or cheat you out of money."

"I can take care of myself, Rick. You are the only man who has ever 'been in my pants.'" She made finger signs for quotation marks. "And you are the only man who will ever get in my pants. I am not going to let Corley McKnight anywhere near my pants or my money. Do you understand that?"

"Yes, I think I understand that," he said, chuckling at her intensity.

The restaurant was extremely busy, but their table was set and waiting for them when they arrived. The waiter came, brought them water, a couple of wine glasses, and the wine list. A few minutes later, he returned with the menu and recommended a few items from it. Rick pored over the selections for quite some time.

"This is kind of pricey, Lizzy, are you sure you want to spend this much money?"

"Well, we're not going to walk out now. Besides, I have an expense account. Relax, darling, I Googled the place and checked the menu before I made a reservation. I knew what to expect. I've heard they have the best steaks anywhere."

"You sure you don't want me to pay for it?" he asked her.

"Oh, you're going to pay for it later, stud."

"What you have in mind is very easy work, baby, for what this is going to cost."

"I'm just happy you came to see me," she said.

"I am too, and later tonight, I'll do my best to make you happier I came to see you."

She smiled and held her water glass up for him to clink with his, as a toast. "I'm going to have the Ribeye Oscar," Elizabeth told the waiter, "with mashed potatoes and asparagus, and I'll have the steak house salad to start."

"Very good, madam," the waiter replied and looked at Rick.

"Give me the Bone-in Filet with mushrooms, mashed potatoes, and asparagus just like my wife is having, but I want to try the chopped salad."

"Thank you, sir," the man said, and he took their menus.

"I hope this is grass-fed beef," Elizabeth said.

Rick laughed. "Do you ever take off work?"

"I never forget how far we've come from letting TV commercials determine how we live and what we eat."

"But what do we do while you're gone? Lizzy, you are our caretaker. Your dad fixes Italian food every night, and now he's into German food. He suddenly thinks he's German. I have to take the kids to Whataburger to ensure they get a non-fattening meal. I may not live until you get back home."

"I'll talk to Daddy. He has all my recipe books there. He can cook meals like I do. You just have to insist he do it."

"We're talking about your dad, you know, Harley Meadows."

"I know," she said nodding her head and chuckling, "I'll talk to him."

They made love again that night, almost desperate love, as if they both believed they would be apart for a very long time. He held her close and kissed her, passionately. "You're an amazing woman," he said. "There can't be another woman like you anywhere in this world."

She laughed at his melodrama. "Most men in love think that about the woman they love, don't you think?"

"I don't know what other men think. I know that I can make love with you and then fall asleep and dream about making love with you."

"Maybe that's why I have a hard time getting to sleep sometimes," she said.

"No, it's more likely from thinking about grass-fed beef."

She laughed and threw her pillow at him.

She fixed a meal for them the night before he left to go back home. Rick opened a bottle of wine, he'd brought with him from the vineyard. After dinner, they sat on the couch and watched a movie. Elizabeth brought a bowl of grapes and set it on the coffee table in front of him. He kissed her and then held up his wine glass, in a toast.

"What are we toasting, darling?" she asked him.

"Us," he said. "I'm proposing a toast to you and me. This is all I'll ever really need in life, baby, you and me, and two glasses of wine."

"That's all?" she said. "That's all you'll ever need?"

He thought for a moment and then reached for the grapes on the coffee table. "And a bowl full of grapes, maybe, just for an added touch."

As quickly as it had begun, their magic weekend was over. He kissed her goodbye, drove to the Richmond Airport, and flew back home.

"You seemed to be in good spirits," Peggy said as Elizabeth got into the passenger seat of the van. "If I didn't know better, Beth, I'd say you look like you got—"

"I did, Peg, several times."

Peggy looked askance at her.

"Rick came in for the weekend, he just flew out yesterday," Elizabeth told her.

"Oh, that's a relief. You had me worried there for a minute. I hope you got all caught up."

"I'll be good for a while," Elizabeth said and giggled.

"Well, judging by the way you're acting now, it looks like he got here right in the nick of time."

"It was a very pleasant weekend, is all I'm going to say."

At the office, Corley began hovering around Elizabeth with her schedule for the month in his hand. "We need to go over this when you get a minute, Beth." He said.

"Go easy on her, boss," Peggy told Corley. "Her husband paid her a visit this weekend, and she can't stop giggling."

The look on Corley's face was not lost on anyone in the office. It was like a slap up beside his head. Peggy noticed it immediately and made a mental note to discuss it with Elizabeth the next time they were on the road.

"You're going south for the next few months," Corley was saying. "Your first event is this Wednesday, and it's in Norfolk. I don't have all the dates set yet, but the cities are: Charlotte—"

"We went to Charlotte a few years back, I think," Elizabeth said.

"Yes, on your last tour, when Rick showed up in Austin and stole you away from me," Corley replied.

Elizabeth laughed, expecting Corley to laugh too, but, when she looked over at him, he was stone-faced.

My gosh, she thought, *he's still bitter about my leaving the company the way I did.*

"Then Atlanta, Charleston, South Carolina, Fayetteville, South Caroline, and Raleigh-Durham, North Carolina. That should keep you busy for the next three months."

Corley leaned over her desk as he showed her the schedule. His after-shave or cologne were pervasive, being applied much too liberally that particular morning, she decided. His hawkish features were deceptive. Corley was not a handsome man, but neither was he revolting. His dark brown hair and eyes, that almost looked black, were his best features. He walked with a practiced swagger, apparently intended to express confidence but, if it had been successful for him to that end, Elizabeth deemed that it was only mildly so.

She knew he had a *thing* for her, but she never acknowledged the attention he attempted to give her. She had only told her husband a little lie when she told him she thought he was wrong about Corley's feeling toward her. Elizabeth was convinced that Corley would never push his desire for her past the flirtation stage.

The green, rolling hills of Virginia had captured Elizabeth's attention as they made their way out of Petersburg, through La Crosse and Bracey, and across the Roanoke River into North Carolina.

"This is really beautiful country," she said.

Peggy nodded. "I grew up in the valley, Roanoke to be exact. You get accustomed to the scenery and eventually don't even notice it. I know Virginia is beautiful, North Carolina is even more beautiful, but people trying to work and make ends meet just don't have time to flip out over hills and trees. Happy, beautiful, people like you, Beth, always love the beauty of nature. Fat girls don't have time for it."

"Oh, come on, Peggy. I'm not going to come to your pity party any longer. You're not an ugly woman, Peg, and you're not fat. Just because that animal back in Baltimore called you fat, doesn't make you fat."

"I need to lose some weight, Beth, and I just haven't been able to do it."

"I'll help you," Elizabeth said, "with some diet suggestions and exercise routines. But it's not like you're obese. You remind me of the actress, Amy Schumer. Do you know who she is?"

"I don't watch movies very much," Peggy said.

"Well, she's an actress, blonde-hair, a little overweight but attractive. You have brown hair and eyes, but you're built like Amy Schumer."

"Then why can't I get a man, Beth?"

"It's the way you dress, Peg. You dress like a man. You need to upgrade your wardrobe."

"You think that will help, Beth?"

"I do," Elizabeth said. "When we get back home, we'll go shopping, and I'll help you pick out some more attractive clothes for you."

Peggy smiled and nodded. "There's a good bluegrass station in this area. I'm going to try and find it and get us some music, if you don't mind."

"If you must," Elizabeth said.

Peggy fumbled with the radio dial for a few minutes and, finally, the one she was looking for came into focus. The song that was just starting was, coincidentally, "The Deep Rolling Hills of old Virginia."

The song was a mournful tale of memories and heartbreak and the guy's mom and dad dying. Elizabeth listened as long as she could and the exclaimed, "Dear God, Peg, please turn that off before I start bawling."

Chapter 21

Annie

Anyway, as I was saying, Ben," Annie continued. "Rick just loved Mother so much that he would always let her have her way. It was like every day for him was their very first date in high school. I remember, many times, I'd be doing my homework at the dining room table, Elizabeth might be reading a book or working on her laptop, Rick would have the TV on, but he'd be staring at Elizabeth. He would watch her until she felt his eyes on her and looked up. She would smile at him and go right back to what she was doing."

"I've been meaning to ask you, Annie, why do you so often refer to your parents by their first names?" Ben asked.

"I'm not really sure, Ben, but HA has a theory about that."

"After mother's book was published—this was after Annie and I were grown, I was twenty-six and Annie was twenty-five. We were both married," Harley Bennett said, "Annie read the book, over and over. She still reads it again about once a year. It is my belief that she got so immersed in the story that she basically just forgot that Elizabeth and Rick were Mom and Dad. And she began calling them by their names. It's become second nature to her now."

"I see," Ben replied. "Well, I guess that's as good an explanation as any. It sure makes an interesting telling of the story. Go ahead and continue, Annie, I won't interrupt you again."

"Oh, that's okay, Ben, now, where was I? Oh, yes, Elizabeth had gone to Virginia to embark on a lecture tour. She discovered that she was still very good at what had made her 'famous.'" Annie held up two fingers on each hand to indicate quotation marks. "And she loved it, she really loved it. Nearing the end of her year-long contract agreement, however, her publisher told her they wanted her to continue the tours. Apparently, they were making a lot of money off Elizabeth's lectures. "Now, Harley, you tell Ben about the other thing that happened. I'm getting a little tired."

"What Annie is talking about, Ben, is this. Sometime, close to the end of Mother's first year on tour, something happened between her and Corley McKnight. It was very bad, and it haunted Mother the rest of her life. Growing up, we never knew all the details. But Dad went to Virginia and brought her home. We never learned what had really happened until the book came out years later. We know now, as do you, since you read her book."

"I do, Harley," Ben replied. "It must have been very hard for Elizabeth to have to live with that and still keep up a happy front for the customers."

"It was hard for her, but she did it," Annie said.

"The publisher took over all of Mother's lectures, the scheduling, paying the venues, and handling all the gate receipts. When Dad went to Virginia to get her, Mother didn't tell him about the new deal she had made with the publisher. She wanted to wait until their lives were less stressful. Corley had been skimming money from the publisher and from Elizabeth, but she ended up okay, financially.

"Truth be known, Rick would have preferred she give it all up completely and stay at home with him and us. But Mother had become an integral part of a rapidly growing movement that had gone far beyond the chemical-free soil concept of fruit and vegetable production and grass-fed beef. She was ready to take on Big-Pharma, Big Ag, and any other *Big* that got in her way."

Chapter 22

Betrayal

2018:

"I got whistled at today," Peggy Boyd said.

"Really," Elizabeth said, smiling at her, "tell me about it."

"It was outside the auditorium while we were getting ready for the show. I went out to the van to call and make sure our room reservation was still good. And while I was coming back into the building, this guy whistled at me. Of course, then he grabbed his crotch and shook it at me, when I smiled at him."

"Well, it's a start, Peg," Elizabeth said.

"Oh, it made me feel good, almost like a hottie. It would have been nicer, though, if the guy didn't look like he lived under a bridge."

Elizabeth chuckled. "You look nice, Peg, you really do. The wardrobe and hair change really make a difference. When we get you back home, you just need to get out and circulate a bit. Men will notice you, I guarantee it."

"As long as you're not with me, maybe."

They were in Fayetteville, North Carolina, for the next-to-last event before Elizabeth completed her one-year contract. About an hour before the start, a man approached her and identified himself as Stuart Pennington, with Earth Publishing. He handed her his business card. Elizabeth glanced at the card, and it did indeed confirm what he had told her.

"I'd like to meet with you—is it okay if I call you Elizabeth, or do you prefer Mrs. Bennett?"

"Elizabeth is fine, Stuart, if I can call you Stuart."

"Yes, of course, that would be fine. The reason I am here is that I need to talk to you about some future plans the company would like to work on with you."

"You mean after my one-year contract is up?"

"Yes, Elizabeth, in light of the past year and the success we have achieved—that is the success you have achieved—we want you to continue lecturing. And, I understand you've been working on another book."

"Yes," she said. "I'm expanding my field to shed more light on how the government's being in bed with Big Pharma and Big Agriculture—and any other mega-businesses that have strong lobbies in Congress—is subjecting Americans to risks of poor health an early death."

"Excellent," Pennington said, "that's the direction in which we'd like to go. So, I'd like to sit down and talk about this in greater depth. Could we have dinner, tonight, after your address?"

"That would be okay, but I usually have dinner with my assistant, Peggy Boyd. Will we be discussing anything you wouldn't want her to hear? She is an employee of SPCFF."

"No, of course not, bring her along. How does the Outback Steakhouse sound?"

"Outback is wonderful, Stuart. Where is the one we'll be going to?"

"I'll text you the address a little later."

It was a Wednesday night, and the restaurant was not extremely busy. They were seated very quickly. After they had ordered, Pennington got right down to business.

"We want to continue the tours, Elizabeth, and we'd like you to do appearances on some nationally-televised talk shows, morning, afternoon, and late-night. How does that sound to you?"

"It's something I'm going to have to sell to my family, Stuart. I made a promise to my husband that I would do this one-year gig and come home."

"I see," he said. "Well, what can we do to make it work better for you?"

"I can't come to Virginia and stay full time, only going home once a month, which didn't work out the way I was told it would."

"What went wrong, Elizabeth?" he asked her.

"Corley kept telling me the schedule and the budget wouldn't permit it. So, I went home about every other month, and my husband came to see me twice. I just won't go through that again."

"Well, the budget should have not been a problem. We figured that into his contract and paid him enough to provide that for you."

"That sneaky sonofabitch," Peggy said, a little too loudly. Heads turned at nearby tables, and Pennington looked shocked. "I bet he screwed you out of a car too, Elizabeth."

"Car, what about a car? You did have a car for your personal use while you were in Virginia, didn't you?" he said.

"No, Stuart, he had Peggy pick me up and take me anywhere I needed to go. It's not a big issue, but it was a big inconvenience to Peg. I don't really get out much anyway. I work at home at night."

"It's an issue for Earth Publishing," he said. "We paid him the money, and it looks like he stuck it in his pocket. So, again, tell me what you need to accommodate us. We need you, that's a given, can't do this without you. What will it take to keep you with us?"

"The first thing is Peggy here. I need her as my assistant. And I want to work from home. I don't mind flying and overnighting or staying two or three days, but I need Peggy and my family."

"What we'll have to do is schedule the events closer together, I suppose. Let me talk to my betters at the company and see how we can work it out. The flying you up and back is no problem, getting Peggy is no problem as long as Peggy agrees."

"You better believe I do, Stuart," Peggy said enthusiastically, "Elizabeth and I are a team."

Elizabeth nodded her agreement.

"The real heartburn is going to be your time away from home. We can only schedule just so many events in a month. I'll get back in the office and butt heads with the bosses and see what we can come up with."

"Thank you, Stuart," Elizabeth said, "I'll be going home after the Raleigh Durham show this Friday."

When Elizabeth got back to the hotel room, she sent an email to Rick.

In Fayetteville, NC, just finished show. Will be in Raleigh Durham Friday for last event. Then I'm coming home. Please kiss the kids for me and tell them I love them.
Oh, and I love you too.
Lizzy-Bee.

"Mommy will be home soon, guys," Rick was saying to HA and Annie when Grandpa Harley walked into the room.

"When will she be here?" Harley asked.

"She has one last event on Friday, that's in Raleigh, North Carolina. I expect that she and Peggy will spend the night there and drive back to Richmond on Saturday. I imagine she'll have to, more or less, debrief at the office on Monday, and maybe fly out then. I'll talk to her before then and find out for sure when she'll be here."

"Do you regret letting her go on her *adventure*, Rick?"

"I don't know, Harley, sometimes I do. I'd rather have her here all the time. Your daughter is just too damned smart. I can't tell her, 'No, you can't go.' That would stifle that wonderful creative talent she has."

"She takes advantage of you, you know."

"I don't think she does it intentionally, Harley. Elizabeth has this save-the-world gene in her that I do think clouds her thinking sometimes."

"It confuses her priorities, I think," Harley said. "You'll reach a point when you're going to have to throw a shock into her again."

"How do you mean? I'm not following what you're saying."

"Remember when you two had decided you would get married in your second year in college?"

"Yes, and she kept putting it off to concentrate on keeping her grades up to four-point-oh and then to work on that farm all summer after her junior year. Yeah, it was maddening for me, but I was afraid if I didn't accept it, I would lose her."

"You wouldn't have lost her. She would have quit it all and married you any time you demanded."

"I know, she told me that, but how could I have done that and lived with myself?"

"It would have been like hiding a light under a basket, to borrow an admonition from scripture," Harley said.

"Exactly," Rick said, "and I think our marriage would have suffered because of it."

"I do too," Harley replied, "you did the right thing, then, by telling her you were breaking up with her. But I feel that she may force you to make that decision again, very soon."

"Oh, I hope not, Harley. I hope she's got this out of her system by now."

"She's written another book and, in this book, she expounds on the evils of Big Pharma, Big Ag, and just about anything the government is involved in. Looking at the success she had with her previous book, the new one could be more successful and more controversial."

"So, what should I do, Harley, hope she's a failure?"

"That's what I'm praying for, Rick."

"Really? I just can't bring myself to do that, it would hurt her too much, I believe."

"There is some big political money behind the movement that is funding Lizzy's success. They own that publishing company and that other company that fronts for them. I'm not diminishing her talent. She is very good at what she does. But what I'm telling you, Rick, is the world is going to try to take her away from you. You'd best start figuring out how to stop them."

After the Raleigh Durham show and book signing, Elizabeth and Peggy had dinner.

"How far is it to Richmond, Peg?" Elizabeth asked.

"About two and a half hours, a hundred and seventy miles or so."

"Let's stay the night," Elizabeth suggested. "We can drive back in the morning."

"I like that idea," Peggy said.

Monday morning, Elizabeth went to the office to clear out her desk, say goodbye to everyone, and thank Corley for his participation in the project. She wanted to leave on congenial terms. Peggy was not feeling well when she picked her up.

"I'll be okay. When you're ready to go to the airport, call me."

"No, Peg, you get some rest. I'll get someone to give me a lift back to my apartment and call the airline shuttle when I'm ready to go. I'm going to hug you goodbye, here at the office. Until I see you again, you take care of yourself."

At around ten o'clock, Elizabeth had finished all her necessary business and was ready to leave.

"Peggy was sick when she picked me up this morning," she told Corley. "I told her to stay home so now I need a ride."

"I can take you home, Beth," Corley said.

She waited by the door as he retrieved his car from the parking garage. In a moment he pulled up to the curb, got out, came around to her side, and opened the door for her.

"You want to get lunch?" he asked her.

"No, thanks, Corley, I have food at home."

"Oh. Come on, peaches," he implored, "have lunch with me."

"Don't call me peaches, Corley," she said curtly.

"Why not, Beth? Jerry and Peggy called you that all the time."

"It was a friend's thing with Jerry and Peg. It's a familiarity I don't have with you."

"But I'd like to have that kind of familiarity with you. Why are you upset with me?"

"I should have a rental car, Corley. The deal was that I was going to be provided a car. I'm not going to do another contract if you're not going to keep your part of the bargain."

"We've just been a little tight on the budget this year, Beth."

"I'm not buying that," Elizabeth said. "It's in my contract, and it's going to be in the next contract. I won't agree to continue this if I can't trust you."

"I just figured that Peggy could take you anywhere you needed to go when you were off work. It's worked out okay, hasn't it?"

"It's been an inconvenience to Peggy quite a bit, I imagine. She hasn't complained, but I know it's inconvenienced her, having to pick me up and bring me back every day. Now today, with her out sick, you have to bring me home."

He arrived at her unit at the Residence Inn. "I wanted to talk to you about the next phase of our project, anyway, Beth."

"We could have talked at the office."

"I wanted to talk over lunch."

"I'm just not comfortable going to lunch or dinner with men who are not my husband, Corley. You have to understand that."

"Okay, I understand that, but can we talk about work for just a few minutes?

"All right, come on in," she said, and he followed her into her apartment. "You can sit at the table. I'm going to put on some more comfortable shoes."

She walked into the bedroom and was retrieving her flip-flops from the closet when she sensed that he was behind her. She stood up and saw that he had followed her into the bedroom. "What are you doing, Corley, why are you here?" she yelled at him.

"You know, Beth, you can't have much with that husband of yours if you're willing to leave him at home with the kids for two years."

"That's none of your business, Corley. Now get out of my bedroom and get out of my apartment."

"No, I want something from you, and you know what it is."

"I am not going to bed with you, Corley, get out of here."

"I can't, Beth," he said, "I need you. You're so beautiful, I'm losing my mind just thinking about you all the time."

Before she could react, he grabbed her, and, with his right arm around her, he clenched her hair in his left hand and kissed her, hard. She struggled to get loose from him, but his quickness had caught her unprepared. His hand pulled her hair harder, forcing her head back as he continued kissing her. He moved her over to the bed and forced her down on it, holding her down with his weight. He started to tear at her blouse, still holding her head captive by her hair. His hand went inside her blouse and bra, and he began fondling her breasts.

Elizabeth was nearly panic stricken by then, and he was hurting her breasts and her head with his hand pulling her hair. She managed to pull her lips away from his for a moment.

"Wait," she said. "Wait, Corley, don't hurt me. Let me take my clothes off."

Excited by her apparent complicity in his effort to seduce her, he removed his hand from her bra but kept his hold on her hair. He kissed her again, and she kissed him back, with feigned passion, she caressed the back of his head with her hand and uttered a low moan to make him think she was aroused. Corley relaxed a bit and released his grip on her hair. He helped her up off the bed.

"It's better this way," he said.

She nodded, demurely and said, "umm huh." Then she punched him in his throat as hard as she could. He grabbed at his throat, started gasping and spitting up blood, and fell to the floor, clutching his throat, trying to lift his head.

Elizabeth called nine-one-one and asked the operator to send the police to her address. "There's a man in my apartment lying on the floor unresponsive."

Operator: "Can you detect a pulse on the man?"

Elizabeth: "I can't tell."

Operator: "Have you tried chest compression?"

Elizabeth: "I did, but his mouth is filled with blood."

Operator: "Police and ambulance are on the way, ma'am."

It was no more than five minutes until she heard a knock on the door. "Two beautiful men in blue uniforms," as she would describe them later to Peggy Boyd, were standing there.

"You called for assistance, ma'am?" one of them asked her.

"Yes, Officer, the guy is my boss."

"What is your name, ma'am?" they asked her.

"I'm Elizabeth Bennett, I work for Earth Publishing and a company called SPCFF. This man is my boss at the last company I gave you. His name is Corley McKnight."

"Tell me what happened, Mrs. Bennett," one of them said.

"He brought me home from work and came in to discuss a new project but didn't want to leave. I asked him to leave and then I told him to leave, and he wouldn't leave."

"So, you did this to him?" the taller police officer asked her."

"He started to put his hands on me," Elizabeth said.

The two cops looked at Corley for a moment and then looked at Elizabeth's disheveled clothing.

"This looks like more than just putting his hands on you, ma'am," the second officer said.

"Hang on a second, Jimmy," the first officer said. Walking over to Elizabeth, he asked her, "Ma'am, my name is William Barrow, but I go by Bill. Did this man try to sexually assault you?"

Elizabeth clearly did not want to answer the question. "I can't file charges against him for that, Officer. He's my boss and—it's just very complicated."

"Well, if he tried to sexually assault you, and I don't arrest him and report it, I could be in big trouble. And he could come back and kill you next time. If I let that happen, I couldn't live with myself. If this is a boyfriend who just got a little rough, then we can handle it differently."

"He's not my boyfriend. He manages the company I work for. He just came on too strongly and wouldn't leave."

"But you damned near killed the guy, Mrs…what was your name again?"

"Elizabeth," she said.

"You almost killed this guy, Elizabeth, you may have. What's his condition, Jimmy?"

"This guy is at room temperature, Bill."

"What does that mean?" Elizabeth asked.

"It means he ain't coming back."

"Oh, my god," Elizabeth exclaimed, "you mean he's dead?"

"Yes, he's dead, and now we have a problem."

"What is the problem?" Elizabeth asked.

"I *know* he tried to sexually assault you, Elizabeth. I'm happy as hell that you were able to defend yourself. Now, I don't want to arrest you for assaulting this guy, but I need you to tell me the truth. He tried to sexually assault you, didn't he?

Elizabeth put her hands over her face and rubbed her eyes for a few moments. Then she answered the officer. "Yes, Officer, he forced me onto the bed and was trying to rape me. I managed to get my hand free, and I hit him in the throat."

"Okay," the officer said, "now we're getting somewhere. Then what happened?"

"He was choking and gasping, so I called nine-one-one, and when you came he was lying there just the way you found him."

"All right," Officer Barrow said. "Are you okay?"

"I need to go home, but I can leave my cell phone number," Elizabeth said.

"Where is home, ma'am?"

"Fredericksburg, Texas," she said. "I have to get home to my family."

"Then I'll need you to wait here for the detective. He will have to talk to you. It's procedure. Give me just a minute, ma'am, I need to talk to my partner about this.

"Let me change clothes. He tore my blouse."

"No, leave it on until the detective gets here, the torn blouse is evidence."

A few minutes later, Officer Barrow and Jimmy, came back into the room. "Okay, Elizabeth, you need to listen to me and try to understand what I tell you. The judges in Henrico County are not rape-friendly judges. What that means is that if this goes to trial, you are going to go to jail."

"Oh, God, I can't go to jail. I have children, my husband, this will ruin our lives. I was defending myself," she said, now on the verge of panic.

"I know you were," Barrow said, "and the good guys won this time. But judges tend to dismiss a rape of a woman by an acquaintance, boyfriend, boss, or whatever. If she knows the guy, they figure it was either consensual, or it was playtime that got out of hand. I'm going to do something that you must not see and must never tell anyone outside this room, not your best friend, not even your husband. I am not going to let you go to jail. Hey, Jimmy, bring that wooden chair over here."

The other officer did as his partner had directed.

Barrow picked up the chair and pushed the seat-back into the dead man's throat and then set it back up next to him. He then tossed the comforter, from the bed, onto the floor at Corley's feet. "He came into your room, tripped over the comforter, and fell against the back of the chair, hitting his throat. It was an accident. Do you understand?"

Elizabeth just nodded. She was about to cry.

"This is how you found him," Barrow stressed.

The EMT folks arrived and took a quick look at Corley. One of the attendants looked at Bill Barrow and shook his head. Officer Barrow asked them to wait for the detective, before removing the man from the site.

Not long after that, a car pulled up outside. "That's the detective, Elizabeth, tell him you found the man in your room, lying on the floor."

Detective Avery Nilsson walked into the room and addressed the two policemen. "Where's the body?" he asked them.

Barrow showed him where Corley was lying.

"You're telling me he tripped and did this to himself?" Nilsson said.

"Yes, Detective, that's what I figure happened."

"Where's the lady?"

"She's in the bathroom, she's pretty distraught."

In a few minutes, Elizabeth came out of the bathroom, rubbing her face with a wet wash cloth.

"Oh, I know you," Nilsson said when he saw Elizabeth. "You're a writer and speaker, Elizabeth Bennett, isn't it?"

Yes, sir," Elizabeth said.

"I'm Detective, Avery Nilsson, and I'll need to talk to you in just a bit, but first I need to speak with my officers outside. If you'll just have a seat, I won't be long. I'll tell the paramedics to take the guy to the hospital."

Outside, after the ambulance had left, Avery looked at the two officers and then said, "You two want to tell me what really happened here. I think I know, but I want to hear it from you."

"The guy tried to rape her, Avery, but she fought back and punched him in the throat. She says he brought her home from the office—er regular driver was sick—and he came into the apartment on the pretext of wanting to talk over some plans for their next project. She went into her room to change shoes, and he followed her, grabbed her, and pinned her to the bed. He had her by the hair and was groping her breasts very roughly. She managed to free her right hand and punched him in the throat. We found him right where you saw him."

"Do you believe her?"

"I want to believe her, Avery. At first, it looked like a boyfriend gone bad thing but, she's married and has two kids and apparently works for the asshole."

"Don't let her looks get your brain caught in your zipper, Bill. I need you to be objective."

"I am being objective, Detective. She just doesn't strike me as a woman who would be screwing around on her husband."

"And what brought you to that conclusion?" the detective asked.

"She has pictures of her husband and the kids in several places around this place and a picture of him where she's wrapped all around him next to her bed. I can show you."

"Okay," Avery said. "I want to believe her too. Damn, she is a looker, isn't she?"

"Try to maintain your objectivity, Detective," Officer Gonzales said, and Nilsson smiled and nodded.

Nilsson and the officers went back into the suite. "I know

you, Miss Bennett," Nilsson said again, "I attended one of your lectures and bought your book. I thoroughly enjoyed it, I have to say."

"Thank you, Detective," Elizabeth said, "and I'm married, I'm not a miss. Please call me Elizabeth."

"All right, Elizabeth, I need to you to tell me how you came to be in the suite at The Residence Inn with the man the police found there with you."

"Corley McKnight manages a company that works with Earth Publishing. That's a publisher that has published one of my books and is preparing to publish another one very soon. My publisher is sponsoring lecture tours I make all over the South. Corley's company handles the logistics of the tours, scheduling, travel, hotel, etc. I also do book signing after each lecture. I had just completed a one-year project and was planning to fly back home today."

"Where is home?"

"I live in Fredericksburg, Texas, with my husband and children."

Nilsson nodded. "So, how did Mister McKnight come to be in your room?"

"My regular driver, Peggy Boyd, was sick today, so Corley offered to drive me home. He asked me to have lunch with him, and I didn't want to. He told me he wanted to discuss some details on an upcoming project. He wanted to come into my apartment. I said okay because I had no idea he would do what he did."

"Has he ever come on to you before?"

"He flirts a little, and I always shut him down. My assistant, Peggy Boyd can confirm that. Corley had never actually put his hands on me until today."

"Okay, go on."

"I told him to sit down at the table, and I went into my bedroom to change my shoes. I was getting my flip-flops out of the closet, and I heard him come up behind me. I yelled at him to get out of my bedroom and out of my apartment." Elizabeth was starting to hyperventilate a bit.

"Are you okay, do you some water now?"

She nodded her head. "I have bottled water in the fridge," she said.

Officer Barrow retrieved a bottle of water and brought it to her.

"Thank you," she told him.

"Go on, Elizabeth," Nilsson said.

"He grabbed me around my waist, grabbed my hair with his left hand, and pulled my head back hard. I yelled out in pain, and he started kissing me. I was trying to get loose from him, but he threw me down on the bed and fell on top of me. He tore my blouse, put his hand inside my bra, and—"

"I understand what he did, ma'am, go on."

"But he was still holding my hair back, and the pain was getting worse." She stopped to take a sip of water.

"How did you get loose from him, Elizabeth?"

"I was starting to panic, so I managed to get my left arm out from under him. Then I grabbed his hair, or collar or something and pulled his head back just long enough to punch him in the throat. He let go of my hair and grasped at his throat. He was choking and spitting up some blood."

"Let me talk to Barrow and Gonzales, for a moment," he said, "I'll be right back. Okay, guys, how do we play this?"

"We can't charge this woman," Barrow said. "Her story is solid. McKnight is not around to refute it, but you know as well as I do, that sending her to trial is going to mean jail time."

"I know," Nilsson said, "so you're willing to swear that the man fell and hit his throat on the back of the chair?"

"He was a clumsy fucker, and a rapist, Avery, he deserved to die."

"Okay, I'll still have to check out the folks she says can support her claim that she never encouraged the man's advances. Let's go talk to her." Nilsson walked back over to Elizabeth. "We have a plan on how to handle this, Elizabeth, but we have to know that you are onboard with us. You have to grasp the seriousness of what we're doing. None of us want you to go to jail, and we're not going to let it happen."

"I killed a man," she said.

"You defended yourself, Elizabeth," Nilsson said.

"I wish Rick were here," she said.

"Rick is your husband?"

"Yes, Rick Bennett."

"Do you want me to call him for you?"

"I don't want to worry him. Will I be able to leave here soon?"

"I have to talk to the DA. There may be some more investigations. The DA will probably want to talk to your assistant…what was her name again?"

"Peggy Boyd," Elizabeth said. "I can call her."

"Let's wait and see what the DA says. I'm going to release you for now, but you should not leave the state until the DA files his report. He will file the report, based on what I tell him. I know it's a bummer for your plans to go home, but why don't I call your husband and let him know? You could use his support. I wouldn't want my wife to have to go through something like this without me being there with her."

"Okay," she said, "thank you, Detective."

Nilsson got Rick's number from Elizabeth and went outside. He was gone about ten minutes.

"Your husband is on his way," Nilsson said when he returned. "Now remember, when you talk to the DA, tell him what really happened. I will advise him of our situation, and if he wants to change anything, I will let you know."

It was two o'clock in the morning when the doorbell rang. She looked through the peep-hole to make sure it was Rick and then opened the door. Rick walked in and immediately took her in his arms, holding her close to him and kissing her on her head, forehead, and cheeks. She began weeping again soaking his shirt with her tears.

"I can't imagine what you've been through, baby. I am so sorry you had to endure that. I don't know what to say except, thank God you were able to fight him off. You must be going through hell right now."

"I killed a man, Rick."

"He wasn't a real man, Elizabeth. Real men don't attack

women like that, especially a coworker and a one who is supposed to be a friend."

"I should have listened to you. You told me he couldn't be
trusted."

"I thought he would just be a nuisance to you, I didn't think
he would try to rape you. But let's not dwell on that now. I
need some sleep, and I know you do too."

They slept late, or what would be considered late for Elizabeth, who was accustomed to getting up around six o'clock in
the morning. It was nine when they got out of the shower.

"You want to get some breakfast, Rick?" she asked.

"Sure, you want to go to the Denny's just down the street?"

"That's fine. Darling, if the police talk to you, don't tell
them you warned me about Corley. That might complicate
things."

Rick thought for a moment. "Why did you let him come in,
baby?"

"It was stupid, I know. My assistant, Peggy, was sick, and
Corley offered to drive me back here. He wanted to take me to
lunch to discuss plans for a new project, but I told him no, that
I needed to go to my apartment. Then when he got here, he
wanted to come in and discuss the plans. I was getting ready to
pack all my stuff and fly out, so he knew I wouldn't be coming
back to the office, and he said it was important. I had no idea
he would do what he did, Rick, you have to believe me."

"I do believe you, baby," he said and hugged her. "You
need to call your dad when we get back from breakfast. He's
worried sick. The poor man was crying when I left. I asked my
sister to come over and talk to him. She brought Dave with
her, Harley loves Dave."

"What if this ruins my career, Rick?" she said. "Oh, I know
you'd love that, wouldn't you?"

"I wouldn't love anything that hurts you, Lizzy. When you
give all this up, I want it to be your choice. Besides, what if
they do find out, what's one dead rapist? No telling how many
men have killed themselves because you wouldn't marry
them."

"Oh, God, Rick, please don't try to cheer me up."

He laughed and hugged her again. "Don't worry, Lizzy, please just stop worrying. I'm not going to let anything, or anyone hurt you."

Elizabeth called Peggy and told her what happened. "They're going to want to talk to you, Peg. They want to ask you about my relationship with Corley."

"That's no problem, Beth. You always acted in a strictly professional manner. Corley McKnight was a scumbag. He was always hitting on women in the office. Angie Herrera quit because he grabbed her ass in the storeroom one time."

"It will help me a lot if you tell them that."

"Of course, Beth," Peggy replied. "I'll do anything I can to help. I just can't believe that Corley is dead. I'm not surprised he tried something with you, though. He's been in love with you since the first day he met you. I'm sure of that."

Elizabeth called Detective Avery to check on her status, and he told her the district attorney wanted to meet with her.

"I know you're anxious to get home, so if you can come meet him today, I'll call and let him know."

Nilsson was waiting when Elizabeth and Rick arrived at DA's office. He introduced himself to Rick. "I'm Detective Avery Nilsson, we spoke on the phone."

They shook hands.

"I'm sorry for the inconvenience, folks," Nilsson said. "We have to go through the procedures. Just tell him what happened the way you told it to me, Elizabeth. Everything will be okay."

The DA, Martin Piccolo, stood up from his desk, when his secretary brought Elizabeth into his office. Elizabeth noticed that he was a tall man, at least as tall as Rick, with brown hair and brown eyes. He seemed like a very nice man. She told him what happened, in exact detail, the same way she had told it to the police and the detective.

"If you can give me a list of anyone in your office who might have some additional input on this matter, I think we can wrap this up and let you get on back to Texas," Piccolo told her.

"My assistant, Peggy Boyd, made a list for me. She worked

for Corey before I started working there. There are five names on the list, and she provided their contact information."

"Very well, Mrs. Bennett, I'll talk to these folks, but I see no reason to hold you up any longer."

"Thank you, Mister Piccolo. I appreciate your understanding."

He shook her hand, got up, and opened the door for her.

Elizabeth thanked Detective Nilsson again and shook hands with him, then she and Rick walked out of the building.

"Let's go home, Rick," she said, "I need to sleep in my own bed."

Chapter 23

Ben Bradley

2065:

So, your dad brought Elizabeth home," Bradley said. "How did that go?"

"Mother was cleared of any wrongdoing, and the DA created a cover story that let Elizabeth off the hook, so to speak," Annie said.

"But that didn't keep her from a lot of torment over it," HA added.

"Yes, I imagine that, for a woman of your mother's upbringing, and with her strong intellectual bent, killing a human being was quite traumatic for her," Ben said. "Even knowing that it was self-defense, she still had to deal with her killing of another human being."

"Indeed, it was traumatic for her. She fretted over that for many years. She credited the support she got from all of us, and Rick and our grandfather, Harley, for her getting through it without losing her mind," Annie said. "Rick wanted her to quit altogether, but Mother was adamant about her cause. She appeared on a local Richmond television morning show. The host and the audience loved her, so much so that they kept her on the entire hour-long program. After that, she was in demand for appearances in shows, all over the country."

"She, apparently, was a big hit," Ben said. "How did that affect her book sales and lectures?"

"Mother made a small fortune, Ben," Annie informed him. "Her book sales went through the roof. But eventually the crowds at her lectures began to thin out, and her publisher decided to end them. They wanted her, instead, to keep making personal appearances and to keep writing books."

"Mother wrote another book, about the 'healthy food' industry, and that was the final one for that," Harley explained to Ben. "She just ran out of ammo on the subject and began writing about our town, Fredericksburg."

"And how did your father handle your mother's fame and fortune."

"Well, Ben," Annie began, "despite being from California, Rick was a very modest and down-to-earth, man. He let her pay off the land they had bought, and he encouraged her to invest her money wisely. Mother put Rick in charge of her money and let him invest it anyway he thought prudent. When Rick's foreman, Carlos Ramirez, died from a heart attack, Rick let his wife and kids live on the new property for free. The kids eventually grew up and left, except for one, who went to work for Rick. They took their mother, Martina, with them and they all took care of her together. Rick bought the trailer house from Martina Ramirez and had it refurbished. Then he hired another foreman and let him live in it."

"Well, thank you, Annie," Ben said, "I'm going to have to get back to my office for a couple of days. But I'd like to come back and take up where we left off, if you don't mind."

"I hope I'm not boring you, Ben."

"No, Annie, not at all, I find your stories fascinating. I'll call you sometime this week, okay?"

"Harley and I will be looking forward to it," Annie told him.

Chapter 24

Cleared

2019:

DA Martin Piccolo, anxious to put the death of Corley McKnight behind him, contacted the names Elizabeth had given him and scheduled them for interviews. The first one to come into his office was Peggy Boyd.

"Thank you for coming, Miss Boyd. This interview will be recorded, if you consent to that. You've already been sworn in so, if you're ready, we can start. Do you give your consent for this interview to be taped?"

"Yes, sir," Peggy said, "no problem.

"How long did you work for Mister McKnight, Miss Boyd," was his first question.

"It's been ten years, now," she replied, "and you can call me Peggy."

"Thank you, Peggy, and how was your working relationship with him?"

"Oh, he left me alone, told me I needed to lose some weight every so often, like I didn't already know that. Corley was obnoxious but, all in all, it was not a bad work environment for me."

"What was his relationship with Mrs. Bennett?"

"Any relationship he had with Beth, that's what most of us call Elizabeth, was all in Corley's mind. He was in love with her, I'm convinced. Every man in the office was in love with her, except for Jerry Meisner. Corley was always flirting with her, but she never responded to him. It was strictly business with Elizabeth."

"Who is Jerry Meisner?

"Jerry worked for Corley before Beth did her first lecture tours. On one tour, a man in the audience approached Beth, after the show, and asked her to marry him, that happened a lot. Anyway, she politely declined, telling him that she was engaged to be married, which she was."

"To the current Mister Bennett?"

"Right, and two guys in the crowd stopped the guy, but that spooked Corley, so he started sending Jerry along with me and Beth, after that, to protect her. Jerry was a black belt in something, and he was as tough as nails. But he became good friends with Beth and took a lot of pride in his job being her protector. He never had any designs on her, or at least he never tried anything with her. He wasn't gay, turned out he was married, and he'd never told anyone. He would have kicked Corley's ass if he'd gotten too far out of line with Beth, and Corley knew that."

"We contacted three of the people, whose names Mrs. Bennett gave us. One name, however, we've not been able to find. What can you tell me about Angie Herrera?"

"Angie was a data entry technician for the company, drop-dead gorgeous and not interested in Corley. But Corley was interested in her. He followed her around like a dog in heat. She wouldn't have anything to do with him. Once he followed her into the storeroom and grabbed her rear-end. She slapped him, and Corley got mad."

"What did he do?" Piccolo asked.

"According to Angie, Corley told her that her work had not been up to his standards, which was baloney, because Angie was very good at her job. But Corley told her he was going to fire her unless she would have sex with him."

"And what did Angie do?"

"Angie quit, walked out that very minute. She filed a complaint with the EEOC, but Corley denied everything, and it just kind of fizzled out. That's what Angie told me."

"We found that Angie had filed a complaint. It looks like it didn't go anywhere because the agency was overloaded with cases and just couldn't devote enough time to really pursue it properly. It just fell through a crack, is my guess. It's too bad, because, had he suffered some consequences then, he might be alive today."

"You mean he might not have tried to rape Beth?"

"Perhaps he would have had more self-control," he said.

District Attorney Piccolo thanked Peggy for her deposition and told her she was free to go. "If I think of anything else, Peggy, I'll give you a call.

He decided not to interview the other three employees of SPCFF. Corley McKnight's penchant for touching female employees, making lewd, unwanted remarks to them, and even putting his hands on them, on occasion, had been confirmed by Peggy Boyd. Piccolo didn't want to involve any more people than was absolutely necessary. But the real nail in Corley's coffin, figuratively speaking, was a report from 1998 that had named him as the defendant in the rape of a young woman he'd met in a bar.

Corley's defense was that the encounter had been consensual. The victim claimed otherwise, and witnesses had testified that Corey had kept plying her with drinks until, by the time they left the bar, the woman could barely walk under her own power. Corley received two years of probation but was not listed as a sexual predator.

District Attorney Piccolo, based on his detective's recommendation, made the decision to cover up the true cause of death of Corley McKnight. He filed a report that said McKnight had gone to the hotel residence of an employee for an unknown reason. The employee was not in the residence at the time. McKnight was able to get a key to the unit from the hotel office because the room was leased in his name. He then entered the residence and apparently tripped and fell against a chair, striking his throat on the back. When the tenant returned, she found McKnight lying on the floor. He appeared to be dead. She called the police, and when officers arrived, they found the tenant waiting outside. An ambulance arrived, and

EMT personnel discovered that the man was deceased. He was taken to the hospital, where he was pronounced dead by a doctor, and subsequently by the coroner. The tenant of the residence was determined to have not been there when the accident occurred and has not been charged with any involvement in the man's death. Piccolo advised Peggy Boyd of his decision to report the death as an accident. He perceived that the woman was so loyal to Elizabeth Bennett that she would not question the action he was going to take.

Elizabeth did not fully comprehend the gravity of the actions the policemen and district attorney had taken on her behalf. They had taken a course of action that, if ever exposed, would certainly mean the loss of their jobs and could, possibly, send them to jail. In time, she would come to realize it. But this day, she was still in a state of shock over what happened and what she had been forced to do to save herself from a sexual assault and possibly being killed.

"Wake up, wake up, you sleepy head, get up, get out of bed," Rick was singing to Elizabeth, the morning after they had gotten back home."

"Oh, what time is it?" she asked.

"It's almost nine o'clock," he said as he kissed her. "Thank you for last night."

"No problem," she replied, "The pleasure was all mine."

"Yeah, I got that impression."

She giggled. "Was I too vocal?"

"You didn't wake up the kids, thank goodness, but you sure made me feel like a million bucks."

"You *are* a million bucks, darling.

"Well, thank you, ma'am, I'd ask for a rematch right now, but we promised the kids we'd go somewhere today. You want to take a shower?"

"Can I get a raincheck, on that rematch, for later tonight?"

"Have I ever told you no to anything?"

"You have not," she said, "and I'm beginning to wonder why I deserve you."

"You don't," he said, and then started laughing at the look on her face."

"You're right, I don't, but I'm glad I have you anyway," she countered. "But don't let this go to your head, I'm still quite a catch."

"You are indeed," he said, "I just have to be careful not to rub you the wrong way, or I'll get a punch in the throat." He immediately regretted his joke when he saw the look on her face.

"I killed a man, Rick," she shouted at him. "I killed a man. Oh, God, what am I going to do now? I killed another human being." She was distraught and crying loudly. "I know I was defending myself, but I have to live with this the rest of my life."

"Oh, hell, baby, I don't know why I said that. I'm a total asshole, Lizzy, I'm so sorry." He tried to take her in his arms, but she pulled away and went into another part of the house.

"Daddy!" she called out to her father.

Harley came out of his room and saw her. She ran into his arms.

"What's wrong, honey," Harley asked, patting her shoulders and back, in an effort to console her. Harvey was perplexed, knowing not what had upset his daughter but knowing that something had upset her mightily.

"It's my fault, Harley," Rick said, having followed Elizabeth out of their room. "I made a stupid joke. I'm an asshole."

"What's wrong with Mommy?" HA said. "Why is Mommy crying?"

The kids had come into the living room, and both were starting to cry too as they watched their mother in obvious distress.

"Harley, will you take the kids outside, so I can try and make up for what I did?"

Harley took the hands of the two children and told them to come outside with him. When they were gone from the house, Rick went to put his arms around his wife, but she pulled away.

"Please, baby, I screwed up, it was a stupid thing to say. I don't even know why I said it."

She came to him, and he hugged her, her head resting on his chest.

"I feel like I just shot Bambi," he said.

She started chuckling and looked up at him. "I just don't want to think about that anymore. At first, I was afraid I might go to jail, and then it hit me that I had actually killed a man. I don't know how I'm going to live with that."

"Consider this, Elizabeth, it might help you see things in a different light. If Corey had succeeded in raping you, he might have killed you."

"Do you really think so?"

"He had to know you would report him. If he was crazy enough to try and rape you, he might very well have been crazy enough to kill you, so you couldn't. We're very lucky to still have you with us."

"He was certainly committed. I had no idea he was capable of doing that."

"I told you he was going to make a play for you, baby. I saw how he looked at you when he was here for those few days."

"Rape is not *making a play* for someone, Rick."

"I didn't know he was crazy. By the way, how did you know how to put him down like that?"

"Jules taught me," she said.

"Your health coach, Jules?"

"Right, you remember, he beat up those two rednecks in the pickup truck. They tried to get me to take off my sweatshirt when we were jogging."

"I remember Jules, and he taught you that?"

"Yes, he did, and I knew I was fighting for my life when Corley came after me."

"You should call Jules and thank him."

"No, I don't want anyone to know about it. I wish I could have kept it from Daddy."

"Your dad needs to know about anything that could have gotten you hurt badly.

"Still, can you just not mention it ever again?"

"Oh, I've learned my lesson, baby, I'll never bring it up again."

An hour later, the Bennett family was hiking up Enchanted Rock, north of Fredericksburg. HA now eight-year-old and his sister, now seven, went running on ahead of their parents, toward the top of the massive rock formation. Rick watched them for a moment. HA took Annie's hand to help her over a rock outcropping.

"Look at them, Lizzy," he said. "If you and I had met at that age, that could be us running up there. HA looks so much like I did when I was his age, and Annie has to be a spitting image of you. It's almost like looking back at ourselves."

"Don't let them get too far away, Rick," she said, and he called to them to come back.

"Why do they call it Enchanted Rock, Daddy?" HA asked.

"Well, son, according to the brochure, these little holes, you see here?"

"Uh huh," the boy said, nodding his head.

"They're not really holes. They're like little cups, scooped out areas. When it rains, these fill up with rainwater. Then moonlight shining on them creates a sparkling effect that can be seen from down on the ground. The original inhabitants of this land all around us saw the sparkling and thought the rock was magical or enchanted. That's why they call it Enchanted Rock."

"I'm hungry, Daddy," Annie said, looking pitiful because Rick always catered to her when she put on her pitiful face.

"Okay, guys, let's go get something to eat. Tell Mommy we're ready to leave."

Harley had lunch ready when they got back home, sandwiches and soup. "Where did you guys go?" he asked HA.

"We went to Enchanted Rock, Grandpa."

"I've been meaning to take them there, Rick, but I can't hike up the thing. My knees are not what they once were," Harley said.

"You do more than enough around here, Harley," Rick told him. "I appreciate all the help you give us."

"I just can't keep up with the kids anymore. HA is so fast, if he gets away from me, I can't catch him."

Rick laughed. "He can't outrun me—yet. But I imagine it won't be long."

Elizabeth announced that she had finally completed her book. It was more than just an addendum to the first book. It expanded it and added so much more that she had learned in the interim since the first one. "I wrote one chapter on my battle with cancer and how I beat it with natural remedies, food, and exercise. I documented the evils of chemo and how it kills more people than it cures."

"I hope you didn't mention the pot," Rick said.

"I left that part out, and it's a travesty how the government impedes the use of a natural cure. It's all because of Big Pharma. They don't want people to get cured of cancer. They just want to sell dope."

"So, what happens now, you send the manuscript to your publisher and then what?"

"They check it for accuracy of content, grammar, and punctuation and for the general flow and readability of the book, and then they print it, I assume. I don't really know what goes into the process."

He was staring at her, and their eyes became transfixed on each other's. "What I need to know, baby, is how long do I have before you leave me again?"

"Oh, Rick," she said, "I've been wanting to talk to you about it."

"But you haven't, Elizabeth, did you really think I didn't know what your finishing the book meant?"

"It's important, what I do, Rick, there are lives at stake."

"Your family is important too, Lizzy."

"I'm not abandoning my family. You *can't* believe that."

"I can't go through another year like this last one, Elizabeth, I won't do it. The kids deserve to have their mother around, all the time."

"It won't be a year," she said, "I'll have a different schedule and format. SPCFF is out of the picture, and the publisher is handling everything. They're doing promotion for the book, booking my events, and handling everything that Corley was doing."

"What does this mean? It sounds like more of a book promotion than a benefit for humanity agenda. Is it really about saving lives or making money?

"It's about both, Rick. What I teach is good for people, that is my motivation. So, I make a lot of money doing it, what's wrong with that?"

"I can't hold your checkbook in my arms and kiss it to sleep at night. Money won't sing a song to the kids at bedtime the way you do. We don't need money, Elizabeth, we have enough to provide the things we really need. All I need is you."

"It'll be different this time, darling, my schedule will be different. I'll be a month on the road and a month back at home."

"I'll believe that when I see it happen. It didn't work out like they promised last time."

"I know, but Corley McKnight is no longer involved in it. Please try to understand, Rick, I have to do this."

"So now you *have* to do it?"

"Yes, it's just something I have to do."

"And it comes before your family? I guess I should have been prepared for this. You left me for four years to pursue an agenda that seemed worthwhile, and now you're apparently prepared to do it again."

She went to him and put her arms around him, buried her face in his chest and began crying. "You know that's not true," she said. "I know you're upset, but your words are cruel. You've never been this mean to me before."

"How long is it until you have to leave?" he asked her.

"Realistically, about six months," she said.

"July, that will put you out of here for harvest. I'd hoped you would be here through July. Well, at least you didn't wait until the last minute to spring it on me, like last time. I appreciate that, I really do. Let's try to live until that time like nothing has changed. I'll be prepared for it when the time comes."

"Thank you, darling," she said, "I hope you'll try to understand. But, in the meantime, we have a vineyard to run. What can I do to help?"

"Besides just being here, what do you want to do?"

"Can I make some sales calls, I mean, do we need to increase our customer base? I've been gone a year, so if you need me to go pitch our product, I'd love to do it."

"Are you sure that, when you start your touring again, your schedule will let you be back home every other month?" he asked her.

"Yes, I made it clear to them that I would not stay away from home for longer than a month at a time."

"In that case, yes, it would help to expand our business since the new acreage will be producing now. But I don't want you going to San Antonio alone. Maybe your dad will ride along with you."

"I'm sure he'd like that," she said. "I'll get on the phone and see about lining up some sales calls."

"Well, okay, peaches, give it your best shot," he said.

"Wait, did you just call me peaches?"

"I did. I think it's kind of cute."

"Jerry Meisner would be proud."

"I wish he'd been there this past year."

"Yeah, me too," she replied. "What happened would not have happened if Jerry had been there."

From mid-July until the end of the month, the Lizzy-Bee was a literal bee-hive of activity. Carlos Ramirez put together two crews to gather the grapes from both locations. Rick barely had time to process Elizabeth's absence from his life.

Once the picking and transport to the winery for processing and storage was complete, however, the vineyard got quiet again. Rick then started to miss her. But in August, she was back home, and he realized that he might be able to live with her being away every other month."

She made no effort to hide her enthusiasm about her latest conquest. Rick played the dutiful husband and asked her to tell him all about it.

"I did five events in July," she told him, going into elaborate detail about her performance and the ease with which she had gotten back into the game.

"Any marriage proposals?" he asked her.

"Nope," she said, "they all seemed to be serious-minded gentlemen. It went very well, no trouble anywhere."

"Are you disappointed?"

"A little, I guess," she said, smiling at him mischievously. "I'm accustomed to getting at least two proposals at every show."

"Must be the name change," he said. "People knew you as Beth Meadows, and now you're going by Bennett. They know you're married and off limits now."

"Or maybe I'm just getting older and losing my looks."

He started laughing. "You're thirty-four years old, Lizzy. Are we fishing for a complement, do you need me to tell you how beautiful you are?"

"No, I suppose not, as long as you still believe it."

"Are you kidding me? I can't take my eyes off of you. I still get dizzy just looking into your eyes."

"Now that sounds like a bullshit line," she said.

"And yet it's true."

"It makes me feel good, regardless, thank you, darling."

"So, what's on your calendar for next month?"

"Oh, I almost forgot to tell you, I'm going to be on a television show."

The Helen McGee Hour was a morning variety show on a local Richmond station. McGee was a middle-aged woman, who had become quite popular and well known, as a news anchor person on the station. Having become adept at conducting personal interviews, and possessing an endearing personality and sense of humor, Helen was offered the opportunity.

Seeing herself as the next Oprah Winfrey, she threw herself into the show with great fervor. And had been so successful that she had catapulted into national venue three years prior to Elizabeth's appearance. When the show went national, a live audience element was added.

"Are you nervous?" Peggy Boyd asked her.

"I'm a little nervous," Elizabeth said, "but I'll be okay. Rick is watching at home. He's going to save my segment on DVD, so the kids can watch it later. They're in school now."

"Just be you, peaches, and you'll knock 'em dead."

Elizabeth was the first guest that morning, and McGee was beginning her intro.

"Folks," she began, "our next guest is a unique young woman whose academic credentials will absolutely blow you away, if her beauty doesn't blow you away first. She's the author of two books and quickly becoming a well-known and respected lecturer and public speaker. Please welcome Elizabeth Meadows Bennett."

Elizabeth stepped out from stage-side to a rousing applause and walked briskly to a waiting chair, sitting right across from Helen McGee. McGee rose and shook her hand and gave her an obligatory hug.

"Thank you so much for coming, Elizabeth," Helen told her.

"Thank you for having me on, Helen. It's my pleasure to be here."

"You have a master's degree in…" Helen checked her notepad, "…bio-molecular engineering from John Hopkins University. Now, what exactly does that mean?"

"My original plan, right out of high school," Elizabeth began, "was to do research in hopes of developing ways to prevent heart attacks. You see, my mother died from a heart attack when I was ten years old, and I became obsessed with that goal."

"But you gave that up to write books and lecture?"

"It didn't happen exactly like that. I had a good friend and roommate at JHU, a young woman named Eva Graham from Pennsylvania. Eva invited me to go home with her one weekend. I met her family, William and Jocelyn, Eva's parents, and Josh Graham, her younger brother. The Graham's raised grass-fed beef and used certain farming methods to prepare chemical-free soil for the growing of vegetable and fruits."

"Your first book says you worked on their farm one summer. That must have been tough on a beautiful, academically oriented student.

"I'm tougher than I look, Helen, I'm from Texas. And yes, I worked all summer with the Grahams, and they taught me everything I know about chemical-free food production. I came to realize, that summer, that I could do so much more for people's health and well-being, by doing what the Grahams do than I could as a research scientist."

"So, you basically changed jobs after getting your master's degree in your chosen field?"

"Yes, I finished my undergraduate work, went for my master's, and then I changed fields. I wrote the first book and, based on its success, I was asked by my publisher to embark on a series of book promotions and lecture tours, which I did."

During a commercial break, Helen told Elizabeth, "You're doing great, Elizabeth. The audience loves you. Can you stay for another segment?"

"Of course, Helen, thank you," Elizabeth replied.

After the break, the applause sign went on and the audience responded as they had been told to do.

"Your second book takes off in a different direction, doesn't it?" Helen said. "Can you tell us about that?"

"When I was twenty-seven, I discovered that I had ovarian cancer."

The audience reacted to Elizabeth's pronouncement.

"But it appears that you came through okay."

"I decided to forego traditional treatment—chemo, radiation, and such and fight the cancer with alternative methods. I had a health coach, a man named Jules Frenkin, a brilliant, wonderful man who saved my life. He gave me an exercise routine and made me stick to it. He did the routines with me, worked my butt off, to be honest. But with that, and changing my diet drastically, the cancer went away. When Jules left after six months, my husband took over, and he keeps me honest and holds me accountable. I still stick to the diet, and I exercise religiously."

"Tell us about your husband, Elizabeth."

"Rick Bennett is the love of my life. We fell in love in high school. He was the quarterback of the football team and is also a brilliant man. Rick got his master's degree in economics from SMU."

"That is interesting," Helen said. "But how did a girl of your knowledge and talents, manage to end up marrying a football player?"

"If you met him, you wouldn't even ask that question. He's the most wonderful man in the world, if you don't count my daddy."

The audience erupted into laughter when Elizabeth said that.

"I'd love to meet him someday. But now, about your second book has a strange name. *They're Trying to Kill Us*. What in the world is that all about?"

"It came from my decision to use alternative treatments for my cancer. Half of the cancer patients who undergo chemotherapy are killed by the treatment, not the cancer. For me, that is unacceptable. Big Pharma, American pharmaceutical companies, the biggest dope dealers in American society, don't want a cure for cancer. It is far more lucrative to treat cancer than it is to cure it. Big Ag keeps pushing the narrative that we are not growing enough food. Society and American farmers accept that, out of economic expediency, and a general lack of knowing the truth. They accept the premise that modified food is safe. This has threatened the existence of the small, diversified family farms that are directly connected to the people for whom they provide food. It has led to the existence of large mega-farms and the use of GMO and dangerous pesticides.

"We have a commercial break coming up," Helen McGee announced. "Stay with us, we'll be right back." During the break, Helen addressed Elizabeth again. "If you can afford us the time, Elizabeth, I'd like to do something unprecedented. I'd like to hold you over for the entire hour."

Elizabeth was surprised. "It would be my honor, Helen," she told her.

Helen called to her producer to clear the scheduled guests. "Invite them back another time and give them some free meal cards or something. I'm not going to cut this lady short. Okay, we are back, and I have decided to hold Elizabeth over for the rest of the hour."

The audience applauded enthusiastically.

"I want to follow up on the GMO controversy, Elizabeth," Helen said.

"This is one of the greatest scams ever perpetrated against the American people, Helen. What Big Ag is doing to us, and trying to make us believe, should be against the law."

"How so?" McGee asked her.

"The GMO and chemical plants present their product with their self-serving research. Granted, most industries and businesses all do that, but what the GMO and its related industries and backers do crosses the line in my opinion. They accuse any person who challenges their findings as being either anti-science or just plain ignorant."

"And they have a strong lobby effort in Washington, don't they?"

"Oh, absolutely. They send their top executives back and forth through the government's revolving doors to ensure that their products hit the market without serious scrutiny. Politicians repeat their claims to keep the donation money coming in."

"You mentioned, back stage, that they have done away with labeling GMO food. Tell our audience about that, if you will."

"People in over sixty countries in the world can choose whether they buy GMO foods or not. Those countries require labeling, but the US does not. Powerful lobbies have convinced, and that means they paid, our politicians to enact legislation that denies Americans the right to know if they are buying GMO food. The bottom line is that big corporations simply control too large a share of our food production industry."

"All right," McGee said, "our time for today is up, and I'd like to thank Elizabeth Bennett, once again, for being on the show today."

The audience gave Elizabeth warm applause, as she left the studio.

While on her last lecture of the month, a man waited in the audience during the questions and comments segment. When the attendant held the microphone up, the man took it out of her hand.

"Yes, Mrs. Bennett," he began," my name, is Sloan Willingham, and I am with *The Inquisitor Magazine*. My question, Mrs. Bennett, is this. Have you ever killed a man?"

The audience reacted with disbelief, and Elizabeth was stymied for a few seconds. This was her worst nightmare come true. She had almost expected it, at some point in time, although she had prayed it would never happen. And yet, here she was, looking at that moment and thinking quickly how to respond. She suddenly recalled something Rick had said, right after the incident with Corley.

"Thank you, Mister Willingham," she said. "I think you might have heard the rumor that several men have committed suicide because I rejected their marriage proposals. There is no truth to it."

The audience burst into laughter, and the attendant took the microphone back from the man. Peggy Boyd asked security to escort Willingham out of the building, and they did, against his protests.

"Where the fuck did that come from, Beth?" Peggy asked Elizabeth after they left the building.

"I don't know, but it scared the hell out of me. What is *The Inquisitor Magazine*, anyway?

"It's a gossip rag," Peggy replied, "in Baltimore, I think. Nobody believes anything they print—two-headed babies, man marries his own grandmother, shit like that."

"Well, I'm not going to worry about it," Elizabeth said. "I just hope it doesn't go any further."

"That was a brilliant response you gave him. He was stupefied."

"I probably should tell Rick about it."

"I think you should," Peggy said."

"Well, we're done for the month, Peg. I'll fly out tonight and see you in a month."

"I'll be ready, peaches. I must admit, I really enjoy working for Earth Publishing. It's so much better than putting up with Corley's shit."

"I'm glad you're happy, Peg, I really mean that."

Elizabeth's plane set down at San Antonio International airport around six o'clock in the evening. She reclaimed her baggage and retrieved the rental car she'd reserved.

Another hour and she would be home. She was thinking about what had happened, and how she was going to tell Rick. Rick would know what to do. He always knew what to do."

Chapter 25

The Tree House

Elizabeth awoke to the sound of hammers, saws, and male voices outside her bedroom window. Rick had already gotten up, and she could smell the aroma of eggs and bacon, drifting into the room from the kitchen. She got out of bed, quickly showered, and put on a pair of shorts and a T-shirt.

Rick spotted her as she came out of their bedroom door. "Good morning, beautiful," he said, "come have some breakfast."

"I shouldn't be eating bacon, you know."

"Two slices never hurt anyone, baby, come on, just two slices."

She consented and sat down and ate her eggs and bacon. "It's better than most of the complimentary breakfasts I get on the road," she said.

"I'm glad you're home, peaches. It will be for a month this time, won't it?"

"Yes, darling, I'm staying home for the whole month. I am working on another book, so I hope that's okay."

"Just so you're at home where I can see you and put my hands on you," he said.

"I'm looking forward to that," she replied, smiling at him coyishly. "Oh, by the way, what is that hammering business I keep hearing?"

"That's the tree house," he said.

"Tree house?"

"Yes, your father is having a tree house built for the kids, in the big oak out front."

"I want to see it."

"Then come on. I'll show you the tree house," Rick said.

Two men were working on a platform, about ten feet off the ground. They had supported it with steel poles, set in concrete. The structure, the floor of the tree house, wrapped around the oak tree, with a gap between the tree and the floor, for the growth of the tree.

Elizabeth was looking up at the gap between the tree and the platform when one of the men spoke to her.

"I know what you're thinking, ma'am," he said. "I'm going to build a short wall around the gap between the tree and the floor, so the kids don't step through it."

"Thank you," she said. "You read my mind. I'm Elizabeth Bennett, what is your name?"

"I'm Seth, Seth Grimmer," the man replied. "I build tree houses."

"I can see that, Seth, I'm happy to meet you. Are you kin to Isaac Grimmer?"

"He's my brother," Seth told her. He climbed down the ladder and walked over to where she and Rick were standing. Pulling a handkerchief out of his pocket, and wiping off his hand, he extended it toward her. "I'm happy to meet you too, Mrs. Bennett."

She shook hands with him. "Please, call me Elizabeth," she said, and he nodded. "So, you build tree houses? I never knew that there are professional tree house builders."

"This is not going to be just any ordinary tree house, Lizzy," Rick said. "Show her your drawings, Seth."

The man took a set of drawings out of his truck and showed them to her.

"Oh, wow, she exclaimed, "this is beautiful. You're an artisan," she said.

"I am, or at least I like to think I am. This design is a traditional one. It will have a walk around porch, that goes all the way around the house, with a fence, of course, to keep the kids from falling off. The finished product will look like an old-style country house, just like in the picture."

"Well, thank you, Seth," Elizabeth said. "I look forward to seeing it when it's finished. I'll try and keep my dad from bothering you. Rick said he has been out here supervising a lot."

"Oh, Harley's no bother. He's a great guy. He's become good friends with my dad. They're both history buffs, so they get along just fine."

The Old German Bakery and Restaurant, on Main Street in Fredericksburg, had become the default location for the weekly meetings between Harley Meadows and Jack Grimmer. Grimmer, being of German descent, knew as much about the history of Fredericksburg as any person in the town. Harley Meadows was fascinated by the uniqueness of the town and had come to love it, even more than he loved Dallas.

"My daughter is thinking of writing about Fredericksburg, if she ever settles down and stops her damned crusading, that is," Harley told Grimmer.

"What she's doing is very important," Grimmer responded. "I wouldn't encourage her to give it up too quickly."

"I'm afraid it's going to affect her family, more than she knows. My son-in-law, Rick, is a very patient man, and he's always let her have her way about almost everything in their lives. He loves her, there is no question about that, but my fear is that he will get tired of having an absentee wife."

"I hope that doesn't happen," Grimmer said "It would be a shame. She's between a rock and a hard place, as the saying goes. She may have a savior complex. That happens to some folks who view their work as a cause instead of just work."

"That's my Lizzy, all right," Harley said. "She thinks she can save the world."

"Causes can inspire you, but they can also leave you disillusioned. I knew people in the army who were in it *for the cause.* I was one of them until I went to Vietnam and saw all the bullshit our government was doing. I lost my enthusiasm for the cause."

"Yeah, I've heard other men say that we were on the wrong side in Vietnam. I don't know much about it. I was only sixteen in 1966, and by the time I started paying attention, I had a wife and two daughters to take care of."

"There wasn't really any good side in the Vietnam War," Grimmer said. "Ho Chi Minh actually believed that the United States would side with him, and he had good reasons for believing that. The French were a European power, interfering in the affairs of a country on another continent. Look at the Monroe Doctrine. We took the position that America would not allow any European nation to invade, take over, or exert any undue influence in any country in the Western Hemisphere. To *Uncle Ho* that translated into his belief that we would view France's presence in Vietnam, the same as we would Germany, or any other European country, taking over Mexico. Eventually, I concluded that the Vietnam War was all about who had the biggest dick."

Harley started laughing. "You're going to have to translate that for me, Jack, I don't understand most of your colloquialisms."

"Well, what it means is that the big shots at the Pentagon wanted to prove that the US could succeed where the French had failed. But when those little bastards shot down my helicopter, the last thing on my mind was the size of their peckers."

"I think I get it now," Harley said, chuckling.

A few days later, at the house, Harley was watching the men working on the tree house and keeping watch over HA and Annie.

"This is going to be my tree house, Grandpa?" HA asked him.

"It is, HA," Harley said, "yours and Annie's."

"But Annie is a girl, Grandpa, tree houses are for boys."

"Don't let your mother hear you say that, boy, she wouldn't take kindly to you ragging on your sister like that. Your mother, and your Aunt Rose, had a tree house when they were little girls."

"Who built the tree house for them?" the boy asked.

"You're looking at him, HA, I built it for them. That was back when I could get around a lot better than I can now."

Harley brought an ice chest out to the picnic table and retrieved several bags from his car. He set the bags on the table and began removing the items from them. "Hey, Seth," he yelled to Grimmer, who was still working on the tree house. "Take a lunch break, young man, I hope you like Church's Chicken. Bring your helper and have lunch with me."

The two men came down from their platform and joined Harley at the table.

"Thank you, Harley," Seth said. "This is very nice of you. We both like Church's Chicken. This guy is Johnny Watters. He's worked for me for a couple of years now.

Harley shook hands with Johnny. "Glad to meet you, Johnny. Dig in and eat all you want, there are soft drinks in the ice chest." Harley made up plates for the two kids and sat them next to him, across the table from Seth. "I had breakfast with your dad, this past Saturday," he told Seth.

"He mentioned that to me. Dad enjoys your meetings, he says you are very agreeable to talk to. He doesn't say that about too many people."

"Well, he certainly gave me something to think about on the Vietnam War. Getting the political perspective on it, from one who was there, is more honest than reading a book or watching a documentary."

"Dad was a helicopter pilot, a warrant officer, and he had some close calls. His helicopter was shot down, in one battle, and he rescued several of his buddies, under enemy fire. He was awarded the DSC for his actions that day."

"The Distinguished Service Cross?" Harley said.

"That's right, he says it was no big deal but most people who know him, think it was a very big deal."

"I think so too, but he seems like a humble man. I guess you just never know about some people. Your dad has quiet strength inside him, and he's very intelligent. That's something a person might not pick up unless you talk to him and get to know him."

"Thank you, Harley," Seth said. "I appreciate that."

Elizabeth received a call from Stuart Pennington, from Earth Publishing, informing her that she was invited to appear on a late-night talk show in New York. It was to be later in the month, after her scheduled lectures in the first two weeks.

Two days before she was scheduled to go back to Virginia, Elizabeth asked Rick to come into their bedroom. "There's something I need to tell you," she said.

"You're not leaving me, are you?"

"No, silly," she told him, "this is serious."

"Okay, tell me," he said.

"It's about the incident with Corley. It didn't happen exactly like I said in my deposition."

He looked at her in shock. "What happened, baby, he did try to rape you, didn't he?"

"Yes, he did, Rick, but how I got loose from him didn't happen like I told you and the police."

"Go on," he said.

"He was on top of me, holding me down. He had my hair in his left hand and was lying across my right arm. I couldn't get it loose from under him, and he was starting to hurt me. I was afraid that I was not going to be able to stop him from raping me. So I acted in desperation, and I said to him, 'Wait, Corley, don't hurt me. Let me take my clothes off.' I was trying to make him think I was giving in to him. He kissed me, and I kissed him back, I just pretended he was you, and I kissed him the way I kiss you. It worked, and he got off me and let me stand up. Then I hit him in the throat. Everything else played out just like I told the police."

"Damn, woman, you are a survivor. That sonofabitch must have had one hell of an ego to think you would give in to him that easily."

"I think he did believe it, Rick," she said. "I believe he thought, all along, that I would eventually give in to his advances. I just never imagined he would do what he did,"

"Thank you, Lizzy."

"I should have told you sooner, but I was afraid of how you would react."

"I'm glad you had the presence of mind to do what you did and thank you for telling me."

Rick drove her to San Antonio, to the airport, and kissed her goodbye. "Don't let this go to your head," he told her. "Fame is fleeting, you know."

"I'm not famous, darling, far from it."

"But you're on your way to it, Lizzy. Just keep your feet on the ground."

"Don't worry about me, husband, I'll be okay."

Pennington met her at the Richmond airport and took her to her apartment at the downtown Residence Inn, where Pennington had relocated her to after the incident with Corley.

"I'll pick you up tomorrow and take you to get your rental car," he told her. "We have a meeting set up to go over your schedule."

"Okay, thanks, Stuart," she said. "I'm going to call Peggy and let her know I'm back in town."

A knock on her door told Elizabeth that Peggy had come to pick her up. When Elizabeth opened the door, she almost didn't recognize Peggy. "Is it really you, Peg?" she said, astonished at the woman's appearance.

"It's really me, Beth," Peggy said. "How do I look?"

"You're beautiful, Peg, absolutely beautiful."

"I've lost twenty pounds and have been doing the exercises you showed me. I wouldn't call myself beautiful, but I sure feel a lot better."

"I think you're beautiful, Peg, so you're going to have to defer to me on this."

Peggy Gail Boyd had grown up in the Shenandoah Valley, in Roanoke Virginia. She was the oldest of the three children of Elias and Gail Boyd, who lived on Melrose Avenue Northwest, in Roanoke. Her two brothers, James and John, were three and four-years her junior, so Peggy was out of high school before her two siblings had started into the ninth grade.

Peggy's early life was as pleasant as could be expected for a plumpish girl who had accepted, early on, that she was not attractive and most likely never would be. Her mother tried to comfort her, on those occasions when she found her daughter crying in her room over some rude and hurtful remark a fellow student had made about her.

After high school, Peggy attended Virginia Western Community College, in Roanoke. Virginia Western Community College was a two-year public college located in the Franklin Colonial neighborhood, of Roanoke. She earned a two-year degree in information technology and worked sporadically for several businesses in the Roanoke Valley area. Disappointed with the lack of what she described as real opportunity in Roanoke, she moved to Richmond when she turned twenty-one years of age.

In Richmond, Peggy rented a one-bedroom apartment and answered an ad for an IT technician at a company called SPCFF, an acronym for, Society for the Promotion of Chemical-Free Food. Peggy was good at her job and enjoyed the work immensely.

Elizabeth and Peggy were on the last leg of a tour that had taken them to Alexandria, Virginia, Leesburg, Virginia, and Gaithersburg, Frederick, and Hagerstown, in the state of Maryland. Their last event was in Baltimore, at the same location they had gone to before, where they had been accosted by three thugs.

"I don't think we should go to Denny's this time, Peg."

Peggy laughed. "Don't worry, Beth, I still have my gun."

"But they won't believe you now. You're much too attractive to pull that off again."

"Men are starting to hit on me," Peggy said. "It's a new experience for me. And I owe it all to you."

"Not really. You did the hard work to get yourself in shape. Just be careful, and keep in mind that most men who hit on you just want to get you in bed."

"I'm being selective," Peggy said. "I'm not under any illusion that the perfect man is going to suddenly come along and want to marry me. I'm not a virgin, you know. I *did it* with a guy several times, when I was in college."

"Rick and I had our first time when we were still in high school," Elizabeth said."

"I can't blame you for that. Rick is a lot better looking than the guy I slept with."

"But it was a good experience for you, wasn't it?"

"Yes, he was not pretty but he was blessed, if you know what I mean."

"I know what you mean," Elizabeth said.

"He made me feel good, but eventually he just stopped calling me. And I wasn't through with him yet."

Elizabeth smiled at her. "Just be patient, Peg," she said. "The right guy will come along, for you. I guarantee it."

"Just my luck, the bastard will come from Baltimore."

Elizabeth received an email from Rick. It was the words to a song, and nothing else. She recognized the song. It was the one he told her he'd heard when he was driving back to Dallas, from Fredericksburg. She googled the song and listened to it on her laptop.

When the song was over, Elizabeth was crying. She answered his email with only two words.

I'm sorry.

At the vineyard, the tree house was finished, and Harley Meadows was making a final inspection. The completed product was a sight to behold, an old-fashioned country home structure sitting in the oak tree in the front yard. It was visible from the highway, if passersby happened to be looking off in its direction as they drove past the property. Rick sent Elizabeth a picture of it, with HA and Annie standing on the wraparound porch, waving to their mother.

"You did a great job on the tree house, Seth," Harley told him. "I guess I owe you some money."

"You paid me half when I started so you owe me a thousand, two-fifty," Seth said.

"Is it okay if I pay you in cash?"

"Oh, heck yes, Harley, that's just fine."

Harley counted out twelve 100-dollar bills and a fifty and handed it to Grimmer. "I really appreciate the job you did. The kids love it."

"No problem," Seth said, "I appreciate the business."

It was "meet the teacher night" at school for nine-year-old HA, and Rick took him to his school to perform that parental duty. As they entered the classroom, the teacher was writing something on the chalkboard and did not see them. She had long brown hair that fell to her shoulders, was very shapely, and dressed nicely. "That's Miss Hunter, Daddy," HA said. When she heard, the boy's voice, she turned around and smiled at them. Rick recognized her immediately.

"Lacey," he said, "is it really you?"

"It's really me, Rick," the woman said. "How have you been?"

"We've been good, Lacey. Wow, I never expected to see you here. My son told me his new teacher's name was Miss Hunter, but it's not an uncommon name, and I didn't make the connection. It's been what, ten years, or so, since you worked at the vineyard?"

"I was in high school when I started, Rick, and then I went to college and worked for you in the summer, between school years."

"You haven't changed much since high school," he said. "So, you became a teacher, I'm glad to know that. And I'm happy you're teaching my boy. I know he'll be in good hands. Why aren't you married, Lacey? You're much too pretty to deprive a young man of the honor of being your husband." The look on her face made him wish he'd not asked her the question. "I'm sorry, Lacey," he said. "It's really none of my business."

"No, it's okay, I appreciate your comment. Can we sit down, I'd like to talk. I didn't schedule any other parent tonight because I knew you were coming with HA."

"Of course," Rick said, and he gave his phone to HA. "Son, why don't you go on the other side of the room and play games on my phone?"

The boy was happy to oblige and scampered off to a desk at the back of the classroom.

"I was married, to a guy I met in college, Texas State," Lacey began. "We got married right after graduation and lived in his hometown, in Tulsa, Oklahoma. I was teaching at a local school, and life was wonderful for a few years. Then Robert, that was my husband, became distant and unwilling to talk and interact with me like he always had before that time. I found out that he was cheating on me with a woman from his job. It got very ugly. I asked him for a divorce, and we got divorced."

"It's hard to believe that a man would cheat on you, Lacey."

"Why, Rick? Men do it all the time."

"But you're beautiful, you're a school teacher, and, as I recall, you were one of the nicest and most amiable people I've ever known."

"That's not always enough. Things happen that we just don't plan on, I guess. I finally got tired of living in the same town where Robert was a constant reminder of our failure at life's most intimate relationship. So I came back home, just before the beginning of the school year. How is Elizabeth?"

"Oh God, Elizabeth, my beautiful, wonderful wife, she tortures me with her career."

"She's gone a lot?" Lacey asked.

"Elizabeth is rarely at home. Her schedule dictates that she tours for a month and then comes home for a month, but it typically let's her come home for only two weeks, sometimes three, in any given month. She does her lectures, and now she's been appearing on a lot of television talk shows."

"Oh, wow, that is impressive. She's so smart, I always felt slightly intimidated by Elizabeth. I'd love to be able to write like she does."

"Her father told me, some time back, that the world is trying to take her away from me. I didn't believe him, and I didn't think much about it, but now I'm not so sure he wasn't right."

"I'm so sorry for that. I hope things work out for you two. It would be tragic if you and Elizabeth do not stay together. My, gosh, you could be the poster-couple for *Happy Marriage Magazine*."

"There's a *Happy Marriage Magazine*?" Rick said.

"I don't know. I just made that up. If there isn't, there should be," she said, chuckling.

"I agree, there should be. Hey, Lacey," he said, "I'm having a dinner at my house this Saturday. My sister, Amanda, is going to have a baby, and she and her husband, Dave, are coming to celebrate. I'd love for you to come, too, if you can make it."

"Of course, I'd love to come, Rick, thank you for inviting me."

Elizabeth didn't like Baltimore, and it wasn't just the incident, in which they had been accosted, that drew her negative feelings about the place. The city seemed dirty and unseemly to her. She had only seen the more dreadful side of Baltimore. The auditorium where the event took place was in a scary part of town, and she just didn't feel comfortable inside or out of the place.

"I made reservations at a Holiday Inn, Beth. I think we'll both feel more comfortable there."

"Good, Peg," Elizabeth replied. "I'm anxious to get back to Richmond."

It was a good show, and there had been great audience participation during the Q and A. Many people in the crowd seemed genuinely interested in the subject Elizabeth was promoting. Both her books, *My Summer in the Dirt* and *They're Trying to Kill Us*, sold several hundred copies. Elizabeth was pleased with herself, despite that her writing hand was aching frightfully from signing so many books. "I'm going to have to have a rubber stamp made, with my signature on it, or I'm going to get carpal tunnel," she told Peggy.

Before she had finished the signing, a man, in the line, approached her and began making lewd comments to her. The man was very large, over six feet tall, even taller than her husband, Rick, and very heavy. None of the men in the line made any move to stop the bully. Peggy went up to him and yelled at him to leave Elizabeth alone, but the man back-handed her and knocked her to the floor. He grabbed Elizabeth and was squeezing her tight against him. She was starting to panic. Before the security guards could get to her, another man grabbed Elizabeth's abuser around his throat, from the back, lifted him off the ground, and slammed him down hard onto the floor. He then threw several punches to the man's face and knocked him out.

Elizabeth had fallen down and was struggling to get to her feet. Peggy, likewise, was just trying get to *her* feet. They both recognized the man at the same time.

"Oh, my god," Peggy, yelled, astonished. "It's Jerry, Beth, it's Jerry."

Jerry Meisner was there, and he first helped Peggy to her feet. Then they both then tended to Elizabeth. "Can you two women not stay out of trouble without me around?" he asked them.

"Are you an angel, Jerry?" Elizabeth said, as she straightened her clothing and brushed her hair back.

"He must be Superman," Peggy said. "What are you doing here, Jerry? How did you know Beth was here?"

"I saw an ad for the event," he said, "and I thought I'd come and see if it was really peaches. I thought you had given up the lecture circuit. What are *you* doing here?"

There was much ado by security about Elizabeth's assailant, and they held him until the police arrived. Elizabeth, Peggy, and Jerry moved out of the way and went to an area removed from the confusion.

"They asked me to come for a year and start the lectures again," Elizabeth told jerry. "Then that year became two years, and here I am still doing it."

"I bet Corley was glad to have you back. He has a mad love for you, in case you didn't know that."

"She knows that, Jerry," Peggy said. "She found out the hard way."

"What do you mean?" he asked. "If he got fresh with Beth, I'll kick his ass."

"You won't have to, Corley is dead."

Jerry looked at Peggy, with confusion on his face, then looked at Elizabeth. "What do you mean?" he said.

"Oh, I really didn't want to ever visit this again, but he came to my apartment on the morning I was leaving to go back home. I don't know what he wanted, but he got a key from the office and went in. I was down the street at Denny's and, when I came back, he was lying on the floor, dead."

After she finished telling him about the incident that resulted in Corley McKnight's death, then about the police investigation and her subsequent clearance from wrongdoing, Jerry was aghast.

"That's sounds like a bullshit story, Beth," he said, "I'm not buying that, sorry. Why don't you tell me what really happened?"

"I can't, Jerry," Elizabeth said. "The police report called it an accident."

"It was an accident, Jerry," Peggy said. "You have to believe us."

He looked at them both with knowing suspicion. "Okay," he said, "it was an accident, I believe you. I don't really want to know what you two are hiding. But, hey, Peg, what's up with you? You're a hottie."

"Oh, I'm n—not," she stammered, visibly nervous from his comment."

"Oh, yeah, you are," he replied. "You look so good, I may have to take you to dinner, but you better bring peaches along to keep me from hitting on you."

"Now, what makes you think I don't want you hitting on me?"

The three of them laughed at Peggy's exuberance over Jerry's attention to her.

"How about we take you to dinner, handsome? It's the least we can do for saving our asses like you did."

"I've never turned down a dinner date with two beautiful women," Jerry said.

They went to La Scala, on Eastern Avenue. After they had placed their orders, Elizabeth and Peggy filled Jerry in on everything that had happened since he left SPCFF.

"Basically," Peggy said, "there is no SPCFF anymore. I work for Beth's publisher. It's been different but a lot more efficient and congenial, since we don't have to deal with Corley anymore."

"I need you to come back, Jerry," Elizabeth said. "I can't handle any more of this uncertainty. Peg and I could have ended up in the hospital before the police showed up. You may have saved our lives."

"That's going to be kind of difficult," Jerry said. "I'm a partner in a business I can't just walk away from. I'd love to go back on the road with you, peaches, but I don't see how I can."

"I understand, Jerry, I do," Elizabeth said, "but I'm worried, not just about myself but about Peggy too."

"We can talk about it and see if there may be some way I can help. Where are you guys going to stay tonight?"

"We were planning to stay at the Holiday Inn," she said.

"I have a townhouse out in Hampden. You should be familiar with the area. It's right close to Johns Hopkins."

Elizabeth nodded her head.

"Why not stay with me? I have a guest room with a king-size bed you both can fit into, comfortably."

"What about your wife, Jerry, are you sure it will be okay with her?

"Well, there's a story there," he said. "It didn't work out for us. We never got married."

"Oh, I'm sorry to hear that," Elizabeth said, and Peggy smiled slightly. "What happened?"

"Her father just couldn't accept an interracial marriage, especially one with his daughter involved in it."

"I'm so sorry to hear that, Jerry. I hope you are not bitter about it."

"No, I'm okay. I always land on my feet."

"Like a cat," Peggy said.

Jerry nodded. "Something like that, Peg," he said.

Jerry's townhome was plush, a two-story, Colonial-style house in a row of townhomes in a very pleasant, tree-lined neighborhood a few blocks from JHU.

"It's a beautiful house, Jerry," Elizabeth told him. "I'm happy that you've done well."

"If I had known you were back on the road, I would have come to Richmond and found you."

"We didn't know how to contact you. Peg tried to find you but with no success."

"Corley and I didn't part on very good terms. I wanted no part of him and his failing company. The man was a piss-poor manager. After he lost his money-maker, that would be you, he went downhill fast."

"Well, like I said, I'm happy you've done well. I want to get your number, so we can stay in touch. But right now, I'm tired. I'd like to get some sleep, if you don't mind."

"Not at all. Let me show you the guest room." He led her upstairs to the guest room. "The bed has clean sheets. You have a bathroom and shower in the room. Should be everything you need, but call me if you need anything else."

"I'll be just fine, thank you, Jerry."

"Okay, I'm going to make some coffee, and talk to Peg a while."

Elizabeth awoke around seven a.m., the next morning, and Peggy was not beside her in the bed. She assumed that Peg had gotten up earlier than she had and had gone downstairs. She smelled the aroma of coffee, drifting up the stairs from the kitchen downstairs. She went down the stairs and walked into the empty kitchen. She poured herself a cup of coffee, added cream, from a creamer that was sitting next to the pot, and sat down at the table.

A few minutes later, Elizabeth heard the knob on Jerry's bedroom door turning and the door being pulled open. She looked up, expecting to see Jerry coming out of the door, but it was not Jerry. Peggy came out of the room, closed the door behind her, and leaned back against it.

She was wearing one of Jerry's shirts and nothing else, except for a full-faced smile. She had the index finger of her right hand, in her mouth, still smiling, which told Elizabeth that her friend was a woman who had been sexually gratified to her complete satisfaction.

She stared at Elizabeth and continued smiling broadly, and with her finger still in her mouth.

Elizabeth smiled back, knowingly and with pleased aston-ishment. She mouthed the words, "You slept with Jerry?" and Peggy nodded, still smiling.

"Oh, my god, Beth," she finally said, as she sat down at the table across from her, "I can't believe what happened to me last night."

"So, Jerry finally noticed you, did he?"

"Oh, he did more than notice me, Beth, he screwed my brains out. It was the most incredible thing that's ever hap-pened to me. I'm so happy."

"I can tell," Elizabeth said. "I want more details when we get back on the road."

Jerry came out of his room, dressed for work, and looking quite handsome, Elizabeth noted. He walked over to Peggy and kissed her, with not a small amount of passion. Then he took out his cell phone. "I want to program your numbers into my phone." Peggy gave him her cell number and, when Jerry finished typing it into his phone, he told her, "I'm going to come and see you every chance I get, if it's okay."

"I would like that very much, Jerry," Peggy said, "thank you for last night."

"Thank *you*, Peg," he said, "now I have to get to work. You guys stay as long as you need to and just lock the door on the way out." He hugged Elizabeth and Peggy, told them how much he enjoyed seeing them again, and left the house.

They were halfway to Richmond before Peggy stopped talking. She told Elizabeth, in intimate details, of her wonder-ful experience in the bed of Jerry Meisner, a man she had loved in secret for so long.

"I'm happy for you, Peg, I really am," Elizabeth said, "but could you maybe find that bluegrass music station again?"

A car arrived at the Lizzy Bee, and Rick went out to meet it. He opened the door for Lacey, and she stepped out, smiling at him.

"Hello, Miss Hunter," he said, "thank you for coming. I wish Elizabeth were here to see you, but I'm afraid Mrs. Ben-nett is out saving the world from itself."

"I would love to see her again," Lacey said, "but I'll come back when she is back in town."

She was wearing a black skirt that came down to just above her knees and a white blouse that fit tightly against her breasts. She was stunning, was Rick's first thought, which he quickly extinguished. He remembered Lacey Hunter as a teenager, still in high school and this woman was definitely not a teenager. "Red or white?" Rick asked her, as he held up two bottles of wine.

"White," she said. "I wasn't old enough to do this the last time I was here."

"Well, you are now," he said, poured her a glass, and brought it to her in the living room.

"I hope you like Italian food," Harley said, from the kitchen where he was preparing the meal.

"I do," Lacey said, "it smells good."

"Oh, I forgot that you never met my father-in-law, Harley Meadows. He's a world-class chef," Rick told her.

Harley raised his hand and waved without stopping his work.

Dave and Amanda arrived. Amanda remembered Lacey and hugged her. "This is my husband, Dave," she told Lacey. Dave shook Lacey's hand.

Amanda and Rick set the table and helped Harley bring the salads and food. Harley's Italian cuisine was a big hit, and they all ate heartily. They talked until almost midnight, then Lacey said she had to go home. Rick walked her out to her car and opened the door for her. "Are you okay to drive?" he asked her. "You look a little unsteady."

"I probably shouldn't have had that last glass of wine, but I'll be okay." He held her hand as she got into her car.

"Thank you, Rick," she said, "I really enjoyed it."

"I'm glad you came, Lacey. When Elizabeth gets home we'll have to do this again."

"You better watch out for that woman," Amanda told him when he came back into the house.

"Oh, come on, Manda, She's HA's teacher, and she used to work for me. I have no hidden agenda in mind for Lacey Hunter."

"Maybe not, but she does," Amanda replied.

Rick scoffed at her suggestion. "I didn't detect any of that in anything she said."

"I don't imagine you did, you were too busy looking at her boobs."

"Amanda, you're imagining things." But he didn't continue the argument because he knew she was right. Lacey was looking at him like a woman in severe need of a man, and he found himself enjoying her attention. She was a beautiful woman now, and he couldn't stop himself from staring at her. He'd tried not to, but she had caught him looking at her several times. Her smile told him that she was enjoying the attention, too.

"I'm imagining that a hard dick has no conscience," Amanda came back at him.

"Dear God, Amanda," Rick said in frustration at his sister's ability to read his mind, "Dave, can't you control your wife?"

"No, Rick, I can't," Dave responded, "and I'm not going to try. My greatest pleasure in life is waiting to see what Amanda might say or do next. I just keep loving her, that's my job."

Chapter 26

Looking Back

2065:

Harley and Annie made a pot of coffee and welcomed Ben Bradley back from his three days in Austin. After getting their coffee, they seated themselves in the living room, and Annie began telling Ben about Elizabeth and Rick, again.

"Mother never told Rick about either of the incidents in Baltimore, Ben. He found out about it when he read her book. He acted like he was mad that she had not told him, at the time, but it was past history by then, so he really wasn't all that upset. Elizabeth continued her lectures, with her faithful sidekick Peggy Boyd, but after a couple of years, the crowd numbers began to dwindle, as did her enthusiasm for the traveling. She was doing a lot of news and talk shows, in New York, and even in Los Angeles. She became quite famous, but she was spending more and more time away from home. Rick became more and more disgruntled, and that weighed on Mother a lot."

"It must have been a grueling schedule for her," Ben said.

"It was horrible, Ben, and it was terribly disconcerting for HA and me. We missed our mother very much. Our Aunt Amanda still worked for Rick, and she became more or less our surrogate mother."

"It seems unfair to you kids," Ben said, "but you don't appear to have any hard feelings toward her for leaving you alone so much."

"Neither of us could ever have had any animosity toward our mother," Annie said. "Elizabeth Bennett was a very special person. She touched people in a very special way. She just made people feel good about themselves. She talked to us just about every night on our laptops and with Skype. We could see her, and she could see us. It wasn't as good as having her with us, but it helped us not miss her quite as much."

"How did your dad manage to get through those times?"

"It was very hard on Rick," Annie replied. "You have to keep in mind that our dad was a very handsome man, and he had a manner about him that endeared him to people, especially women. Rick was always being hit on by women. They flirted with him, and on those rare occasions when he struck up a conversation with one, they would sometimes proposition him. It was humorous to watch. He'd be there with me and HA right with him. They had to know he was married, but some woman would actually make a move on him. He never surrendered to temptation, at least as far as I know," Annie said, "but he came very close one time. Well, I should tell you this first. Before he and Mother got married, Rick did go to bed with a woman from Austin. She had stopped by the vineyard and, when Rick told her about Elizabeth being into the permaculture thing, she gave him mother's first book. Mother was using a pen name, Beth Ann Meadows, at that time, and Rick wasn't completely sure if the writer of the book, was Elizabeth, or not, despite the similarity of the names."

"Anyway, when HA was nine years old, Rick met his teacher, a beautiful woman who had worked for him and Elizabeth at the vineyard. Her name was Lacey Hunter and Lacey was six years younger than Rick and was divorced. Lacey fell in love with Rick, told him she had always had a crush on him, when she was working for him. She let him know what she wanted, and it was more than a one-night stand, or a one-night lay, as the case may be." Annie chuckled at her own joke. "Now, I don't know if Rick ever did anything with Lacey Hunter or not," she continued. "If he did, he never told Elizabeth, or anyone else, but Lacey was crazy in love with Dad, and, even though I was only eight at the time, I could see that he was attracted to her. You didn't read anything about them, in the book, because, like I said, he never told anyone, and neither did Lacey."

"So, what do you think, Annie?" Ben asked her, "did he, or didn't he?"

"I don't know, Ben, I think he probably did, but HA says no."

"Well, I wouldn't venture an opinion on it either way. From what you've told me about your father, I think he was a decent man with an extreme amount of love and patience for your mother."

"He was that," Annie said, "he loved her very much."

Chapter 27

Coming Home

2019:

Dave Braddock owned a water well drilling company, along with his brother Jerry Braddock. Their Uncle Eddie, the brother of their mother, Elise, had willed the business to the two boys when they were teenagers. They began working for him right out of high school, and by the time Uncle Eddie retired, the two men were running the business for him.

Eddie died in 2001, and the Braddock brothers inherited the company. They had done well and provided a good living for themselves and for their widowed mother. Dave married a woman named Patricia, who went by Patty, when he was twenty-years-old. The marriage was doomed to failure from the very beginning. Patty had issues with her self-image, and she suspected Dave of cheating on her. The man had never been unfaithful to her, but Patty accused him constantly, getting angry to the point that he often had to restrain her, physically, from assaulting him.

Long story, short, Dave asked Patty for a divorce, and she attacked him again. While he was restraining her, once again, Patty stumbled over a chair and broke her wrist. She called the police, and they took Dave to the station. They released him right away, however, because Patty's behavior was well known to just about everyone in Fredericksburg.

"I had my officers bring you in, Dave, to get you away from your wife. I know you didn't hurt her, and you won't be charged. Just try and stay away from her until your divorce is final. It will save you a lot of trouble, and me too," Chief Ferguson told him.

"Thanks, Danny," Dave said. "I'm sorry for the trouble. I'll stay as far away from her as I can."

Dave's fortunes made a turn upward early one afternoon while he was shopping at the local Walmart. He noticed a young woman shopping in the same aisle he was in. She was pretty—he noticed that first—with brown hair that fell to her shoulders. He guessed her to be about five feet four and barely weighing more than a hundred pounds. But the hundred pounds were arranged perfectly, as perfectly as Dave had ever seen on a woman, he concluded. He watched her for a short while, being careful not to let her see him watching her.

She rounded a corner and went to another aisle, and he followed her. Dave was smitten with the woman, and he couldn't believe it himself. He was about to leave the area, being concerned that she might figure out that he had been following her and accuse him of stalking. But before he could walk away, she called to him.

"Sir," she said, "can you reach something for me, on the top shelf?"

"Sure," he said, but instead of reaching up and retrieving the item for her, he put his hands on her waist and lifted her up, so she could get it herself.

She started giggling. "Oh, well, I guess that's one way to do it." He held her up for a moment. "Are you going to put me down?"

"I'm sorry," he said, "I hope I didn't offend you, but you are just so damned pretty, I couldn't help myself."

"Who *are* you?" she asked him.

"My name is Dave, Dave Braddock, what is your name?"

"I'm Amanda Bennett. I work for my brother at the Lizzy Bee vineyard, not too far down the road."

"Amanda," he repeated her name, "Amanda is my favorite name."

"Oh, it is not," she said, "you're a bullshit artist."

"Well, it's my favorite name, now, since you put it that way."

She giggled again. "You have a nice smile, Dave Braddock," she said.

"You wanna have some lunch with me, Amanda?"

"I'm not hungry, but I can have some coffee or tea, or something."

"I was hoping you'd say that," he said, "when you're ready to check out, we'll go."

"I'm ready now."

They paid for their purchases and walked to the parking lot.

"If you'll ride with me, I'll bring you back to your car."

"I drive that green Ford one-fifty," she said, pointing in the direction of her truck.

"You drive a Ford one-fifty? Oh, now I *know* I love you," he said.

"You mean you weren't sure until you saw my truck?"

"I was pretty sure," he said. He opened the door to his truck, and she got in. He turned left on 290 and headed back toward town. "You are over twenty-one, aren't you?"

"No, I am twenty-one."

"Okay, that's good, thank you for coming with me."

"Thank you for asking me, Dave. Hey, this is a nice truck. What is it?"

"It's a Toyota Tacoma, double cab. I like this truck. It gets good gas mileage, and it runs great."

He took her to a local café. And the waitress came to take their order.

"I'll just have coffee," Amanda said.

"Same for me," Dave replied.

Amanda looked at him, askance. "Oh, you 'are' a bullshitter. You're not even hungry."

"I had to meet you," he said. "Let me take you to dinner when we're both hungry. Will you go to dinner with me, Amanda Bennett?"

"I would love to have dinner with you, Dave, yes, I will go to dinner with you."

He explained his situation to her, about his marriage and the trouble his wife had caused him. "I want to start off being honest with you," he told her. "I am in the process of getting a divorce, and the papers should be here any day now. Once I receive the papers, sign them, and send them back to the lawyer, I will be done with her."

The attraction was mutual between them. Amanda fell in love with the rough-cut, powerfully built man, and he fell hard for her. She gave up her virginity to him, less than a month after they started dating. From that day on, she never looked at another man, with any sort of romantic inclination. He treated her like she was the only woman in the world, and to Dave, she was. Amanda was a little bit crazy, but she was crazy in a good way. She had no filters and would say whatever came to her mind with no consideration that someone might be embarrassed by her outbursts.

They dated for almost a year before she told her brother, Rick. Dave was five years older than Amanda, and that made him two years older than Rick, and Rick had concerns. His concerns were eventually dispelled after he met Dave and got to know him.

Amanda prattled on endlessly about Dave to her sister-in-law, Elizabeth. "He's just wonderful, Elizabeth. He makes me feel good about *me*, he fills me up."

"What do you mean, he fills you up?"

"I mean he fills me up. He's got a huge—"

"Okay, okay, I get the picture," Elizabeth said.

Amanda kept him smiling through each day and happy to go home at night. They were a perfect couple, and almost everyone who knew them agreed enthusiastically. They had now been married nine years, and their passion for each other had not dimmed one bit.

His world was shattered, however, one morning before he left for work. Amanda was in the bathroom, and Dave heard her yell out to him. He immediately ran to her to see what was wrong.

"I think I lost the baby, Dave," she said, sobbing and holding her stomach.

Dave called for an ambulance and EMTs checked her out. "She's okay," the paramedic told Dave, "but she did miscarry. I'm really sorry, Man, tough break."

"Oh, God, Dave, I'm so sorry."

"You don't have to be sorry, baby. It's not your fault. Shit happens. You didn't do it on purpose."

"But I wanted to give you a son," she said, still crying.

"And I wanted that too, Manda, but we'll try again. Don't blame yourself."

But there would not be another time. Amanda discovered that she could not have children. Doctors told her that, if she became pregnant again, it might kill her.

Dave accepted it. "I still have you, baby," he told her. "You're all I'll ever need. I can't take a chance on losing you."

A late-night talk show, on CBS, that was entitled *America Tonight*, invited Elizabeth to do a segment on the show. The host was slick, ex-actor, named Zeke Graham. Graham was a bore, who was more convinced of his own talent than his movie producers apparently were. Regardless, Elizabeth and Peggy boarded a plane at Richmond Airport and flew into JFK in New York City.

Two people met them at the waiting area outside the terminal. The woman introduced herself, first. "I'm Samantha Freeman, Elizabeth, and this is Jeff Howell, and we're with the Zeke Graham show. We'll take you to the studio, and after the show, we have a room for you at the Marriott Marquis.

"Hi, Samantha," Elizabeth said, "this is Peggy Boyd, my assistant."

"Do you have bags to pick up?"

"No, we travel light, we just brought carry-ons."

They took them to a limo, and Jeff opened the door for them in the back, Samantha got in the back with Elizabeth and Peggy, and Jeff drove the limo. Elizabeth made mental notes on the route from JFK to the CBS studio. While Samantha went over some details about the show, Elizabeth noted that they took Interstate 678, to 495.

"What's the name of this tunnel we're going through?" she asked Samantha.

"This is the Queens Midtown Tunnel," she replied.

"I'm trying to remember the route, in case I ever come to New York with my husband. I want him to think I know my way around."

Samantha smiled and ignored her comment. "Now, Elizabeth, let me tell you a little about the host of the show. Zeke is an actor, but he doesn't make movies any longer. Have you seen any of Zeke's movies?

"Honestly, Samantha, I'd never heard of him until I got the call from your scheduler. I don't go to a lot of movies."

"Zeke is a bit of an egomaniac," Samantha told her. "There is no foundation for it, in my opinion, but he is certainly sold on himself. You don't have to pander to him—"

"I don't pander to anyone," Elizabeth said.

"No, I don't expect you to, but you might express some interest in his movies. He'll love that."

"I thought I was asked to be on the show to discuss my books and my mission."

"Oh, of course," Samantha said, "just be yourself, Elizabeth. It will be awesome."

Elizabeth and Peggy were waiting in the side wing for Elizabeth to be called to the set. Zeke did his monologue and then began Elizabeth's introduction.

"Ladies and gentlemen," he said, "we have a special guest tonight. This lady is the author of two books and has been on speaking tours for a number of years. Her mission is to make Americans aware of the benefits of chemical-free soil for food production. She promotes grass-fed beef and has taken on the agriculture and pharmaceutical industries in her effort to rid the world of GMO as the norm in American food production. Now, if the men will stop drooling long enough to listen to this lady, you might learn something. Let's welcome to the stage, Elizabeth Meadows Bennett."

"That's your cue, Elizabeth," Samantha said, "take the seat right next to the desk."

Elizabeth stepped out and began walking across the stage. The audience applauded, and some shouted. A few men whistled and cheered as Elizabeth took her seat.

Zeke shook hands with her and took a sip of coffee then began. "I have to tell you, Elizabeth, I could tell by the audience reaction, that you are not what they expected. You're very attractive. "How did you get into such a 'dirty' business?" He made air quotes to emphasize the word, dirty.

Elizabeth retold her story, quickly and as briefly as possible, about her work on the Graham farm. "I wrote my first book, which I entitled, *My Summer in the Dirt*, based on my experiences that summer," she told him.

"And I understand you began lecturing on the preparation of chemical-free soil."

"I did, Zeke, and I still do.

"I read your book," he said, "and what I found most interesting was how they are able to produce grass-fed beef on a relatively small amount of acreage. Could you talk about that?"

"The process is called paddock rotation." She gave her quick overview, of the process and they broke for a commercial.

During the break, Zeke made small talk with her. "Have you ever thought about becoming an actress?" he asked her.

"I've never done any acting, so no, I haven't given it much thought," she told him.

"That's unfortunate," he said," you're really beautiful. You do know that, don't you?

"That's what my husband tells me," Elizabeth said.

"Well, you're doing great, so just keep on doing what you're doing."

"Thank you, Zeke, I appreciate your having me on the show."

"My pleasure," he replied, "you're going to be good for my ratings."

Elizabeth laughed. "Business is business," she said.

The break ended, and they were back live. The audience applauded as they began again. Elizabeth figured they had an applause sign that told the crowd when to clap. She was not so self-centered to believe that their spontaneity was all about her.

"So, tell me, Elizabeth, you have a PhD from Johns Hopkins, is that right?"

"No, I have a BS from Johns Hopkins. I dropped out, before I got my PhD, to start doing what I'm doing now."

"I see, that was my mistake," Zeke said. "You are now taking on Big Ag and Big Pharma?"

"Yes, I'm trying to expose the dangers of GMO food and the benefits of getting back to locally owned family farms that have a direct connection with the consumer. I'm also trying to teach people how the medication-manufacturing industry is doing more to prolong poor health among Americans than they are doing to help."

"How do they get away with it, Elizabeth?"

"They buy politicians, Zeke. The Ag and Pharma lobbies in Congress are powerful and have a death grip on the American people. Do you realize that more people die from the traditional cure for cancer than from the disease itself?"

"No, I didn't know that," Zeke said. "It sure gives us something to think about."

And that wrapped up Elizabeth's segment on the show. Zeke thanked her for her appearance, shook her hand, and she walked off the stage to rousing applause.

"Jeff will take you to the hotel," Samantha told her, "and here's my card. You have an afternoon flight tomorrow. Breakfast or lunch, or both, if you choose, is on us, so enjoy yourselves. Jeff and I will pick you up at one o'clock to take you to the airport.

Their room was on the fortieth floor of the Marriott Marquis. They slept late and then got up and showered, got dressed, and went to lunch. Their room was on the south side, so they had a great view of Midtown and Lower Manhattan. Elizabeth decided that she and Rick must come to New York, one day, maybe on their wedding anniversary.

Elizabeth called Rick and told him about the show. "I was watching, baby," he said, "the kids and I watched you together."

"Wasn't it kind of late for them to be up?"

"It's an hour earlier, in Texas, besides, they wanted to see you. You were great, Lizzy."

"Thank you, darling, the host was a lot nicer than I expected him to be."

"He kept staring at your legs," Rick said, "but then I was too."

"I didn't really notice. He seemed to be genuinely interested in what I had to say."

"It was your legs he was interested in, Lizzy. It's their job to appear interested in what their guests have to say. I guarantee you, he's forgotten everything you said. But I bet he remembers your legs."

"Oh, God, Rick, I miss you so much. I wish I could wrap my arms around you, right now."

"Then come home, baby, I miss you too."

"I will, just as soon as I finish this tour. I have two more shows, and I'll come home for a month."

"You promise?"

"Yes, I promise," she said. But Elizabeth was not prepared for the next curve that life would throw at her.

She was finishing her last event, looking forward to going home, when a familiar face approached her in the book-signing line. It was Sloan Willingham, the reporter who had asked her if she had ever killed a man.

"Hello, Mrs. Bennett, do you have anything to say about Corley McKnight, before I run the story in my magazine?"

"What is it you think you know, Mister Willingham?" Elizabeth asked him.

"I know that you killed him," the man said.

"You don't know half of what you think you know. Why don't you just leave me alone?"

"I have a right to know, Mrs. Bennett. Will you tell me what happened when he died?"

"I have nothing to say to you, and you should leave, or I'll call security."

"Corley McKnight raped my sister, Mrs. Bennett."

Elizabeth was stunned when she heard that. "What?" she said, disbelieving what she had heard.

"Corley raped my sister, Julie, in 1998, and it ruined her life. Please, I know he tried to rape you, and it will be justice for her if I know he died trying to commit another rape."

"I'm sorry, Mister Willingham, but there are reasons I cannot tell you what happened to Corley McKnight."

"I know you can't go on record because they called it an accident, but I just want to know, for my sister."

"What about the magazine story?" she asked him.

"There is no magazine story. I don't work for *The Inquisitor*. I just made that up to shock you into telling me the truth." He showed her a picture of his sister, Julie, when she was nineteen before Corley raped her. Then he showed a picture of the woman as she looked now.

"My God, Mister Willingham, I'm so sorry, that poor woman."

Willingham was dejected and was looking down, almost as if he were praying.

Elizabeth turned the picture over and scribbled something on it. "I hope your sister finds some closure for this and is able, eventually, to put it behind her."

"She never has, and she never will," he said, "Thank you, ma'am, I won't bother you again."

In July, during harvest, Rick received a call from Billy Ramirez, the oldest son of Carlos Ramirez, Rick's long-time faithful foreman. Carlos had collapsed in the field, and Billy ran to the trailer to call Rick.

"Did you call nine-one-one, Billy?" Rick asked him.

"Yes, sir," the boy said, "they're on the way."

"I'll be right there Billy." Rick called Amanda in the office, "I'm going to the Luckenbach property, Manda," he told her, "Carlos Ramirez just collapsed in the vineyard. I'll keep you informed."

When he arrived at the property, the ambulance was there, and they were putting Carlos inside for transportation to the hospital.

Rick ran to the ambulance. "What can you tell me?" he asked one of the attendants.

"Don't know yet," the man said, "he was unconscious when we got here. We gave him aspirin, intravenously, now we need to get him to the hospital. We'll do CPR on the way."

Rick went to the trailer, where Carlos' wife Martina, was frantic and crying. Billy was trying to comfort her. "Come with me, Martina. I'll take you to the hospital." He got her and Billy into the truck, called Amanda, and asked her to come and watch the smaller children, and then drove to the hospital.

Carlos was dead before the EMTs got him to the hospital. He had died from a massive heart attack. Rick held Martina in his arms, while she wept inconsolably. Billy Ramirez was stricken, by what had happened to his father, and he went to them. Rick put his arm around the boy and held them both until a nurse came over and asked him about insurance.

"Billy, take care of your mother while I go do the paperwork for them."

The boy persuaded his mother to sit down, and he sat down beside her and held her as she continued sobbing.

"What is your relationship to Mister Ramirez, sir?" the nurse asked him.

"Carlos works for me, my name is Rick Bennett, here is my insurance card. Carlos is on my group insurance plan. Any expenses, the insurance doesn't cover, I'll take care of."

"We'll need to talk to the wife regarding Mister Ramirez's final disposition, Mister Bennett."

"She may not be up to that right now, let me ask her?"

"I don't have any money, Rick," Martina began telling him when he asked her about picking a funeral home to take Carlos to.

"Don't worry, Martina, Carlos has insurance, and, if it doesn't cover everything, I will."

Carlos was taken to a local funeral home and was buried in Greenwood Cemetery. Rick paid for the plot and helped Martina arrange the funeral.

The woman was terrified. "I have no money. What am I going to do, Rick?"

"You're going to not worry, Martina," he told her. "Billy, I don't speak Spanish, explain to your mother that all of you will be able to stay in your home, for as long as you want to. You won't have to pay rent or for any utilities or anything else. Tell her not to worry. I will take care of everything."

The boy related the message to his mother, and she became less distraught. She hugged Rick around his waist—being a very short woman, at least a foot shorter than Rick—and cried on his chest.

Billy Ramirez was seventeen-years-old, at the time, and he asked Rick to let him work on the vineyard. "Papa taught me everything, Rick, he showed me how to run the irrigation system and water the plants just right, and not waste water. I can work and pay for my family living here."

"Don't you go to school, Billy?" Rick said.

"Yes, sir, I do, but I'll work after school, and I'll get up early to water the plants. My brothers, and my sister will help me chop the weeds and check the plants for bugs. Papa taught me how to do it."

Rick and Billy arrived at an agreement on salary for Billy. Rick helped Billy get his driver license, so he could use his father's truck on the vineyard work and to take his siblings to school and his mother to buy groceries and other household needs.

Rick sent Elizabeth an email, not wanting to tell her on the phone. It was cowardly, he knew, but expedient.

Dear Elizabeth, I'm sorry to bring you this news in an email, but I just didn't have the energy to tell you on the phone.

Carlos Ramirez had a heart attack and died today, and also, Amanda had a miscarriage and lost her baby.

I love you, Rick.

Elizabeth had precious little time to dwell on the bad news. It was a terrible blow, but she knew that Rick would take good care of Carlos's family, and that Dave would be comforting and loving to Amanda. Elizabeth would make up for not being there when she got home.

When she returned to Richmond, she called DA Piccolo and asked to come in and talk to him.

"I've been approached by a man who asked me about Corley McKnight."

"What did he say, Elizabeth," Piccolo asked.

"The first time he stood up in the audience, for the Q and A, and asked me if I'd ever killed a man. I deflected the question, the audience laughed, and security hustled him out of the building. Then this past week, he showed up again in my book signing line and told me that Corley had raped his sister, back in 1998. I expressed sympathy for his sister but told him I couldn't tell him anything different from the police report. He looked beaten and like the life was gone out of him. I came to see you as soon as I got back in town."

"Okay, you did good, if he contacts you again, be sure to let me know."

"I will," she said, "thank you, Mister Piccolo."

Later, in her office, Elizabeth turned to Peg. "I'm going home for a month, Peg," she said."

"I'm glad to hear it, Beth, you need a break."

"You seem to be in good spirts, what's up with you?"

"Guess where I'm going, Beth?"

"Well, judging by the smile on your face, and that finger in your mouth, I'd say you're going to see Jerry Meisner."

"Bingo," Peggy said. "He called me last night and told me he missed me. Can you believe that, Beth? Jerry called me and asked me to come and see him."

"Why not, Peg? You're a good-looking woman, and apparently very good in the sack, for him to call you like that."

"I'm going to make him very glad he called me, Beth."

"Yes, I expect you will. Have fun, Peggy Boyd."

When Elizabeth arrived at the San Antonio Airport, Rick was waiting for her. "We're spending the weekend in San Antonio," he told her.

"I'm up for that, where are we staying?"

"I have a room for us at the Courtyard Marriott, on the river," he said.

"What a pleasant surprise," she said, "thank you darling. I needed this."

"We're on the fifteenth floor. The back of the hotel is right on the river."

They checked in and took the elevator up to their room. "I only have one change of clothes with me. I hope you are not planning to go to a fancy restaurant."

"You'll be fine, baby, we can buy you some more clothes, if we have to. How do you like the room?"

"It's very nice," she said. "I like it."

"Good," he said, as he sat down on the bed and leaned back against the headboard. "Now, take off your clothes."

"What?"

"Take off your clothes."

"Are you serious?" she asked him.

"Yes, I am serious. I want to see you naked. I haven't seen you naked in a while, and I want to see you naked."

She began unbuttoning her blouse as she looked at him seductively. He stared into her eyes until she took off her bra, then his eyes wandered down her body and joyfully drank in her beauty.

"Now come over here."

He sat up on the side of the bed. She came to him and wrapped her arms around him. The sexual chemistry between them was electric.

When their passion was spent, she told him, "We haven't done that in so long, I'd almost forgotten how good you are at making love."

His arm was around her, and her head was laying on his chest.

"I was desperate for you," he told her.

"That was incredible, darling. I've missed you so much."

"It's time for you to come home, Elizabeth," he said sternly.

"I know, Rick, I will."

"When?"

"There's just so much to do. I have five more talk show appearances to make that I've already committed to."

"I've always let you have your way, baby, because I am so in love with you that I have no rationality, where you are concerned. But now it's time for you to come home."

"I know you don't share my passion and sense of urgency about my work, but you've always accepted my desire to make a difference in people's lives. I just wish you would try and understand how I feel about it. It's important."

"Your family is important, too, Lizzy, I'm important too. I think you are blinded by the lights."

"I don't know what that means, Rick," she said.

"I don't think you're doing this for the *cause* anymore, I think it's all about you, now."

"That's not fair, Rick. Do you really think I'm that superficial?"

"I do," he said. "I think you love the attention, being the *star*, and having people, men, telling you how beautiful you are. I think you've gotten caught up in the *show*, and it's no longer about a cause. The cause was just a means to a higher end."

"That hurts me terribly, darling. If that's what I have become, I certainly didn't intend to become that. But I do have commitments."

"You committed to a one-year tour and book promotion. That was three years ago, Elizabeth. Your world has passed me by. It's passed the kids by, too."

"Then tell me what you want me to do, and I'll do it."

"I want you to quit, not in a year, but now. I want you to come home, write books, drink wine with me, and make love every day."

"Make love every day?" she said, looking up at him and smiling.

"Every other day, maybe—okay, twice a week."

In Baltimore, Maryland, at the home of Jerry Meisner, Peggy was sitting at the table, in the breakfast nook, drinking coffee. Jerry was making breakfast for them. He finished his work and brought two plates to the table then went and took a tray of biscuits out of the oven.

"I'm really glad you came, Peg," Jerry said as they ate their breakfast.

"You're not as glad as I am, Jerry," Peggy told him. "You are super fantastic in bed. I can't begin to tell you how you make me feel."

"It's mutual, baby," he said.

Peggy felt a rush come over her when he used a term of endearment to address her, instead of calling her by her name. She played casual and made no indication that it was anything but common practice, for him to do that. But her heart was pounding, and she was sure that he could hear it.

"I want to talk to you about something," he said.

"What is it, Jerry?"

"I've been with a lot of women, Peggy, I think you know that. But every romantic relationship in my life has been superficial, all about getting women into bed. Did I enjoy it? Yes, I did."

She started snickering.

"At least I thought I did," he continued. "Now, I'm not so sure about that. I'm forty-years-old, and I don't know much, but I do know I can't go on like this forever. It's probably too soon to be talking about getting married, but if you would consider moving in with me, we might talk about that, if you think you want to."

"Are you serious, Jerry," she almost yelled at him. "I've loved you since the first time we met. I'll do anything you want me to do, move in, get married, it doesn't matter. I'll be the best thing that's ever happened to you."

"Well, I love you too, Peggy," he told her. "Will you marry me?"

"Yes, yes," she said through the tears that were streaming down her face, into her mouth, and down her neck. "I would love to marry you. It's all I've ever wanted, or imagined, could happen."

Elizabeth called Stuart Pennington and told him she was not going to come back to Virginia. She asked him to cancel her appearances on the talk shows and the rest of her lectures.

Pennington was philosophical about it, disappointed, but understanding. "You made us a lot of money, Elizabeth. You put us on the map. I understand your need to get back to your life. I wish you nothing but happiness and good fortune."

"Thank you, Stuart, I appreciate the opportunities you gave me," she said, "I'll never forget it."

HA was now fourteen. She finally noticed that her son—her baby boy, her first born child—was now taller than she was. HA derived immense pleasure from that fact. Annie was still a few inches shorter than her mother and was not bothered by it.

Elizabeth began doing research on the history of Fredericksburg. She had decided to write about little-known historical events and people who had been important to the town and had added, in some way, to its personality and persona.

"You'll need to talk to Jack Grimmer," her dad told her. "He knows a lot about the history of Fredericksburg, he's lived some of it, actually."

"I will, Daddy, thank you. I want to write about things no one has thought about, yet."

"I'm glad to have you home again, baby," Harley said.

"It's good to be home, Daddy, this is where I belong."

Chapter 28

Back to Earth

Sloan Willingham, the man who had confronted Elizabeth about the incident in which Corley McKnight ended up dead had accepted that he was not going to gain any closure for his sister, Julie. After Corley raped her, her life was never the same again. A life of dependency on alcohol and drugs left her a wrecked human being. Unable to get close to any man and afraid of entering into relationships of any kind for fear of being betrayed, she sleepwalked through her life and never really recovered.

Her brother, Sloan, supported her and paid for countless therapy and counselling sessions, all for naught. She became an almost crippling burden to him, but he never faltered in his compassion and his zeal to gain closure and some semblance of life, for his older sister.

The news reported that Corley McKnight had died in a freak accident in the apartment of a company employee. Claims were made that he had tripped and fallen against a chair, struck his throat on the back of the chair, and had died at the scene. Willingham had been suspicious of the police report.

Not long after the incident, the police report gave the name of Corley's business, and Willingham looked up the address. Upon arrival at the SPCFF, he found the staff cleaning out their desks and beginning to close up shop.

"What's going on?" he asked the first person he met.

"Out of business," the man said.

"Why, what happened?"

"The boss died."

"Oh, my goodness," Willingham replied. "I'm so sorry to hear that."

"Can I help you, sir? I'm Herman Nichols, I used to work here."

"I was interested in getting some information about your business. I want to know more, about the permaculture business your company promotes."

"I can give you some brochures, if you want," Herman said, and he went to a file cabinet to retrieve the items. "The best advice I can give you is to check out one of these lectures by Elizabeth Bennett. Elizabeth is a writer and speaker. She conducts lectures on the subject. She really knows her stuff." He handed the man a brochure that had Elizabeth's picture on it.

Willingham perused the brochure for a moment. "She's a very attractive young woman," he said in a factual sort of way, not expressing any inappropriate interest in Elizabeth.

"Oh, she'll make your mouth water, in person," Herman said. "Ol' Corley never got his hands on that, although he tried awfully hard."

"How did Mister McKnight die, if you don't mind me asking?"

"He died in her bedroom," Herman said, pointing the brochure."

"Did she kill him?"

"No, of course not. She was gone, and Corley went to her apartment for some unknown reason. When she returned, she found him in her bedroom, laying on the floor, dead. The police determined that he had tripped, fell against a chair, and hit his throat on the back of it."

"That's kind of strange, don't you think?"

"It's downright bizarre," Herman said, "especially him being in her bedroom. Corley had it really bad for Elizabeth. He was a little strange. He'd get mad if anyone in the office even looked at her like they were...you know...slobbering over her."

Willingham was even more suspicious of the police report after talking to Herman Nichols. He was sure the woman had something to do with McKnight's death. He decided he would attend one of her lectures and confront her about it.

After two attempts trying to get Elizabeth Bennett to admit to him that Corley McKnight had assaulted her, and failing both times, he gave up. He was certain of his suspicion, but the woman was obviously protecting a cover-up on her behalf by the police.

About a week after his last attempt, to solicit a confession from Bennett, he was coming out of the grocery store with a basket full of goods. He pushed the basket to his car and was taking out the items and putting them in his car. A man walked up behind him, put his hand on Willingham's shoulder, and shoved what felt like a pistol into his back. From his reflection in the car window, Willingham could see that the man was wearing sweat pants and a dark hoodie. The hoodie was pulled up over his head.

"We know about your attempts to confront Elizabeth Bennett," the man said. "I'm not going to ask you your reason, but if you don't forget you ever heard her name, the next time I walk up behind you, it will be to put a bullet in your head. Are we clear?"

Willingham, shaking from fear, nodded his head. "Yes," he said, "I understand."

So, that was it. He knew he had to give up on ever getting even a slight degree of closure for Julie. He'd hoped that, if he could prove to her that Corley McKnight was a sexual predator, it might make her realize that what happened to her was not her fault. Now he had to give it up or lose his life.

It was Wednesday morning, and Elizabeth had told her father she would go with him to his regular weekly breakfast with Jack Grimmer at The Old German Bakery and Restaurant.

"I'm going to write a book about a select few prominent citizens of Fredericksburg, Mister Grimmer, and my dad said I need to put you in it."

"Well, I'm not so sure the city fathers would share you fa-ther's opinion of my alleged prominence, but I would certainly be honored to be in your book, Elizabeth, and please call me Jack. What do you want to know about me?"

"It's going to take some time, Jack," she said, "would you be willing to come to my office at the house?"

Grimmer consented and, the next day, met her at the Lizzy Bee for an interview.

"How long have you lived in Fredericksburg, Jack?" she asked him.

"Well, let me think. I moved to Fredericksburg not long af-ter I came back from Vietnam, a few years. It's been about thirty-two years, I'd say."

"And what brought you here?"

"I had a friend who lived here, who was active in the local theater group, or theatre—" He spelled it for her. "—they call it the Fredericksburg Theatre Company. My understanding of the word is, as I have been told, that the British spelling is used when referring to the building, or an organization. That might be all wrong, but that is what I was told. Anyway, I came to Fredericksburg for a visit and tried out for a role in one of the plays."

"So, you were an actor?"

"I wanted to be an actor, in high school," he told her. "Af-ter graduation, I went to New York to get on 'Broadway.'" He emphasized the word Broadway with air quotes.

"So, did you get on Broadway, Jack?"

"I did," he said, "every time I took the bus down to the Macy's at Herald Square to my job in the bakery."

She began chuckling at his self-deprecating humor. "Did you manage to get in any plays?"

"I was an extra, in a couple of Off-Broadway productions, but no speaking parts. The next Laurence Olivier, I was not destined to become."

"How did you end up in Vietnam?"

"I joined the army. I had no desire to go to Vietnam but joined the army because my father had been in the army air corps, in World War Two. I wound up in Germany, at a place called Bamberg, which is in the northeast corner of Germany, north of Nuremberg. It was cold, I mean very cold. And I was a Texas boy who was not used to that kind of cold. On one exercise, they sent helicopters to transport us to the battle area. I was sitting in that warm helicopter, watching those pilots, all dressed up in their Sunday best, just as warm as toast. When my gang had to get out of the helicopter and jump back into the cold German winter, those pilots flew off in their warm helicopter. I went the next day and applied for Helicopter School."

"And they sent you to Vietnam?"

"After I became a pilot, they did. I was assigned to the Three-Thirty-Third Assault Helicopter Company, based at Soc Trang, in the Delta."

"You flew a Huey?" Elizabeth asked him.

"Right you are, missy, the UH-1D, a troop carrier. We mostly carried ARVNs, that's soldiers of The Army of the Republic of Vietnam."

"Daddy told me your helicopter was shot down, and that you saved everyone and won the DSC."

Jack looked puzzled. "I didn't tell him all that. I told him my aircraft was shot down, but nothing more than that. Are you sure you heard him, right?"

"I'm sorry, Jack, Daddy said your son, Seth, told him that."

"Oh, yeah, that's possible," he said, "My boys sometimes talk too much. Several of our aircraft were shot down, my troop commander, and a good friend of mine, Captain Simmons, was killed and a lot of other people, most of the ARVNs were killed. The actual conflict bore little resemblance to the combat report."

"But you did receive the DSC? Daddy told me that's the Distinguish Service Cross, just one level down from the Medal of Honor. That's right, isn't it?"

"Yes, that's right, but you have to understand, there is a great deal of BS associated with the awarding of medals. There was a major in charge of the operation, and he wanted to get a medal to look good on his resume. The overall commander of the operation was in a helicopter, flown by a Viet-

namese general, above the battle. He was observing our land-
ing and kept telling Captain Simmons to set down too close to
the tree line. The enemy was in bunkers just inside the tree
line. Captain Simmons tried to tell him we needed to set down
farther back, so the troops would have time to form up and
move in. The commanding officer would have none of it, and,
as a result, when we landed, we were immediately under fire.
Captain Simmons's ship was shot down, and when I started to
withdraw, I was hit, and my aircraft went down. The major
was in Captain Simmons's aircraft, which had come down on
its side, and he scratched his leg getting out of the ship. All of
us, who were not dead or wounded, formed a perimeter, and I
took the M-Sixty out of my ship and set it up, in case the enemy attacked us. What saved our hides were the F-One-Oh-
Fives out of Saigon. They came in carrying napalm, a lot of
napalm, and burned them up. It was beautiful, and horrifying,
at the same time. I'll never forget the screams of those men in
their bunkers, being cremated alive. For them to award me the
DSC, the commander of the operation, the major, had to receive a medal." He received a purple heart, for the scratch on
his leg, and the Silver Star for his actions in the battle. They
gave me the DSC."

"I hope you don't think that cheapens what you did, Jack,"
Elizabeth said.

"No," he said. "I don't, I was just glad to get out in one
piece."

After Grimmer left, Elizabeth thought about what he had
told her. The older generation was so different from hers. Here
was a man, who according to his own son and Elizabeth's father, was a true American hero. He had saved lives in a terrible
ordeal, and he played it down like it was not really such a big
deal. She had never known anyone like that.

With Grimmer's help, Elizabeth was able to put together a
list of twenty-five people, men and women, who had contributed to the unique greatness of Fredericksburg. All the people
on the list, except for one, were just ordinary people, no politicians, and no exceedingly wealthy individuals. They were men
and women who, like Jack Grimmer, had lived their lives qui-

etly, making and keeping friends and never seeking to bring more attention to themselves than was their due. She remembered a scripture from the bible, *Let another man praise thee, and not thine own mouth, a stranger, and not thine own lips.* She had to google it, to find the location in the bible, which was, Proverbs 27:2.

The only name on her list of ordinary people, who was anything but ordinary, was Chester W. Nimitz, a Fredericksburg native, born February 24, 1885, died February 20, 1966, in Yerba Buena Island, in San Francisco Bay, California.

Nimitz was a fleet admiral, in The United States Navy, who became Commander in Chief of The United States Pacific Fleet, in World War II. Elizabeth listed three of Admiral Nimitz's quotes.

Uncommon valor was a common virtue.

God grant me the courage not to give up what I think is right even though I think it is hopeless.

A ship is always referred to as "she" because it costs so much to keep one in paint and powder.

It took Elizabeth a year to complete the book. She struggled to come up with a title. Rick gave it some thought and suggested a title, with a sub-title.

Inconspicuous Heroes
Who Walk Among Us

"I like it," Elizabeth said.

"Who are you going to ask to publish it for you, Lizzy.

"I'll probably self-publish and put it on Amazon."

"Good, a publisher might want you to go all over the country, signing books."

"I'll have to do promotion myself, Rick," she told him, "if I want to sell any of them, I mean."

"What does that mean?" he asked.

"Don't worry. I doubt there will be much of a market for this book, outside of Fredericksburg and the Hill Country."

Elizabeth was right. The book sold less than two-thousand copies. She was disappointed, but not devastated.

"Now you know how I felt, baby, when my book bombed," Rick said. "You're not used to losing, are you?"

"I wasn't expecting a best-seller, but yeah, you're right, I don't like losing."

One afternoon, Elizabeth was working on her computer when she received a phone call. The voice on the other end was a woman's voice. She seemed hesitant to speak and cleared her throat several times before she spoke. "Hello," the woman said, "I found this number in my brother's things, and I don't know who this is."

"My name is, Elizabeth Bennett. Will you tell me your name? Maybe I can help you out."

"My name is Julie Willingham, and my brother, Sloan, had a picture of me with your number on it. I don't have a clue, why he had it."

"Is Mister Willingham okay, Julie?" Elizabeth said.

"Sloan died about a month ago. Do you know anything about this?"

"Oh, I'm so sorry, Julie. I gave your brother my number, and I was hoping he would call me. You see, he contacted me about the death of Corley McKnight. He told me that Corley had sexually assaulted you, many years ago, and he was convinced that Corley died trying to rape me."

"Sloan was thinking that, if I knew that Corley was a rapist and had tried to rape you, it might help me deal with it. He wanted me to understand that it was not my fault, what Corley did to me."

"Yes," Elizabeth said, "that's what your brother told me too."

"Okay, thank you," Julie said, "I just called to see who it was. I guess it doesn't matter anymore. Sloan was more obsessed with finding out that Corley was killed committing another rape than I ever was. It ruined my life, but I knew he was a rapist because he raped me. I didn't need to know any more than that. I'm just happy that he didn't rape you, too, Mrs. Bennett."

Elizabeth spent a moment, in deep thought, trying to decide how to respond to the woman. Finally, she spoke. "I am too, Julie, thank you for calling. I'm really sorry about your brother."

Two years after she left the lecture circuit, Elizabeth began to examine her life. In his efforts to bring her back home, her husband told her she was no longer doing lectures for the stated cause, but rather for ego. She eventually realized that he was right. She was glad to be back home. She loved her life, but she did miss the attention, the whirlwind, the constant motion. She enjoyed people fussing over her, complimenting her, and telling her she was either smart or beautiful. It was a rush and was exciting.

The Bennetts, Rick and Elizabeth, had led charmed lives, blessed lives. Having met and fallen in love in high school, to Elizabeth, it seemed that their lives had been orchestrated, programmed somehow, to always work out right. It had been magic, their love never faltered, and they had disagreed rarely. They just always seemed to win life's lottery.

Elizabeth wrote two more books, after *Inconspicuous Heroes*, on little-known events in Fredericksburg history. The books made money but never came close to her first two on the cult-like genre she had promoted with such passion. She learned that she simply had no passion for the mundane or the commonplace. Her past success occurred because she had put her soul into everything she did. The world's interest was in her, the woman she was. They wanted her, not what she could write about forgotten history. Men fell in love with her, and it was exhilarating, although her deepest love never diminished for Rick Bennett. Rick had remained hers, for all those years she was away from him. He stayed on their vineyard and made his wine and waited for her. But coming back to Earth had its price and its reality.

The fog of real life visited Elizabeth, coming in on little cat feet, as Carl Sandburg put it. Walking into the house, she found her father, Harley Meadows, lying on the floor, lifeless. The frantic efforts to revive him, the ride to the hospital in the ambulance with him, brought the fog of life into Elizabeth's world. All the success, the oratorical skills, personality and passion for life, could not stop the fog from rolling in, uninvited and unannounced.

Harley Meadows was sixty-five-years-old when he left the two girls he loved so dearly. He was buried in Catholic Cemetery, in Fredericksburg.

Life goes on, even for those who try not to notice.

Rick and Elizabeth were eating lunch, that she had prepared when Rick's cell phone rang. His facial contortions told her that something was wrong. "Where is she, Dave?" he said, starting to hyperventilate. "I'll be right there, don't panic, Dave. I'll be there with you just as fast as I can." He hung up his phone. "Come on, baby, we have to go to the hospital."

"What happened, Rick," Elizabeth asked him frantically.

"Amanda's been hurt. We have to go to the hospital."

Dave was sitting in a chair, the waiting room, bent over with his head in his hands. He was sobbing, loudly, and shaking. Rick and Elizabeth went to him quickly and put their hands on his shoulders.

Dave looked up. "I should have killed her, Rick," he said through his sobs. "I should have killed that bitch."

"What happened, Dave, what happened to Amanda?"

"Patty, it was Patty, I should have killed that bitch."

Elizabeth looked around and saw a doctor behind the receiving desk. "Can you tell me what is going on with Amanda Braddock, Doctor?" she asked.

"Are you related to her, ma'am?"

"Yes, she's my sister-in-law."

"She's in surgery right now. Amanda was shot, in the back."

"Shot?" Elizabeth exclaimed, in disbelief. "What in the world—"

"I don't know any details, ma'am," he said, "They're trying to save her life right now. I'll let you know as soon as I have more information."

Dave eventually calmed down to the point where he could tell them what had happened to Amanda. "We were in the diner on Two-Ninety, on the San Antonio side of town. Patty, my ex-wife, came in screaming at me and threatening to kill me. She had a gun, I didn't think she would use it. She's always been nutty like that. But she came toward me, pointing the gun at me. Amanda jumped in front of me and threw her arms around my neck. Patty fired one shot. It hit Manda in the back. I should have killed that bitch, Rick."

Two policemen walked into the waiting room. They knew Dave and approached him. One of them sat down beside him and put his arm around Dave's shoulder. The other one went to the nurses' station to get an update on Amanda's condition. Rick went to talk to him.

"Officer, I'm Rick Bennett, Amanda's brother, can you tell me what happened?"

"The best I can figure, Mister Bennett, from what folks at the diner told us, is that Dave's ex-wife showed up at the diner, brandished a weapon, and threatened to shoot Dave. His wife, your sister, started yelling, 'No, no, don't shoot my husband.' She jumped in front of him and took the bullet in her back. A couple of customers in the diner took the ex-wife to the floor and held her until we got there. How is your sister, any word yet?"

"I don't know," Rick said. "The doctor said he would let me know when he knows."

"Poor Dave, he was on the floor, holding his wife in his arms, rocking back and forth, utterly out of his mind."

"Dave and my sister are very close. They're crazy about each other."

The bullet hit Amanda in the right shoulder and broke her scapula. The wound was determined to not be life-threatening, but her recovery would take weeks, if not longer.

Rick called his parents, Adrian and Leeann, and they arrived about six hours later. Rick greeted them when they came into the waiting room. Dave immediately started apologizing to Amanda's parents. "It happened so fast, Adrian," he began, "I didn't have time to make Amanda get down in the seat. She jumped in front of me, trying to protect me. Oh God, I wish Patty had shot me instead."

Amanda came out of surgery and was moved to a room in the hospital. The doctor recommended that no more than two people be in the room at one time. Elizabeth had left earlier, to pick up the kids and take them home. Rick suggested that Dave and Leeann go to Amanda first. The sight of Dave Braddock, this big, bear of a man, leaning over her daughter, kissing her head, and bawling like a baby moved Leeann to tears, and she left the room.

"I think we should leave him alone with Amanda," she told her husband and son. "He is really hurt by this."

"I knew he would be, Mom," Rick said. "You have no idea how crazy he is about Amanda."

Many months later, when Amanda was home and out of danger, Elizabeth cornered Rick in the office. "I need a name for my book, Rick," she said.

"Which book, baby?" he asked.

"The big book, the story of our lives, I'm almost finished with it."

"But our story isn't finished yet," he said.

"Well, I can't wait until we're dead to finish it."

"Good point, then just put *To Be Continued*, as the epilogue."

"I'll do that, darling. I'll be wrapping it up in a couple of months."

"A couple of months? I thought you said you were almost finished."

"I've been working on the book for fifteen years, two more months is like the blink of an eye."

"Fair enough, don't rush it." Rick cleared his throat. "I'm going to ask Billy Ramirez to take over running the business," he said.

"He seems capable enough," Elizabeth replied, "and he has a business degree, now, thanks to you."

"It was an investment. The other kids have all gone and taken their mother with them. Billy is planning to get married soon and have kids. I'm going the help him buy a house, a nice house, wherever he wants it—in town, out in the country, whatever he wants. Billy has been a good employee since his father died."

"And what are we going to do, with you not working so much?"

"Go places, where would you like to go?"

"Wherever you're going will be fine with me," she said.

"I'd like to go back to California and visit my grandparents' graves."

"Sure, darling, if that's what you want to do. Can I come with you?"

He scowled at her. "I'm not going anywhere without you," he told her.

In recent years, they had remodeled the house and added a Gazebo in the front yard. Rick liked to take his coffee with him, in the morning before dawn, and watch the sun come up in the east. In the afternoons, he and Elizabeth would drink wine and watch the sun, after it had made its trek across the sky, go down in the west. One evening, they were there performing what had become an almost daily ritual for them. Elizabeth had filled up a bowl with grapes, and they were sipping wine and munching on the grapes.

"I've got it," he suddenly exclaimed.

What?" she said,

"A name, a name for your book. I have a name for your book."

"Tell me," she said, "what is it.

"*A Bowl Full of Grapes.*"

"That's fitting, isn't it?" Elizabeth said. "It pretty much sums up our lives together, after all these years. We're back to you and me, two glasses of wine, and a bowl full of grapes."

Chapter 29

A Bowl Full of Grapes

2065:

Mother published her book, Ben. She was fifty-Two when it went on sale. Because Elizabeth was so well known around Fredericksburg, it seemed like everyone in town bought a copy, except for the cheap bastards who borrowed it from someone else, that is."

Ben started laughing. "You sure have a way with words, Annie," he said.

"She has a foul mouth, Ben, that's what she has," HA added.

"Maybe so, Harley, but it's very endearing. So, if your mother was fifty-two, there had to be a lot more story after the book was published."

"Oh, yes," Annie said. "She could have written another book about them after that. But she didn't want to. She said that was enough for the world to know about the love story of Rick Bennett and Elizabeth Meadows. She added that as a subtitle to the book right before it was published and began selling on Amazon."

A Bowl Full of Grapes
A Love Story

"Then you're going to have to fill in the blanks for me, Annie. What ever happened to Amanda?"

"Aunt Amanda recovered from her injury. It took a long time for her to get full use of her right arm again, but she did eventually. Her happiest time was the first time she was able to put both her arms around her husband, Dave. My goodness, how she loved that man. Dave died when he was sixty-two, and Amanda never got over him. She never remarried, although she was only fifty-seven at the time of Dave's death, and she had a couple of offers. Our paternal grandparents, fortunately, were not alive to experience their daughter's passing, ten years later. It broke Rick's heart to lose Amanda, but he went on living. Elizabeth had to go to Dallas, Austin, San Antonio, and Houston, for book signings, but Rick went with her. They traveled a lot, Elizabeth wanted to go back to New York, and she and Rick went several times.

"He took her to Paris and Hawaii, that was about the only places Elizabeth wanted to go. They were content to stay at home on their beloved vineyard. Rick hired Billy Ramirez to run the business, after it became more work than he could handle. Billy worked for Dad until Billy retired. Then Rick sold the Luckenbach property and just bottled enough wine to serve Fredericksburg and a very small area around the town. And they lived happily ever after," Annie said.

"I wish I could have met them, Annie," Ben said. "They sound like fascinating people."

"Well, you can, Ben," she replied. "Rick and Elizabeth are still alive."

"You're serious?" he asked incredulously. "Where do they live?"

"Well, they live at home, of course. They would never leave their vineyard."

"Would it be possible for me to talk to them?"

"I don't see why not. They're not recluses. Do you know where the Lizzy Bee is?"

"I have the address, but I guess I didn't do my homework. I hadn't thought about asking you until today. I didn't know they were still alive."

"Oh, they're still alive. When they first fell in love, Elizabeth asked Rick if he would still love her when they were eighty years old. He told her he would, and that he was going to live until he was eighty, just to prove it to her."

"That's amazing," Ben said, "truly amazing. Well, folks, I guess that just about wraps it up. I want to thank you both for affording me the time and for sharing so much of your parents' lives with me. It's been a fascinating time. I've spent with you. I plan to go see your parents, just as soon as I'm back in Fredericksburg. I will send you a free subscription the magazine with a copy of the one with the story about Rick and Elizabeth. It's been a delight, thank you again."

Epilogue

Ben slowed down as his GPS alerted that he was approaching the Lizzy Bee Vineyard. He turned into the driveway and approached the house slowly. Off to the right, he saw the remains of what was once an exquisite tree house, now showing its age. It had obviously been allowed to grow old, resting in the huge oak tree where once the Bennett children, and their children, played noisily.

Not far away, a gazebo sat in stark contrast to the tree house. The gazebo was either a new structure or had been meticulously maintained. It looked as if it had been recently painted. Two people were sitting in the gazebo.

It was mid-April, and a warm breeze blew quietly across the yard, bringing an inviting and pleasant feel to the world. Ben got out of his car and walked toward the two people who were sitting in the Gazebo.

"Hello, folks," he said, as he drew near to them, "My name is Ben Bradley, and I'm looking for Mister and Mrs. Bennett."

"You're looking at them, Mister Bradley," the man said. "I'm Rick, and this is my wife, Elizabeth. What can we do for you?"

"I'm with the *People of Texas Magazine*. I've just spent the last two weeks speaking with your son and daughter, in Dallas."

"Annie mentioned that you would be coming to see us, Mister Bradley," Rick said. "You're here about my wife's book?"

"I am," he replied, "and please call me Ben. My magazine wants to run a story on Mrs. Bennett's book, along with a profile of you both, since you both are the main subjects of the book."

"Lizzy has always enjoyed attention, Ben, so, I imagine she will be okay with that."

Rick Bennett stood up, to go to Bradley and shake his hand. His six-foot two-inch frame was stooped somewhat, but he was still an imposing man. His hair had turned white, and his handsome face had acquired some wrinkles.

Bradley noted that Rick's handshake was strong, stronger than he had expected. "Come and meet my Lizzy, Ben," he said.

"It would be my honor," Ben said.

They walked up to the gazebo where Elizabeth was sitting. Time had not dimmed the bright blue eyes. They still had excitement and passion for life in them. And they still observed the world with wonder and anticipation of the possibilities that every new day offered. Her white hair, no longer as blonde as sunshine, was still beautiful.

Ben understood, immediately, why Rick Bennett had fallen in love with such a woman. "I have to tell you, Mrs. Bennett, that you have two children who love you very much."

"Oh, you didn't have to tell me that, Ben, they tell me that every time they call me. They are wonderful children, always were. Harley and Annie never caused us any heartache, not once in all their lives. My husband and I were blessed with wonderful children and grandchildren."

"I read your book, ma'am, that's why I'm here."

"Which one, Ben?" she asked him.

"The one about your lives together, yours and Rick's,"

"Oh, that one," she said and curled up the corners of her mouth. "I should have written an addendum to that book—several, maybe. We've done a lot of living since that book was published."

"I'm sure you have," Ben said, "and I'm happy to get to meet you both."

"You mean before we died? I bet you thought we were dead, didn't you, Ben? Be honest, now."

"I didn't know you were alive, Elizabeth, until Annie told me, but I am happy that you are. I want to do a story about you, about your book and you, if you don't mind."

"No, I don't mind," she told him, "I think that would be nice."

"I just need to ask you a few questions and take some notes, if you're up to it."

"That'll be fine, Ben, whenever you're ready."

"How long have you and Rick been married, Elizabeth?"

"Fifty-six years, Ben, we've been married fifty-six years."

"What contributed the most to your being able to stay married for such a long time, when a large percentage of marriages these days fail after just a few years"

"Well, I'd have to say it was the mutual love and respect that we had for each other, the same desires, and needs, and great sex."

Ben started laughing. "I sort of gathered that from reading your book, Elizabeth."

"I married a real stud, Ben. That man right there," she began, pointing at Rick, "he was the—I probably should let that drop right there."

"I understand," Ben said, "I think it's pretty much common knowledge that you and your husband had a wonderful love story to tell. I'm just glad you told it and told it so eloquently."

"Well, thank you, Ben, it took me fifteen-years to write it, give or take a year or so, and when I finished it, I felt like the story was just beginning."

"I've heard a lot of writers say that same thing. They never feel like the book is completely finished after they finish it."

"You have to stop somewhere and sometime. I expect our story will be over soon, but until it is, we will keep on loving each other and being thankful that we got together in the first place."

"That's a nice outlook on life, Elizabeth," he said, "Now, can you tell me what was the thing that held your marriage together for so long, in addition to being in love, I mean. There had to be some contributing factors."

"Well, Ben, I'd have to say it's the same things that we have today. We'll always have each other, two glasses of good wine, and a bowl full of grapes within arm's each. We really don't need anything else."

About the Author

Jack Sprouse is from Dallas, Texas, although he now lives in Lewisville, a few miles north of Dallas. He studied American History at Texas Tech, in Lubbock, and his fields of greatest historical interest are the American Civil War and World War II. He served in the United States Navy as a crewmember on an ASW (anti-submarine-warfare) patrol aircraft. Writing fiction is his passion.

Sprouse just loves making stuff up (his mom used to punish him for doing that when he was a kid). He has written two books of historical fiction (Adventures in Time Book I: The American Civil War and Adventures in Time Book II: The American West—these are both Walter Mitty type stories in which he places himself back in time as a war correspondent following historical events and interviewing the major players in those events; two books of original poetry, The Quiet Place and Dreams of a Forgotten Man—both books contain approximately fifty original poems on various subjects: Life, love, friendship, relationships, war, conflict, tragedy; and several novels: *The House Wren*, a saga of a fictional Texas family; *On Neptune's Wings*, a love story set in the 1960s against the backdrop of a US Navy Patrol Squadron; *Magnolia Road*, an improbable love story between a girl from Vermont and a rancher from Colorado. She is purposeful and dedicated to her chosen calling in life; and *Clare*, about a twenty-four-year-old woman who faces life with quiet confidence and inner turmoil; experiencing love, hurt, uncertainty, sexual harassment in the workplace, and tragedy. He is currently working on several ideas for new books.